money
Wanders

Eric Dezenhall

THOMAS DUNNE BOOKS
St. Martin's Press ❧ New York

THOMAS DUNNE BOOKS.
An imprint of St. Martin's Press.

www.stmartins.com

Design by Michael Collica

Library of Congress Cataloging-in-Publication Data

Dezenhall, Eric.
     Money wanders / by Eric Dezenhall.—1st ed.
       p. cm.
    ISBN 0-312-28275-3
   1. Organized crime—Fiction. 2. Washington
(D.C.)—Fiction. 3. Atlantic City (N.J.)—Fiction.
4. Public opinion polls—Fiction. 5. Grandfa-
thers—Death—Fiction. I. Title.

PS3604.E94 M66   2002
813'.6—dc21

                      2001054335

10 9 8 7 6 5 4 3 2

for donna

author's note

Whenever fictional characters are placed in familiar settings as they are in this book, it is tempting to speculate about whether they are based upon real people and events. For the record, *Money Wanders* is a work of fiction derived entirely from the author's imagination. I made up everybody and everything. Among other creative liberties, I portray Lucy the Elephant, a beloved Jersey Shore monument, as an underworld hideout. This is pure fantasy. Lucy is a solid, upstanding pachyderm and is operated as a tourist attraction by the community of Margate.

—E.B.D.

These days you apply for a license to steal from the public. If I had my time again, I'd make sure I got that license first.

—Charles "Lucky" Luciano,
in exile, Naples, Italy

A boy can be two, three, four potential people, but a man is only one. He murders the others.

—Mordechai Richler,
The Apprenticeship of Duddy Kravitz

book one
play it down

Keep your filthy hands out of Atlantic City.

—New Jersey governor
Brendan Byrne to
organized crime, on
the passage of casino
gambling, 1978

Eye in the Sky
Atlantic City, New Jersey

"They think they can fool everybody."

E VEN A TERRIBLE MAN WANTS TO LEAVE HIS KIDS SOME-
thing," my grandfather, Mickey, ranted at me as if he were
the Jersey Shore's answer to Solomon the Wise. His accent was
coarse, like petrified wood: "Terrible" rhymed with "gerbil."

"What terrible man?" I asked.

"Mario Vanni. He wants to talk to you."

"*Vanni?* Why?"

Mickey shook his head in surrender as he watched my feet. I
had begun to straddle back and forth, digging the heels of my boots
into the red-brown carpet.

"Settle down already!" Mickey concluded, "What are you doing,
a rain dance?"

"How the hell can you expect me to settle down?" I snapped. "Irv
the Curve made it sound like you were taking your last breath when
he called." Deathbed summonses and their attendant speeches had
become routine for Mickey ever since my business took off. "And
now you tell me this about Vanni."

Mickey bit down hard on a pickle, decapitating it, as if his being
almost a century old were the pickle's fault. Mickey didn't sound
like himself; he seemed faded, his tracking off center—like a video

dub of who he once had been. He chewed in slow motion, which made me think that maybe he really was sick this time. He then popped a green tablet that I hadn't seen before into his mouth. Now I felt like a vulture.

Television monitors winked and blew tinsel kisses from along the wall. Mickey and I were alone in the room where he watches over the Golden Prospect, the casino he opened when Jersey made gaming legal. Ninety-five years old and he can't wait to get here every day. He complains about the pressure, but it's all he knows, it's who he is.

The "Eye in the Sky" feeds into in this room. It's a phrase the pit bosses use to describe the cameras that track everyone in Mickey's gambling kingdom. He didn't officially own the Golden Prospect. He was listed in company records as the bell captain, a nuance he loved. Once when I brought some friends home from college, Mickey met us in the lobby in a bellhop's uniform. He loaded all the bags onto a cart and waved his fingers at a few FBI guys who were watching. *"See!"* was all he said.

Mickey couldn't be listed as the hotel's official owner because he fled the country in 1975 to dodge an indictment involving gambling junkets to the Bahamas and God knows what else. I was thirteen at the time and had left the United States with Mickey and my grandmother, Deedee. My parents had died a few years earlier. Deedee was gone, too, now.

Irv the Curve, Mickey's voice to the outside world, had called me this morning and told me to hurry down the Shore. Irv made it sound as if Mickey had had a stroke. He didn't actually say "stroke," he just used sentences that ricocheted me into thinking this. I shot out of my office in Washington, D.C., and drove north on I-95, making it to Atlantic City in two hours and forty minutes. This was exceptional timing considering that I would rather be pecked to death by Boardwalk pigeons than be jerked through the wilderness again by Mickey. I had lived in Washington since I graduated from Dartmouth, but came home to the Shore often, however reluctantly. After years of political work, I had my own polling firm, the Jonah P. Eastman Group, which specialized in maverick Republicans.

My hip began to itch, and it took me a second to realize that the little E-mail device I carried on my belt was vibrating. I unhooked it and read the tiny screen.

"What are you looking at?" Mickey asked.

"I just got mail."

"What the hell are you saying, that you got mail on that little matchbox?"

"Yeah. It's just a friend checking in. You remember Trouble, right?"

"Trouble, sure . . . Wait a minute—if you got mail, where's the envelope?"

"No envelope, it's just words." I held the little device up for him. He snarled at it and looked the other way.

"My taffy shop downstairs wants to do this gadget thing, a websty."

"A Web site."

"Yeah, Web site. People came into that shop for sixty years because they smelled the saltwater taffy. How the hell can you smell saltwater taffy across a goddamned wire? Next thing you know, you'll be able to play with girls on a computer. You know what I'm talking about," he added furtively.

"You can do that now, Pop."

"Girls on a computer? Without the clothes? You're shitting me! So that's the bait with this Internet"—*Innernet*—"a buncha kids looking at girlie pictures. I knew it had to be something like that." Mickey thought for a moment. "But how do you get all the nice perfume? *Aaah!* In the lobby, they have a computer where you can press a button and the machine says, 'Take a walk on the Boardwalk.' "

"So?"

"So? It's not taking a walk on the Boardwalk with the air and the pigeon shit, it's a cartoon! I'm glad I won't live to see it."

"What do you mean, Pop? You *did* live to see it."

"Every generation has its swindle. Mine had Prohibition. Yours has those damned gadgets. Enough with that. How's business?" he asked.

I hesitated before answering. Things were not going well, and answering Mickey's question truthfully would upset him. To the extent that my business still existed, it lived in this little E-mail pager strapped to my hip. I could always nurse the old guy back to health by telling him how great things were, what awards I had won, what big shots I had met. Mickey's pride in me took on biblical proportions, especially after a polling stint I did in the White House in the eighties. (I won my whiz kid reputation then by conducting a poll demonstrating how in certain settings, President Reagan could make even liberals "feel good.") One moment Mickey would order me to "stay down there and build your life." Then he would call and ask me if his big-shot grandson had forgotten his "beat-up old Pop Pop." Mickey's violent zigzag from pride to punishment caused me to crash perpetually between self-congratulation and an all-too-real impulse to kill him myself and get it over with. To complicate matters, I could never tell whether he was relieved or hurt that none of the big shots ever found out that I was the grandson of Moses "Mickey" Price, "the billionaire Atlantic City gangster known as the 'Wizard of Odds,' " according to KBRO-TV reporter Al Just in Philadelphia.

In his state, I decided that lying to Mickey (he'd know) would have hurt him more than the truth, so I told him.

"Business isn't great. I'm on the outs with my big governor client. A polling technique I used in another campaign backfired, and some folks are making a whole ethics case out of it."

"*Ethics?*" Mickey studied the remains of his headless pickle.

"Ever since the *Post* said that I engineered the last Congressional sweep with my America Delivers platform, I've needed another hit."

Truth be told, I needed more than just another hit. After my campaign fiasco made the news, all of my other clients suddenly began to embrace "alternative strategies," that is, strategies that didn't involve me.

"Yeah, Elvis? I have news for you. You can make a living without hits. Your problem is that you believed the *Post*. You're all like dope addicts down there. Don't mistake yourself for somebody historically significant. Hits!"

"Anyway, I was thinking about moving up here and taking over, moving you out, seeing as how you're so sick. I could be the *capo di tutti frutti*, the Big Kugel. Maybe I'll talk it over with Vanni." I thought this might make him laugh.

"Now don't get smart. You didn't go off to your fancy college to come and work with me. This is no life for, you know, guys like us. We got out of that in the forties." *We.* Our Crowd. Tribesmen. Jewish racketeers. Mickey said this with a straight face, then summed up: "You had other choices, Jonah."

"So did you, Pop."

"Entrances are wide, exits are narrow. And who's got the ethics problem, Justice Brandeis?" Mickey let forth a sharp, pickled growl.

"Pop, what did you mean about Vanni wanting something for his kids?"

"Christ, I dunno," Mickey mumbled to his pickle. "I don't know anything anymore. All I know is I got a goddamned canker sore in my mouth," he announced, blinking up at me from his chair.

"Then don't eat pickles." This was the only way to handle Mickey. He only understood commandments. He glanced off at the wall of frantic convex screens.

He called this room "the Eye" for short. It was about fifteen feet wide and thirty feet long. Along one wall, thirty TV monitors were stacked in three rows of ten. They were hooked up to cameras that covered the whole casino floor. If Mickey's guys didn't like something they saw, they had their choice of ten red phones that could call right down to the floor. Mickey watched the screens like the kids watched MTV.

A great Lenni-Lenape Indian tapestry was draped against the wall opposite the monitors. Mickey had bought it from the tribe before I was born. A small plaque at the ornate tapestry's base read LENNI-LENAPE SWADDLING BLANKET. He loved the thing.

I took a seat across from Mickey. He began nibbling at the pickle stump again, looking like an elf with snow white hair that had eroded in step with the Atlantic City shoreline.

He was wearing a green Dartmouth sweatshirt and khaki pants. A Patek Philippe watch was strapped tightly around his left wrist. A turquoise and silver band hugged his brown middle finger. Mickey always wore loafers. He said you could tell who was who by his shoes. The FBI wore thick, clunky tie shoes that were forever chasing after sleek loafers. "Loafers are nice and easy," he once said. "Slip 'em on and slip 'em off. Run to the next thing, you know?"

Mickey's eyes were a warm green, the only feature I had inherited from him. I was taller and my features were smaller and of no obvious ethnicity. His nose split his face like the wedge in the middle of a sundial. Nearly a century of walking and worrying had kept him thin. He had chain-smoked until he was eighty, which had also kept the weight off. Mickey's nemesis, the reporter Al Just, had said on the air that Mickey was "a cross between your favorite tailor and Napoleon."

Mickey's voice echoed like the Boardwalk at dusk. I didn't have his accent anymore. Mickey had been vigilant about making my speech untraceable, as if I could be jailed for it. He was ashamed of how he spoke, which was one reason, I think, why he relied on Irv the Curve to do the talking.

Mickey rolled his chair across the room to a white porcelain sink in the corner of the Eye. He proceeded to wash his hands with antibacterial soap, a long-standing habit of his. He then took a long hit from an oxygen mask that appeared from a drawer next to the sink. I had seen him do this before, but he never used to breathe in this long.

"Just look at you in the cowboy boots. In New Jersey no less."

"South Jersey. They're not actually cowboy boots. They're Australian roping boots. I've worn this kind since those summer jobs at the racetrack." (*It'll be good for you to trample around in a little shit, Jonah.*)

"Slide over the pickles."

Mickey took out a laser pointer from his breast pocket and beamed it on the little bowl with the Golden Prospect logo. Mickey's nurse, a mountainous black woman named Odessa, had gotten him the laser pointer so he wouldn't have to walk over to the TV screens whenever he saw something.

"So *now* you want the pickles."

"Right. Pour me some of that water?" He shot the laser onto a pitcher.

Mickey kept the laser on the pitcher. It looked like I was pouring a string of blood. My wrist jerked with a nervous spasm, and some of the water flowed over the side of Mickey's glass.

"You ever been in a tidal wave?" Mickey asked, sliding over a crested napkin.

"No. Have you?"

"Nah, but remember what I told you about waves."

"Move toward them, not away."

"Right. Get in close and ride it. You run, it crushes you. You always liked to fight things bigger than you, but you don't fight tidal waves."

"If all this talk is about Vanni, then just tell me."

"You play tidal waves different, if you can believe that," Mickey persisted.

"I can believe it. What do you believe, Pop?"

"Do I have to believe in something?"

"Sure."

"All right, I believe in something."

"What?"

"None of your businesses."

Mickey shut his eyes then popped them open wide, urgently leaning across the table to grab my hands. I remember the first time he did this to me. It was after my mother died, when I was twelve. He had just given me a lecture about having to be tough. He reminded me that he had lost his daughter, too. Deedee told him if she ever heard that "tough business" again, she would kill Mickey herself.

Mickey's eyes were slowly turning red and welling up. His tears weren't falling and I wondered if he had a little drain behind his eyes the way sinks do to prevent overflow. "Always get inside a big wave. They hit you hard but they show you what you've got." Mickey picked up his laser and wiggled the red light at my chest. "Up close is the best way to play the variables."

"I can't watch over you," he added. Two large pearls of tears now slid down his tan cheeks. No drain. "I can't tell people what they can do and can't do anymore. I can't stop what I can't stop. You've got to find a place for yourself. The Shore isn't for you. Sounds like you pissed off those hoity-toity Republicans with that bull head of yours. You don't have patience for the broads you meet. And don't get me started on those cowboy boots—"

I wanted desperately to change the subject. I turned and studied the monitors on the wall. One of Mickey's boys had left a radio on. It was playing Springsteen's version of Woody Guthrie's "This Land Is Your Land." I gently tapped Mickey's knuckles.

"Pop, do you hear this song?"

"What about it?"

"My counselor used to play it on the guitar when I was in summer camp in the Pine Barrens. There's a line about 'walking that ribbon of highway.' I thought the singer said 'Ribbonoff Highway,' like there was some old guy named Ribbonoff who had built a highway and named it after himself."

Mickey's eyes dragged across me. My reminiscence had not registered. My throat tightened up, and suddenly I felt dizzy. I had a history of vertigo. Sometimes it came on strong and other times it passed over me, but the anticipation was always there. I stood and held on to the table, which helped straighten me out.

"Hey, Pop, you look tired. Why don't you lie down? I'll take you up to your apartment."

Mickey held up his hands in forfeit. "There's no billion dollars, Jonah."

"What? A billion dollars?" I involuntarily laughed. The local press loved to speculate about where Mickey had hidden his stash ever since Al Just first discovered how sexy talk about gangster cash could be. Whenever his ratings fell, Just could always draw the region to its TV sets by injecting the phrase "new information about Mickey Price's hidden stash" into any story. I had long since come to regard the notion that Mickey had big money as a suburban legend—South Jersey's answer to the D. B. Cooper story. Another wave of vertigo fell through me, then dissolved like the breakers.

"Reporters. I remember that Al Just when he was Alvin Yutzel tagging along with his father, Mouse Yutzel. Mouse worked for me, you know."

"I know."

"Reporters are *momzers*. They think they can fool everybody."

"They *can* fool everybody, Pop," I said.

"You can fool all of the people who want to be fooled all of the time."

"I know. So why does everything come back to that story?" Mickey was obsessed with the "billionaire" label that had been affixed to his head by KBRO. He didn't respond.

Mickey didn't want to go to bed. He wanted to watch the evening news with "that nice-looking Peter Jennings," so I sat him down on the sofa up in the penthouse. Odessa awaited Mickey, puffing up a pillow so that he could sit back. He looked like a Lilliputian next to her. I flipped on the television.

"How old are you, Jonah, you thirty yet?" Odessa asked me.

"I was thirty-eight a couple of months ago. I was born during the big storm in March of sixty-two."

"Knocking on forty," Mickey said in the background. "Don't kid yourself."

"Hoo-eee," Odessa said. "That storm almost knocked the whole city into the sea. God musta seen something goin' on he didn't like. But you still look like a child. Like a child."

"Where's my pointer?" Mickey asked.

Odessa rolled her full-moon eyes. "Him and that damned pointer," she said, as if Mickey weren't there. She found it sticking out of his pocket and handed it to him. "I'll leave you boys alone to talk about all the pretty girls."

Mickey's eyes quivered between life and sleep, open (as if by accident) and then soldered shut. His rich South Jersey voice degraded to a whisper. "Listen to me, Jonah." *Lissena me.*

I sat beside him and he held my face in his hands. His fingers smelled like burnt paper. "That old story. The guy. The piney guy." Pineys were inhabitants of the South Jersey Pine Barrens, a strange lot by legend. "He walked in the woods. Things didn't go so hot with a broad at a dance. He threw his hat in the air. It got caught in a pine branch. That story. He pulled the branch down. Like a lever. Ground opened up into another world. Another world."

"What pine branch, Pop?"

"You get in close. *In* the tidal wave. Run toward. Not away. Listen to the gypsy music," Mickey opened his eyes and smiled broadly, tapping his skull. "You'll talk to Vanni and listen. Choices . . . well, you don't always have 'em. Believe me. What did I do? What the hell did I do? Look, look, Vanni's like you. He's got his noodles up there. We all want what's best for our kids—*mishpocha*, *famiglia*, Yid or Italian, same thing. It's a whole other story with those young banditos he's got. But they don't know the gadgets like you do. Mmm. Ah, you'll figure it out. You'll do whatever. Now go and run."

Mickey's eyebrows were arched toward his scalp. He wore the same expression that he did when listened to his klezmer music, the gypsy tunes of Eastern Europe's Jews. The look was a facial drawbridge connecting pleasure and peace. I felt that if I pressed him any more about Vanni that I could kill him. The silver-blue light from the television slid along Mickey's closed eyelids like a line of feathered showgirls.

Odessa reemerged and rolled her eyes again, as if Mickey babbled this way often. "You go out and get some fresh air," she said. "It's a nice night on the Boardwalk. You go for one of your runs and get some salt air, show off those muscles for the girls. Win a trophy like you used to," she said, pointing to a photo of me at a high school track meet. "Mickey, he sleeps this time a night. You go on, now."

I was disarmed by how well Odessa knew me. Like Mickey, she knew what I did when I was upset: I ran. Odessa kissed my cheek and shooed me away, the flick of her blue-black anchor hands more commanding than Mickey's voice had ever been. I changed into running gear, and Odessa shooed me away again. The letters of my college alma mater rose and melted gently across Mickey's chest, in step with his breath.

"Go on, now."

Cash Flow Temples

"I did not see my trade as a science, I saw it as a weapon."

⸱

I PEERED OVER THE SHOULDER OF A KID IN THE HOTEL LOBBY
taking a virtual walk on the Boardwalk on the computer Mickey
had spoken about. I could see why the thing pissed him off. On
screen, the Boardwalk was antiseptically perfect, with an occasional
shit-free cartoon pigeon head-bobbing across the planks. I stepped
away and set off on a monster run from the Golden Prospect in
Atlantic City to the southern tip of Absecon Island. It was an
eleven-mile trek there and back. The Boardwalk would take me
as far as Ventnor, then I'd have to run out onto Atlantic Avenue for
the remaining four miles or so down to the point.

It was late May and the Boardwalk was desolate except for a
rabid rollerblader who almost bowled me into oblivion. Dew
hugged the tall steel lanterns placed about fifty yards apart along
the waterfront. The square blue newspaper vending boxes made
me think of big, lifeless tumbleweeds, as if I were running in a
mutant, millennial Dodge City. A fresh sling of bird shit dripping
down the side of a railing made the Boardwalk smell like failure.
I was back *here*. Atlantic City, that blend of Oz and Calcutta—a
town that had imploded the grand, hand-sculpted hotels of Irving

Berlin's America and replaced them with the gilded cheese of Engelbert Humperdinck and Donald Trump.

This was my first run down the Shore as a political pariah, and I needed it. About a month ago, I had fallen out of favor because of a poll I did to get people to admit that they wanted to elect a racist senatorial candidate in an Arizona Republican primary. My client was the New Republicans Committee, an ad hoc group concerned about the rise of hateful rhetoric from within the party. They wanted me to find out how Republican voters really felt about coded talk on race, religion, class, and sex. The committee's suspicion was that the same voters who claimed to repudiate hate politics secretly welcomed it. I assured them that I had an unconventional polling technique that could get at the root of this. I knew that they intended to release the results of my work during the primary in order to inspire the nicer Republicans to get out and vote. They were afraid of what Straun, the bigoted candidate, would do to the party in the general election. If he won. My job was to make sure he didn't.

Rather than approach voters with the neutrality attendant to most polls, my people infiltrated on-line chat rooms as if they were just plain country folks standin' in line at the Piggly Wiggly. "How you gonna vote, bud?" (as if we didn't know). When the good people of Arizona thought they were "talking" to one of their own—with the added benefit of Internet anonymity—they let loose with their true feelings, which were right in line with Straun's. I quantified what we learned and packaged it in poll form.

The day before the committee was to release it—with our spin—I began getting calls from reporters asking how the poll was conducted. A mole within my client's shop had leaked my summary memo and sent it out over the Internet. They sought to neutralize my poll by alleging that my methods had been corrupt. I acknowledged my unorthodox approach but defended its accuracy. I was summarily blasted by the Society of Public Opinion Professionals in the press. My client fired me, echoing the concern about my tactics they full well knew about.

The ostensible issues at hand were my ethics and improper methodology. I understood why Straun's supporters wanted to discredit me, but the motives of my fellow pollsters were less obvious.

I knew what was going on, though: They were my competitors. By conducting the poll the way I did, I had smashed the aura of tweedy probity that was essential to my racket's collective self-esteem. They fancied themselves scientists. In order to maintain that aura, they needed to suck ass with the media and feign respect for the public. I felt no such obligation. I did not see my trade as a science, I saw it as a weapon—one used because I was retained to *win*. When my colleagues weren't drunk on lobbyists' liquor, they saw things the same way.

Straun lost, which was my client's wish. Once the poll became public, even the racists opposed the racist out of fear they would look like racists. Surreptitiously getting chat room confessions may not have been nice, but it was accurate. My effectiveness had been my downfall. When the scandal hit the papers, my other clients, including the Republican presidential front-runner, stepped away from me despite my earlier electoral success with the America Delivers program. In the current political climate, being accused of doing something that "raised unanswered questions" was as lethal as getting caught banging a collie. My clients didn't formally fire me, they just didn't take my calls. This is how you got whacked in Washington, indirectly and without a word exchanged or a shot fired. You had to sniff it out because no one would confirm it. Sure, I had been a hot item on the news shows after the story broke— for one evening—giving me a temporary fix of ratings heroin. Then, nothing.

My serial shitcanning led to another occupational hazard of political consulting: The only people who get paid are the hot guys. It was universally accepted that losers didn't get paid because they had no recourse. Meanwhile, I still carried K Street office overhead and a few contract employees without a dime coming in. It was a crushing reversal from where I had been: Jonah Eastman the "Poll Vaulter," as the *Post* had once called me, who could smell victory no matter the client's odds. All I could smell now was slick pigeon shit.

My career postmortem skidded to its conclusion as I passed the great cash flow temples of Longport, residential monuments built by Main Line wheeler-dealers to avenge some vague injustice suffered in a high school hallway long ago. They were gratuitously huge, each new one boasting more windows and decks than its neighbors to the north. I stretched on a strip of sand that faced Ocean City, which floated on the glow of the sunset a few miles to the south.

My Uncle Blue Cocco's little ranch house was wedged between two cash flow temples (CFTs, as Mickey called them) only a few hundred yards from here. Blue had been Mickey's Sicilian partner since Prohibition and the *éminence grise* of the Mid-Atlantic Mafia. He had never been the titular boss, Mickey explained, because the minor increment of prestige hadn't been worth the major increment of heartache: The Feds mainly wanted the bosses, not their aides. The temples appeared to be squeezing Blue's place like a coastal zit. No one dared utter a word, though. The noisy boys and their meretricious wives in their CFTs knew better than to fuck with the quiet ones like Uncle Blue.

The sudden shock of cold white sea-foam on my running shorts bolted me upright. Mario Vanni wanted to talk to me. *Christ.* I began running back north to the Golden Prospect with sand and water in my shoes and tried to make sense of Mickey's spooky rant about a man in the woods. Had Mickey met with Vanni in the woods? It made no sense.

The Longport firehouse came up quickly on my left. It sported its familiar sign: EVERY MAN MUST GET TO HEAVEN HIS OWN WAY.

When I returned to Mickey's apartment, he was leaning back in the corner of his sofa. His left hand was cupped over his face. Tears had streamed down from his eyes and fallen toward his ears. One drop had fallen onto the shoulder of his sweatshirt and had begun to expand like a pond ripple. His right arm was extended over the side of the couch. His fingers were open, and his watch rested precariously on his palm.

Odessa emerged from the kitchen, crying. Behind her was Fuzzy Marino, glum and mammoth like Jupiter, rubbing his temples. In his midsixties, Fuzzy was the baby of Mickey's Shore crew.

"*What?*" I asked, accusingly.

Fuzzy held out his gorilla arms. "When I got here, he was gone. I'm sorry, Jones."

While I stood over Mickey, numb, Fuzzy called Glick's Funeral

Home. Fuzzy told Glick's attendants that if one reporter or Fed tried to sneak in and take a picture of Mickey dead, they would be "shipped out" next. Photos of dead gangsters had become collectors' items and had a way of turning up in true crime books. Bugsy Siegel lying on his chintz sofa with his eye shot out. Carmine Galante with his cigar hanging out of his mouth covered by an intestinal blanket of linguini bolognese. Paul Castellano on the sidewalk outside of Sparks Steak House, his eyes open and blood trickling down his face. Philly's Angelo Bruno, mouth agape in shock, one eye slightly open in a final peek at Snyder Avenue in early spring.

I helped Fuzzy and the paramedics carry Mickey on a stretcher to the roof of the Golden Prospect via elevators I never knew existed. Even in death, Mickey had to sneak around. The Golden Prospect's huge helicopter—Mickey had named "her" *Goldie*—waited to whisk Mickey off to Glick's. As the rotors blew my hair wildly, I found myself jealous of Mickey: His heart stops and he's off. . . .

In the guest room, Odessa held me. She was sobbing and almost crushed my chest. I was so focused on breathing that I had not begun to compute Mickey's death. Fuzzy interrupted us, handed Odessa a wad of cash, and suggested she go back to her apartment.

Fuzzy sat next to me on the guest bed, causing the mattress to tilt toward the Atlantic. Tufts of hair reached out behind his neck like claws, which was why we called him Fuzzy. I held Mickey's watch in my palm.

"He got this in Paris," I said. Mickey, Deedee, and I had lived in Paris during our exile.

"I know he did. They framed him up good on that skimming deal," Fuzzy volunteered. "The old guy made saltwater taffy," he added with a wink. I guess he thought this would make me feel better. Saltwater taffy had been Mickey's legitimate business. By the time we'd been chased to Paris, I knew Mickey did more than make taffy. He told me that once when I inquired years ago. I had just come home from a track meet.

"What's your job?" I had asked him as he read *Barron's*.

"Molasses," he'd said without looking up. When Prohibition ended, Mickey had converted his molasses stills into saltwater taffy plants. I didn't buy the frame-up line but didn't want to debate with Fuzzy. Besides, I had suspected even twenty-five years ago that the Law had been right, a hypothesis that I always linked to my vertigo. Kids are literal—you can't spin them.

"You still have that beanbag chair?" Fuzzy asked.

"No. Somebody stole it from my office a few months ago. Probably the cleaning crew." I had bought the beanbag chair at a thrift shop in Pleasantville when Mickey, Deedee, and I returned to America. While my friends were inflicting their freedoms on civilization, I had been shuttling around the world to keep my grandfather out of prison. Embossed onto the chair's vinyl cover was a fading procession of rainbow-colored cartoon partridges, the TV *Partridge Family*'s logo. The Partridges were pecking airily along the beanbag after a larger Mother Partridge, whose chest was puffed out, celebrating her mod brood. "C'mon Get Happy"—the family's mantra—dotted the vinyl in decaying felt below the Partridges.

Fuzzy shifted, and the perfect silence of the room was interrupted by the chipmunk whine of the mattress. "What an old pile a rat shit that beanbag chair was!" Fuzzy bellowed. It made me laugh. "What's with you and that thing?"

"When we left the country, I felt like I had missed the seventies." The truth was that I had been gone for the ninth and tenth grades, but these were critical years.

"Didn't miss much, Jones." Fuzzy had called me Jones since I was young. Some of my friends had picked up on it and began calling me Jones, too.

"When Mickey first saw that chair, he said I was rebelling. Like it made me Patty Fucking Hearst. I once caught Mickey sitting on the damned thing. I saw through a crack in my door."

"No shit?"

"Yeah, he was looking up at Blue. You know what he said? He said, 'Blue, I feel like a blintz.'" The mattress bounced twice as Fuzzy's chest heaved with a two-syllable laugh.

"So Blue says back, 'You look like a fuckin' blintz.'" Another double laugh.

"Hey, Jones," Fuzzy said apologetically, "Irv the Curve's going to call you. He wants to meet. Talk about arrangements. You gonna be okay?"

"What else can I be?"

When Fuzzy departed it was like watching the Grand Tetons walk out the door. You didn't see guys like that anymore. Guys who were all guy. Guys who didn't worry about cholesterol because they would kick its ass if it ever became a problem.

I stood on Mickey's twentieth-floor balcony, facing south toward Longport. You would think I'd be crying, but I wasn't. In the movies, when wise guys die there are always these great displays—people making pasta, swearing vengeance, and hugging each other. I couldn't cook, and I didn't want to kill anybody. I had no siblings. Parents gone. No woman, either. Irv the Curve would grill me about women to dodge the subject of Mickey's death.

From this elevation, the Boardwalk looked like a thin, drawn-out flag. It was made from three types of materials. The oldest boards were a splintery brown, rotted hollow in some sections. The second oldest planks were made of silver sheet metal with tiny ridges to grip your shoes or the wheels of a bike. Then there were the newest boards, which were a blond wood that hadn't been corrupted yet by the elements. A year from now the blond wood would be brown. I used to wonder why they didn't do the whole Boardwalk in sheet metal so that the elements wouldn't get through, but I preferred the Boardwalk hammered together on an ad hoc basis. It was good for people to see the damage, to see that the whole thing was capable of collapse.

The kitchen phone rang. When I picked it up, it slipped from my hand. The receiver smelled like Bengay or some old-mannish elixir.

"How you doin', Mr. Brooks Brothers?" a soft voice asked.

"I'm all right, Irv."

"Let's you and me meet. Whaddayasay we go to that place in the A.M.? The old haunt. You know, down there near the elephant. You can get your omelet. You know where. Nine in the A.M. You can run it off later."

Arrangements

"I lived to be this age in my line of work because I'm good at seeming."

THE SCENT OF THE BOARDWALK ROSE SHARPLY TO THE BALcony—a potpourri of peanuts, cotton candy, popcorn, and molasses. Even in the morning Atlantic City was ready for the evening's recreation. Daylight was a rite of passage to get to night. Depending on the breeze, these smells could overpower the sea air, not the kind of sensation you could squeeze onto the little Boardwalk computer tour downstairs. It netted out a thick, sweet smell, the molasses dominating. A blonde woman in a tight black outfit rollerbladed from the south beaches. I could hear the furious hum of her wheels and the jerk in sound as the Boardwalk changed from wood to metal. An old couple hobbled out of her way, frightened, as she rocketed by. I grabbed the binoculars that Mickey kept stashed under the table and focused on the blonde. She looked seventy. This kind of thing was happening to me more and more. Usually it was a woman who looked like a knockout from a distance but up close turned out to be twelve years old or something.

I sat on the balcony and opened up my laptop. It took me about twenty minutes to bang out a short obituary of Mickey. Despite what had just happened, I was very clearheaded. Maybe it was because writing stuff like this meant that my professional self was overtaking the man. In the copy, I emphasized Mickey's origins in taffy manufacturing and titled the piece, "Farewell, Taffy King." Fuck 'em if they can't take a joke. I found a photo of Mickey taken in the early seventies: He was waving from the second-story window of his Taste of the Shore Taffy shop, his headquarters for many decades before the Golden Prospect was built.

I threw on an oxford shirt, khakis, and old boots and dropped off a disk with the obit and the photo of Mickey in the Golden Prospect's business office. A frizzy-haired secretary promised that she would place it on Atlantic City On-Line, a popular Web site.

I drove my Cherokee the five miles south down Atlantic Avenue to Margate. Irv didn't need to name the restaurant. The boys always talked as if their shorts were bugged, so after a lifetime, I picked things up.

The place was Murray's, a deli that hadn't changed its menu or its furniture since Chester Alan Arthur or somebody had a corned beef and Russian dressing there a million years ago. It was on the street front of a ten-story condo building on the 9000 block of Atlantic Avenue at Decatur, near Lucy, the giant, six-story, steel-plated elephant that had been guarding the beaches from intruders since a speculator named Lafferty put her up in 1881. First-time visitors to the Shore had been known to drive into telephone poles upon encountering Lucy's hulking grayness. There was even a story about a German spy who came ashore from a submarine one night during World War II and ran screaming back into the Atlantic when his flashlight illuminated her.

Lucy was a perfectly proportioned elephant magnified ten or twenty times. She once served as a hotel, but stress to the structure and a lack of care shut her down in the late 1940s. People in Margate got together in the seventies and restored her, although I wasn't sure what went on inside anymore.

Across the street from Lucy there was a new billboard, inappropriately placed, I thought. It featured a man with blow-dried black hair and a mustache who was hawking furs and staring down at me, with three peroxide blondes in soft-focus admiring him from the background. BARRY SILVER. FURS, the sign read in bold gold letters. He had this smarmy look on his face, as if we should buy his furs because he had banged his three biggest fans. I had a theory that BARRY SILVER. FURS was precisely why the Jewish girls in college catapulted themselves into the arms of wheat-haired men with nicknames like Rowdy or Hoot.

Irv the Curve Aronson joined up with Mickey after Irv's boss, Dutch Schultz, was gunned down at the Palace Chop House in Newark. Irv saw Mickey as a brother, although I never heard Mickey reciprocate the sentiment. He read a lot, like Mickey, but was far more articulate. Mickey liked having him out front when it came to dealing with the politicians.

I opened the door to Murray's and was blasted simultaneously by the air-conditioning and an overplayed Yiddish song called "Romania, Romania." Whenever it played, Mickey would remind me that he was born in Romania and had fled after some god awful pogrom. Yes, that's right, I would acknowledge. "Romania. Land of the gypsies," Mickey would say.

Murray's was divided into two sections. A deli was on the right. A restaurant was on the left. I strolled down the aisle of the deli that featured the divine scents of fresh corned beef and coleslaw and the violent sight of tongue in a frosted window. Waves of elderly—and other assorted diminutive—people stood in line taking yellow numbered tickets, waiting for America, sliced lean, and shooting across looks of conspiracy and betrayal at the heavyset man behind the counter when he didn't call their numbers.

After admiring for a few seconds the stacks of borscht bottles piled in one of the freezers toward the back of the deli, I headed back to Murray's entrance to find Irv the Curve. I was a medium-sized guy, but I felt like a linebacker wading through all of these little people, who seemed to part as I cut through them. They had old faces, not just in the sense of being elderly, but of being from another time. The men looked like permutations of Alan Arkin. The women looked like Elton John circa 1975 with their glitter and oversized glasses. As they moved aside, I had this strange sense that I was being wheeled through at great speed on an old pushcart. *Aaah, Romania, Romania, Ro-MAYN-ia!* When the last wave parted, a meticulous-looking old man with sad red eyes, a knowing smile, and ears like flesh-tone question marks (holding a *Racing Form* as if it were a holy edict) stood smiling next to a shimmering box of

Rolaids balanced on the edge of the cashier's counter. I watched the little people tittering at each other and silencing their unruly children at the sight of Irv the Curve.

Irv was handsome in a way that only a very old man can be. In fact, I could not imagine that Irv the Curve had ever been young. God had created him to be at precisely this season in his life. A man of extraordinary self-discipline and vanity, he didn't have any fat on him, not that I had ever seen him without clothing. Forever on display, Irv wore fine clothing even on the beach in the summer, occasionally rolling up his pants when he needed to speak with someone away from the crowd, by the water.

Everything in Murray's seemed to pick up tempo when Irv the Curve held out his arms. Waitresses scurried to get our table ready. Plates and utensils danced like cartoon characters to a booth in the back. Random people shook his hand and rushed forward to hug and kiss him. He responded as if he knew them all, his eyebrows rising and falling with each new greeting.

"Hey, Irv," I said with an embrace.

"Shush, Jonah, you shouldn't say names."

"What's the big secret? Everyone here knows you."

"Nothin'. I'm just so used to sayin' that. Here we are back at the old haunt. You grew, *shaygets*." *Shaygets* meant a gentile male. Irv shook his head as if to wake himself up. Waitresses scurried in fast-forward to get Irv's table ready.

"You saw me last week."

"I had a growth spurt around your age. I got to around five-five."

"You're five-five?"

"I *was* five-five."

"You still look like Paul Newman to me, Irv."

"Hey, pal, I looked like Paul Newman before Paul Newman. I see you got his watch. You know, your grandfather's. That's nice. And, look, a few gray hairs on you." Irv flagged a hostess who gestured with a flourish toward a booth and we were seated.

Irv toyed with the pickle bowl. "So we lost our holy man," he said. "I talked to Glick's. You all right?"

"A little hollow."

"I'm sure. I'm sure."

"I picked out a suit."

"Which one? He liked blue. Hated black. Said black made you look like a hood."

"I got the one he bought for my graduation in eighty-four. There's a shirt and a tie he bought with it. He got a pair of Allen Edmonds shoes a couple of years ago that he never wore. He said he wanted them for a special occasion."

"Now's pretty special."

"Right. Then there's socks and underwear and an undershirt."

"Why the hell's he need an undershirt?"

"He always wore one under a business shirt. He said the starch made him itch."

"He's not itching now."

"I'd feel better if he had it."

"Fine. So what's your thinking about the funeral?"

"Simple. Gravesite. It's springtime."

"I dunno. You'd be standing out there with all the *shtarkers*. We've done a helluva job low-keying your ties to Mickey. It's never caused you any trouble. You standing with me, old Blue, and the others may not square with your political friends. Vanni will show up, you know, but that's outside talk." Outside talk: code for the Sweet 'n Low on the table could be bugged.

"I don't think people will make the link between Mickey and me. I'm not that famous."

"Don't kid yourself. People talk. That Al Just, or whatever he's calling himself these days, has been dogging us for years. Chased you all outta the country and cost you a nice American boyhood. His father, Mouse Yutzel, could fuck up a slice of rye toast."

"Mickey was ranting about Al Just."

"People think things. The life is sexy when it's sexy, then somebody uses it against you when it's not so sexy."

"Then what?"

"Then we show 'em the view."

I dropped the butter knife I was fiddling with.

"Show 'em the view" was a phrase Mickey had used. It meant to take a troublemaker up to the top of the Tacony Palmyra Bridge and hold him over the side until he got the message.

"I'm kidding, Jonah." Irv smirked like a kid who just short-sheeted a bed. It was Irv's way of changing the subject. "Let's try and talk cheerful. So, how's the broad that I met that time?" he asked. I had brought a woman up from Washington last summer for a few days. She was a knockout, a rising star at a satellite company.

"Not so hot. I couldn't make it work."

"Not with a broad like that you couldn't."

"You thought she was that bad?"

"She'll make kasha outta you."

"You seemed like you liked her when we had dinner that time."

"I lived to be this age in my line of work because I'm good at seeming. Seeming is what I do. When I was shlepping those suitcases to Zurich for your grandfather, do you think I seemed like I was carrying Fort Knox? No. I seemed like a nobody. That's why I'm eighty-five. Anyway, life takes care of things. A broad like that, her power's between her legs. Yours is between your ears. That's a bad match. Now, whaddaya want?"

"I want someone who wants to settle down."

"No, no, what you want to eat, that omelet?"

"Sure."

A waitress in her sixties with a beehive hairdo, orange lipstick, and matching orange glasses appeared from behind a smoked-glass wall. She had been at Murray's forever. She called everybody "Doll," "Dollsy," and once in a while "Dollsner." Her name may have been Marie, but I had been calling her Dollsy for years, and she got a kick out of it. Irv ordered a ham omelet and a cup of coffee. I got the spinach omelet and grapefruit juice.

"Yeah, that girl was a smorgasbroad."

"Smorgasbord?"

"No, smorgas*broad*. For her, life's a buffet. A buffet of men. She's always looking for what's under the next steamer. Never stops. Can't stop. Had them in my day, too, only nowadays they're everywhere. I see them come down from New York and Philly from their jobs. They believe everything they read in *Cosmopolitan* magazine. They think God's going to come up to their table with a little pad and take their order like he's their own chef. There's only two ways to deal with a smorgasbroad. For a guy like you, you stay the hell away. She sees you have a heart and cuts it out. Why? Because that's what she does! She's a smorgasbroad!"

"I'm with you on the concept, Irv."

"Guys like Benny Siegel and Carvin' Marvin in his day were good at it. See, you play cool, aloof—"

"I tried that once—"

"And you failed, so shut up and listen. A smorgasbroad *wants* to be deserted. It confirms her fix on the world and allows her to do what she really wants to do."

"What's that?"

A smack on the head with a *Racing Form*. "She wants to be a smorgasbroad because that's what she adds up to."

"Christ. Are they all like that?" I asked, getting depressed.

"No. Your Deedee and your mother weren't smorgasbroads. They were real ladies. They're just not many of them anymore."

Dollsy brought our breakfast. Irv and I ate without speaking. There was nothing awkward about it, just that we were perfectly content to eat. When there was nothing left, we agreed to a graveside funeral. It was to be held at the same cemetery in Ventnor where Deedee and my parents were buried.

"I guess I'll go back, call Rabbi Wald, and check Mickey's mail or something."

Irv leaned across the table and bopped me again on the head with his *Racing Form*. "Mickey never got mail. What the hell's wrong with you? Anyway, call the rabbi."

As we exited, who but BARRY SILVER. FURS himself strolled by. I held my glance for a few seconds because I didn't immediately tie him to the billboard and thought I might have known him from someplace. Suddenly I recognized him. He then did something with his eyebrows and a twitch of the shoulder that communicated quite clearly that I must have known who he was and been impressed to see him in the flesh. I wanted to knock him on his ass.

"Jonah, we'll have to screw with his sign." Irv and I had had a long history of seeing who could come up with the cleverest way to alter signs without getting caught, usually dumb little restaurant postings.

On the concrete steps in front of Murray's, Irv curiously swept the street with his eyes. I could have sworn a vein next to his left eye twitched. He smiled broadly and then cupped his mouth, scratching his upper lip.

"Hey, there's something I have to tell you now."

"Is it about Vanni?"

"Yeah. He wants to talk to you. Mick told you, huh?"

"Yes. What does he want?"

"Don't know for sure. But you've got skills, the mind wars with the public, the airwaves. My guess is the answer lies in that."

"What do I do?" I felt my colon fall to my toes and spring back up to my throat.

"You'll meet him at the funeral."

"I don't want to deal with this guy. I'm a political pollster for God's sake."

"Yeah, and I'm Alan Greenspan! I think I'll go home, take a piss, and lower interest rates. What the hell's wrong with you? You'll talk to Vanni."

"At the funeral?"

"I'm sure he won't want to talk there, but he'll like you. He's not like those red-eyed punk animals he's got that have no respect for commerce," Irv said, echoing the common fears about the new wise guy generation. "It's blood over money with them. When Vanni wants to meet, you'll meet. It's not like a choice, like choosing between Dartmouth and Haverford—"

"I didn't say—"

"You go is all! Vanni's Shore outpost is inside Lucy," he said, pointing with his *Racing Form*. "The Elephant."

Klezmorim

"It's reasonable to believe men want to kill you."

I ARRIVED AT THE CEMETERY EARLY, PARKED MY CHEROKEE ON Atlantic Avenue, and headed across the street to the Boardwalk to collect a ration of sea air before the service. May down the Shore is a peculiar mixture of sadness and bounty. It is desolate for the most part, and everything echoes. But there is hope, the promise of summer. In spite of the echoes—or maybe because of them— euphoric high school kids raged down the Boardwalk on roller-blades and skateboards to the puzzlement of recoiling visitors. A teenage boy and girl emerged, laughing, from under the Boardwalk. Their cheeks were rosy, and their hair was a sandy mess. I was furious with them because their worlds were made up of wonder and seaside delight, not death.

The steady stroking of the waves lulled me into a daze that made me temporarily oblivious to the lives around me until a soft voice retrieved the moment.

"The ocean looks a lot closer than it used to," the woman in the black cotton dress said, barely audibly.

"It *is* closer," I said, as the surf washed beneath us.

We were both holding on to the railing of the Boardwalk. A thin layer of broken clouds let rigid blue rays of light stir the ocean like celestial eggbeaters. To the north, a helicopter buzzed over the casinos, probably a high roller who had lost a fortune the night before being whirred above the beach to see how small everyone else was, too.

"You're klezmorim!" I said, startled, when I saw that the woman was not alone.

"We are. You must be Jonah."

The woman who spoke to me was hauntingly beautiful, not every man's "type" for certain. My mother and Deedee would have thought she was pretty. She had translucent olive skin, an upturned Main Line nose, and large fawn brown eyes. Her bone structure was delicate, hinting at the blue-blooded hunt country and somewhere else that I couldn't place. I followed each curve on her face, unrelenting because I was wearing sunglasses that I assumed masked my fascination. She wore a medallion around her neck of silver and turquoise. That she was a klezmer musician was wildly, unbalancingly dissonant. She had a guitar. She was also wearing paddock boots, the kind worn for horseback riding. A mousy-looking woman standing beside her had a violin. A little bearded dude had a clarinet.

"Jonah," Doe Eyes said, "I am sorry about your grandfather. Mr. Aronson—Irv—called for us. He asked us to play two songs at the service. It's something your grandfather wanted. Mickey used to like to listen to us when we played at concerts on the Boardwalk. Gypsy music, he called it."

Doe Eyes bloomed for me at her mention of Mickey's name.

"You knew Mickey?" I asked. I stiffened when I realized how desperate I probably sounded.

"Not well, but we would talk at our concerts." I envisioned Mickey conducting this band from wherever he was. Death was an obstacle, not a deal breaker.

Doe Eyes swayed a paddock boot behind her ankle. "So how do you know the ocean's closer?"

"When I was little, I read about erosion. I used to go to the Atlantic City Library and take out books on regional geology. In the mid-eighteen hundreds, Jersey was a mile wider to the east.

Here's another number for you: Four hundred thousand cubic yards of sand are drained southward every year toward Wildwood. The beach is getting wider down there."

"Sounds like you worried about it." The word "worried" throttled a memory in my brain. *Mario Vanni wants to talk to you. . . .*

"Still do."

"We probably ought to head to the cemetery," Doe Eyes prodded, and we began our mournful retreat across Atlantic Avenue. A college-age couple swiveled their heads in offense as a skateboarder shot by.

"The shoebies can't handle the speed," I told Doe Eyes on our walk.

"Shoebies?"

Mickey had said "shoebie" was from decades ago when people brought their beachwear in shoe boxes and got changed in their cars. They have since graduated to backpacks, but they still looked like shoebies to me.

I pointed out to the klezmorim the gravestone of Puggy Feinberg, the jester of Mickey's gang. Chiseled into the granite beneath his name was Puggy's eternal message to the living: "What are you lookin' at?" Doe Eyes brought her hand to her lips, stunned by Puggy's irreverence.

A new figure soon emerged from behind a nearby grave post. Like a Shakespearean king, he held his arms out, a long, black raincoat hanging from his back like a cape. My Uncle Blue. His brittle white hair blew gently in the ocean breeze. I split from the klezmorim when Blue's twisted mouth formed my name. Blue had had a stroke a few years ago that slackened his face gruesomely. I hugged him and could feel his vertebrae against my palms. It was like embracing the skeleton that hung in the back of a high school biology class.

As I shuffled in step with Blue toward the grave site, an amused old woman who looked like Phyllis Diller stood on the sidewalk and studied a tabloid headline reading, "Farewell, Lenape Warlord." It was a similar headline to the one I had written for Atlantic City On-Line. Beneath the headline was the photo of Mickey I had given the hotel secretary.

"Lenape warlord" was a reference to the Indian tribe that ruled

South Jersey and eastern Pennsylvania hundreds of years ago until William Penn's son Thomas chased them away using a bogus land measurement. "Penn *shtupped* the Lenape good," Mickey once told me. He was upset about it and tended to lecture anyone who would listen about the Indians. "That old chief Lapowinsa had to carry the bones of his dead tribe from here to Wilkes-Barrre, the ass crack of the nation," Mickey had raged. "This whole land is a swindle."

A host of familiar old souls began lining up at Mickey's service. Unlike the Lenape, these guys didn't do a lot of walking. They drove in Cadillac Devilles of assorted colors ranging from mulberry to white diamond that they parked along the grass next to the cemetery driveway. This tidal wave of *alter kockers*, old farts, drifted toward the grave site. Irv the Curve fell in line next to Blue, me, and the other geriatric minstrels. God, I couldn't believe they were still alive, but here they were, spooking the coast like old warriors lining up for their ration of face paint.

There was Carvin' Marvin Kushner (Cadillac color: mulberry), who was smooth with women and fast with a stiletto, but wouldn't kill on the High Holidays; Louie "Kid Knish" Marks (sterling), who ate like a horse but never gained weight; Mort the Snort Stein (moonstone), so-named because he sniffed when he spoke; Timmy "the Mick" O'Malley from Pleasantville (emerald green); Fuzzy Marino of Margate (canary yellow); Sid Goldman (Turkish magenta), who also was called "the Mick" for reasons I never understood; Isidore "Darth" Schnader (Harvard crimson); Rhymin' Hyman Reznick (sable black), a moron of breathtaking proportions who liked to use important-sounding words—incorrectly—while handicapping horses and making small talk. When I got my White House job, Rhymin' Hyman counseled me that Washington was a snake pit: "Remember," he said, "Don't ever let anybody circumcise your authority."

A pocket of acute sadness festered in my abdomen. It felt like it was moving down, down through me, trying to find a place to escape. It was too big to squeeze out of any one place. The struggle liberated an inconvenient question: Would I suddenly begin to miss the Shore now that my only reason to be here had died? Despite this intrusion, Mickey's funeral was no place for genuine expression. Tears? Not a chance. I would sooner have worn a pink tutu than cried. Today, I was one hundred and fifty pounds of salt water that had to remain bottled. This was not a crowd that possessed pity.

Twenty yards to the north, two men in suits emerged from the back of a white Mercedes with crimson seats. One of them was Mario Vanni. Who wanted to talk to me. I swallowed hard. Vanni was the boss of the Philadelphia–South Jersey Cosa Nostra, if you believed that sort of thing, and I did.

I put Vanni in his early fifties. He had a widow's peak at the top of his forehead, a deep tan, and quizzical eyebrows. Vanni reached into his breast pocket and slid out a black pair of sunglasses. He whipped them onto the bridge of his nose. The man walking with Vanni smashed a cigarette beneath a thin loafer. He wore a dark European suit that sucked in the sun and radiated it back a shade or two duller. The guy appeared to be my age and had the sleek pinched head of Doberman. He craned his neck the way jocks do when they warm up.

As Vanni moved closer, I was thunderstruck by his dress. He was wearing a perfectly pressed white button-down shirt with his dark blue suit. The getup was almost certainly from Brooks Brothers. I knew those deep weaves. Vanni looked like a banker, with the exception of his sculpted ethnic face. There wasn't a trace of a belly on him, suggesting he preferred health clubs to social clubs.

I stood between Blue and Irv as Vanni and his attack dog approached the grave. Blue held out his arms, and Vanni embraced him.

"Sorry about Mick," Vanni told Blue in a rich local accent, which neutralized his attire. "He was a real great man, a hundred percent." *A hunnert p'cent.*

"They broke the mold," Blue said.

Vanni—and the slick Robin to his Batman—nodded in agreement.

"You know our friend Noel, don't you, Blue?" Vanni gestured toward his young associate. I knew who this man was now but had never seen him before.

Noel bowed his head and smiled respectfully to Blue.

Vanni turned to me, pulling off his sunglasses. Blue took a step forward, "Jonah, this is Mario Vanni."

"Hey, Jonah," Vanni said. "I wanted to show my respect for your grandfather. I hear you got his brains."

"I'm not sure about that, but I'm glad that you came." He stepped forward and embraced me. I felt my blood flow abruptly halt. Standing nose to nose like my father might have, Vanni quietly said, "When things settle, you know, we'll talk. Need a little advice. Say you want to ask a favor in private. Come down to the big elephant. That all right?"

"Sure." I stiffened my legs to redirect the corpuscles away from my temples, where my cells felt like they had hidden for cover.

When Vanni backed off, I got my first steady bore on his eyes. They were the warm and intelligent brown high beams of a hotshot Little League coach. I could see why men followed him but was bewildered by his demeanor. Vanni reminded me of many of the successful Italian Americans I met every day in business and politics—the senators, doctors, lawyers, professors who were no more tied to the mob than Doe Eyes the klezmer player.

In the distance, an outraged driver on Atlantic Avenue suddenly blared his horn, protesting the slow-moving traffic. Vanni's eyes went hard and black at the sensory blitzkrieg. In a millisecond, his eyes shot across a subliminal message like the ones you used to hear about when one frame in a movie read, "Buy Popcorn," and people supposedly got up and bought it. Vanni's message to a long-vanished driver was, "I'm gonna put you in a fuckin' scrap crusher." But as quickly as it had come, Vanni's surge of rage disappeared and his Little League eyes returned.

Noel extended his hand and stated his name. He had long eyelashes that gave him a vulnerable look, offsetting his brutal body and bone white incisors. Noel, he of the ringing jingle bells name, did not smile broadly, which would have been inappropriate to the occasion, but I saw enough of his teeth to be unnerved. The son of a bitch had a diamond embedded in his right upper eyetooth. It was drilled right in there. I had the impulse to cover my throat.

According to the papers, Noel was Vanni's *consigliere*, an amazing feat for a man so young. His position was some kind of concession to the Young Turks, the hotheaded faction that Noel led. I felt queer thinking it, but the guy was sexy in a terrible way. I could see gorgeous women liking him, the kind that pay attention only when they're being defiled.

Having heard stories about Noel, I once asked Mickey what he knew about him. "A guy to watch," was all he said, flicking his nose.

Rabbi Wald—Friar Tuck to Mickey's merry band—emerged from behind a seawall of shoulders. He had on a conservative black suit and a tie with tiny pairs of dice on it. He began a Hebrew prayer without even gesturing for silence.

Wald had been tossed out of his Philadelphia congregation years ago because he had beaten up his popular understudy. Knocked him flat after a kid's bar mitzvah lesson. Not long after the incident, we ran into Wald on the Boardwalk, and he was wearing a leather bomber's jacket. "That's my rabbi," Mickey told no one in particular walking by.

I snapped to attention when the rabbi told a story of meeting Mickey in a Haddonfield park called Birdwood. The first-ever complete dinosaur skeleton had been unearthed there in 1848, and Rabbi Wald eloquently, however oddly, linked Mickey to the extinct beast before saying "Amen."

As the rabbi said *kaddish*, the prayer for the dead, I looked past him toward the Boardwalk. Near where the klezmorim had first emerged a few hundred yards away, a solitary figure in black, of exaggerated length, stood with his back against the sea. His skin was dark. Long, black hair fell around his shoulders. He held a black hat in his hand, down by his belt. *Mickey had mentioned a man in the pines with a hat.* Babble, Jonah? The man's hat appeared to be vaguely Western; something glittered beside a feather on the hatband. The wind danced through him in a way that made his suit fan out from his bones. His hair blew wildly as he arched his head backward to face the clouds.

The rabbi finished his prayer and turned toward the klezmorim who began their doleful "*Mein Ruhe Platz*" (My Resting Place). I was distracted from the solemn, atavistic figure on the Boardwalk by the guitarist. She had begun to sing. Her eyes matched her voice—expansive, soft, and touched with sadness.

She was looking at me. I thought so, anyway. I turned to see if there was someone behind me whom she recognized. There wasn't. I nodded at her, and she smiled a touch more, but it did not disrupt her singing. I smiled back, I think, at her feet.

I turned back toward the Boardwalk. The dark man with the hat was gone, vanished. The klezmorim began their second piece, called *"Miserlou."* It was about a princess wandering in the desert looking for her lost love.

Noel slipped behind Vanni and moved toward the Boardwalk. He then did something very strange. He motioned with his eyes and grinned at me. With his eyeteeth catching the silver sunlight, Noel turned toward Mickey's casket. His eyes widened in a "How 'bout that?" kind of expression. My heart began racing at speeds that I hadn't felt even when I sprinted at the end of a run. Then Noel rubbed his thumb against his index finger in a financial gesture and brought his hand up to his heart. He concluded this bizarre ritual with an exaggerated frown, the empathetic kind you make to a child who's just scraped his knee. Noel's lower lip then retracted like the wing of a fighter plane to its normal position, and I felt as if I had vanished from his consciousness.

The music stopped. I abandoned Noel and instinctively stepped toward the grave, kissed my fingers and touched them to the coffin. Doe Eyes nodded in agreement with my sorrow. Yes, Jonah, this *is* sad. My heart's gallop had shifted down to a canter. The distraction of Doe Eyes made me think it was possible that I might have gone temporarily insane and interpreted Noel's gesture to mean something other than sorcery. I stepped back from the grave, and Blue took my elbow.

"Let people think you're crazy," Mickey told me once when we discussed paranoia. "It is reasonable to believe men want to kill you."

Two sinewy gravediggers—I took them to be pineys—began cranking a lever on the silver frame and lowered Mickey's casket, the eternal shoe box, into the ground.

Blue tugged at my shoulder, moving me backward. I was surprised by his strength and almost lost my balance. "Son, I've had a lifetime of death," he said. The statement caught the attention of one of the gravediggers, who wore a black derby that was both comical and chilling, as circus clowns are to kids. We watched the casket lower.

Rhymin' Hyman the idiot stuck his Jell-o-y head over my shoulder. "Yeah," he began, "Mick said you went off and became a big shot. Said you shouldn't be so impressed with those Washington people. He was right. After all, Jonah, they put their legs on one at a time." Blue and I squinted at him in disbelief. "Anyhow," Rhymin' Hyman continued, "Mick said he was proud a you with all the success. And look, there he is," Hyman concluded, pointing toward the yawning earth. The burial vault cover was lowered with a pulley onto its mate, emitting a definitive concrete belch.

Blue nudged me aside without so much as a nod of etiquette to Rhymin' Hyman. Unlike me, Blue knew what to ignore, which was true wisdom. I felt a magnetic impulse to ask, "What did you mean, 'And look, there he is'?"

"Look, Jonah, how about me and a couple guys take you out to Carmine's tonight," Blue said. "I got a little room, all right?"

"Okay."

Blue grabbed my face like I was a child. "Yeah, we'll take care of you." He let me go and backed away slowly toward his waiting driver.

The klezmorim slowly glided across the cemetery toward the outer gates. I caught up and thanked them. The man identified himself as Jerry. The mousy-looking woman was Rachel. Doe Eyes's name was Edie. Edie Morris.

As we spoke, a heavyset woman with sunglasses and a camera ducked toward me and snapped my photograph. She looked like the warden of a women's prison. This emboldened a pack of camera crews, who came forward. Punishment. This was punishment for me thinking thoughts about Edie at my grandfather's funeral.

I walked toward Edie and put my hand on the small of her back. I needed her as a shield, to say to the reporters, "I'm going somewhere with this woman and it would be impolite to interrupt further." Surprisingly, they stood down as we slipped out of the

cemetery. Irv the Curve and the boys gave the crews a conse-
quential look.

"Thanks for getting me out, Edie Morris."

"Happy to help. It was a slick move. You've dealt with reporters
before, I guess."

"My little gift."

A cloud broke apart in between two high-rise condominiums,
sending rays of blue light onto the windshields of the cars filing
out of the cemetery. The white Mercedes with Vanni and Noel in
the back pulled out. Vanni held his fist against his ear in a "call
me" signal. I solemnly waved back. Noel gave his hand a friendly
wiggle, along with an unctuous grin. A red light from somewhere
inside the car caught the diamond in his fang and made it wink at
me. Noel, my buddy. I watched in a daze as the Mercedes disappeared onto Atlantic Avenue.

"Yoo-hoo?" Edie said, waving a hand before my eyes. When I
faced her, a warm wave of familiarity filled me. She was the only
thing that "fit" into the climate. Attractions between men and
women must be elemental, neither rational nor "appropriate," that
watchword of millennial sensitivity. I couldn't identify the enzymes
that were zinging back and forth, only that I was being persuaded
by visions of Mickey listening to a klezmer concert that Edie and
I had been well acquainted.

"Well, I'm going back to Mickey's place to clean things out."

"Sad work."

"Right. Off to another funeral for you?" I was hoping that this
would come out sounding funny. It hadn't.

"No, home."

"Where's home?"

"Near Batsto."

"In the barrens?"

"In the pinelands. We say pinelands now."

"Sorry. What do you do there?"

"I teach music."

"To whom?"

"Children."

"Really. How many do you have?"

"I have none. Of my own. You?"

"Just one. Me."

"You're one of those men, are you?"

"Actually, no. I've been middle-aged since kindergarten."

"I'm sorry to hear that."

"So am I. You ride horses, don't you?" I asked.

Edie's features morphed into surprise. "Yes, why?"

"Your paddock boots. I used to have a pair like that. When I rode." This was an obtuse way of suggesting a future to myself, if not to her.

"Oh."

We both stood silently. There was something adolescent about it.

"Well, I'll let you know if I decide to take up the harmonica or something."

Bad Facts

"I need you to help spin me out of all that past crap."

THE HAMMERING STRAINS OF GEORGE THOROGOOD'S "ONE
Bourbon, One Scotch, and One Beer" pounded out from the
window twenty feet above me in Lucy the Elephant's ass. The
rumble made me think of Frat Row at Dartmouth. When I spotted
an oversized man without a neck standing at the base of Lucy's
thick rear leg, I stopped reminiscing about college.

I decided to see Vanni immediately after Mickey's funeral. I
wanted to know what was on his mind so I could bring it up with
Blue and Irv that night at dinner. In my life, patience had never
offered much of a payoff.

My anxiety about meeting Vanni transcended anything that I
factually knew to be true about him or why he wanted to meet
with me. It was a Darwinian nervousness that I had seen crease
Mickey's brow over the years. It had its roots in chronic historical
tensions between the Jews and Italians.

After Prohibition, Italian rackets had supplanted Jewish ones.
The Italians had a centuries-old management structure that the
Jews lacked. That structure was called Cosa Nostra, or Mafia. The
Italians respected and tolerated Mickey, but the purists among
them resented that he had held on to Atlantic City as if it were

Masada. Complicating matters, Mickey wasn't really a regional boss and hadn't been since the 1930s. He had no real "turf," which had always been the defining point of gangland power. While Italian men like my Uncle Blue Cocco didn't care, less visionary members of Blue's union didn't "get" why prehistoric Mickey Price still held so much sway. Street turf had become almost all Italian as the Mafia structure took hold in America.

When Prohibition was repealed, Mickey and his crew found themselves in a gangland diaspora. Mickey began to focus on gambling, tourism, and finance—trades that required no territory. He cut in many Italian partners to the satisfaction of most, or else he would have been dead.

On top of the strategic friction between the Kosher and Cosa Nostras, there were ancient insecurities on the part of Jewish and Italian men that always throbbed beneath the surface. Jews were smart but weak; Italians were dumb but strong—or so the racist logic went. These notions had caused Jewish wise guys to engage in displays of violent, warped masculinity (Murder Inc. was run by Jews), while Italians like the diminutive Carlo Gambino went out of their way to demonstrate genuine brilliance. Truth be told, there were plenty of dumb, tough Jews and smart, weak Italians, but realities never defused the tension.

As I stepped toward Lucy, this narrative was fully registered in my DNA: An Ivy League–educated, Republican White House–trained pollster, who was the grandson of the biggest Jewish crime boss of his day, had to—*had* to—tweak at this ancient percussion.

"You lookin' at somethin', chief?" the neckless man beside the elephant asked me in a gratuitous South Jersey confrontation. He shrugged his shoulders, to which his head was directly soldered, presumably to remind me of my insignificance to him.

"I wanted to see Mr. Vanni," I said.

"You wanna see Mr. Vanni?" he shrugged again.

"Yeah."

"Whattayou, a comedian? You Jerry Steinfeld, smart guy? Or are you sellin' Girl Scout cookies?"

"No. I'm Jonah Eastman. Mr. Vanni and I spoke a little while ago at my grandfather's funeral. I wanted to ask him for a favor. He knows I'll be coming by."

I got a tick of recognition. "You Mickey Price's kid?"

"Yes, sir."

"Why the fuck didn't you say so? What am I, a babbo? Yeah, I seen you on TV doing public relationships and shit."

"Would you tell Mr. Vanni that I'd like to see him?" I gave him my best tombstone eyes. Fuzzy taught me how to do this when I was getting picked on in seventh grade. Fuzzy said the key to tombstone eyes was not to squint or growl, but to look like nothing mattered. "The eyes should just be there."

No-Neck smirked at me and rapped on the door that was welded to Lucy's leg. The door opened.

"Tell Mario Mickey Price's kid wants to talk to him," he said to a black opening.

The door closed, and the big guy looked me over.

"I'm Frankie Shrugs," he said, unprompted. No shit. "You heard a me?"

"Frankie Shrugs. It sounds familiar. I think my grandfather mentioned you."

"Yeah?" Frankie adjusted his collar.

"I think so. Yeah, it sounds familiar to me. Maybe my uncle Blue said something."

"Blue, huh?" Frankie Shrugs was pleased at my recognition. My butt-sucking technique was clearly transferable from Washington to South Jersey. "You politics guys are full a shit. You're worse than us guys."

"I'm on a break from politics. I got straightened out."

Frankie Shrugs laughed with a tommy gun heh-heh-heh. "Straightened out" was a term wise guys used for being inducted into a crime family.

"You're so straight you come to see Mario in your Ivory League pants."

"Hey, we Ivory League guys have to stick together."

Lucy's door opened. A wiry, ferret-faced punk stuck out his nub of a chin. This was my invitation inside. Frankie Shrugs stopped me with his gorilla hands before I stepped inside.

"Hey, chief, I gotta frisk you."

I stopped and held my arms out, degraded as hell. The White House had sensors. I had a killer patting me down to make sure I was safe. He pulled at my shirt, presumably feeling for a wire.

Frankie Shrugs gave me a light punch in the shoulder. "Okay, you behave yourself."

The ferret guided me inside the giant elephant, her belly swollen with full-term killers, and shut the door behind us. We walked up a creaky spiral staircase that hugged the inside of Lucy's fat old leg. He stopped me at the top and stared at me moronically. He held his fingers out in a "wait a minute" gesture. He then made a sweeping motion with his hand, inviting me in.

Noel stood at the door of a small waiting room. He was wearing a tight, short-sleeved black shirt and jeans. He must have peeled off his funeral Armani fast. His skin stood out from the darkness of the wall behind him. Noel's body looked like one of those mechanical display Swiss Army knives they have outside of cutlery stores in the malls, with thin moving blades and edges. Every function sliced, ripped, or punctured.

The ferret tapped my chest. He had long fingernails. "You don't got any bugs on you, do you, genius?"

"Listening devices?"

"Yeah. Listening devices." He smiled at Noel, apparently to make fun of my use of polysyllabic words.

"He's fine, Petie," Noel said. "Jonah, good to see you." I felt surprisingly calm. Maybe down deep I liked having my life threatened. Noel was glad to see me. I shook his hand. It felt like barbecue tongs. A cigarette emerged from nowhere, and Noel asked if I had a light.

"No, I don't smoke," I said.

"Healthy. That's good," he said and took a matchbook from Petie.

"Keep the fuckin' matches already," Petie said, annoyed, when Noel attempted to hand them back to him.

"What's with you, Petie?" Noel asked.

"Can't you afford a fuckin' lighter instead of bummin' off everybody for Crissakes?"

"Take a fuckin' walk on the beach," Noel said, swatting Petie back down the stairs.

Noel gestured toward an archway within the elephant's neck that I took to be Vanni's door. My feet slid across thick shag carpeting. I had watched the Partridge Family on this type of carpet when my mother was still alive. A stream of light quivered on the burnt orange wall next to the door like a laser. I could not tell its source. Inside Lucy's torso, Vanni's office was actually bright and large, maybe about fourteen by eighteen feet. The main light source was the rear—as in ass—window. Secondary light came from reddish recessed lamps embedded in the floor. Air-conditioning flowed from vents from below. Lucy's belly must have been a maze of wires and ducts.

The boss was sitting behind a large mahogany desk with his back toward the window. Vanni was wearing a blue button-down shirt, open at the neck, khaki pants, and tasseled loafers that he had propped up on the side of the desk.

"I wanted to thank you for coming to Mickey's funeral." I laughed involuntarily. "I always wondered what was inside here."

"Just what you'd expect on the inside of an elephant. Furniture, air-conditioning. Can you imagine the FBI tryin' to climb in an elephant's ass to put in a bug?" Vanni cackled like a bad kid. "It was Mickey's idea, you know. This place."

This is why they were called wise guys.

Vanni's eyes widened. He gave Noel a comical look of enthusiasm and brought his feet down from the desk. This brought Noel from the doorway to an oversized white leather sofa Vanni had placed under a watercolor print from the bicentennial.

"I was honored to be at Mickey's funeral," Vanni said. "He was a great man."

"I wanted to ask your advice on something in private before I go back to Washington soon."

"I understand." *Unnerstann.* Vanni locked eyes with Noel. "You want to be in private, you said?"

"Oh, I don't want to be out of line with Noel or anything. It just involves something with my grandfather."

"Sure. Sure." Vanni winked at Noel, who winked back. Despite the playful eye gestures, the sinews in Noel's jaw tightened at the affront, and he vanished.

Vanni moved from behind his desk to the other guest chair that was next to me. He moved like a cat. Not a prissy household cat, but a panther, calculated and efficient.

"Look at you." *Loogit chu.* "You look like a movie star," Vanni said. "All decked out for the White House."

I felt like a goof and said nothing. "The tie, the shirt, the shoes. Where'd you come from?" he cackled. He seemed awfully genuine, as if he had dressed me himself. "Aw, I'm just babbling."

I didn't want to ask Vanni why he had called me here because I didn't want to know. I wanted to get out fast. Between my years living with Mickey and, more recently, during press interviews, I had learned how to navigate dead air. The key is to get comfortable being silent: Sooner or later the other guy will open his yap. In the silence, Vanni's eyes were transformed into black missiles preparing to launch atop a slow, deep burn.

"Thanks for playing along. I wanted to see you in private because I have a problem that I don't want the whole world to know about. Anyhow, Jonah, your grandfather was a smart man." Fire one. "He was smarter, I think, about you than he was about himself."

"About me?"

"Yeah, about you. You went off to Dartmouth. You should have seen Mickey wearing that shirt of his"—*shirtahis*—"so proud and all. You worked in the White House. He should have been proud. Shit, I'm proud of you. It's not because you're my kid, you understand, but you're *like* my kid. You follow?"

"I'm not sure that I do."

"See, Mick never went straight, no offense. Couldn't pull it off. He was always what the Casino Control Commission called an 'undesirable operator.' Some of the old Jewish guys like Moe Dalitz and Sam Tucker went straight. Out in Vegas. They didn't have *points* in casinos"—Vanni snarled the word "points"—"they had shares. *Shares.* You read me?"

"Yes."

"We Italians, we got a problem. I'm trying to solve it here. It's why we're talking. We had this old system, an organization that ran back a thousand years. There's a lot of pride going on there. The old-time Italians wanted guys like your grandpop out of the business because they had this mental prejudiced attitude. They got their kids involved with the thing. *La mala vita.* Dumbest fuckin' thing I ever heard. Mick didn't involve you. What my people should have been doing is getting out. If they couldn't get out themselves, they should have got their kids out, like Mickey did with you. Follow?"

"I do."

"Me, I'm not an Ivy League kind of guy like you, if you don't mind my saying. But my kids are like you. My daughter went to Penn. Angela. She graduated from Villanova Law last week. That's her up there." Vanni pointed to a picture. I nodded in the direction of the photo. Vanni's daughter was an attractive young woman with fine, dark features that were not done justice by an oversized graduation cap hovering above her head like a deformed halo.

"I can see why you're proud of her. You should be." Vanni arched his eyebrows in appreciation. He could tell that I meant it and that I knew this struggle.

"My boy's at Rutgers for another year. Chris. He's doing well in business classes. He has as much to do with my thing as you did with Mickey's, know what I mean?"

"You won't regret it."

Vanni tugged nervously at one of the buttons on his collar. "Anyhow, I got these Young Turks working for me. Your age and younger even. You heard of them?"

"I know the problem from the papers."

"Guess what? They all want to be fuckin' gangsters. I'm going in fuckin' reverse here! To be a gangster anymore is an acid trip. There's nothin' left in the life but the fantasies about the life."

I winced sympathetically. "They watch the movies."

"You're damned right they watch the movies. But life ain't a movie, is it, Jonah? The Italian people get all worked up about Mafia movies. You know what my problem is? My problem is that they're right. I don't want to be called a gangster any more than Mick did."

"Mickey liked his work, though. He didn't want to be called a gangster, but he didn't exactly try too hard to switch jobs. We used to talk about that. I'm just being straight with you."

"I know you are. That's why we're talking." *Tswhywertalkin.* Vanni leaned toward me conspiratorially. He whispered, "I can't leave my business to my kids. I mean, what are they going to get, a bunch a refrigerators we heisted off a truck in King of Prussia? Are they going to get *shares* in Fidelity Bank? The best a guy like me can do, Jonah, is casinos. The casinos started with names like Bugsy, and now they've got names like Hilton, Sheraton, ITT. I got the money but not the reputation. I'm the lowest of the low, no better than a drug pusher."

"Have you been accused of that?"

Vanni's eyes narrowed. "Never been accused in court, but, you know, there's always talk. The more I deny it, the more people believe it."

"Maybe you're denying the wrong things."

"How's that?"

"If you want someone to believe something is true about you, deny it. It's all in what you really do and what you deny you do. You get people asking questions: 'Is the sky blue? Is the grass green?' I dunno anymore."

Vanni's leg commenced a nervous bounce. He was excited, like a little kid waiting for permission to go downstairs to open his Christmas presents.

"I'm a fuckin' genius, you know that?" he said, leaning forward and pinching my cheeks. "I'm a genius because I know where to find geniuses. That brain of yours . . . I swear to God. Beautiful brain!" Vanni stood and kissed my scalp and plopped back down again. I felt like a schmuck.

"Follow me," he said.

We left Vanni's office and climbed a tiny collection of nervous wooden stairs that led to a ceiling hatch, the kind that accesses an attic. Vanni pushed it open, and it made a loud thunk as it hurtled through the daylight. In moments, we were standing on the deck atop Lucy. Vanni pointed with his palms to the north where the Atlantic City skyline stood like concrete dominoes against the sky. His eyes were filled with furious saline, which may have been a swift reaction to the breeze, or it may have sprung from somewhere desperate inside. The wind blew through our hair. It felt glorious and, for a nanosecond, I couldn't imagine there being a higher place on the globe. My barometric delight shattered when Vanni began speaking into his palms, which he held against the north.

"See, Jonah, they won't give me a license. I need a license, which is why I'm in this fuckin' elephant to watch over things down the Shore, *farshtayn*." Yiddish for "Do you read me, college boy?"

"That's why I need you. You know what to admit, to deny—all that shit! I've got a misunderstood image. If the commission meets with the anger of the public, if the public thinks I deserve a license, I get one."

"Mr. Vanni—"

"Mario."

"Mario. You said yourself that I have no role in this life. Why are you sharing these things with me?"

"Because I need you to help me. You know what to do here with the public opinions to spin me out of this life. You said it yourself. Admit, deny, admit, deny. You're creative."

"That's where everybody has it wrong. I create nothing. I *conduct*. I'm a conductor who depends on a good orchestra and a certain mood in the audience to get my clients good face time. I think you overestimate me."

"I estimate you just fine. Jonah, I need that license. I'm up again this September. Now it's May. We've got a few months to deal with all these bad facts. The commission better have a damned good reason for rejecting me. Face time. That's good."

"Do you have a criminal record?"

"Yeah, Lewisburg."

"That's a powerful reason. Mickey was denied a license, and he never spent a day in jail."

"I need you to help spin me out of all that past crap. Play it down."

"I don't mean to sound like a smart-ass, but that's a lot of past crap to spin you out of and to, uh, play down."

"Nah. I know it's not easy. And I've got the cash to buy serious talent."

"This is a scary proposition. If my clients thought I was mixed up in your business, I'd be finished. I don't know how else to say it. There are also guys out there like Noel who don't think much of guys like me."

"Don't worry about Noel."

"Well, I am. I don't like the way the guy looks at me. I'm in politics. I can read guys like that, although in Washington, they don't shoot you, they smear you. To work for you—"

"I understand there's been some problems down there lately. Washington."

I felt my Adam's apple go spastic in my throat. "There have been problems. They're fixable problems."

"Ethics, right?"

"That's how it's being framed."

"Framed, right. I saw the article from that Arizona paper. I saw what you did. Know what I think?"

"Actually, no."

"I don't think it was an ethics thing. I think you've got people who don't like you because you're a threat. You know how to get at the truth about people, get 'em to talk. Nobody wants the truth, do they, Jonah?" His mind was whirring.

"I understand the reasons why people follow your requests. And you know that I know that. If I don't work for you, do I end up facedown in a bowl of borscht?"

"My proposal is that I'm your client. You're my . . . conductor. You don't have to put me on your Web site if you don't want." Vanni winked.

"And if I am unable to focus on your case right now?"

"Irv said you were a ball-buster. Christ. It don't have to come to anything like that. Borscht. It's a business proposition here." The missile blackness of Vanni's pupils returned. "Do those Republicans who are busting your balls know what that *P* in your name is for?"

And here was the threat. My middle name: Price. I'm nailed on an ethics charge, and then word gets out that I'm tied to the rackets. Which I am, whether I am or not. My family background had never before hurt me in politics. Then there was Noel and his fang. Vague threats all, but all threats.

"Sure, some do,"

"But with what happened with the poll, somebody could say you learned those tricks from your grandpop. Lotta corruption around here. Atlantic City. Camden, with ABSCAM and all. Philly."

"They could say that."

"A fuckin' mess . . ."

Again, Vanni did one of his palm points to Atlantic City. It was a grandiose, quasi-literary moment. It was the quintessential American syllogism that straddled the underworld and high society alike: If only I had you, then my life would make total sense. . . .

I asked Vanni for a day to think it over and left the viscera of Lucy the Elephant feeling partially digested.

Money Wanders

"You go free when they fear you."

I FOUND A PARKING SPACE IN FRONT OF CARMINE'S. I HOVERED
like a ghoul beneath the red and white awning and read the
menu that was posted on the front window. There was a young
couple sitting on a raised veranda feeding each other cannoli. I was
scanning the desserts when a sudden bear hug from behind held
me aloft. I felt my heart stop. As soon as I felt the ropy hands of
Carvin' Marvin, it began to beat again. Fuzzy Marino was standing
right behind him.

"How's it hangin', College?" Carvin' Marvin asked. That was
Marv's name for me: College. A great-looking guy with thick silver
hair, an aquiline nose, and a cleft chin, Carvin' Marvin was a jock.
He played tennis, gave me horseback-riding lessons when I was a
kid, and teased me relentlessly about girls. The guy was frozen in
adolescence and still wore Speedo bathing suits on the beach. He
could get away with it, too. Carvin' Marvin often had a girlfriend
in her twenties, something that amazed Mickey's gang, who were
more inclined to complain about feminism or their prostates. Carvin' Marvin was fine with feminism if it could get him laid.

I answered with a what-are-you-gonna-do face that I had plagiarized from Mickey.

Carvin' Marvin and Fuzzy guided me into Carmine's. The maî-
tre d' offered up an obsequious wave. Fuzzy grunted and pushed
me gently into the private room in back. A redneck type with electronics gear gathered his equipment together and tried to adjust a
painting of the Leaning Tower of Pisa. He couldn't figure out that
the damned thing was supposed to be leaning. He gave up and
said "all clear" to Fuzzy, who pulled out a wad of cash and gave
him a few hundred dollars.

"FBI won't hear shit today," Fuzzy said. Blue and Mickey had
always been relentless about having places swept for listening devices.

Marvin and Fuzzy held the backs of two chairs and surveyed
the baskets of focaccia and breadsticks on the table. A palpable
transfer of power occurred when the shadow of my Uncle Blue in
his straw fedora straddled the doorway. Irv the Curve stood behind him.

"Well, if it ain't Peter Pan and the Lost fuckin' Boys," Blue said,
grabbing my cheek. Everyone was seated, and Blue flicked a bread-
stick into his mouth and held it with his teeth. It made him look like
FDR with his cigarette holder. There was little discussion while the
guys read the menu. I tried to picture them in a classroom as kids
learning to read. Little bitty killers learning about consonant blends.

A waiter took our orders while a tough-looking young woman
brought in a plate of antipasto "onna house." The discussion
quickly turned to politics. The boys all handicapped the next election, hinting that "my" guy, meaning the Republican, would win.
Blue looked skyward and began shaking his fist, which served as
an exclamation point on everyone else's sentences.

"You can't treat the public too nice," Blue said. "That's wrong,
see. The public wants to be lied to. Lied to!"

"Lied to like cheap broads," Fuzzy echoed. "So here's to liars
and cheap broads," Fuzzy toasted with an invisible glass, which got
a laugh out of everyone, including Blue.

"I'll factor that into my advice for clients," I said. "If I get them
back."

Within minutes, we were stabbing antipasto and Caesar salad with
anchovies, and the subject turned to cheap broads in Havana. Fuzzy
and Carvin' Marvin recounted their favorites, who had names

that sounded more like tropical drinks than human beings. Ginger the Raven, Bambi Red and Bambi Gold, Leopard Kate, Sugar, Tink, Foxy Marie, Pat the Cat, Midnight Rose, and Debbie.

"What's so funny?" Carvin' Marvin asked me.

"All those fancy names and then Debbie. She wasn't Debbie the Demon or anything?"

"No. Just Debbie," Carvin' Marvin said clinically.

"Where do you suppose she is now? Debbie," I asked. They all looked at me like I was a nitwit.

"Just like Jonah," Blue said. "Always worried what happens to the broads."

"Who the fuck knows where Debbie is now?" Fuzzy added. "She's gotta be seventy years old or somethin'. You want us to look her up for you, Jonah, so you can write her a poem? Sir Lance-a-fuckin'-lot, I swear." They smirked at me. Years ago, I composed a poem for a girl and I was still catching hell for it.

After dinner, as Blue made his last piece of tiramisu vanish from his plate, I brought forth my agenda item.

"Uncle Blue, I need your advice on something. It's about a meeting I had today."

"Yeah?" Blue said. "Already?"

"Yes, sir."

"Brass balls you got," Blue said, carefully folding his napkin and touching his fingers together in prayer. Carvin' Marvin and Fuzzy read this as a signal for them to leave and rose from their chairs.

"We'll go out on the memorandum and have a drink," Carvin' Marvin said. He must have meant the veranda. The two men left. Irv and Blue hunched forward.

"I met with Vanni," I said.

"What'd he want?" Blue asked.

"He wants a casino license. He thinks I can help get him one by swaying public opinion."

"The kid wants to go straight," Irv said.

"The kid?"

Irv said that to them, Vanni was a kid.

"He opened up to me about his kids and everything. He said

he wanted the best for them, and the best he could do was get a casino license. I couldn't believe he was telling me all this."

"He trusts you," Blue said. "You two share a problem, see. Getting respectable. Only you're closer to it than he is. He admires you. He knows you're a smart kid. So, what are you gonna do?"

"You're natural partners," Irv concluded. "I hate to say it. Both looking for a place in America. He wants a straight business."

"I don't want to go to work with Vanni. Mickey always kept me away from gambling. I want to drive back to Washington and try to start my business back up."

"Did you tell Vanni this?" Irv asked.

"I was respectful, but he knows how I feel."

"So how did you leave it?" Irv asked.

"I told him I needed to think it over."

"But you're not going to work for Vanni."

"Hell, no. What do I know about casino licenses? Why would I want to get mixed up with something like that?"

The two men gave each other exclusive looks.

"What else did Vanni say?" Blue asked. A crooked grin twisted across his face.

"He said something about people knowing about what my middle initial stands for."

"Price," Irv said. "So, you don't play ball, the world knows that the pollster with the ethics case is mobbed up. A lot of your old friends who didn't know feel betrayed. Not a good cascade of events."

"No, and then there's something that Noel did at the funeral. Noel"—the name made me swallow hard—"gave me this big smile. He rubbed his fingers together like this." I demonstrated the money gesture. "Then he looked over to Mickey's... Mickey's casket and didn't look back at me. You know that I know enough rules not to get myself in trouble, but I don't know everything. I didn't know what Noel was doing, or if he was doing anything at all."

"Was Noel in the room when Vanni told you what he wanted?" Blue asked.

"No. I did what Vanni told me to do at the funeral and said I wanted to meet him in private."

"Vanni told you this at the funeral?"

"Yes, when he hugged me."

Blue began twiddling his fingers as if he were playing an upright keyboard or working an abacus. Irv was calculating, too, but he did it with his lips, which formed soundless words like "beep, bop, boop."

"Okay, Jonah. I think I'm getting the big picture here," Blue said. "Vanni wants his casino license. He wants you to fuck with the people's minds, or whatever you do, to hedge the outcome of the commission's decision this, uh—"

"Comes up in September," Irv volunteered.

"Right. In September," Blue repeated. "You don't play ball with him, he can get word out that you're tied in with Our Thing, which fucks with your chances of coming back to Washington after all that poll shit."

"Understood, but what's Noel's beef with me?"

Irv pulled a *Racing Form* out of the salt air and slammed me on the head with it. "You're the political genius. What do you think Noel wants?"

"Noel's the bad cop. Vanni wants me to feel safe only with Vanni, is that it? Noel's there to remind me that I need Vanni."

"Maybe," Blue said.

"Don't assume it's all coordinated," Irv admonished. "Those guys hate each other. Noel's an accommodation."

"Right. Vanni mentioned the Young Turks."

"What does this tell you?" Irv repeated Noel's money gesture.

"Noel thinks I have Mickey's money?"

"So, do you have the money?" Blue asked.

"If I had the money, you'd know, wouldn't you?"

"Why would we know?" the two men said simultaneously.

The table began to sway away from me. I felt like I was falling forward. I grabbed on to the table to steady myself. I could see that the room wasn't moving for Blue and Irv, that I alone was tilting toward the edge of a cliff.

I excused myself, not even thinking about protocol. I fumbled along a small hallway and into Carmine's bathroom. The bathroom seated one and had a cross on the wall above brass soap holders with the kind of molded soap bars that nobody touches. Strange for a restaurant. I looked into the mirror, the type with the golden veins running throughout. My face seemed to be cracking up and sweat started pouring out. A ringing in my ears grew into a roaring. My hands shook badly. I felt my throat tighten up and the little muscles near my eyes started pulsating. I quickly turned on the faucet and began splashing my face with water.

I tried to grab the soap, which was at the end of the sink, but it fell into the pink toilet. Somehow I had also knocked the cross off the wall into the toilet. I began coughing and pulled myself up next to the toilet to retrieve the cross. It kept slipping from my hands, and I finally clasped it because it wouldn't fit down the pipe. The soap bar was gone.

I stood up mortified at my unwitting sacrilege and ran the cross under the sink faucet. I quickly dried it off on a paper towel and began washing my hands. My vertigo probably didn't last two minutes, but it felt like two hours.

I had always thought of Mickey, Blue, and Irv the Curve as a unit. And they were. But I always considered that unit to be absolute, the perspective of a little boy looking up at a sculpture of gods who were carved from one slab of granite like Mount Rushmore. These guys either didn't know about Mickey's money, or they did and had no intention of telling me.

But how the hell could I work for Vanni? I thought about climbing out a kitchen window and making off to a Virginia plantation where a lobbyist I knew trained horses. I could shovel dung in obscurity and lead a rich inner life. I liked the ring of that: rich inner life. Screw reality. Doing so, however, would have screamed guilt from the rooftops, and I had committed no sin against any of these men. I returned to the archway of the little room where Blue and Irv the Curve were waiting. Before I entered, I listened from the other side of the wall to the men talk.

"Underneath the gloss, Blue, the kid's his mother."

"Yeah, but our life won't kill him. From the inside, you know?"

"Nah, Jonah's healthier. He runs."

I walked into the room and coughed so Blue and Irv would stop talking.

"You all right, kid?" Irv asked.

"Sorry for running out. I'm a little rattled."

"Good," Blue said. "Smart guys worry. The man who tells you not to worry is the one who wants to kill you. So what are you gonna do?"

"I want to make a clean break. I want to go to Vanni and say I just can't work for him. The consequences are the consequences."

"You don't have enough to walk away, boychick," Irv said. "Do the math. Calculate assets and liabilities. On the assets side, you got your talent. You've also got some hotshot contacts in Washington. Vanni wants your talent, and he'd hesitate—a little—before whacking a guy who would draw heat. Now, liabilities. You've got nowhere to run. You've got a guy who would kill you. Will kill you if he wants. Make it look like a suicide like they did with that White House lawyer. You don't have enough leverage to chase him away."

"The calculations say you've got to work for the guy," Blue concluded. "Gain leverage as you go. You go free when they fear you. You don't know enough to be feared, and it's not like we can go in and make it go away. Don't work that way. Vanni would have never gone to Mickey in the old days when he really had the juice. Nah, you'd be walking down the street one day thinking everything's okay. Thinking even if it's not okay, you're smart, you're fast, you're alert. Uh-uh. No. All of a sudden some fat kid with a Sno-Kone pops two slugs in your head before you can even piss your pants."

"Honest to God I don't know about any money. With all the billion-dollar talk, Mickey brainwashed me that there is no money."

"Good thing, too. We know nothing," Blue said. "There's no will, you can bet on that. The money wanders. It wanders around. It don't stay noplace, like in a will. When guys like us go, anything we got goes back into the pot."

"Noel must know that."

"You'll throw him off that bridge when you get to it," Irv said. "You're thinking sane, and you want the for-sure answer right now. That's the problem. Noel isn't sane, and we don't know anything yet. Noel thinks what he thinks. Vanni wants what he wants. The only way to get rid of a guy like Noel is to make him somebody else's problem. It may not be such a bad idea if Noel thinks you have the money. It may give him some reason to keep you healthy.

Other than that, right now you don't know a fuckin' thing. All you know is Vanni wants your help."

"Then you're just like us," Blue said sorrowfully. "Showing your value every day just to stay alive. Living every day not knowing, doing shit so that you can know more to make the next move."

"You know what Hamlet said, Jonah?" Irv asked with his eyes closed. " 'By indirections find directions out.' You find out answers by jumping in a fight, fucking up, and doing it better as you go. We'd be the first to tell you if you had other options. The only one we see is doing this gig for Vanni—and seeming to embrace it—finding out more as you go. The best we can do is whisper in your ear along the way."

"Not a great option," I said.

"No, but the best option given what we know. The facts a life, Jonah," were the final words that seeped from Blue's contorted lips.

I sat, covering my mouth with my hands. I did not know at this moment if these men were my friends or my enemies. I did not kid myself: With Mickey gone, their first loyalty was not to me. Old times' sake played no role today. They were loyal to business. Regardless of what I asked Blue and Irv, I would not know who they really were in all of this any time soon. Either way, I had no choice but to stay close, engage them, and grow accustomed to not knowing.

Who Are You, Fuckin' Mannix?

"People must look at you and see their own struggles."

MICKEY'S DOORBELL RANG TWICE. IT WAS SIDNEY WAGNER, the manager of the Golden Prospect. Mickey had transferred Sidney, a tired-looking functionary, here from Las Vegas in the late seventies. He was an operations guy, not a gangster, and Mickey had needed men like Sidney to be on-the-books executives. I called him Sidney Blintzes because he would always bring blintzes up from the kitchen for Deedee. In the old days.

Tall and stoop-shouldered, with a thick head of silver hair like a Brillo pad, Sidney's basset hound eyes conveyed an acceptance of his place in the world. He tended to sigh and smile after completing a sentence.

"Howdy, Sidney. Things all right?"

"Usual *mishegoss*. How are you holding up?"

"I'm not sure it's hit me. I'm jumping into my work. I've lost people before. I'm a pro at it."

"Not a great thing to turn pro in."

"No."

"Speaking of pros, you want company? I can make a call."

"No. Thanks, though."

"You got plans?" Sidney asked, looking above my head. I smelled something deeper than a shiva call.

"I have a campaign in this area, and then I'll be in Washington before long." Sidney nodded rabbinically without looking me in the eye. "You need Mickey's apartment, Sidney?"

His tired yellow eyes jerked up at me.

These guys were always surprised the first time they realized that I could think like Mickey, "see around corners," as Blue once put it. It was true, though. Like a track coach once taught me, you jump before the hurdle, not at it.

"Guys are asking," he whispered, pained.

"What did you tell the guys?"

" 'Give the kid time,' I said."

"How long does the kid have?"

"End of June, if that's kosher."

"What do you say, Sidney, you and me fight these guys?" I offered a broad smile of surrender accompanied by a feeble gun gesture.

"Knew you'd be a mensch. Look, it's May. You have a month. We'll get a mover for you. If there's anything else, any favor I can do, you let me know."

"I will, Sidney."

The move was a matter of protocol, but it served a critical purpose. It sent a message to all of the Golden Prospect's investors, from the boys in Philly to tribute recipients in New York, that the torch had passed smoothly and that their dividends would keep coming. It was nothing personal, but the very notion that a member of Mickey's family could be living off their rightfully stolen annuity disrupted a long-cherished order.

I began loading Mickey's shoes into a box for Goodwill. They were almost all loafers. There was also a pair of sneakers in the back, black Converse high-tops. I had no memory of Mickey ever wearing these. What the hell did he do in them? I couldn't imagine he was playing pickup hoops with the kids at Atlantic City High. He clearly had worn these sneaks, though. There was dirt jammed in one of treads. The discovery got me thinking again about Mickey's final rant about the woods, but his clues registered no meaning.

On a shelf in the back of the closet, there were two wooden boxes, one small and square, the other long and slender. Inside the small box was a stainless-steel thirty-eight-caliber revolver with a two-inch barrel. The long box contained a rifle. There was ample ammunition. Odds were that neither weapon had been registered.

I held the revolver in my palm and coughed up what may have been a laugh. A gun is really a dumb and practical little tool. At first, just glancing at it, I felt no fear. But then I thought about the holocaust that bursts from one mechanical click. Pointed outward, remote-control style, another life gasped to white noise. Pointed inward, my life and all its narrative would be gone with a click. To take a life was humanly colossal but logistically simple. What must a man be made of to point this outward and squeeze? And what switch in his mind could make it point inward? Where does a poll-ster point a gun? My mind was turning over jokey questions that had no punch line.

I began to think I was getting a message: Keep the guns. It wouldn't be such a bad idea to carry around the revolver. There was a small holster that I could shorten and strap to my ankle. Alive and running was better than tortured and dead. Besides, I had fired this gun before. Mickey had had it for years. When I was little he had it in a lockbox with a punch code—my birthday. I remember breaking Mickey's code when I was about sixteen. All I could think about at the time was that *this* was the criminal genius who helped mastermind the Kennedy assassination, according to Al Just? I had sneaked out into the Pine Barrens a few times and fired it. I wasn't a bad shot, which had saddened Mickey when I finally confessed that I had known about it all along. All he could say was, "Your grandmother wanted the shiny stainless steel. I told her we should go with the black because it doesn't catch the light, and you can hide it better, but did she listen?"

As I loaded five bullets into the gun, I heard Mickey's voice ring in my head: "Who are you, fuckin' Mannix?" A tear fell from the corner of my eye onto the tip of the trigger. These guns were now the closest thing that I had to parents.

Odessa had left Mickey's turquoise ring on his dresser. The sil-ver had turned greenish with pickle juice. I washed it off with soap and water and slipped it onto my ring finger. It fit snugly, and I liked the Western motif. Searching through Mickey's drawers, I found his old undergarments. Every pair was spotless. There was also a tiny blue velvet pouch. I opened it up and emptied it out on the dresser. A large diamond rolled out, about three carats. I remembered this stone. There was a whole story behind it. Bugsy Siegel had given it to Mickey. I slipped the diamond back into the pouch and tucked it away in one of my shoes.

I pulled out a digital phone from my breast pocket. I actually had a phone in my breast pocket.

I had to call Edie Morris before I could really think about what was happening to my life. I could have called from the hard line in Mickey's apartment, but I didn't want the FBI critiquing how I asked a woman out. The digital in my pocket was unlikely to be tapped. Directory assistance gave me her number in Batsto. Just do it, don't think.

A voice like linen answered.

"Hi, I'm calling for Edie Morris."

"This is she."

"Hi, she. This is . . . Keith Partridge. We met at a funeral. I'd like a music lesson."

"Really? Do you still play guitar, Keith?" She posed the question sweetly, as if I were one of her young students.

"I don't."

"I see."

"How about having dinner with me, then?"

"I'd like to, but the Keith Partridge I know vanished years ago. I'm not one for phantoms."

"This is Jonah."

"I know."

"How's Friday?"

We agreed to go to Braddock's Tavern in Medford. It was a hike, but I wanted to get away from the Shore, and Medford wasn't that far from Batsto.

Edie directed me from the Atlantic City Expressway to her place. It was all of two turns, from Route 623. I wrote the directions on one of Mickey's old *Racing Form*s. It seemed easy. I thought there must be something wrong with her. It was easier to settle tobacco litigation than it was to set something up with a woman in

Washington. Smorgasbroads. When I hung up after speaking with Edie, I missed her until Irv the Curve's ice-cold words detonated again in my ears. *Mario Vanni wants to talk to you.*

"Good afternoon, Frankie Shrugs."

"What's up, Eastman?" Frankie Shrugs said, lazily swatting a bug against Lucy the Elephant's leg with a *Philadelphia* magazine.

"Is Mr. V. here?"

"Yeah. He said you could be stopping by. Says you're the man. I'll see if he's ready." Frankie Shrugs vanished into the elephant.

I'm the man. God, tell me this is a joke, that I am not actually here. I greedily sucked a few units of sea air into my lungs. Get *in* the big wave.

A meaty hand waved me inside. No frisking this time. I was, after all, the man.

"What's this, the fuckin' book-a-the-month club?" Frankie Shrugs asked when he saw that I was carrying an old book.

"Just a little homework assignment the boss wanted."

"Homework, huh?" Frankie Shrugs bellowed.

I had slipped a handwritten note for Vanni inside. The book was *The Image: A Guide to Pseudo-Events in America.* It was first published the year I was born. The author, Daniel Boorstin, had a theory that the public had ceased to differentiate between real news and events that were manufactured for the purpose of getting news. The note inside read:

> *Mario:*
> People don't fight for others. They fight for themselves. People must look at you and see their own struggles. Strip away the elephant and you're just an ambitious kid looking for his place in America. People *get* that.
>
> *Jonah*

I found Vanni alone in the covered throne atop Lucy's back. He was working out with weights. He wore a Villanova Law sweatshirt and gray shorts. A white bandana was wrapped across his head, and a citrus cologne violated the sea air. He looked like Captain Kidd.

"Self-improvement, Jonah. That's the key." *Zatz uh key.*

"How often do you work out?"

"Three times a week with weights. And I do treadmill three or four times. Guys my age don't burn it off the way we did when we were your age."

"If you don't mind me asking, how old are you?"

"I'm fifty-one. 'Bout you?"

"Thirty-eight."

Vanni pointed at me. "You blink a few times and, *bada-bing*, you're fifty-one, too."

"I'm starting to realize that."

"What's that there?" Vanni asked, pointing to my book with his chin. "You gonna read me a story?" Vanni sat and ran a washcloth across his neck.

"It's a book I'm lending you. I carry it around in my briefcase. There's a note inside. The bottom line is that I'll do it. I'll try to help you."

"I got money, you know." He said this with a touch of guilt in his voice.

"I know you do."

Vanni vigorously toweled off his hands before accepting the book. "*The Image*," he said. "I like that. But will it get me my license?"

Vanni wasn't my first results-obsessed client, but he was the first who would torture me with a cattle prod before slitting my throat. As I knelt close to Vanni to consummate our conspiracy, I thought about how long it would take for me to die after having my throat slit. Would I lose consciousness right away, or would I watch the blood drain around me for minutes?

"Mario," I said, faking confidence with every larcenous muscle in my body, "if people think their license—*their license*—is being denied them . . . you'll get *your* license. *Capisce*?"

Vanni caressed the silver spine of *The Image* and shook my hand fraternally. "I'll read this book," he said. He wiped the corner of his eye with a sweaty knuckle. "Swear ta God, I will."

Mick-e-leh

"Who the hell is DELVAC?"

CHERRY HILL, NEW JERSEY, WAS AN HOUR'S RIDE ON THE
Atlantic City Expressway, which sliced across the Garden
State from the Golden Prospect. Cherry Hill was a notoriously
flashy Philadelphia suburb known for its material aggression and
the water tower with the town's big red name mooning travelers
along Route 295, lest anyone in the galaxy forget where he was. It
had been the headquarters of the "Pizza Connection" heroin ring,
the home of the once-torched Garden State Race Track, not to
mention the proving ground for America's first indoor megamall.

I would meet Cindi Handler at Ponzio's restaurant. Cindi had
become a powerhouse publicist in Cherry Hill. She would be my
fox on Vanni's Machiavellian program; the lion would arrive soon
enough.

I felt safe in Ponzio's because it was so bright. The counters
overflowed with pastries that I wouldn't eat but found comforting
to look at. Seeing all this stuff meant that there were people who
thought life held sufficient promise that they would be able to eat
all that had been set out here. Maybe this is why Americans loved
eating: the hope.

I had known Cindi since we were kids at Camp Hilltop in Medford. Cindi had seen me at my worst. She was the only one who saw me cry over my family's—Mickey, Deedee, and my—exile in October of 1975. Our departure coincided with the release of Springsteen's "Born to Run," which Cindi and I interpreted, in a fit of adolescent self-absorption, as being prophetically linked. We even signed our letters, "Tramps like us. . ." Before my family boarded the airplane for Paris, I had bought a copy of the current *Time* and *Newsweek*, featuring dueling covers of Springsteen. I was despondent: the youth of Jersey was exploding onto the national scene, and I was bolting the country to keep my grandfather-the-killer out of the clink.

The tears came upon our return from Paris. I stayed over at her modest split-level house in Kingston Estates. In her family room, I grilled her about what the papers said about Mickey after we fled. She resisted telling me. Finally, she whipped out what became known in the Price household as "the Record."

A Borscht Belt comedian had become famous for a week by distorting the oft-distorted lyrics of the Hispanic folk song "Ma-tilda" and replacing "Ma-til-da" with the Yiddish diminutive of Mickey, "Mickeleh." Cindi saved the forty-five that the comedian had released upon our flight from the country. The shtick had gotten a lot of play in Philly and South Jersey. Its rhythm and lyrics injected themselves into my life sporadically, during a run or a shower, or while conducting a focus group. I could handle Mickey being a feared gangster; there was something badass about it, which was tolerable to an adolescent boy. But I couldn't tolerate him being thought of as a petty thief who could be jabbed by a vaudeville reject.

> *Mick-e-leh*
> *Mick-e-leh*
> *Mick-e-leh, he took de money and run Venezuela*

So went the chorus.

> *From Bahama out to Reno*
> *We play in Mickeleh's casino*
> *Mick-e-leh, he took de money and run Venezuela*

Never mind that we went to Paris; the point had been made.

At first, Mickey would hum the song, much to Deedee's and my amazement.

> *Greenbacks, Mickey got a ton of*
> *He's the Shore's biggest gonif*
> *Mick-e-leh, he took de money and run Venezuela*

"What are you so proud of?" Deedee finally asked Mickey. He calls you a *gonif*." Yiddish for thief.

Mickey went white. "He says 'pontiff,' like pope of the Shore," he argued.

"I hate to disappoint you, Pius the Fourth, but it's *gonif. GONIF!*" Deedee said.

For the remainder of the day, Mickey played the record over and over, insisting that the comedian had said "pontiff." The following morning, Deedee pulled the smashed record from the trash, kicked her fire-engine red heels up on the table, lit a cigarette, and declared, "Was I right or was I right? Listen to him. *Pontiff!*"

> *Mickey say I make no one poorer*
> *Why, I just a little schnorrer*
> *Mick-e-leh, he took de money and run Venezuela*

I had found sanctuary with Cindi because she was not a woman who considered happiness to be a noble pursuit. Her parents were intellectuals, always researching something and writing but never making any money. In fact, I suspect she hated the happy and loved me because, as she once put it, "You've got issues."

I spotted Cindi walking down the narrow walkway outside the restaurant. The business suit she was wearing made her look sleek and in charge. Her thirties became her. Tall and slightly pear-shaped, Cindi exercised like a fiend, but it never altered her figure, which was neither excessive nor lacking. It was a structural issue, not a weight problem with her. Her wavy black hair fell to her shoulders; you would call it neither long nor short. Her features were delicate but not delicate enough to make her beautiful.

Cindi hugged me hard. Tears appeared in the starting blocks of her eyes but didn't fall.

"I'm so sorry about Mickey."

"I know you are."

"I went back and forth about going to the funeral but decided against going. I know so many media, and with all that's going on with me—"

> *Mickey say go and throw de dice down*
> *I split de money with de paisans*
> *Mick-e-leh, he took de money and run Venezuela*

"Did something happen to you?"

"My adolescent parents happened to me. I'll tell you later."

"At least you've got them."

"You're right. I'm sorry."

"You were smart to stay away. I always told you to stay away from—you know."

"I know, but I felt like a shit heel."

We had not let go of each other.

"I learned a long time ago that I couldn't hold people to uncommonly heroic standards of friendship."

Cindi nodded in a way that made me think of a dance at Camp Hilltop. The memory made me feel warm and sad; warm because I always adored this person, and sad because I never imagined that I would be old enough to have decades-old memories of anything.

Cindi registered us with the hostess, an exhausted woman who looked to be in her sixties but was probably twenty-eight. A handful of patrons pushed with their chins toward the front of the line as if the line's existence had been a terrible mistake that did not apply to them. Cindi rolled her eyes at the class warfare.

"I usually don't like to have lunch here because I don't want to hear how much everybody made last year," she said. Cindi could rail against Cherry Hill for hours. And she still had that *voice*. It was the sexiest voice I had ever heard. In the PR business, most flacking is done over the phone. I was convinced that Cindi seduced everybody into attending her events and running her stories with the combination of her brains and her voice.

We proceeded back toward a booth facing Ellisburg Circle, arm in arm, which embarrassed me a little.

"How's the world of flackery?" I asked her.

She sighed, "How many South Jersey jewelers can I inflict on the world? I pitched the New Jersey Tourism Board, which would have been a huge account, but I didn't get it. I don't think they liked my slogan."

"Which was?"

"New Jersey: You Got a Problem with That?"

"Nice. Very homespun. What could they have been thinking? Is there something else you'd rather do?"

"Yeah, but my father just decided at seventy that he needs another doctorate. They don't have a dime, Jonah. My mother wants to kill him. I'll be supporting them until they die. And that guy I lived with, Shawn—did you meet him?"

"No."

"We had a joint account at Dean Witter. Well, it ain't joint anymore. He cleaned me out and opened a candle shop in Sausalito. His true destiny . . . You look good," Cindi said as we sat. "Still running?"

"Faster than ever," I said, tugging her long, hot hands.

"You said that way too seriously."

"As serious as what I've got strapped to my leg."

"Oh, Jonah," she said, batting her eyelashes.

"It's not strapped to that part of my leg. Feel down near my calf." I rested my leg on her side of the booth. Cindi reached under.

"Is that what I think it is?" she said turning a pale shade of something approaching mauve.

Cindi slid her hands across the table and placed them on top of mine. "A gun, Jonah? A gun? Are you really in danger or, are you flipping out about Mickey?"

I leaned forward. She met me across the table, practically nose to nose.

"I can only tell you so much, for your own protection. But there's a guy from Mickey's world who thinks I have his money or something—which I don't. Other than Mickey's watch and his music, and a few other things, I got nothing and won't get anything. At least I don't think so. Anyway, the media over the years have said he had—"

"A billion dollars."

"Right. It's horse shit. I need you to help me with something tied to some rough guys, and it'll be a nice business for you. You'll be paid well, you won't be doing anything illegal, and you'll learn more about your friends in the media than you ever imagined. Have you ever leaked stories?"

"Jonah my love, I've got a bladder full of stories." Despite her bravado, Cindi appeared tense.

"Good. I'm doing a little polling now to nail down a few hunches about message. When I get the results, I'll share them with you. What I'll need you to do is tip off the press about certain events, most of which will genuinely take place. These reporters will be indebted to you for the scoops. The risk to you is not a legal risk."

"I don't know, Jonah. You keep saying that."

"I know I do. There's no law against trying to get a bad man a good reputation. The only thing you'll have to be careful about is having media people wonder where you got your tips."

"Where *did* I get my tips?"

"A smart reporter will only care if your information is good, which it will be. Usually."

"Yeah, but sometimes reporters can turn on you. They may decide to do the story about me and the leaks I'm putting out, or come after you. They love mastermind stories—Mickey Price's hotshot grandson returns to *la mala vita*."

"That's why we'll need the Internet. We need to make this story a fait accompli so that nobody asks why they're covering it. We just need to trigger it. We can also focus on one reporter, a desperate sort not prone to doing homework. We need a guy who'll carry a story line."

"*We*, huh?"

"I need you."

"What you need is an evanjournalist. I have a theory that there are two kinds of reporters. Talmudists and evanjournalists. Talmudists wrestle with the truth. Evanjournalists can only crucify or deify along with their agenda. They don't check. They just run with whatever sounds good. You know that better than anybody with what that Al Just did. He hasn't had a hit in years. Didn't his father—"

"Work for Mickey, yeah. Mouse Yutzel. We need to get an asshole like that, a rabid guy on a holy war. Then we'll have our buffer, DELVAC."

> Mickey cry that he go bust
> But he got a billion say Al Just
> Mick-e-leh, he took de money and run Venezuela

"Who the hell is DELVAC?" She pronounced the moniker as if it were someone's name: Del Vac. I envisioned a seedy crooner in a lounge on Admiral Wilson Boulevard in Camden.

"The Delaware Valley Anticrime Coalition."

"Never heard of them."

"That's because I made them up on the Atlantic City Expressway. We need a virtual organization, not an actual one—a group that's assumed."

"We again?"

"I. I need it, and I really need you."

"Go slow with me. Who's in the coalition?"

"Concerned citizens, that kind of shit."

"Who finances DELVAC?"

"Ah."

"Jonah, this is scaring me."

"They'll never even know who you are, I swear."

"Do I want to know who they are?"

"No. You want to get paid."

She leaned in, kissing close, and whispered, "Vanni?"

I nodded.

"What kind of money would I get paid? Enough to load up my retirement account? Shawn took fifteen years of savings." She suddenly looked like a woman nearing forty.

"I'll raise the money for the coalition itself. We'll talk about your fees in a second. What you'll do is call the press on the auspices of DELVAC but then happen to mention stuff that you heard in the context of talking about something else."

"That could work."

"It will work. People hear what they want to hear and look the other way at what they don't. What kind of retainer do you get, say, for a three-month project?"

"An average is five thousand a month. I don't get the big hot-shot clients like you do. I get local developers and furriers."

"How about an on-the-books payment of two thousand a month and an off-the-books payment of twenty-five thousand?"

"*Per month?*"

"Uh-huh. Do you know any computer whiz-kid types? I need an electric sniper, a dweeb who can fire bullshit all over the Web."

"Hell, yeah. My neighbor's kid works in the computer lab at Mount Misery, that summer camp out in the pines. He's a junior counselor or something."

"What does a kid like that make?"

"Practically nothing."

"We can greatly improve his standard of living provided that he keeps his mouth shut."

"He's a computer geek. He doesn't have any friends, believe me."

"Good. Have him register a domain name, jerseydevil.org. The name is available, I checked this morning from my laptop. Have him play with some Web site designs, devils and shit. A gypsy will drop by your office and give you three fat envelopes totaling seventy-five thousand dollars for three months of work. The account exists, token fees exist, but the big money doesn't."

"Jersey's shaped like a boomerang, Jonah. It always comes back."

"I know."

"I don't want it coming back on me."

"There are so many layers, I don't see how it can. If it comes back on anybody, Cindi, it'll be me."

Cindi glanced out the window in the direction of a McDonald's we used to go to all the time, usually after a disappointing dance. A man with puffy silver hair and bricks of gold dripping from his neck and arms parked his black Mercedes along a yellow curb beneath a sign reading No Parking. Cindi snorted.

"You know, you ran away to Dartmouth to get away from this."

"Mickey picked Dartmouth."

"He had an accomplice. If it hadn't been Dartmouth, it would have been Williams, or some other place where you couldn't find pastrami if your life depended on it."

"You were never much for this area yourself," I reminded her.

"I know. My parents chased Ph.D.s the way everybody else around here chased currency."

"Isn't it amazing how prejudice from the inside out is familial, but prejudice from the outside in is genocidal?"

"It's true. We can disapprove of our own, but we won't act on it. With other people—you don't know what they'll do with their hatred."

Cindi smiled like a vice cop. As a kid she had worn her victimhood like a burnt prom corsage. As a grown-up she could hide her rage and harsh judgments beneath layers of wit, pluck, and simple Chanel suits. For a flash I wondered whether I should have married her. She was still single.

"Time provokes hard questions," she responded.

> *Mickey, he clean out de slots*
> *Took so much money you could plotz*
> *Mick-e-leh, he took de money and run Venezuela*

Almighty Message

"The police said they can't do anything."

DESPITE THE INFLUENCE THAT POLLING HOUSES HAD IN PUBlic discourse, their offices were always drab and stark. Perhaps this was to mask their power. I was using the Populace Group on Walnut Street in Philadelphia.

My mission today was the Almighty Message—to know what would move people from point A to point B, to probe raw nerves using a research methodology I had branded "Basic Beliefs." The message would inevitably have its provenance in anxieties, Darwinian cues rooted in enzymes as opposed to analysis.

About fifty interviews would be conducted during the next week. I would attend a handful of them. I wanted to watch a subject who was likely to be hostile to Vanni and one who would tend to be receptive. I also wanted to observe different demographics. I picked a single white woman in her fifties who described herself as an accountant's aide and a churchgoer. She lived in West Philly. I also picked a Hispanic man in his thirties who was the manager of a clothing store in Center City. Finally, I would observe a local grandfather.

The interviewing psychologist, Eliza Baird, was a soft-spoken woman in her forties. She came across like a social worker who was uniquely impressed with your trenchant views, your pain, and your proposed solutions to what ailed the world. I told Dr. Baird she was working on a legal case—a potential truth—but she did not know the name of the defendant or what crime he or she was alleged to have committed. She did not ask further questions. Had she asked, I would have told her that full disclosure could have made her vulnerable to having to testify in a trial. If she stayed ignorant, this vulnerability would be reduced significantly. This was not unusual to do in focus groups; the interviewer's ignorance of the client made her truly unbiased.

Despite her gentle demeanor, Eliza Baird was tough and shrewd—good attributes, because pollsters tend to suspect that they know what people are thinking before the research has been conducted. I had worked with her five years ago on a corporate crisis involving high-pressure toilets that people claimed were sucking them downward if you flushed while seated. (I polled for private corporations in between my political work.) She had recommended that we do something to give people a greater sense of control, which included a recommendation that consumers stand when flushing to avoid being within "suction range." I had wanted Dr. Baird to ask interview subjects whether they would be embarrassed to sue a toilet maker for getting sucked downward if they flushed while seated. She hadn't been shy about rejecting my suggestion on the grounds that it divulged the client's position and could prejudice the research.

Today's interview arrangement was standard. Dr. Baird was sitting at a wooden conference table with her back toward a large mirror that ran almost the width of the conference room. I sat on the other side of that mirror beneath a camera that filmed the proceedings.

The observation room was equipped with notepads and a laptop computer; the latter could be used to send notes to Dr. Baird, who also had a laptop in front of her. There were bowls of unhealthful food like cookies and candies, as well as soft drinks. There were also low-sodium pretzels, probably an accommodation to some health-freak advertising executive who had become porcine after years of focus groups.

The middle-aged woman, Evelyn Woulders, went first. Dr. Baird began by putting Woulders at ease and telling her about the proceedings. She explained that she was conducting opinion research and that her goal was to determine what Woulders valued, to get a sense of her moral priorities. She mentioned that Woulders's comfort level with various issues would be tracked, in part by monitoring her skin temperature through rubber rings. There was a reliable correlation between surface body temperature and anxiety. Dr. Baird further explained that there might or might not be representatives behind the mirror taking notes on what she said. Woulders looked at the mirror and twitched a little. She reminded me of someone who might believe that the CIA had placed a microchip in her molar. Finally, Woulders was told that Dr. Baird did not know precisely how the research would be used or who the client was.

Dr. Baird, almost invisibly, slipped two rubber rings on Woulders's fingers and began with small talk about her family. Woulders had never been married and had lived in the same neighborhood since she graduated from high school. Her mother was still living and in relative good health, and she spoke frequently with her two sisters, one whom lived in King of Prussia, Pennsylvania. Her other sister lived in Cinnaminson, New Jersey.

"Do you like where you live?" Baird asked.

"Oh, yes, very much."

"Is it your dream place?"

"Oh, I wouldn't say that."

"What would make it a dream place?"

"A few palm trees. Maybe a nice lottery win."

"Do you play the lottery?"

"I never used to. I'm embarrassed to say that I've started to."

"Why now?"

"My nephew moved in with me not long ago. Maybe that's what sparked it."

"You want to win the lottery for him?"

"Not just for him."

Woulders's nephew had just been laid off by a big company in Delaware.

"Had he worked there long?" Dr. Baird asked.

"About ten years."

"What did he do there?"

"He handled the machinery that makes bottles."

"How is he adjusting to the situation?"

"All right, I guess," Woulders replied. "David has a couple of bucks saved up, but he feels demoralized, like he'll never work again."

"Why exactly was David laid off?"

"Oh, you know the way things are going. There's no loyalty to workers anymore. It's just the bottom line. It's all computers now."

"What's all computers?"

"The money. People who make computers make the money. Except the bosses. Guess how much the head of David's company made last year?"

"How much?"

"About five million dollars."

"Do you think he'll find work soon?"

"He'll find something," Woulders said, looking off toward the focus group mirror. It made me feel guilty about judging her as a nut earlier. Her hands were resting on top of her purse. "It's just that nowadays you don't know what young people will do with their spare time. He walks around the neighborhood, which isn't what it used to be. And every day he goes to lunch at Burger King. They're not as cheap as they used to be, you know."

"Tell me more about your neighborhood."

"Well, it's always been pretty quiet, nice people. We just had a robbery on our block last month. That used to never happen. The police said it was kids looking for money for drugs. It's awfully scary. The police said they can't do anything right away, just that they'll keep looking."

"Why do you believe things have gotten worse in your neighborhood?"

"It's a lot of things, really. There's not as many good jobs these days. People who commit crimes are let right out. They have more luck than people who are trying to find jobs. When I was a girl they used to throw them in prison, and that was that. Nowadays, nobody cares. They'll probably give them jobs at a fast-food place."

I didn't know what Miss Woulders's quarrel with fast food was, but her comments about crime were disconcerting. She'd never support Vanni.

I leaned over the laptop and typed Dr. Baird a note: ASK HER WHAT SHE THINKS OF WHEN SHE THINKS OF CRIMINALS.

A *ping* reached Dr. Baird's computer and she took a moment to read the message.

After finishing up a few questions about Woulders's neighborhood, Baird asked her about the causes of crime and whether some crimes are worse than others, which I thought was a clever way into it.

"Sure, some crimes are worse than others. Those drug people are the worst. And that awful man who killed the police officer that all the movie stars got behind. That's wrong." Woulders hesitated a few moments. "No, I think it's the drugs. That's the thing that really scares me because it makes people wild. That's the thing we never had to think about growing up." Woulders's anxiety level jumped when she spoke about crime but fell back down when she spoke of her neighborhood.

"What kind of crimes did you have to think about growing up?"

"None really. I mean, sure, you heard about things. You heard about someone getting killed or robbed, but it was never in your neighborhood, you know? Then people would get killed in drunk-driving accidents, but that's not really what you're talking about, is it?"

"It's what you want to talk about that counts."

"Oh, that's right. I'm the star here," Woulders cackled primly.

I sent another message to Baird: QUERY CRIMINAL GROUPS IN THE REGION, THE MOB.

"You know, I read something about a crime group getting more powerful," Baird said, as if it were an afterthought.

"Really? I didn't read about that." I propped up closer to the mirror.

"Now I have to think. Yes, I'm certain that I read something about a Philadelphia criminal group being watched closely by the FBI."

"Huh, that's really something," Woulders said. "I read the paper and listen to *Action News* every day."

"Hmm," Dr. Baird said to Woulders. "It was some mob thing, I think."

Woulders's eyes widened a bit. "Oh, Vanni," she laughed. "Sure,

I read about him. I thought you meant *crime* crime—a drug ring or something. I know about that Vanni." The body heat monitors were still level.

"Are you concerned about organized crime?"

"Maybe a little."

I typed: QUERY ATTITUDES TOWARD POLICE.

"What kind of thing are you talking about when you think of crime?" Baird asked.

"The kind of people who bring down the neighborhood and make things unsafe. What we want is stability. I'm not afraid of a bunch of guys having coffee in some social club. Those are really just neighborhood guys wearing Skin Bracer that never grew up. I am not a prejudiced person, you understand." Woulders looked at Dr. Baird, strangely hurt and defensive, her shoulders tensing up. The monitors measuring Woulders's body heat shot way up. We had hit upon something very visceral that would not translate into words. Baird waited a few seconds before responding.

"Why do you think I thought you were prejudiced?"

"Oh, oh. I know you don't think I'm prejudiced. At least I don't think you think that. But you never know how people read things." The monitors indicated a great deal of anxiety. I made a note on my pad: "They need villains. Probe scary names in follow-up poll."

"Can the police help?"

Woulders rolled her eyes. "They have their own agenda."

"I see."

I typed a note on the laptop for Baird: PROBE SCENT OF SKIN BRACER.

"Why do you say the men wore Skin Bracer?"

"Oh," Woulders released her shoulders and took a deep breath. "Those old-fashioned fellows with their Skin Bracer and Aqua Velva. They thought they were Romeos. They weren't. Just old-fashioned lugs who only hurt each other, if they hurt anybody at all. It makes me think of the fifties and early sixties. Before the president was shot.

"Actually," Woulders laughed, "you didn't have any drugs when those guys—guys like Vanni—were around. They were part of the scenery." Down fell her body heat.

I jotted on my pad, "Rely on disaffiliated to carry message."

• • •

Steve Fuentes's interview began at about eleven. Dr. Baird gave him the same opening explanations and disclaimers that she gave Evelyn Woulders. Baird asked him to talk about his work. He obliged gladly by explaining that his family was from Puerto Rico and came to Philadelphia when he was three years old. His father was a maintenance facilities director for the Philadelphia school system. His mother was a homemaker whom he described with great affection. His body temperature was cool when he spoke about his family.

Fuentes had worked for the International Scene clothing chain since he graduated from a local community college fifteen years ago. He was sharply dressed with a European flare and wore stylish glasses that gave him a more serious look than he would have had otherwise.

He had started at International Scene as a salesman and had become manager of the store about two years ago.

"Look, you've got people, okay, who want what I have but who don't want to work for it. You know, I wasn't exactly handed a trust fund."

"Very few of us were," Dr. Baird said.

"Just when I start coming down on people, though," Fuentes said, "I start feeling bad. I mean, somebody could say rotten things about my family, too, because we're minorities and all. So I've got to—we all have to—be so careful not to throw it down on one group or another."

During the course of Fuentes's interview, he expressed sentiments about crime that were not unlike those of Woulders, despite their diverse backgrounds. There was a lot of goodness in these people and a heaping dose of underlying anger. There was no question that they had impulses toward bias—biases that could be exploited—but they also recognized that these biases were harmful. Whatever I cooked up, assuming the other interviews went like this, I couldn't shove it down their throats. I had to tweak people but let them reach conclusions privately.

"I have nothing against others trying to make it in America. Look, my family was from Puerto Rico. We came here with nothing. But we didn't terrorize the way some people do. We gave something." Up shot his body heat.

· · ·

The last subject up was an eighty-one-year-old man named David Fine. Bald and stoop-shouldered, Mr. Fine was a retired carpet salesman from Bala Cynwyd. He and his wife had just come back from a vacation in Spain. He flirted with Dr. Baird for a few minutes and suggested that he really wasn't a retired carpet salesman but a bull fighter. If she'd like to see him in action, they could run away to Pamplona together. It was cute, and I felt kinky watching from behind the mirror, especially after Dr. Baird told Mr. Fine that someone was watching.

"I take it all back," Mr. Fine said. "I don't want to get sued for sex harassing. I read about that. Let's be honest, in my day we called it flirting." Visions of Edie Morris leapt past my eyes. I thought she would like Mr. Fine.

"In mine, too," Dr. Baird agreed. It gave her a perfect segue into the interview about what Mr. Fine valued as a senior citizen.

"At this stage, young lady, I'm not afraid of dying. Let's be honest, I'll just be laying there. When you think about it, what's the big deal? Do I get upset about being asleep? Of course not, I'm asleep! I think a lot now about being a good person. Maybe I always did. I'm not sure. But now I want the slate clean. Not so much because I'm going to hell, which, by the way, I don't believe in. But I want my life to have meant something other than that I shlepped around the planet for so long. I've been cleaning things up. I told my daughter, who is fifty-five if you can believe, that I was sorry I was on the road for some dance show when she was in high school. I told her, not because of hell, but because I want her to pass along to my grandchildren that David Fine was a good man who offered up something good that they should try to do, even if I'm not rich from inventing some computer chip or whatever the hell they're making these days.

"What scares me is my grandchildren living. Even though I won't be there to see it, I care about how they'll drive down the road. I care about them being safe. Everybody says spend your money, live life to the hilt, but I think about those kids. I want them to go to college, which, let's be honest, I didn't. So I socked a little away." Fine's body heat rose.

"I saw this book about what a great thing it is to die broke, to spend it all. Maybe this is smart by today's thinking. And I'm not saying you spoil your children, but if you can give them something to be safe, you do it, am I right?"

"I'm here to listen."

"So listen. Let's be honest, I don't care who you are, you care about how God sees you. Even if you don't believe in God you believe in God. When you get old, you start believing in God even if it's not a religious God. I guess what I'm saying is that you care about the footprints you leave on the carpet. That's what I used to tell people who said they wanted to buy a carpet that didn't leave footprints. Impossible, I told them. What you want, let's be honest, is to leave good footprints, not no footprints."

"What are good footprints?"

"Footprints that show you were there but didn't track in dirt. I mean, what's the big deal if a carpet gets worn down eventually? We all wear down. But these people who drag in dirt or wear golf shoes on soft carpet—what that says is they're careless in the true sense of that word. Without care. I don't see why that's such a virtue. People say 'I could care less' like they should get a prize. Even at my age, I'd go to war with guns and knives rather than care less. That I care, that I worry, let's be honest, keeps me alive. I'm glad I worry about my grandchildren, to tell you the truth."

Mr. Fine could have been Mickey's benevolent younger brother, a nonterrible man who wanted to leave something for his children. I wanted to burst through the one-way mirror to ask him if Mickey's fading riddle made any sense. Was there money, Mr. Fine? Did you know a man in the woods, Mr. Fine, who didn't do well with a woman at a dance and disappeared into another world? And if the man in the woods didn't have the money, what did he have, and what, Mr. Fine, did gypsy music have to do with it?

By the end of the day, I had sat through enough interviews that I felt I could speed up my Vanni program. My synapses were kindling with longing for my grandfather, the sight of Noel's diamond-studded fang, and the scent of Mario Vanni's Skin Bracer.

You're in, Dude

"We need you to be the good old days."

WHAT'S THIS?" *WHUTTZIZ?* MARIO ASKED, TAKING THE BOT-
tle of Skin Bracer from my hand. With his other hand, he
shoved aside a stack of cash on his desk.

"It's your new aftershave."

"This shit?"

"Yes. Just for a while. I'm having more tests done, but it seems
that people associate it with the good old days."

"So what?"

"We need you to be the good old days. And the future."

Vanni nodded with an incredulous grin. "Oh, yeah, the pseudo-
events. That's good stuff. . . . I don't understand a thing anymore,
I swear to God."

"I'll help you understand. We have to get you ready for the media.
I'd like to bring in a camera crew to train you for interviews."

"Interviews? You gonna get me on Barbara Walters?"

"You never know."

I handed Vanni a sheet of paper. "You'll find some recommen-
dations here. You'll need help from your associates to do these
things. I usually don't write things down, but I know you're
not used to operations like these so you may want to mull it over."

In my memo, I had grossly oversimplified the conclusions of the Basic Beliefs research because Vanni wasn't an on-the-other-hand kind of guy, and most opinion research fell into that squirrely netherworld where absolute conclusions were hard to reach. There were clear trends, however. People didn't know where they belonged, they didn't know whom they could trust.

In the verbatims, one young mother of three from Blackwood had said, "I don't know where the South Jersey suburbs end and the Shore begins anymore." An older man from Bucks County said that he bought a computer, but "I didn't trust the young fella that put it in. It was like he was trying to put one over on me." When Dr. Baird asked what the "young fella" had done to make him feel that way, the man from Bucks County admitted with a chuckle that he didn't really know.

In other cases, the spirit of protest, especially in the college-age interviewees, struck me as being a fashion statement more than a true expression of disenfranchisement. Several college kids hearkened back to "when things were better"—in the 1960s. This was odd, given that most of them hadn't been born until the early 1980s. Nevertheless, it was clear across many demographics that folks *wanted* to take to the streets and weren't too picky about the crusade that got them there. Their fears about disintegrating boundaries, evaporating industry, and the boom of a gadget economy appeared to fuse together in a generic hatred of violent criminals, not so much because violent crime was on the rise, but because it was something that everybody could agree on.

Vanni gave a glazed nod to my memo, rubbed his eyes, and sighed. "Look, Jonah. Do me a favor. Take Noel out to lunch and tell him some of the basics from the research. Don't tell him the endgame, the license, just tell him it's about image. With that shit he puts up his nose, you never know what he'll actually hear."

"Won't he suspect something?"

"Shit, yeah. He's smart that way. But if you don't talk to him, he'll be pissed, and I can't deal with the Turks right now."

"Well, I'm sure I can smooth things over. Noel trusts me," I said insincerely.

"Yeah, I know. You're buddies. Don't worry. All things resolve in time." Vanni grabbed a stack of bills and currency, stuffing them into a shopping bag. "I'm socking away money for our little program."

"Good. We'll need it."

On the way out of the elephant, it occurred to me that it was the first time I had worn my gun in Vanni's presence. I had not been searched, nor had I anticipated being searched. We had strangely grown at home with one another.

Noel loafed with Frankie Shrugs and a few others on lawn chairs that were scattered in the mealy gray penumbra that Lucy cast in the June sun.

"Noel, how about lunch?" I asked.

"How about it?" he answered, sparking low-grade laughter from the other boys at his rapier wit.

"Mario wanted me to keep you posted on a few things."

"How's Macko's?"

I knew Macko's Subs on Ventnor Avenue and found the suggestion chilling. I used to eat there all the time when I was in high school or home for the summer during college. I had notions that Noel knew this and suggested it on purpose as some sort of mindfuckery. Never mind that Macko's was a perfectly logical suggestion for lunch. It had been a popular place for decades, but in my raw state I began routinely interpreting everything as part of Noel's plan to kill me.

Macko's was another rectangular sub shop where the smells of Italian sausage and salt air collided. There were a handful of booths lined up along a wood-paneled wall. A jukebox stood in back and familiar local but nameless faces toiled in the oniony steam behind the counter, including the requisite kid who was proudly cutting school to work there. The Shore was a magnet for short-term thinkers: The young sea babes coming down from the mainland probably thought this slicky boy was quite a catch—the cute guy from . . . Somewhere Else.

Noel and I drove separately, he in a black Mercedes convertible. He lit up a cigarette the moment he climbed into his car. He rode in back of me, only feet from the rear of my Cherokee. I kept speeding up to see if he was conscious of the closeness. He sped up, too. He was right on me, his car jerking forward. I waved to him in the rearview mirror and he waved playfully, psychotically back.

I got to Macko's first, Noel having stopped a block back. I chose a booth (facing out). I practiced crossing and uncrossing my legs for fear that if I sat the wrong way, my gun would go off and I'd blow Noel away by accident. He would fall face down into his hoagie, which the witnesses would pronounce in the pinched Philly-Jersey twang, "hyewgee."

Noel, looking batlike, entered the restaurant and hugged a young but used-looking woman who was wearing an apron. She was hurrying out the door.

"How's that pretty daughter of yours?" *Doorter a yers*. Noel the community relations manager.

"She gets braces next week. I'm working overtime to pay the damned orthodontist."

Noel scratched an eyebrow and frowned the way he had at Mickey's funeral. A handful of hundred-dollar bills appeared from nowhere, and Noel handed them to the woman.

"Karen," he began, "maybe this'll make a dent in those tooth bills. If you know what's good for you, you'll take it quietly," he added with a wink. "You got a light?"

Karen accepted the cash with a quiet thank-you, seemingly more in terror than appreciation. She coyly handed Noel a book of matches and vanished from the restaurant.

Noel, pleased with his charity, took a seat across from me. The proprietor offered a thank-you-for-not-killing-me nod of "respect" from across the counter.

"We learned some good stuff in a poll I did for Mario," I volunteered.

"Yeah?"

"People are scared of crime and losing their jobs, and worried about rich people getting everything."

"You needed to do a poll to tell you people don't like rich fuckers?"

"It's nice to have confirmation."

"Christ, and they call *us* racketeers."

"We'll go to the press soon with some stories. We need a bad guy, a receptacle for all kinds of fears."

"Receptacle. Good," Noel said with an eye roll.

The owner took our order. Macko's was a place where you knew what you wanted before you came in, or you didn't come in. Noel ordered a tuna sub, light on the mayo. Can't have too much cholesterol in your bloodstream when you're chopping guys up and throwing them in Barnegat Bay. I ordered the same.

"So, Jonah," Noel began, "how are you doing with your grandfather gone and all? You doing all right?"

"It's not easy. He raised me."

"I know, I know," Noel said, concerned, his diamond eyetooth catching a brown spark from the Cokes that the Macko's kid put before us.

"You know, Noel, you did something at Mickey's funeral I've been meaning to ask you about."

"Yeah? What's that?"

"You went like this." I made the finger-rubbing money gesture with my thumb and forefinger.

"Nah. I did that?"

"Yeah. I was wondering what that meant."

"Get outta here."

"You did that, sure. I'm sometimes a little slow, so I wanted to ask you what it meant."

"Don't know. Don't know. You're jumpy, college boy?"

"It's a jumpy time."

"You come into any money after the old man died?" Noel flicked around a plastic knife.

"I wish I did. After all that talk about Mickey having a billion dollars, all I got was his watch. I guess you know better than I do about how inheritance works in that life."

"No, I don't know. Tell me, how do these things work? Tell me now."

"My Uncle Blue said everything goes back to the partners."

"Yeah? Fuck him," Noel growled. "Fuck him. I'm a partner. I haven't seen dime one, and you've got some nice suits."

"I don't know what to tell you. I'm out of my league in this area."

"You're in our league now, genius. You're with us. Can't you play by our rules?"

"I'm just helping out."

"You're in, dude. We don't want you feeling unwanted. I'd be real sad if you felt like you weren't one of us. Of course, like anybody, you have to pay your club dues, which are more than you're paying. You're charging *us*. That ain't right."

"Mario asked me to work with him. It's a standard client-vendor relationship."

"Client-vendor, huh?"

Midmeal, I excused myself to go to the claustrophobic rest room in the back of the restaurant. I felt hot all of a sudden and washed my face. Beneath greenish fluorescent light, I thought I looked old—older than I had this morning. As I dried my hands, the door flew open, breaking the weak little hook that posed as a lock. My heart racing, I swung around and found myself suspended against the wall with Noel's hand around my throat. He held the point of a stiletto against my eye. Any impulse I had to defend myself deflated when I felt the tip bounce against my eyelid. So much for the revolver around my ankle, which was a hemisphere away.

"Fuck Mario," Noel coughed into my face. "Fuck Mario and fuck you. I'll waste you and chop you up so fast the birds in the Pine Barrens won't have time to shout 'buffet.' You got that?" Noel asked, his hot spit speckling my face. For the first time, I smelled him. Close up, he reeked like a landfill.

"What do you want?"

Noel's red-and-yellow-swirled eyes widened as he drew his knife several inches away from my eye. He actually looked bewildered, as if he could not answer my question. I envisioned the barrel of my revolver in his eye and pulp flying out from the back of his head. I wanted this.

"Just tell me what you want?" I repeated. "I don't know. I don't know."

Noel shook his head the way cartoon characters do after they're hit on the head with a mallet and stars fly out. He dragged me against the wall toward the toilets. The room stank something fierce. It was an olfactory monument to urine.

"The money. The money," he repeated. It was an afterthought.

Irv the Curve had been right. With these guys, violence was the end, not the means. I felt the blood gather in my head and thought my brain would explode out my eyes. Was this possible?

"Let go . . . Ah, I don't have it, but I'm looking."

"Take some time to think about it," he said, his jugular vein swelling. Noel backed off. Fear for my life converted into a sense of emasculation, as if my whole seventh-grade class had been watching. The pricks win, I thought. Why do the pricks win? "You'll come up with something," Noel concluded.

The logic of insanity. You don't debate the insane, you stay away from them. To hell with their difficult childhoods and chemical imbalances; I believed in evil. I fell back into the booth and felt around for my gun. It was there. I wanted to shoot Noel. I wanted to see the look on his face when he acknowledged, if only for a split second, that a bullet was hurtling into his brain. I wanted to see the surrender in his expression. I wanted to see his body quiver with every shot I fired into him.

But I didn't shoot. I didn't shoot because a sickening thought churned somewhere deep down: What if he didn't care? What if Noel saw me shooting him and his eyes went flat? If it just didn't matter. This is what people never understood about madness, that communicating solved nothing. Communication presumed lucidity, and not everyone possessed it. Avoidance was rapidly declining as an option here. I didn't see how it was possible. Two months ago, I was buying air time for Senate candidates. Today I was contemplating where to buy lime and dispose of a body. And I was passing off Noel as the lunatic?

Noel tapped my hands gently, the way a girlfriend would. The reversal in climate was menacing in itself.

"All I'm saying is that I can help," Noel continued, as if there had been no violence. "I can be like a coach. I'm just trying to help you out here. Like you're helping us out with something we don't know about with this poll stuff. You just don't know everything yet. That's all."

My sad sandwich uneaten, I slapped down a gross overpayment and left Noel alone to eat my lunch.

Categorical Denial

"It was during the MOVE trial that I first learned the word 'dreadlocks.'"

AFTER MY BASIC BELIEFS INTERVIEWS WERE COMPLETE, I RAN a survey asking broader audiences about the names of local criminals they currently feared. I listed a few well-known criminals, including Mario Vanni, plus a handful of made-up names I had cooked up to evoke some of the fears—of guns, drugs, and crazy men—that had surfaced during Eliza Baird's interviews: Ruger Dan, Monkey Hooch, Cokey Joe, Two-Slug Nick, and a gang I named the Angel Dusters. I had used the same technique in this poll that had gotten me fired from the Arizona Republican campaign. I had surveyors sidle up to folks in shopping malls and on-line, make friendly conversation, and see what they said. It wasn't scientific, but I got what I needed.

For one thing, people didn't appear to be terribly frightened of Mario Vanni. In fact, a lot of people smiled when his name came up, a reaction that I couldn't easily interpret but was somewhat consistent with what I had found in the Baird interviews. In this round, many folks were expressing considerable fear of a character I had fabricated and named Automatic Bart, who was described on the survey reference sheet simply as a "drugged-up maniac who runs a narcotics and extortion gang." The idea was, on one hand, to reinforce the public's free-floating fears, while, on the other, attempting to assess what kind of monster the people themselves would conjure up. Once a villain could be defined, we would pit him up against Mario Vanni. Who made people smile.

We began with Cindi's little computer-geek neighbor—an electric sniper she referred to only as Dorkus—at Mount Misery Summer Camp. Using the handle "Mad in Marlton," Dorkus shrieked in an Internet chat room that his brother had been killed by Automatic Bart. He was the same brother who had been laid off from a refinery in Swedesboro. Soon Dorkus had a handful of his pasty buddies echoing how their lives, too, had been terrorized by Automatic Bart, adding in a few validating rants about the rich getting richer. They offered ubiquitous symptoms of the gangster's presence—unexplained broken windows in the neighborhood, unknown new faces in the shopping malls, and mysterious laughter in the night.

We supplemented the on-line effort by whispering Automatic Bart's name using Vanni's men throughout the Delaware Valley and Shore Points. The name would suggest chaos and smoky clouds rolling over William Penn's statue posed eternally atop Philadelphia's City Hall, allowing no building, by ordinance, to stand taller than Penn's iron hat. The name Automatic Bart offered the specter of a clutching hand reaching from the sea and pulling the Delaware Valley, its good people and their jobs, under to wherever the hand came from. Even the mob, according to our whispering campaign, supposedly didn't know what to do about Automatic Bart. People here relied upon their racketeers the way voters claimed to love their congressman but hate Congress. Wise guys were *our* racketeers. Automatic Bart was something else entirely.

The first time the region ever saw Automatic Bart's name in print came with a telltale twist. It initially appeared as a small story that ran in the *Camden Journal On-Line* under the headline, "Hammonton Cops Deny Racism." It was placed next to a story featuring a Campbell's Soup spokeswoman denying that the mammoth company had plans to move its operations out of Camden, a rumor we had floated on-line. The police in Hammonton, a small Jersey town midway between Philadelphia and the Shore, had arrested a Hispanic man for some petty crime. While being brought into the courthouse for arraignment, the man, one Alfonso Gutierrez of Pemberton, claimed the police had accused him of working for Automatic Bart.

Cindi first learned about Gutierrez's arrest from a random South Jersey weekly that one of her interns monitored. She alerted me, and we made contact with Gutierrez through a Vanni operative. Vanni posted Gutierrez's bail; in exchange Gutierrez would mention Automatic Bart.

"They see me talk to a man in dreadlocks and that makes me a runner for Automatic Bart," said Gutierrez in earshot of a green *Camden Journal On-Line* reporter Cindi had tipped off about his release. On-line editions of newspapers were almost always staffed by cubs who were dying for a story to catch the eyes of the *real* newspaper's editor. "My advice is don't go talking to a man of color. That makes you a drug runner," Gutierrez added.

The Hammonton police chief, Robert Dunne, "categorically denied any deplorable acts of racism" on the part of the Hammonton police, which just confirmed for African Americans that life in the Delaware Valley was the same old shit.

Once the story ran on-line, Dorkus & Company—ostensibly victims of Automatic Bart's—ginned up the Internet chat rooms and carpet-bombed the *Camden Journal* with E-mails demanding broader coverage. The *Journal* then ran Alfonso Gutierrez's Automatic Bart quote in its print edition the following morning.

Local crime reporters in the Delaware Valley began asking their sources a chilling question: "Why haven't the authorities located Automatic Bart?" No matter the answer, we won.

By leaving his description opaque in our whispering campaign, the Delaware Valley, with the help of Alfonso Gutierrez, had rapidly decided that Automatic Bart was, in fact, black. A wave of nausea passed through me. We hadn't asked Gutierrez to describe Automatic Bart, only use his name. But his invocation of race and dreadlocks—combined with the Hammonton police chief's ostentatious stab at diversity-mindedness—tapped a wellspring of on-line panic that went back at least a quarter century.

During a 1978 shootout in the Powelton Village section of Philadelphia, a radical black group called MOVE had killed a white police officer named James Ramp. Every member of the group used the last name Africa and had grown long, terrible dreadlocks. Nine MOVE members were convicted of Ramp's murder and were sentenced to a billion years in prison. How you felt about the verdict depended upon your race. Whites called it justice. Blacks called it business as usual.

This was the Philly that Mickey, Deedee, and I came home to after our time abroad.

It was during the MOVE trial that I first learned the word "dreadlocks." This collection of letters terrified me. There was the word "dread," which made me think of death wrapped inside ropes of black licorice hair, and there was "lock," which reminded me of "warlock." Other kids who watched the news had the same morbid notions. The dreadlocks allowed us to be terrified of MOVE without conceding that our terror was tied to race; after all, we'd be scared of white people with dreadlocks, wouldn't we?

MOVE's dreadlocks tapped on Philadelphia's shoulder again in the spring of 1985. On May 13 of that year, the Philly police went to arrest a handful of MOVE members. They resisted, so the police flooded the house with water from fire hoses. Within seconds, bullets began whizzing around Osage Avenue. The cops fired back with automatic weapons and smoke bombs. When this failed, Mayor Wilson Goode ordered a police helicopter to drop a bomb on the house. One observer said the tar roof melted within seconds. When the flames had been doused hours later, sixty homes in the neighborhood had been destroyed, two hundred and fifty people were left homeless, and eleven MOVE members were incinerated. Only Birdie Africa and Ramona Africa were known to have survived, but there had been intense debate about the body count, with suggestions that a MOVE member had escaped only to be tortured and killed later by the Philly police.

There was a great public uproar after the incident with the political left and the media hammering at the police and Mayor Goode for genocide. The requisite comparisons to Hitler were raised, all contemporary deaths now being called holocausts. That Mayor Goode was black was the only thing that prevented the whole city from going up in flames. An outraged Al Just was on the air throughout the MOVE bombing, now sporting a sad little ponytail that resembled stray nose hairs more than it did dread-locks.

Just's indignation was lost on many Philadelphians. I remember a bunch of knock-around guys smirking on the Boardwalk as they read the headlines. No words were spoken, but their expressions conveyed, "It's about fuckin' time." This sentiment was aggravated by raw memories of the 1982 slaying of a white police officer named Daniel Faulkner by a former Black Panther who now called himself Mumia Abu-Jamal.

Within days after Alfonso Gutierrez's arrest, the chat rooms in the Delaware Valley sprang to life as the region weighed in on Automatic Bart. One posting reminded others that the body count after the MOVE bombing was never resolved. A liberal-minded chat room visitor interpreted the lack of resolution as murky proof that the Philly police had indeed tortured and killed an escaped MOVE member. A swaggering racist entered the chat room and decided that the person who escaped was, in fact, Automatic Bart, or Barton Africa, who now controlled the region's drug trade. "The hophead bleeding hearts are just afraid to call a spade a spade!" he summed up, which only inflamed the on-line accusations.

I felt a bubble of acid drift through my chest as I scrolled through these messages. I tried to picture Automatic Bart. I could begin to see his dreadlocks, but not his face. I thought about Mickey and the man in the woods. Nothing was clear, except that a massive but shadowy narcotics empire had supposedly metas-tasized, a business sector that the traditional mob had supposedly avoided. This was a nostalgic urban legend, but one Al Just, who specialized in phantoms, and Vanni's public seemed desperate to believe in their Skin Bracer fog. I had begun to consummate this illusion.

Vanni's Best Angle

"You can't keep the big guy on camera too long."

Ican't fuckin' believe i'm letting you do this," Mario
said in disbelief, his eyes darting around at the elephant bowels
he called an office.

I handed him a copy of the day's *Philadelphia Bulletin* and
showed him a quote from the Delaware Valley Anticrime Coalition.
DELVAC (Cindi, for now) had E-mailed a statement on electronic
letterhead calling on law enforcement to pay attention to "the new
criminal organizations of which we know little." It quoted a community college professor Cindi dug up. Vanni rubbed his temples
and smirked tentatively at a reference to Automatic Bart as an "unknown and potentially lethal force."

"Mario, you may need to show your skills on TV to address all
of this," I said.

"Who am I, Jay Leno?"

His arms up above the archway, a pit-stained Noel grinned a
conspiratorial that's-just-Mario grin. Still raw from my Macko's encounter with Noel, I had decided not to tell anyone until I had
thought the whole thing through. Right now, I felt degraded in
addition to threatened and didn't think that tattling on Noel was

the kind of thing men like Vanni, Blue, and Irv respected. These were men you approached with your solutions, not your problems.

"We may also want to provide the media with footage of you that we like so they can portray you in the best light," I added.

"Best light? All my lights are pretty good."

"We're now in show business whether we like it or not. I need to put you under a little pressure to get you used to how the media work. I don't mean to be disrespectful, but they don't fear you. The only thing they fear is low ratings. In fact, they want you to threaten them. It's good for ratings."

"I'm not threatening nobody."

"That's good. You'll need to show that on camera."

As I briefed Vanni on additional highlights of my public opinion research, a freelance camera crew from Philly set themselves up inside Lucy's large intestine. I assured Noel that the video guys were clean and would not be filming Vanni's office. Keep the tapes, I told him. "It's okay," Noel assured, "I trust you." It was as if the knife in the eye incident at Macko's had never happened.

One of the video guys was named Eddie and the other called himself Diamonds, I gathered because of the diamond stud in his ear. I was comforted by their Philly accents: Eddie and Diamonds knew who Vanni was and appreciated the consequences of yapping about their intrapachyderm adventure.

There were two chairs set up interview-style and two cameras facing the chair where Vanni would be seated. I wanted a sense of how he would look from several angles. We had two Sony video monitors connected to two VHS machines. Eddie and Diamonds had also brought several lights so we could test how Vanni handled realistic interview settings.

Vanni, Noel, Frankie Shrugs, and a few other killers watched the setup with an arrogant sort of amazement.

"What, are we makin' a *Die Hard* flick?" Frankie Shrugs asked.

"Hey, you know Bruce Willis is from around here," Noel said. "Penns Grove. Maybe we could get him to do another sequel," he added, anxiously absorbing the action.

"Yeah, he really wants to leave Hollywood for this place," Frankie Shrugs laughed. Noel didn't like that a bit. There was an existence *out there* that he, Noel, did not govern, let alone participate in. This upset him because the core of his mental operating system was the illusion that he ran the world, or at least that the world revolved around him. This was vintage gangster logic: we control everything. As if these men had had a choice between Yale Law School and crushing kneecaps. Vanni, on the other hand, knew that gangsters were small time.

Vanni wore a sports jacket. He asked everyone except the camera guys and me to leave. Unable to express anger toward Vanni, Noel and Shrugs glared at me.

Vanni eyed the cameras and the heavy-duty equipment and whistled in amazement. "Some setup," he muttered. I gestured toward one of the guest chairs, and Vanni and I sat down with Vanni squinting straight into the hot square lights. Eddie stepped forward and hooked a mike to Vanni's lapel.

"That's a microphone," I explained.

"No shit, Marconi," Vanni laughed. "I never had somebody walk right up to me and put one of these on."

Diamonds pinned a mike on me. "Jonah," Diamonds said, "the hum of the air-conditioning interferes with the quality of the tape."

"Don't worry," I said, "the media wouldn't trust footage from Mario that's broadcast quality. We want it a little rough."

In the first round, I asked softball questions. I focused on Vanni's wife and kids, and his childhood. He did fine, but he wasn't great. He kept tugging at his chin.

"Diamonds, how long did that session go?" I asked.

"Eight minutes."

"Why does how long matter?" Vanni wanted to know.

"Some people break down on camera after a while, and I need to know your boiling point," I explained. "Let's go again. Roll tape. . . . Mr. Vanni, tell me about your job."

"I'm a businessman," he said.

"Every tough guy dishes out that cliché. What business are you in?"

"Different businesses," Vanni said, looking hurt. "Dry cleaning, waste disposal, vending and pharmaceutical supplies."

"Talk in full sentences please."

"Christ. I've got different businesses. I've got businesses in dry cleaning, waste disposal, vending and pharmaceutical supplies."

"Good."

We continued at this pace for another seven minutes.

Vanni asked for water. "Am I doin' all right?" he added.

"You're solid," I said. "Are you ready to go another round?"

"Sure, Rocky," Vanni said with a quick punching gesture. He was impressed with himself.

"Three, two, one, go," Eddie said from behind the camera.

"Are you a made member of the Mafia?" I opened.

Vanni's eyes widened and he sat up straight in his chair. "I don't know about anything like that."

"I think you do. Law enforcement believes that you are the *capo di tutti capi*, the boss of all bosses, of the Philadelphia Cosa Nostra family."

Vanni turned his head toward the door, but there were no button men to vindicate him.

"Are you the don of the Philadelphia–South Jersey Mafia family?"

"No."

"Who is?"

"I don't know about any Mafia."

"How does one become a made member of the Mafia?"

"Beats me. Sounds like a smear against Italians."

"Who said anything about Italians?"

Vanni shrugged.

"Have you ever killed anybody?"

"No."

"You've never killed anybody?"

"Who told you I killed somebody?"

"If I told you, what would you do to him?"

"I'd probably ask him how he heard such a thing. . . . I had a manslaughter conviction when I was a kid."

"Did you whack him, clip him, burn him, ice him, or what?"

"Nah, I'd never ice nobody—anybody, I mean."

"Could I join the Mafia?"

"I dunno."

"Could you hook me up with some connected guys who could get me an application or something?"

Vanni sneered.

"The government says you run a criminal enterprise. Do you?"

"They have a thing against Italians, I guess."

"You've applied for a casino license in the past and have been turned down. Why?"

"The commission's prejudiced against Italians."

"There are other Italian casino owners, Mr. Vanni. Some of the leading prosecutors and law enforcement agents in the country are Italians. Are they prejudiced against Italians? There's no evidence whatsoever that the Italian people have any empathy for you at all."

"Every race has got Uncle Toms, right?"

"Did you know a man named Nicky Scarfo?"

"Yeah, I knew the guy, so what?"

"Some people say you set him up so you could get his job."

"People say shit. Stuff. People say stuff all the time."

"Why should law enforcement leave you alone?"

"Because I'm just a guy breaking his neck to run a business. Some government people don't like my suits or the car I drive so they come after me. I mean, there's drug dealers out there, and they come after guys like me."

"It's been said that you deal drugs."

"Never. Never."

"You wouldn't work with people in the drug business?"

"No."

"What does your pharmaceutical supply company sell?"

"Pharmaceutical supplies."

"What kind of supplies?"

"The pharmaceutical kind."

"If you had a clothing store and you sold shirts, would you admit you sold shirts?"

"Why not?"

"Then why won't you tell me what kind of drugs you sell?"

"It's not your business."

"But you just said that if you had a clothing store, you'd admit you sold shirts."

"I don't sell drugs."

"Then what does your drug supply company sell?"

"I've got business whizzes that do the details. I'm a financial guy."

"Anything a financial guy wants the public to know before we wrap?"

"Yeah. I hope the people understand that guys like you with your fancy words and tricks don't fool anybody."

"Thanks for being with us."

When we cut, I could see a vein on the left side of Vanni's forehead pulsating. Tiny beads of sweat had broken out around his hairline. His facial expression was a disquieting combination of menace and vulnerability, as if he were saying, "I'll bust your fuckin' head open with a crowbar and, by the way, how'd I do?"

I pre-empted his question by telling him he did fine. Vanni left the room. He knew that once I reviewed the tape, he'd be coming back in to have me record sound bites that tapped in to some of the things learned in my polls. The videotape would be distributed via satellite to the broadcast media at the right moment.

Eddie and Diamonds reconfigured the study so that the two monitors were side by side and we could watch Vanni handle the same interview from the two different angles and draw conclusions.

After a few minutes of watching Vanni on the dual monitors, Diamonds said, "From the right, Vanni's features look softer."

I agreed. When shot from the left, his eyebrow was arched in a way that made him look sinister. Even his smile from that side revealed an eyetooth that appeared more like a fang. From the right, however, there was a curvature to his face that made him look more like those hardy Italian Little League coaches of my boyhood Aprils.

Frankie Shrugs hauled his freighter of a body past the room, and I called him in. I asked Eddie to freeze the monitors on Vanni so that we could review the same expression from two different angles.

"Frankie," I asked, "which shot of Mario do you like better?"

Pleased to be a player, Frankie Shrugs contemplated the dual monitors and pointed to the one that captured Vanni from his left. "I like that one. Looks like a badass there. Looks like a good fellow, you know?"

I gave Frankie Shrugs a thumbs-up and thanked him. He vanished into Lucy's esophagus.

"This confirms it, guys," I said. "Frankie likes the left so we go with Vanni's right." Eddie and Diamonds nodded.

"Do you notice anything else funny on the tapes?"

"No," the guys said.

"Reverse the tape, would you?"

As the tape speedily rewound, the two men looked at each other. Eddie said, "He tics a little, don't he?"

"That's what I think," I said. "But not right away."

We played a few interview segments at real time, and I noticed that Vanni took on a different mien after a while. We sped through a few more clips and again confirmed that the twitching, which I had never noticed in person, indeed seemed to get more intense toward the end of an interview. I didn't associate the tic with anything medical, like anxiety. Rather, it seemed to be more of a churlish expression of frustration or boredom. It was just a sideways movement of the head, a minuscule shrug, and a flash of a snarl. What was with these guys and the shrugging?

"Eddie," I asked, "clock the average time until Vanni starts snarling."

Eddie fiddled with a few buttons. "We average out a snarling start time of four minutes. As the segments go on, he starts that shit earlier."

"Okay, freeze Vanni at the time he starts ticking. Match up the frame side by side so I can see the same expression from two angles," I said. Diamonds adjusted the monitors manually, which made Vanni's voice sound like a robot on Valium. I shivered a little and the other guys made a similar facial expression to the one you see when the TV coroner whips back the blanket in the morgue.

In the frozen frame, we now noticed something on top of the snarl: Vanni's eyes blackened and hardened. His eyebrows moved closer together. His left eyelid appeared to droop. His lip curled in a way that showed his teeth, specifically, the left eyetooth that looked like a fang. His jaw was thrust slightly outward, and his two lower incisors seemed pointy, too.

Diamonds leaned forward and, after looking over his shoulder, said conspiratorially, "Jonah, my man, you can't keep the big guy on camera too long." He was right. Our campaign could contain nothing spontaneous.

Taken in very short cuts, Mario could be good. I'd have to make him ubiquitous in frequency but not in duration. Too much duration would make him familiar and suck away the mystery I thought we needed. By keeping the show short and frantic, we'd be the media's only source for Mario stories. But we could still make Vanni *look* like a spontaneous media star who openly welcomed scrutiny if we carefully repeated the distribution of controlled pixels, the basic visual elements. This would have to be a summer blockbuster—we'd get our initial bounce on-line and be out of the newspapers before mid-September's nip. I scribbled a few messages on a pad and invited Vanni back in to film him in short bursts. From the right.

After the training, I collapsed in Mickey's guest room and slept off my terror. I awoke at dusk to go for a short Boardwalk run. Night slipped into Atlantic City like a fugitive and crept along the Boardwalk. The sky reminded me of an old navy curtain Deedee once had in a guest room.

I didn't want to be without my gun, but couldn't easily run with it in shorts. Screw it, they wouldn't get me on the Boardwalk.

Taking my first step, I nearly was run over by a rollerblading sharpie I took to be a middle-aged lawyer from Philly. He sped toward a flashing billboard in the distance, one that announced casino winnings and the name of the winner. BETTY WILKINS— $15,000 PAYOFF AT RESORTS, a cultural cousin of BARRY SILVER. FURS and his obsession with display.

I bent down to tie my sneaker, but I hated stopping in midrun. While crouching, I saw the little wheels of a rollerblade bump by me at eye level. A few feet away, I saw another type of wheel hobble feebly past. It was a rolling chair being pushed by an old man with a scrunched orange face.

Rolling chairs were wide wicker carts that held several tourists and were pushed slowly down the Boardwalk by old guys who looked like Popeye. This face was in the job description. Even the black rolling chair pushers looked like Popeye. And I remembered a few female pushers who looked like Popeye.

Rolling chairs had been around since 1887 and had come into fashion seventeen years after the Boardwalk was built by a hotel owner named Alexander Boardman. Mickey had told me that the man's name was not connected to the word "Boardwalk," but I didn't believe him. I had already begun singing "This Land Is Your Land" at summer camp and knew all about the Ribbonoff Highway: Big shots liked to name things after themselves and that's all there was to it.

At first the Boardwalk was a small, collapsible number that would go up in the spring and be taken down in the fall. Today it was sixty feet wide and six miles long, the oldest and biggest Boardwalk in the world.

Running south, I passed a young couple with their toddling son squeezed between them in a rolling chair. I felt old. I vividly remembered sitting in between my parents in a rolling chair on the Fourth of July. It must have been around 1968, a time of unrest for the rest of civilization but a perfect, peaceful time for me. There was a moist nip in the air, and old Popeye gave Mom and Dad a burgundy blanket that covered me up to my neck. I'm almost certain I was wearing a red, white, and blue cowboy hat.

A terribly old and diminutive man and his regal-looking wife, both beneath blankets, waved in sad slow motion as their rolling chair was pushed by. A policeman walked a few steps in back of them.

"Look at that man, Jonah," my mother said. "Look. Look. Wave." I craned my head above the blanket.

"Bye-bye," I waved.

The tiny man, who reminded me of Mickey, executed an eensy wave as my father identified him with awe as Mr. Berlin. I nodded in appreciation because there was a town in South Jersey by that name where I had gone with my dad to have his car inspected.

"Does Mr. Berlin own that town where we took the car?" I asked.

"No, Jonah," my father laughed. "He writes songs about America. 'God bless America, land that I love,'" he sang. "He loved Atlantic City. Even had his honeymoon here, but he likes to be very private."

I turned around to try to see Mr. Berlin. I waved, but he was gone. . . .

My memory short take ended when I spotted a man in the window of a pale motel extending his hand and patting it flat against his open mouth, the way children do when they make Indian sounds. I imagined the sound he might have been making, a high-pitched *Woo woo woo woo woo*. It made me think of the vanishing man on the Boardwalk at Mickey's funeral and the elusive man in the woods. If Noel didn't get me, perhaps these ghouls would. Whoever they were, they were coming for me, I just knew it. There was only one thing worse than a failed spin campaign, and that was one that grew larger than its creator. I envisioned lynchings throughout the Pine Barrens. They would get poor Odessa, old Mr. Fine. My heart began to race, so I turned back and sprinted past the happy young family in the rolling chair toward the Golden Prospect, where I sweated in Mickey's chair until my resting pulse returned.

Edie Morris of Batsto

"I believe that heaven and hell are lived here on earth."

I WASN'T THE FIRST *SHTARKER* IN SOUTH JERSEY," MICKEY TOLD me once over cabbage soup at Murray's. I must have been in junior high because my mother was still alive, sitting next to him. "Jersey was the muscle for the revolution." Mickey then made a gazelle-like transition to some of the region's successful prizefighters: Jersey Joe Walcott; Joey Giardello and his son, Joey Jr., who both moved like lightning; Mike "The Jewish Bomber" Rossman; Joe Frazier and Sonny Liston had trained in Philly; and Muhammad Ali, who lived for years in Cherry Hill. As the years went by, Mickey added Philly's mythical Rocky Balboa, as if his celluloid appearances had made him real.

The region had first seen bloodshed in revolutionary times. Edie Morris's little village of Batsto was the nucleus of the War of Independence. The weapons that George Washington used against King George's Redcoats were manufactured in Batsto. What the barrens lacked in the natural resources for farming they made up for in iron, which was mined from the South Jersey soil and molded into cannonballs.

I was almost certain that I had been to Batsto on a school field trip once, but my mind had mashed all of the field trips to the pines indecipherably together. The trees appeared to be in the same condition as they had been when I was little—healthy but tired. The pine trees were arboreal *alter kockers* that held a thousand legends in their knots: legends of gangland stills and murders, camera-shy pineys, and Jersey devils. Edie lived on the second floor of a small, rust-colored apartment building. It was within two miles of old Batsto Village.

As my right foot pressed the truck's accelerator, my left foot jittered in anticipation of this evening, and I knew why: I am not shrewd with women and tend not to pursue unless I see a future. At twenty-one, I saw this romanticism as a weakness; at thirty-eight, I still did but now knew that I wasn't hardwired for smorgasbroads. Mickey hadn't been, either. He married Deedee young. After her funeral, he had said, "That was that." Exact words.

I stepped down from the Cherokee feeling murderously self-conscious about the pistol strapped to my ankle. I climbed a set of stairs and lightly tapped Edie's door. She opened it within fifteen seconds, looking serene in a red sundress and flat brown leather sandals with thin straps that exposed her feet. My Australian boots had a slight heel on them that made me about her size, which meant she would be taller than I was had I not been wearing the boots. What would she think of me if I were shoeless, if we both were shoeless? Height wouldn't matter while we were seated or lying down, not that I should be thinking about lying down. Turn it off, Jonah.

"Nice Cherokee," she said. "I saw you pull up. Go off-road a lot?"

"Never."

"Then why the four-wheeler?"

"Washington shuts down in the snow. One flake and people act like it's Armageddon."

"I saw you sitting there. You could have knocked earlier."

"I'm always early."

"A planner of contingencies."

"It's always good to factor in disaster."

"Planning one?"

"Always."

Edie's furniture was an eclectic mixture of old wooden tables, which struck me as having come from her family, to contemporary touches such as a puffy off-white sofa that faced an outdated TV and a VCR. There was a pile of library books atop an ancient dining room table.

Edie caught me studying the place.

"Any questions?" she asked.

"No," I said, startled. "I just wanted to see where you live."

"This is where I live. It's a place."

Climbing into the Cherokee, Edie swept her dress under her and folded it over her legs. Her calves were long, brown, and toned. Riding horses will give you that tone, but it can also warp your legs. In the summers when I rode, I'd find muscles that I had not been aware existed. I wiped my forehead on my way over to the driver's side with a red bandana I had in my back pocket. I had a vague sense that I had been staring for an hour at her legs and imagined she noticed. As soon as I opened the door, I fixed my eyes on the rearview mirror, pretending to notice something curious. I pulled the door behind me, and it hit me on the side of my ass, a casualty of my hyperthinking.

"Tell me what you actually do in Washington." She said "Washington" disapprovingly.

"I read minds," I said as the Cherokee rolled toward Medford.

"And you get paid for this?"

"When I get paid, I get paid well."

"You don't always get paid?"

"No."

"Why not?"

"Politicians don't always have money." (Say what you will about Vanni, he paid.) "Even when they do, they can't manage it. In exchange for payment, they sometimes send other clients to me. Or they let me go on TV and do my genius shtick in order to attract more business."

"That's right, I saw you once."

"How'd I do?"

"You're slick. On TV. Not in person. I don't get that."

"People are tricky. I met a guy once who killed his brother but who cried when his dog died. Figure that out."

"I can't. You've met wonderful people. Your grandfather worried about you," Edie said. I could see she was looking at me sorrow-fully.

"How did you know that?"

"He talked. He used to come and watch our little concerts when we played at the Shore. He said that you liked the song *'Miserlou.'* He would stay and talk to us afterward. He liked me."

"What did you talk about?"

"We never talked long, but when we did it was about you. He told me to watch you on CNN. That's how I saw you."

"That's when you saw me be slick."

"Yes. I rolled my eyes, if you want the truth."

"Then why were you nice to me at the funeral?"

"You weren't in control like you were on TV. You looked like a lost little boy in a department store."

"Did you know who Mickey was?"

"They told me."

"Who's they?"

"The other klezmorim. I couldn't believe he was what they said he was. He was so sweet. He looked like an elf or something. I told my parents they shouldn't believe everything that they heard."

"You told them about Mickey?"

"Yes. My mother said he was the biggest gangster in America." Fifteen seconds of silence.

"He raised me, you know," I said.

"I know."

Edie shook her head the way I did as a kid sitting down to take the college boards. *You've got issues.* Much work ahead.

Braddock's Tavern was located on Main Street in Medford and looked exactly the way a Braddock's Tavern on a street called Main would look. The restaurant operated out of a big old two-story house that must have dated from the early 1900s. It sported a yel-low brick facade, heavy shutters, and an old-fashioned bar inside, where patrons could wait while the staff prepared their tables. The sidewalks were old and bricked, and it was hard to find a parking space on the pinkish and narrow streets.

A middle-aged man with curly black hair guided us up a narrow staircase to a tiny room that sat no more than twelve. Edie and I were seated adjacent to a fake fireplace.

"What else did you and Mickey talk about?"

"Nothing big. He loved talking about the pines. I told him how I used to go with my parents to pick berries."

"Berries?"

"The pines are bad for farming, but the cranberries and blueberries are terrific if you can get through all of the mud."

A preppy-looking waitress stopped at the edge of our table, introduced herself as Jenny, and took our drink orders. Edie confidently ordered merlot, and I, who abhorred alcohol, ordered the same.

"Tell me the tale of Edie Morris." A waiter placed two crimson glasses before us and retreated to the kitchen. "You don't look like an Edith."

"I'm definitely not an Edith. Just Edie."

"Do you have a middle name?"

"Yes, but I don't know you well enough to tell it to you. It's too weird."

"I see."

"I'm the baby in our gang. Two older brothers. I grew up in Pilesgrove—"

"Cowtown?"

"You know Cowtown?"

"Hell, yeah."

I loved this. Some guys wanted a woman from Sweden; I couldn't imagine there being anyone more exotic that a cowgirl from Jersey. How great was this? I had been to the Cowtown Rodeo as a kid. Cowtown was an air bubble of the Wild West plopped down by some joke of fate in South Jersey.

"My dad owns a lot of property around there. We always rode horses. We weren't competitive like those people in Devon or Bucks County. We rode Western, usually, just to relax. We roped and all. Three years ago, I opened my own music school to teach kids guitar. Did you ever ride at Cowtown?"

"Not there. Mickey had me take lessons from a friend of his at the Atlantic City Race Track."

"I bet you didn't know many girls like me growing up."

"The girls I grew up with just wanted to rope a Mercedes. Seeing you playing klezmer music was freaky," I added randomly.

"Why?"

"Because you don't look Jewish," I said.

"Neither do you, really."

"What religion are you, anyway?"

"Methodist. You?"

I shook my head, comically resigned. "I don't know what the hell I am. What do you believe?"

"I believe," Edie said instantly, "that heaven and hell are lived here on earth. You didn't touch your wine."

"I don't drink."

"Then why did you order wine?" Edie asked.

"I always like to have things in reserve in case someone needs something."

Jenny the waitress presided over this exchange with a forced smile.

We each ordered a pasta mix called "straw and grass" and spoke of South Jersey and klezmer music throughout dinner. I recognized almost all of the songs in her repertoire and was able to tell her what they were about. I knew enough Yiddish words to distinguish between a happy melody and a sad one.

The discussion turned to books during a humid after-dinner walk to an ice cream store a few doors down from Braddock's Tavern. We walked back and forth along Main Street until one in the morning. We agreed to exchange a book that we each felt the other should read. She had a book for me at home.

"I do not want to take you home, Edie, but I also don't want to wear out my welcome."

"If you don't want to take me home, what do you want to do with me?"

"I want to know if I earned a few hours on horseback. For Sunday."

"You did," Edie responded quickly, gazing somewhere beyond my ear.

"I'll drive to your place and then follow you."

I was reluctant to kiss Edie good night, so I didn't. Still too shy. She asked me to wait for a second at her door. She went into her apartment. When she returned she handed me a small book called *Happy All the Time* by Laurie Colwin.

The very title of the book depressed me because I suspected that such a state was impossible. Happy all the time? Was she insane? I hadn't even kissed Edie yet, but I was already equating the success of the evening with impending doom because I had so little experience with successful evenings. I began to project how I would say good-bye to her, end things. She would be better off meeting another music teacher, somebody with whom a duffel bag filled with corpses didn't come as standard issue. She deserved a soft, steady life, a front door with ground-up flowers in a little pink bag of potpourri. Not me. Not with all this.

book two
philadelphia
bleed 'em

"A boy has never wept nor dashed a thousand kim."

—Dying words of Dutch Schultz,
Newark City Hospital,
October 24, 1935

Photo Op

"Solid, respectable funding was just assumed."

FROM WHERE CINDI AND I STOOD ON THE DRIVEWAY, WE could see that there had been at least three additions urgently stapled on to the McNee house in the Exeshire Leas section of Cherry Hill.

Cindi had met Rhoda McNee, the matron of the house, on a committee to beautify the median strips on Route 70, a PR project of a local real estate firm. McNee had been the first to respond to an advertisement Cindi had placed in the *Shopper's Guide*. She had aggressively taken command of the effort "like it was the Cuban Missile Crisis," according to Cindi. "She may be what we're looking for," she said when I explained whom we needed to "run" DELVAC. For the time being, we had gotten away with distributing unsigned statements from the group, but it was only a matter of time before the press wanted to touch a warm body.

"Here goes," I said the moment I saw the Exeshire Leas sign.

In a perfect British accent, Cindi chirped, "I myself grew up on an estate but summered in the Exeshire Leas. Tell me, Jonah, have you been to the Leas?"

I didn't respond.

Cindi had been successful as a publicist because she understood the people of the region as they actually were, as opposed to how they wanted to be seen. She knew what impressed them, and what impressed them was display. For example, Cindi had counseled a builder to emblazon the phrase THE SUCCESS ADDRESS in huge gold and red letters on a water tower near his new development. The place sold out immediately. She had driven me to the damned thing once and grinned vindictively at the spectacle.

Cindi had also advised a local hotel to get vanity plates on its limousines reading CLASS. The fleet had CLASS 1, CLASS 2, and so forth. "In this town," Cindi told me once, "class is defined as hemorrhaging overstatement." Indeed, there was a small gilded sign at the foot of the McNees' driveway that boasted the given name of the dwelling: Beau Monde.

We could tell precisely where the builders had broken through by a slight difference in the color of the outside paint. The front was done in brick, but the rear was plastered with aluminum siding.

A uniformed, defeated-looking woman of Hispanic origin answered the McNees' front door and escorted us to what she referred to as the "greenhouse," where iced tea awaited us. One addition put a family room at the rear of the McNee residence. A two-story foyer had also been added at the front. Its floor was covered in white marble, veined throughout with golden tributaries that culminated in a delta of sixteen-foot-high mirrors. The entry staircase had been realigned to give it an aristocratic curve where it had once been L-shaped, if the boxy shape of the room was any indication.

The third addition to the McNee residence was the garage. Judging from the lines, it had once been a standard two-car garage with a giant double door that snaked up into the ceiling. Through some architectural prestidigitation, it had been transformed into a four-car garage with four separate doors, as if to underscore that the garage was capable of housing four vehicles, lest anyone gliding by underestimate its capacity.

On either side of the McNees' place were houses that had, at one time, been similar in layout. The one to the east had a Tudor shtick going on the outside, and the one to the west flirted with something Renaissance.

Rhoda McNee—I put her at about fifty—was a tall, slender

blonde woman in a jogging suit that had probably yet to endure as much as a brisk walk. Her gait was regal, with one hand flapped down in a pose that would have been considered a little queer had she been a man. In her other hand, she carried a copy of *Town & Country*, which she set down on a silver demilune table next to a martini glass that bore fresh lipstick marks. Atop her head was some twist of metal that I took for a quasi tiara. Tiara—as in what a queen might wear. I had never seen anything like it.

"Oh, hello, Cindi," she said, as she floated through the foyer to the greenhouse as if she were on a dolly. "And who might this dashing fellow be?"

"This is my colleague, Jonah," Cindi answered. Rhoda McNee slid her hand out toward mine and held it a bit longer than was appropriate. "Enchanted," she said. *En-SHOT-tid*. The accent blended high-society England with the express checkout line at any South Jersey Shop-Rite.

"Nice to meet you," I said, playing the role of an unconfident assistant.

"Let me give you a tour of our humble commode," McNee began. "Our help supposably has it all in order before Mr. McNee returns." Rhoda took us around for what seemed like an hour. I froze my face in a hollow grin as she explained the origin of many of the "pieces" decorating the place, including a freaky sculpture she described as being "modren." Cindi asked questions about each of them, delaying the tour. I instinctively rubbed my ankles together. The gun was there. I didn't know whom I wanted to shoot more, Cindi or Rhoda.

We passed a black-and-white photo of John and Bobby Kennedy huddled in the Oval Office shadows. Rhoda noticed that it caught my eye and said, "I just love that picture of the boys," with excruciating familiarity. "The McNees are originally from Boston. A big clan, you know. My father-in-law knew old Joe. What a character, but a very imminent man."

As McNee prattled on about faucets and pieces and "ghastly contractors," I scanned the house for more character references. Front-group patsies had certain, well, qualifications they had to meet, and we couldn't wing it with someone who would be ultimately shilling for the rackets.

I was looking for three qualifications in particular. First, I wanted someone who might logically be concerned about whatever issue we were cloaking her in. The charade had to make sense. Second, I wanted someone who needed the notoriety sufficiently that she wouldn't ask too many questions. Questions like, "Who are you?" "Who funds you?" "What do you want?" Finally, I wanted someone who would ultimately wear out her welcome with the press. My thinking here was that when we were done with our shill, she could vanish. Any attempt by her to resurrect the issue would be met with a roll of the eyes by the media and public officials alike. She would inevitably misinterpret her fame as a permanent arrival and become a pain in the ass.

I preferred well-to-do housewives for stunts like this because the press didn't think to ask them about their backers. Solid, respectable funding was just assumed. Also, I had found that reporters are less likely to interrogate a woman than they are a man; there is something intrinsically un-American about doubting a homemaker. That Rhoda McNee was an unreflective social climber with an unsteady South Jersey–Piccadilly Circus accent and inventive word usage was even better. There is no one harder to challenge than a crackpot with a galloping sense of destiny.

Rhoda also wouldn't want anything untoward surfacing about her connections to Vanni, not that she would ever know she had any. If things got rough, she would do all that she could to cover up any link.

In a room that she referred to as the "parlor," I noticed a year-book from Merchantville High School from the midsixties. Merchantville was an old middle-class suburb of Camden. I had run a few track meets against them in high school.

"Merchantville High. Who went there?" I asked.

A hurried McNee answered, "I did—and here we are back in the greenhouse." She's dragging us around her place for an hour and the minute I mention Merchantville, she hauls us into the "greenhouse" like somebody had detonated a skunk in the "parlor."

I sat back at the wrought-iron "greenhouse" table and listened like an intern as Cindi cut her deal.

"Rhoda," Cindi began obsequiously, "I have a handful of clients who are concerned about crime in the region—"

"And they certainly should be," Rhoda said. "Something must be done to stop it. People need empowerment, don't they? Somebody has to come up with an anecdote to crime."

"Exactly. As you can imagine, they are concerned not only in a passive sense, they would ultimately like to be known for their contribution." Cindi rolled her eyes at her own remark as if she were letting Rhoda in on some great Machiavellian secret about the corporate desire for publicity. Rhoda volleyed back with a knowing smile, and I crinkled my mouth like an assassin trying to look like I, too, was in on the darker deed.

"Believe me, Cindi, I know how things work."

"I know that you do," Cindi sucked back. "Anyway, I don't know why or how they'll want credit for their anticrime efforts. My sense is that they will just list themselves at some point as members of the Delaware Valley Anticrime Coalition, or DELVAC. But that's not the big thing right now. What I have to do is get this group off the ground for a few months—with minimal funding—in order to see what course it takes."

"Sure," Rhoda said.

"Anyway, we need a leader, a spokesperson. Someone who is known in the community and who is willing to sponsor a Web site and be interviewed on camera."

"Like *Action News*," Rhoda stated knowingly.

"Exactly. Like *Action News*, or even national outlets like *USA Today* once things get going. We're planning events with the governors of New Jersey, Pennsylvania, and Delaware. I have offices that, for the time being, can be used as a clearinghouse for press calls, news releases, and things like that. I also have someone who can design DELVAC's Web site—"

"Good, Cindi, because I don't know a thing about computers."

"Don't worry about that. What I don't have yet is a prominent member of the community to spearhead the whole group, and I wanted to come to you first. Ooh, you know who would love Rhoda, Jonah?" Cindi blurted out in a not-so-secret aside.

"Who?"

"Yvonne in the Life section of *USA Today*. She loves Kennedy family friends—"

Rhoda said nothing. Cindi gave her no time to object, sustain, or overrule. I let Cindi's cunning ride.

To the extent one could even call it a deal, it was done inside of a nanosecond of the mention of *USA Today* and the Kennedys. Cindi and I listened to Rhoda prattle on for another half hour after we had her. Growing impatient, I cautiously pressed a button on my pager with my elbow, hoping that Rhoda wouldn't notice. The pager sounded and I mock-read the little screen, annoyed. There was no message, I just wanted to get the hell out.

"Cindi, we have to call the *Bulletin* reporter."

Cindi knew what I was up to. This was an acceptable interruption to Rhoda McNee, and she allowed us to scoot out feeling secure that she had discovered a tributary to Hollywood. Rhoda McNee photographed for Vanity Fair by *Annie Liebovitz*. As we pulled out of the McNees' driveway, Cindi balanced my chin in her hand and asked me, "Who the hell from Merchantville speaks with a British accent?"

The Atlantic City Expressway was desolate, and I made it from Cherry Hill to Ventnor in forty-five minutes. I met a haggard Mario Vanni at a beachfront park. Noel strode up seconds later. The moment he arrived, he asked a park worker who was picking up litter if he had a light. The man did and helped Noel fire up a cigarette.

Cindi had arranged to have a publicity photo taken of Vanni by an old wire service photographer named Lloyd Hernsen. He was, according to rumor, an alcoholic who was doing freelance work at the casinos. He covered mostly prizefights. Cindi said he was still well connected with the wire bureaus and got pickup from time to time.

Hernsen met me at the park. He was a ginger-colored little man with a red nose and watery eyes. I explained that a "very photogenic guy" would be sitting on a bench playing with kids. I offered him twenty-five hundred dollars if he'd take a few shots and attempt to place a photo with the regional photo wires at the right moment.

Cindi had arranged for three different children to be on hand. I suggested variety. She rounded up a Hispanic little girl, a black little boy, and a mentally disabled boy. The black child and the visibly retarded child were over the top. I paid their parents handsomely and sent them off. Little Carmela Diaz stayed. Somehow, shooting with the Hispanic little girl was less wrong. Somehow.

I parked Vanni's Mercedes beyond the park bench so the smiling grille would be visible in camera shot. We had Hernsen shoot Vanni from his right, of course. I emphasized that we needed the car in the shot. We shot for about twenty minutes with Carmela.

We then drove in a caravan to Vanni's beach house in Margate. In the rearview mirror, I saw Noel speeding after us in his Mercedes. Paul and Diamonds from the video crew set up shop on the boss's short, lush front lawn. Vanni pulled his Mercedes into his driveway like he was coming home from work, played with his dog, and walked toward the cameras when I yelled, out of vision, "Mario, Mario, c'mere." Vanni shrugged his shoulders as if to say, "What the heck," and moved toward the cameras and answered a few questions amid a throng of neighborhood well-wishers that milled around behind him.

My questions included a few token hardball shots for which I had prepared Vanni.

"Hey, Mario, are you the boss?"

"I'm not even the boss of my own house. My wife, Rita, she's the boss."

He nailed the questions in a few tries, better than I had expected, and Paul and Diamonds headed off to the studio in Atlantic City to edit the b-roll footage. Later in the week, they shot the footage to a satellite somewhere over the Gulf of Mexico to be held for eventual broadcast. Cindi delivered a copy to Dorkus so he could work it into the Web site he was designing for Vanni.

The next day, Hernsen gave me two photo choices. There was one showing Carmela with her head leaning against Vanni. I didn't like it. Why would she do something like that, just walk up and lean her head up against a man she didn't know as if she were resting? The kiss seemed more logical. You could see how a little girl could meet someone, a grandfather type, and peck him on the cheek. So I went with the kiss, which would come in handy at a low moment in our little jihad.

• • •

Jimmy Mack did odd jobs around South Philly, and I had an especially odd one for him. He wasn't a violent guy or anything, just
a random character in his early thirties who swept up at social clubs
and made deliveries for connected guys with legitimate businesses.
Vanni found him for me after I reviewed the photos of Carmela
Diaz. Hernsen had done a good job, but the photo was too campy
to lead with. I could use it, but I needed something more provoc-
ative.

While I hadn't figured out a plan for its deployment, I knew
from the opinion research that I needed a strong, if indirect, pro-
Vanni visual. It had to convey many of the things that had to be
conveyed without enumerating facts so specifically that they could
easily be questioned or, worse, proved false. The optics had to
validate the worldview of an anxious public in a way that folks
would *feel*, but never say, "I told you so."

I had been ruminating about legendary photographs, losing sleep:
the dark-haired college student screaming as she knelt beside the
body of another student who had been killed by the National Guard
at Kent State; the Viet Cong man being shot in the head by a South
Vietnamese general, wincing as the bullet smashed into his temple;
the Cambodian girl running naked after being napalmed; John-John
Kennedy and his chubby knees saluting his father's casket; the
masked Black September terrorists in Munich; Neil Armstrong's silver step into the Sea of Tranquillity. . . . Then it clicked: Rodney
King. Nothing the LAPD did to offer "context" for King's beating at
the hands of the police—such as the charge that King had been violent—had done a damned thing. Spin worked only when there were
no witnesses. People saw what they saw.

I shot back into Philly shortly before sunset, resenting every
mile of the Atlantic City Expressway.

Jimmy Mack held the video camera unsteadily as he focused on
the dusky scene outside of his apartment window on South Street.

"Hold it a little unsteady, Jimmy," I directed.

Jimmy tilted the camera slightly to one side.

The man out on the street looked a little like Frank Zappa.
Cindi had picked him out from a local theater troupe in Wilmington. His precise ethnicity wasn't clear, especially since some of his

features were obscured by a long black wig and a fake mustache and goatee. Cindi had scuzzed him up somehow with ash, and he looked dirty. I could smell him from across the street.

Dirty Zappa made menacing small talk with the two junior high kids that stood before him, a white boy and a black girl. He held out an object that reflected slightly. He waved it before them in a hypnotic way. The kids eyed it passively and then suddenly flinched.

A silver-haired man the size of a continent hulked into Jimmy Mack's camera view. He parted the two kids and pointed at whatever Dirty Zappa was holding. A smaller, darker-haired land formation of a man entered the picture and took hold of Dirty Zappa's arm, grabbing what appeared to be a small plastic bag away from him. The silver-haired continent shooed the two children away from the scene. Jimmy Mack's camera followed them until they vanished.

The camera swung back to Dirty Zappa, who was now suspended against a brick wall by the continent, who held him by his throat. Despite the position of Dirty Zappa's hands, which unequivocally conveyed surrender, the continent and his partner knocked him to the pavement. Jimmy Mack's camera captured the blows that followed against the backdrop of a grainy bluish light. The continent knelt down and pounded Dirty Zappa in the face until his accomplice kicked the skinny predator off of the sidewalk into the street. There was no sound.

"Lock it up good, Jimmy," I said. "I'll be in touch."

Cowtown

"The land is honest."

WHY *GOOD-BYE, COLUMBUS?*" EDIE ASKED, TAKING THE BOOK from me in the parking lot of the Cowtown stables.

"Read it and we'll have a little book club. You'll analyze my selection of *Good-bye, Columbus* and I'll analyze *Happy All the Time*. I'm a quarter way through."

"What do you think of it?"

"I don't know, they're all nice people. I'm trying to figure out why you chose it for me."

Happy All the Time, which I had been reading in the purple hours of the morning, followed the journey of two offbeat couples, artistic types.

"Life can be this way. It's not all swindles and setups," Edie suggested.

"I don't know how far a person can run from his own nature."

"It doesn't hurt to question?"

"Oh, yes it does."

Edie put *Good-bye, Columbus* on the passenger seat of her car and loped toward the stables. I followed.

Edie's thoroughbred, Squaw, stood sixteen hands. A gray filly, she nodded temperamentally when Edie brought her out of the barn. Squaw didn't seem pleased to meet me, judging from the way she kept bobbing her head.

"You'll be on Maverick. He's over there," Edie pointed with her crop.

Standing suspiciously behind a sliding wooden door was a middle-aged, deep-bay-colored quarter horse. I put Maverick at fifteen hands. He didn't look much like a Maverick.

"Jonah, can you tack him up?" I didn't answer right away, having forgotten that my name was Jonah. I was strictly on wise guy parlance these days and had come to believe that I was either College or Jones. "Yoo-hoo," Edie prodded.

"I haven't tacked a horse in years."

"Well, here's your big chance." She held Squaw's reins with her right hand and put her left hand against the waist of her tan riding pants. Edie had on an old pair of black tall boots and a Cowtown Rodeo T-shirt. Her hair was pulled back into a sun-bleached ponytail that fell beneath her riding helmet.

I slid open the massive cage door to the stall and quietly approached Maverick. He didn't move. Good sign. Maverick's English saddle rested atop a post that stuck out of the stall at a slightly raised angle. It made me think a lewd thought, but my brain returned to the challenge at hand when a dark-complexioned boy handed me a riding helmet. I spoke to Maverick for a few minutes very quietly as Edie watched.

I took the saddle, protective cloth and all, from the erectile post and flopped it on top of Maverick, who didn't move. Having things and people dropped on him was his fate, and he had accepted it. The animal's eyes blinked just once, resigned, as if to say, "What are you gonna do?" I reached beneath the horse and fastened the two straps beneath his barrel.

"Thanks, Maverick, for being gentle," I whispered. He responded by taking a violent piss that splashed against my boots and jeans.

"This would be Maverick relieving himself," I said out loud.

"They do that," Edie said from the central walkway, where a portable radio was playing Sister Hazel's riff on Fleetwood Mac's

"Gold Dust Woman." A few vague sniggers echoed through the barn. I chose not to associate the Southern-twanged mirth with anything that I had done.

The Southern lilt usually immobilized visitors to this part of Jersey, where country boys, with their protruding Adam's apples and narrow yellow eyes, were almost as common as they were in the South. In this confused pocket of mankind, swaggering city dudes and hair-trigger country boys were cultural bookends, married by Puggy Feinberg's linguistic belch: "What are you lookin' at?"

Within minutes, having successfully mounted on a block at the end of the barn, Edie and I were out trail riding. Edie sat upright on Squaw, her head framed in a halo of sunlight that left white dots in my eyes, sculpting the image of an ancient goddess—Inca, Maya, or some other glistening and long-vanished civilization. If Blue and the boys had seen my moronic expression they would have shot me on the spot, perhaps justifiably.

Edie wrestled with Squaw a few times, but Maverick was behaving.

We rode through the pine woods with Edie leading. Occasionally, Maverick stopped to chew on leaves. I kicked Maverick on. Sometimes he moved, other times he kept munching.

"Who's riding whom?" Edie asked.

Angry, I grabbed a branch myself and used it as a crop, rapping Maverick on the ass. The animal was unnerved by my aggression and glanced back, a little hurt.

"You don't ride me, Maverick," I said under my breath.

We vanished deep into the June shadows. There was an immediate hill, and I instinctively remembered how you were supposed to rise in the stirrups and lean forward on a horse while traveling up an incline.

"How long has it been?" Edie asked, her voice echoing off the trees.

"How long has what been?" My answer was a little defensive, and I cringed.

"Riding."

"I haven't been on a horse since I was eighteen."

"You're not bad. Really."

"I wanted to be a cowboy, you know? The land is honest."

Edie's ponytail swayed in between her shoulder blades. Her cotton shirt was beginning to show signs of perspiration. I strained the part of my brain right behind my eyes to imagine her without a shirt. I pictured a smooth back, perfect skin, the right degree of definition to her shoulders. Her muscles would arc gently, not at the sharp, hurtful angles of workout queens. Edie continued, "The land really is honest, isn't it?"

"If you fall from your horse on your ass, you're on your ass. There's no other interpretation. You're either on your horse or you're on your ass."

"I bet that's why you're not married yet." Edie jerked Squaw to a stop. She dropped her jaw. "Oh, my God, I'm sorry."

I halted Maverick. "Sorry for what?" Edie turned Squaw deftly with heel pressure and faced me.

"I'm sorry for that."

"Don't be sorry. Just tell me what you meant. I'm interested."

She brushed aside a string of renegade hair that had fallen from beneath her helmet. A ray of sunlight cut between the trees and fell across her face, making her look like an island nymph I would paint if I could paint island nymphs.

"I just meant that you don't trust easily. That's all I meant to say. And that the ground . . . the ground is something that you always know where it is and that must be important to you given what you've seen." Edie looked away from me, steamed with herself. I pressed my legs against Maverick and inched up alongside Squaw. I leaned to my side, and Edie met me between the narrow but deep chasm between the animals. I kissed her still mouth, which was arched into a pout, presumably from her perceived faux pas. Her lips turned up at the sides in midkiss when she realized that her hip-shot observation about my social status was welcome.

"What you said is true. I'm not really a good-standing member of the twenty-first century and that's why I'm not married."

"Why aren't you in good standing?" Edie asked, her confidence easing back.

"Socially, I'm wired like a farmer. Early to bed, early to rise, that kind of thing."

"And that's important to you?"

"Normalcy is important to me. It's exotic. It's as exotic to me as adventure is for some people. I've had enough adventure for a thousand lifetimes. So why hasn't some cowboy gotten down on one knee and said, 'Jersey girl, let's go!'?"

She kissed me hard. "Haven't met the right cowboy."

In the stable lot, Edie reached into the backseat of her car and displayed three newly budding birds of paradise. The flowers had long necks like swans. There were streaks of orange and blue on the buds of the flowers, which were closed like cupped hands. Wisps that reminded me of glowing fingers were prying at the openings. I stared at them like a nitwit.

"They're for you," she said.

"For me?"

"Yes."

"Why?"

"Why not?"

"No one's ever given me flowers before," I said, still staring at them.

I held them the way new fathers hold infants—at arm's length, like dripping radioactive matter.

"Why is your hand trembling?"

I said nothing.

Edie followed me back to Mickey's, where we set the flowers in one of his Indian vases and showered. Separately. We walked to the Princeton Antique Bookstore in the heart of Atlantic City. It maintained the oldest collection of Shore memorabilia in existence, including obscure books about the region's history. It was here that I had read about the 1929 conclave Mickey had organized with Lucky Luciano and Al Capone. I had also discovered the text of Dutch Schultz's death speech and haunting final words: "A boy has never wept nor dashed a thousand kim . . ." The store's owner did not whitewash this city's past and I had always admired him for this. I never told him who I was, but he knew. I am a whiz at recognizing those who know, but I cannot explain empirically how. I was the only kid who walked in that store that he was happy to see. It wasn't because I was Mickey's grandson; it was because I loved the books.

I took Edie to Dock's Seafood for dinner. Afterward, we got ice cream for dessert, and she gave me a rough time about ordering a vanilla cone. She ordered some tropical number that looked more like fireworks than food. I took Edie's hand, first by the pinkie, then gradually acquired more fingers when I detected no resistance. We stepped onto a nameless pier and took a seat facing England. I let go of her hand and reached around lightly supporting the back of her neck as if I held a Fabergé egg. With my free hand, I stroked her eyelids shut. I kissed her once, for just a moment. I felt myself shiver and hoped she didn't notice. My eyes shut as I moved back.

Edie turned my head to the side and whispered in a quiet, foggy voice, "You kiss like a poet."

"A poet?"

"You kiss like a poet. I see through you," leveling her statement with a pointing jab.

I didn't know what to say, so I stood and tugged Edie upward. We walked back to the Golden Prospect and talked into the night on Mickey's balcony. The breakers pounded. I ran my fingers over the pale veins in her hands. She wore her nails short, but they were curved and polished in a two-toned way that revealed a slim white line around the top edges.

We fell asleep at two in the morning, inside on Mickey's big old sofa. Sleeping next to someone on a sofa, even if it is someone you are falling in love with, is not comfortable. But I wasn't about to move. Every time I shifted even slightly, I feared that Edie would spring up in betrayal and decide that we should sleep apart. She did not. Morning rose quickly, and I began to feel the old Jonah (the young Jonah?), the brash Poll Vaulter, awakening from the dead.

Trouble Comes to Town

"Mickey and muddy shoes don't add up."

SORRY I ALMOST BLEW YOU AWAY," TROUBLE TOLD ME AN HOUR after he almost cut me in half with an Uzi outside of the Oval Office. I had been a staff pollster at the time. That was sixteen years ago. Greg "Trouble" Hartwell had been a Secret Service agent posted outside the hallway door to the Oval Office. He looked familiar to me, South Jersey familiar—he wore a mask of distrust that begged, "C'mon, just try it, pal." I placed him at a track meet in Camden or some other place where there were many other black kids like him. So I approached. As I did, I reached into the breast pocket of my suit to remove an envelope that I was to deliver to the press office. I inadvertently covered my blue security pass to the White House West Wing. Trouble reached into his suit jacket and pulled at something audibly metallic. I stopped cold and showed him my hands and my security pass. He nodded like a hard ass and let me by.

On the way back from the press office, I asked him if he was from South Jersey. He stood firm beside the curved Oval Office door and said, "Yes," checking me out with narrowed eyes. The Secret Service guys were trained to anticipate hustles and distractions, even when there weren't any.

"I won't bother you when you're on duty, but I know I have seen you somewhere before. I'm Jonah Eastman. From Atlantic City."

Trouble smiled a little. "Greg Hartwell. Camden."

"Did you run cross-country?"

"Yeah, I did."

"So did I. Ventnor High. I work over in Room 166 in the Old EOB."

"I remember you. Middle-distance guy. Collected a few trophies."

"So did you. Too many. They called you Trouble."

"They had other reasons for calling me that."

Trouble dropped by that afternoon with his apology for being cold, but I had long understood the Secret Service's professional posture. Agents who were nice to you in the cafeteria would shoot your eyes out of the back of your head if you weren't where you were supposed to be. Trouble and I became friends after that and took long runs around the monuments when our breaks coincided.

Trouble had left the Secret Service around the time Clinton took office. It wasn't political; he was now wrestling with some problems with his wife and sick daughter. Dawn was six and had cystic fibrosis. He also said he had been doing some "security consulting" off and on for the mayor of Camden, a guy about our age who had grown up with Trouble. The mayor, not unlike his predecessors, was perpetually under indictment and alleging conspiracies to frame him. That Trouble had done work for a character like this was selfishly gratifying. Despite his Secret Service pedigree, he was a local guy like me who did what he had to do when Fate got nasty. Trouble was to be the lion to Cindi's fox on the Vanni campaign.

Trouble stepped out of the train at the old Atlantic City station in a Brooks Brothers polo shirt and khaki shorts. He looked a little thin and his hair was longer—taller—than when I had last seen him a few months ago. He hugged me but didn't smile.

"Brooks Brothers shirt," I said. "You snooty WASP."

"What can I say? I'm a polo-playing daddy from the Radnor hunt country. What's up, Jonah?" Trouble offered me his Secret Service eyes, the ones that saw a pistol in every pocket and a sniper in every window. I grabbed the smaller of Trouble's bags.

"I've got a guy who wants to kill me."

"Tell me something I don't know," he said, staring straight ahead.

"How'd you guess?"

"Let's skip the bad movie line where I tell you how I was trained to know things like this. By the way, nice heat strapped to your ankle. What's his beef with you?"

"He wants to be boss. He thinks I'm his nemesis standing in the way. The boss is competent. Now, I'm doing a project for the boss—"

"No way you're in with these guys. No way. Oh, God."

"No. Oh, Moses. Anyway, with me on the scene, he can make a case that the boss is hanging around with Mickey Price's preppy grandson who's not passing Mickey's cash around."

"You know he's saying this?"

"Let's skip the bad movie line where I tell you how I was trained to know things like this," I said.

"Uh-huh." Trouble stopped for a second. The muscles in his calves made him look spring-loaded. His eyes came alive, too. "Where's the plan?" We began walking again.

"It's up here," I said, pointing to my skull. "I'm figuring it out as I go. I need to protect myself. Two of us aren't going to make it to the High Holidays."

"What about those old guys, Mickey's partners like that Blue?"

"Blue doesn't have authority over Vanni anymore."

We climbed into my Cherokee and headed for the Golden Prospect.

"Jonah, why don't you go straight to the FBI right now. Right now. Tell them what's going on—"

"Not an option."

"Why not?"

"What do I have? I can't prove the guy wants to kill me, and if I start making noises against Mickey's world, then I'm really dead. What am I going to do, wear a wire and then spend the rest of my life in Kansas working in a Jiffy Lube?"

We brought Trouble's bags up to Mickey's apartment. I gave him Mickey's muddy sneakers in a plastic bag. Once we were out on the Boardwalk, I asked him to check them out with one of his forensic kits.

"Mickey and muddy shoes don't add up. See if you can find out if there's anything special about the dirt."

"Will do."

"How's Dawn?" I asked, clutching Trouble's shoulder.

"Good enough but no better," he said sorrowfully. "Any extra cash couldn't hurt. The gig with my mayor friend in Camden is up."

"Should I ask what you did for him?"

Trouble gave me a disgusted glare. "Criminal defense work, we'll call it. He was acquitted on the charge I helped him fight."

"Mazel tov. And Jessica?"

"It's not like when we first met, I'll tell you that much. I guess I didn't turn out to be the warrior she thought she married. She freaked out a little when I did work for the mayor. When I brought back my suitcase filled with rancid clothes, she knew I'd been digging around in his enemies' trash cans, looking for records, any shit that could acquit him. I found it all right, but only after tossing aside used condoms and files stained with coffee grounds. I stayed in the shower for a week. . . . I don't know how anybody can be tough enough to handle a sick baby."

"I can't imagine." I sensed that Trouble didn't want to go any farther. "I met a girl," I volunteered.

"Naw. Where did you meet her?"

"Mickey's funeral." I looked away. "She's a musician. She played that old gypsy music he liked. She's not another desperado."

"Good. Choosing a desperado is choosing to be alone. Never mind that ratio shit you hear about Washington." Washington was known for having four women for one man, a statistic that hid more than it told.

"I know. It's strange: you take a hundred men and a hundred women and put them in a room, all one hundred men want the same one woman. The problem is she wants all of them, too."

"That's why she's a desperado. What's your girl's name?"

"Edie Morris. We've seen each other a few times. I wish all of this other stuff wasn't going on so I could see her more."

"Other stuff like saving your life tends to stand in the way."

Trouble and I walked for an hour. I told him there was serious money in it for him if he helped with his end of the program to save my life. I explained exactly what I needed him to do, and he was comfortable with it in an exhausted way. Maybe he didn't want his law enforcement career as much as I had supposed. Or maybe when you're depressed, you don't care. He had brought enough artillery to stop a Panzer division and plenty of radio equipment to intercept the necessary frequencies I needed him to track down.

Things at DELVAC were going fine, according to Cindi. Dorkus and his electric snipers were having a blast screwing around in chat rooms. DELVAC's Web site, also created by Dorkus, had begun to run a new feature: Citizens could send in via E-mail examples of things they were doing to make the region safer from crime. Kids could draw crayon pictures of safe neighborhoods and mail them to a post office box. Dorkus then scanned them onto DELVAC's Web site. We prominently featured one Magic Marker drawing of stick-figured schoolchildren running away from a factory with the word DRUGS blaring in neon.

Cindi and I talked in code a few times a day, even though we were each at pay phones, me in one of the casinos and Cindi either at Ponzio's or the Cherry Hill Mall. We kept our talks short enough to handle five dollars in quarters. We never used E-mail to communicate with each other.

"You'll hear from me in the next few days, Cin. You'll just need to do one thing now. Alert a really good friend that he'll be hearing from a reliable source."

"Then what?"

"Tell your really good friend that you've never met the source, which will be true, and become a hero when your source's prediction turns out to be true."

Despite my intention to regulate media access to Vanni, there was a core issue I decided that I had to address with him: his potential for rage. I sat him down and engaged in shameless flattery.

"I'll tell you, Mario, you could have been a senator. The camera loves you."

"Nah, quit blowing sunshine."

"It's not all sunshine."

"Not all sunshine? What did I do wrong? I thought I was a senator."

"You're good, but I found something where the press can trip you up. See, you're used to respect. You're used to being treated well. These media people, they don't even respect kings and presidents. They scream at them, they chase them around shouting questions. . . . Look, do you have Xanax or Valium?" I asked.

"I take Xanax when I fly. I've got some here somewhere. You need some?"

"No. I want you to take a small amount."

"Why?"

"Because your face tenses up on camera. I want to smooth that out. Trust me."

Vanni called for some water, and Petie brought in a cup. As Vanni found a Xanax and popped it, I set up a small video camera behind my chair, which would give the pill a few minutes to take effect.

"What's your point with the face tensing, Jonah?"

"My point is that you—like a president or a king—aren't used to being abused and may snap. If you snap on camera, Mario, we're screwed. Losing your temper on camera is dangerous. Anyone who snaps on TV looks out of control. If you end up looking out of control, the only thing people will see is an angry man who people say is a gangster."

"I thought I wasn't going on camera for long."

"You aren't, but things will come up. I have to protect you."

"*You* have to protect *me*?"

"Yes."

"He's my bodyguard all of a sudden," Mario said to his watch. "How do you protect me?"

"I have to thicken your skin. You have to show me that you understand the attacks on you are business, they're part of the game. To get you riled. That's what Sam Donaldson tried to do with Reagan all the time—get him pissed off."

"Reagan stayed cool."

"Right, he did. He stayed cool because he knew it wasn't personal."

"You don't think I can stay cool?"

"No Italian can stay cool."

"What was that?"

"I said that Italians can't stay cool. They have to beat the crap out of people to show how tough they are."

"What the fuck's wrong with you?"

"You're a Mafia boss. You're trying to look respectable, but you're no better than a common drug pusher selling dope at a grade school."

Vanni's jaw fell slack. He glanced around inside the elephant, but there was no one there to glance back. It was just the two of us.

"I'm no better, huh?" he finally said.

"You gonna hit me, Mario?"

He looked away.

"What kind of money do you make on drugs?"

Vanni rubbed his temples and said nothing.

"Hey, Mario, you gonna drag me out to the Pine Barrens and chop me up? Let me tell you something, friend, if I'm a reporter, I chop you up, you don't chop me up. Reporters aren't afraid of you. Reporters aren't afraid of Osama bin Laden, they're not afraid of you."

"I get the point, Jonah."

"I said that Italians were hotheads. You didn't refute that. How do you feel about how you represent all Italians, how you portray them as hotheaded killers?"

Mario held his hands together, as if in prayer. "That ain't fair," he said calmly. "That's not fair."

"Don't you feel bad about smearing all Italians with the taint of the Mafia?"

"I don't like the prejudice. I don't like the prejudice toward me, and I don't like the prejudice toward Italians."

"But you, sir, *cause* a lot of that prejudice by being a mob boss."

"I am not a mob boss."

"Don't repeat the negative, Mario," I told him in counselor mode. "You're no choirboy, are you?"

Vanni grinned, aw-shucks style. "No, I'm no choirboy."

"Don't you think your reputation hurts Italians? Don't you think that reputation hurts your wife and your kids?"

Vanni sighed. "What do I say here, Jonah?" he asked softly.

"You say what you believe in your heart. Don't think. Feel. Don't take the question personally, but give the answer personally."

"Yeah, okay, I'm embarrassed?"

I leaned forward, squinted, and cocked my eyebrows. I looked at Vanni like he was the biggest dumb ass in America. "You're embarrassed."

"Yes. Yes, I'm embarrassed. I admit it," he said vulnerably.

"What are you embarrassed about?"

"I'm embarrassed about what my name does to my family. What it does to other people." Vanni's face twitched, but in a hurt way. It wasn't sinister.

"What are you going to do about it?"

"I'm going to do what I can. I don't know what I'm going to do. I don't want people looking at my kids and thinking that they're mobsters. They're not. I don't want people saying Italians are mobsters when they're not. It's not fair the way you said we're all hotheads. An old Italian man teaching science class at a grade school is not a hothead. He's teaching molecules, or whatever. Shame on people who would say such a thing. Shame on you, in fact. Shame on you."

Vanni sat back and folded his hands in his lap. He was staring at the floor. His lips were trembling. I rose and put my hand on his shoulder. Vanni looked up at me. He was silent, maybe even scared.

"I wasn't kidding," I said quietly.

"About what?" he asked, depressed. "About Italians and mobsters?"

"I wasn't kidding about you having it in you somewhere to be a senator, something like that."

"It's too late for me."

"Yes, it is, but it's not too late for your kids, and someday your grandkids. You're good when you answer with your heart. Keep doing that. You can't beat these press people with your fists; they'll kill you. If you answer the way you just did with me, you'll take them down. You'll give them nowhere to go. Jesus, Mario, they'll never see it coming."

As soon as Vanni left, I slowly reviewed the new footage on the video recorder's tiny screen. No ticking.

If the Mob Is Killing Drug Dealers, Should We Stop Them?

"The world spins around nicely without people like him."

J-MAN," TROUBLE SAID OVER THE PHONE. "WE GOT A FLOATER in the Delaware. Can you get down here?"

"Give me ten minutes."

I timed the lights on Atlantic Avenue so that I made it through every one without getting nailed by a red light. The trick is to go the speed limit, which no one around here appreciates. Trouble stood on the deck of a green house on Quincy in Margate. His rented studio was accessible from an outdoor staircase that went straight up to his deck.

Trouble's living room looked like a fencing operation for RadioShack. Every electronic gadget that had ever been invented was strewn about the floor in a way that, knowing Trouble, was organized to some specific end.

"Your floater's a brother, early twenties, shot a few times in the head and chest. Been down there a few days. He'd puffed up like that marshmallow guy in *Ghostbusters*. This the kind of thing you're looking for?"

"It's exactly what I'm looking for."

"Good. By the way, Jonah, cranberries." Trouble held his hands out like a vaudeville comedian.

"What do you mean, cranberries?"

"On Mickey's shoes. I chipped off all of the mud and looked at it under a magnifying glass. There were little cranberry bits in the grooves. Does that mean anything?"

Frankie Shrugs sat on a lounge chair at the base of Lucy's feet reading *People* magazine. I recognized the chair as matching those used by a restaurant down the street.

"Frankie, you up for a little caper? I need you to make a call. I've got the quarters."

Frankie Shrugs had been warned about my potential need for him, but I could tell by the marbly brown inertia in his eyes that he never actually thought it would happen.

"Seriously, Frankie, Mario knows all about it."

"All right, all right. Let me tell the guys." Frankie entered the elephant and shouted something up Lucy's gullet. The only words I heard were "fucking Jones."

Al Just was walking his yellow Labrador on Spruce Street in Center City Philadelphia, wearing khaki pants and an old blue oxford cloth shirt; both shirt and pants were wrinkled. As chronicler of the Philly mob scene, Just had had a full-time job during the 1970s chasing Mickey around. In the early 1980s, when the war broke out after Don Bruno's murder, things got so hot for Just that there was speculation he'd move up to the networks. His star turn never materialized. Things were a lot slower these days. Mario Vanni's power was supposedly growing, but nobody had a handle on him. He was cold and secretive about his business operations, and so far Just hadn't interviewed him. Nobody had. The mobster wore button-down oxford shirts—figure that out. Just, who fancied himself as Philly's answer to Indiana Jones (in addition to his ponytail, he had a developed a thing for leather bomber jackets), had tried to pin his future on covering Vanni, but there wasn't a lot of blood flowing on the streets, something his producer, Davis Fox, didn't forgive him for.

Cindi had told me all about Just's woes. Gossip about which reporters were up, down, and out in the Delaware Valley media inevitably found its way into her voice mail. Other Philly reporters like George Anastasia had gone out and written books and magazine features about the mob wars of the 1980s and 1990s. Just hadn't reaped the benefits of the civil war that followed Angelo Bruno's killing. Unlike Anastasia, he wasn't much for digging: He was all for the cinematic pose, a man with perpetually flared nostrils who understood that his job description lay more in the realm of entertainment than journalism. He had been known to peel back his lip on camera, Bogart-style, and liked to be filmed cocking his eye and swaggering down sidestreets, as if a movie soundtrack were pulsing in his mind. Just raids a mob hangout to the strains of the Rolling Stones' "Gimme Shelter." Just saves a baby from a fire to the Fabulous Thunderbirds' "Tuff Enuff." He was the textbook evanjournalist, a reporter by title but an egomaniacal preacher hellbent on foisting his own brand of justice on the region.

As Davis Fox told him over a drink at Smokey Joe's, "It's not your job to get the story right. It's your job to get the story *first*."

Just's pager went off at a few minutes after nine. It was Davis.

"I just talked to the Sunday intern at assignment," Davis said. "Some Joe Pesci impersonator keeps calling for you, saying he knows about some murder. He says it involves Vanni. He wants you to be at your home number at ten o'clock."

"A wanna-be?" Just asked.

"Don't know, Al. I didn't talk to him. See what's up."

Just was back in his townhouse by twenty after nine. In his late fifties, Al was too old to get too excited at every tip but too young to give up hope. At a minute before ten, his phone rang. He picked it up and pressed the Record button on his miniature taping device.

"Al Just?" the gruff voice asked.

"You got him."

"Some scumbag is gonna turn up in the river. Mario Vanni had him hit because he's selling drugs around schools. Thought you should know."

"How do I know you're on the level?"

"I'm *not* on the level, Lois Lane. I'm the kinda guy you talk about."

"Fine. We're on the QT."

"QT? What's this, Adam fuckin' Twelve? I'll let you know some good stuff. That's how you'll know I'm on the level. I'll be in touch. By the way, love the ponytail, sweetheart. That's good shit."

Philadelphia police officer William De Felice was walking along the Delaware River waterfront near Newmarket earlier that same morning when he saw a red flash bobbing in the water about thirty feet out. For a moment, he thought it might have been a bag of balloons held over from last evening's Society Hill Theater Festival. But the bobbing was heavy. Discarded plastic tended to skip along the surface. This thing, whatever it was, was inert.

De Felice waited. As the orange summer sun floated above the factories across the river in Camden, he noticed two puffy brownish items straddling the red object in the water. He walked twenty yards back to his patrol car and retrieved his binoculars. Returning to the river's edge, De Felice adjusted the binoculars on the red and brown swirl in the water. Slowly, he lowered them and held them in his left hand. With his right hand, he reached for his radio and reported his discovery. It was the bloated body of a small-time drug dealer named Norvular LaMonty. Trouble had intercepted this transmission and the dialogue that followed.

That night, Al Just reported on the murder, conservatively linking it to a "possible mob war a-brewing." In the freeze-frame of his wrap-up, I detected the grin of a preadolescent baseball fan on opening day.

Later in the week, three shots rang out in the men's room of Lazy Jake's bar in Audubon, New Jersey, fifteen miles west of Philadelphia. Thirty-one-year-old degenerate Steve Vernon dropped dead, his brains floating down a river of blood in an old-fashioned wall-length urinal. A small article appeared in the *Camden Courier* about the demise of the lifelong troublemaker.

The gruff wise guy called Just again, this time at his office.

"Yo, how ya doin', Lois Lane?" the emasculating voice asked.

"What do you have for me?"

"Well, your buddy Mario had a guy named Vernon clipped in Audubon, in South Jersey. Another drug-dealing school pusher. Mario don't like that. You may want to check with an old lady named Doyle in Audubon. She turned Mario onto Vernon. Said he was ruinin' the neighborhood."

"All right, I'll look into it. But what's the endgame here? Why are you telling me this?"

"New sheriff in town, Ace." Click.

DELVAC called for an on-line discussion of the crime wave in the region. In one of the attendant chat rooms, Dorkus posted a highly embellished rap sheet for Norvular LaMonty linking him with numerous murders and, of course, Automatic Bart. Dorkus and his summer camp geek patrol offered kudos to whoever bumped off the viral LaMonty.

Later in the day, KBRO ran a story about two drug deaths being investigated. The police department spokespersons separately acknowledged that both murder investigations and all possibilities were being explored, although Vanni had yet to be questioned.

In time for the news cycles that followed, we urgently released a statement from Mario Vanni on his lawyer's letterhead. We posted the statement at Vanni's new self-spoofing Internet address, jersey dcvil.org.

FOR IMMEDIATE RELEASE
   Statement by Mario P. Vanni Pertaining to Recent Incidents Involving Narcotics Peddlers in the Philadelphia Area

   I have always supported the death penalty for drug crimes and believe Norvular LaMonty and his cohorts got what they deserved. While I had no hand in their demise, I cannot lie and say I feel bad about it. I hope anybody else who sells drugs to kids meets the same fate, although I won't personally do anything against the law to enforce my beliefs.
   I call on the media to stop trying to drag my name through the mud with all these murders. My wife and I would like a break from all of the phones and doorbells ringing. I also hope the media will not waste more time trying to get sympathy for men like LaMonty who have no regard for children. The world spins around nicely without people like him.

DELVAC's new boss, Rhoda McNec, also released a statement on-line: "DELVAC deplores the unjust murder of anyone, even if that person is a danger to our children. We hope that the authorities and the people of the Delaware Valley will recognize these incidents as a plea for help from a community in desperate need of justice."

It didn't take long for Just to track down Mrs. Phyllis Doyle in Audubon, New Jersey. He headed over late Wednesday afternoon in his beige 1985 Honda Accord hatchback, a car he had been planning to scrap for years. Mrs. Doyle lived in a pale blue ranch house with old furniture with plastic slipcovers that smelled like they had just left Du Pont's factory. She greeted Just hesitantly and invited him inside.

"Mrs. Doyle, I won't keep you, so I'll get to the point. A man called me and said you may know something about the death of a man named Steve Vernon."

"I didn't know him," Mrs. Doyle interjected sharply.

"Why would someone say you knew him?" Just asked.

"I don't know."

"It doesn't make sense to me. Mrs. Doyle, I don't want to make you uncomfortable, but this person also said this may have something to do with Mario Vanni."

Mrs. Doyle stood up and looked out her window, fiddling with a chain around her liver-spotted neck. She quickly sat down again and looked at Just almost angrily. "I didn't do anything wrong."

Somewhat surprised, Just shook his head. "Mrs. Doyle, it never occurred to me that you did anything wrong. I was just given your name as someone who might have some insight. Have the police been to see you?"

"No. No police."

"Mrs. Doyle," Just said, "I am bound not to reveal my sources as a journalist. The Supreme Court protects that right. If you tell me what you know, I can protect you. If you were to talk to me on camera, I could put you behind a screen and garble your voice with a computer."

"You'll need to prove that to me before I tell you a thing."

Just pulled from his ancient backpack a ratty copy of Justice Douglas's lead opinion in *Farr* v. *Pitchess*, concluding that a journalist cannot be held in contempt of court by refusing to disclose his source. He had used this document often over the years. There was something about seeing the words "Supreme Court" that started people yammering. Just then handwrote a short agreement with Mrs. Doyle that he would never reveal her as his source.

Al Just's feature story ran that evening with Mrs. Doyle appearing—or not appearing—behind a shadowy blue screen with her voice sounding like a character from *Star Wars.* The story opened with Just walking the streets of Philadelphia with a hologram of Mario Vanni lording over the city's skyline. Beneath Vanni's chin was the story's title: "Vanni Drug Ban." Mrs. Doyle spoke about writing a letter to Vanni pleading for his help in ridding her town of drug dealers. Just, wearing his bomber jacket despite the summer heat, referenced the spate of on-line rumors about the possible return of MOVE activist Barton Africa.

The following day, the *Bulletin* ran a story aping Just's blockbuster contention that a gang war had broken out in the Delaware Valley. The article featured photographs of Vanni in recent years along with references to sources that KBRO's Just had, in fact, reported first. The *Bulletin* had lifted textually what KBRO had reported visually, an expanding phenomenon.

Authorities Puzzled over Rash of "Playground Pusher" Murders

Some Say Vanni Ordered Hits

AUTHORITIES ARE investigating a potential link between the murders of a growing number of Delaware Valley drug dealers and reputed crime boss Mario Vanni.

Sergeant Mike Hall of the Metropolitan Police Department urged caution in jumping to any conclusions. "The fact is that right now we don't have a shred of evidence against Mr. Vanni in these cases."

Since last weekend, four bodies of drug dealers have been discovered, which have prompted the recent speculation. Last Sunday, the body of Norvular LaMonty, 22, of Strawberry Mansion, was found floating in the Delaware River near Newmarket Square.

Last Tuesday, Steve Vernon, 31, a reported South Jersey drug dealer, was shot to death in a bar in Audubon, New Jersey. And on Thursday morning, the bullet-riddled corpse of Hadji Banrup, 40, was discovered in a Dumpster outside of Benjamin Franklin Junior High in Manayunk. Later that day, Atlantic City police reported that Darnell Bose, 28, was found with his throat slit in a halfway house on Vermont Avenue. One source claimed that the once-popular antidrug slogan "Just say no" was written in Bose's blood on the mirror above the urinal near where his body was found.

All of these men had drug records and, according to sources, had been said to deal drugs to schoolchildren. There has been speculation that the slain men may have been linked to the elusive former MOVE member Barton Africa, who is believed to have escaped from the May 1985 Osage Avenue massacre. Africa is alleged to have entered the local underworld and is known on Badlands streets as "Automatic Bart."

The reason for the speculation around Vanni has more to do with his long-standing intolerance for drug pushing to children. A source who has been providing reliable information to the Al Just of KBRO-TV claims that Vanni has heard from members of the community who have asked him to help eliminate drugs from area schools. An elderly South Jersey woman who has become a confidential source to KBRO admitted on last night's newscast to having written to Vanni asking for help. "I wrote to him and asked if he would he help try to get rid of the bad element around here, because the police don't do anything."

As Al Just frantically searched for evidence that Vanni was actively bashing druggie heads, I authorized Jimmy Mack to release the digital version of his videotape to KBRO. I wanted to do it this way to make Just worry that the video of Dirty Zappa's beating could be—may already have been—sent out all over the place. When Jimmy Mack followed up with a telephone call to assure the reporter that he had not E-mailed the video elsewhere, Just became more obsessed with exclusivity than with vetting the footage.

Jimmy Mack, unshaven and oblivious in demeanor, delivered the hard copy of the videotape to Al Just after the dinner-hour newscast. Just hungrily reviewed the tape and interviewed Jimmy Mack, disguising his face with a digital mixer, about how he had captured the beating on tape.

Just's colleagues, in the meantime, tracked down the two kids who were in the videotape, who confirmed (off camera) that Dirty Zappa had tried to sell them a "smelly little bag." KBRO couldn't locate Dirty Zappa, who had cleaned himself up and gone to Tahiti with his girlfriend on Air Vanni.

The top story on KBRO's evening news featured Al Just breaking the Jimmy Mack tape.

"The war on drugs has taken a new—and disturbing—turn. Several nights ago, a South Philadelphia resident filmed the following scene showing two burly men emerging from Happy Mike's social club on South Street, a legendary Mafia haunt, and beating a man who was attempting to sell two schoolchildren a bag of what may have been marijuana."

The Jimmy Mack tape ran for two minutes, quivering just enough to appear amateur but focused tightly enough to make it clear that two Mafiosi were shooing away a couple of kids from a bad actor holding a small bag, and then kicking the piss out of him.

KBRO's camera panned the facade of Happy Mike's, which showed a handful of Continent types embracing, shrugging, smirking, and refusing to comment, every tic a Darwinian confirmation that the mob had taken care of Dirty Zappa. Once Just had broken with the tape, Jimmy Mack E-mailed it to Dorkus, who put it on jerseydevil.org for easy downloading worldwide.

I counseled Vanni against making any statement whatsoever about the Jimmy Mack tape: Let the whole thing remain visual, let it tug at the imagination, and don't corrupt it with spin. The people had demonstrated that they would know what to think.

The following Monday evening, Bill Maher, the comedian who hosts the talk show *Politically Incorrect*, asked his panel the question, "If the mob is killing drug dealers, should we stop them?" Cindi began routing via E-mail a nonsensical joke she made up to media friends around the country, with the Jimmy Mack footage attached digitally. The joke made its way up to Jay Leno, who opened his monologue by asking the nation, "How many Philadelphia drug dealers does it take to screw in a lightbulb?" The answer: "None, there aren't any."

Killer Flacks

"We're gonna kill two birds with one spoon."

A T THE ABANDONED CARPET STORE ON WELLINGTON IN
Ventnor Heights, there were still carpets slung over display
racks, giving the appearance of an indoor desert with miniature
tents. Noel had recommended the place. Insisted on it.

Between each carpet rack, there was a small metal desk with a
telephone. Here in the remnant wilderness, I assembled my dis-
ciples of flackery who would alert the regional media about Mario
Vanni's upcoming Jackie Kennedy–esque tour of Lucy the Elephant. Cindi had provided me with her special list of media contacts.

I had Trouble sweep the location for potential listening devices
and, once he determined that it was clean, I loaded up my crew,
which consisted of Frankie Shrugs, a new guy with hooded eyes
called Sally Kisses, and the ferret-faced Petie. I had Petie pull the
van into the rear of the strip mall and back it up to the rear door.
We exited one by one, carrying various pieces of equipment, mostly
shredders. The store's front windows were papered over so that no
one could see in.

I asked them to take their seats on the carpet mounds and, like

George C. Scott at the beginning of *Patton*, I gave them a pep talk and their orders.

"Okay, guys, our job today is to get as many media people as possible to cover Mario's tour of Lucy tomorrow."

"He ain't letting people inside Lucy," Frankie Shrugs bellowed.

"Not directly. It's a virtual tour," I explained. "Computers. We're taping Mario walking around the elephant and we're just going to run it tomorrow like it's live, like it's happening at that moment. We've got to get media to report on it so that everybody goes to this one Web site at the same time.

"I'm going to give you each a list of reporters to call in the Delaware Valley. I want you to ask for the person whose name is highlighted. If that person's not there, then ask who's taking that person's place.

"When you get to the right person, all you have to say is, 'If you log onto jerseydevil.org tomorrow morning, Mario Vanni will talk to the public.'

"Now, they may try to ask you questions. They may say, 'How do I know you're for real?' If that happens, all you have to say is, 'Fuck you then. You don't believe me, don't log on. It's no skin off my ass.'"

Sally Kisses spoke up, his brown eyelids not fluttering once during his tommy gun verbal delivery: "Hey, I can't remember all that shit."

"Don't worry," I said, "I have it all written down." I distributed the scripts to them. "Now, when you're done today, I want you to give me back the sheets because I'm going to shred them in this machine."

Sally Kisses reviewed his pitch sheet. "I'm confused here," he said. "I see here it says 'no skin off my ass,' right?"

"Right," I said.

"Isn't it supposed to be skin off my *teeth?*" Frankie Shrugs asked.

"That's one expression, but I want you to stick to the script."

"I want to say skin off my teeth," Sally Kisses said. "I think the ass thing here is wrong."

"Okay, fine, say 'teeth' if you want, but I want everybody else to stick with the script."

"Why the fuck does he get to say 'teeth' and we all have to say 'ass'? That ain't right," Frankie Shrugs complained. I sensed by the way Frankie Shrugs leered at Sally Kisses that the two men did not like each other. Given that Mario had Frankie Shrugs guarding the elephant and serving as his Mafia mole to the press, I assumed that the big guy was loyal to Mario, while Petie and Sally Kisses must have been "with" Noel.

"Because that's the way I want it. You guys say 'ass' because it sounds tougher than 'teeth' and that's what I'm getting at here," I explained.

" 'Ass' is tougher than 'teeth' you think?" Sally Kisses asked.

"I think so."

"So, Jonah, you think I'm less tough than these guys, that's why you let me say 'teeth'?" Sally Kisses was really pressing.

"I thought you wanted to say 'teeth,' Sally."

"Not if you think I'm half a fag. I won't say 'teeth'; I'm gonna say 'ass.' "

"Okay, Sally, say whatever you want."

"I mean, I clipped more guys than Shrugs, so he shouldn't get to say 'ass' and not me."

"*Stugots*, Sally," Frankie Shrugs spoke up. "My ass you clipped more than me. How many you done?"

"I put away six," said Sally Kisses proudly, "if you count the guy who had the heart attack when I lit his hair on fire, then seven. Would you count the guy whose head I torched, Jonah?"

"You bet I would."

"You ain't done no seven," Frankie Shrugs huffed.

"I done four and I'm ten years younger than yous," Petie weighed in with his contribution. "Don't that count for somethin'? I'm a fuckin' child progeny."

"I prostate myself all over your feet," Sally Kisses said, genuflecting.

"Now, Petie, you call Philly radio stations," I cut in, attempting to regain control. "Frankie Shrugs, you call Philly newspapers and Philly TV. Kisses, I want you to call Jersey papers and Jersey radio. I'll do Jersey TV. They're yours." Everyone took his list and grabbed a few pens.

Petie stormed through his calls. He was impressed with his progress and smirked at me. "Good, ain't I?"

"Petie, you're not only a progeny, you're a goddamned cretin, you know that?"

"Damned right."

Sally Kisses was doing well, too. He stayed with the script and even cut out the curse words. He came off like a nervous wise guy informant imparting confidential information, which was good.

As I made the rounds toward the front of the store space where Petie was working, a shadow moved outside the papered-up windows. I watched the figure for a few moments, wondering if he was a Fed. Then a knock came on the glass door. I froze, hoping that he would go away, then I heard Petie slam his phone down, clearly audible to the lurker outside. "Jonah can kiss my ass," he said. He had had enough real work for a half hour.

"This virginal tour is bullshit," Frankie Shrugs echoed.

I heard another phone slam down as I made my way to the door and imagined myself telling Vanni and Noel that my assignment for them had failed. I had been pushing Vanni hard lately and was very conscious of crossing a line. The shadow hovered. The store began to tilt with my damned vertigo.

My brain went into fast-forward, and it was a cold night in the Pine Barrens. I had a shovel and was digging. There were roots and stones making it a hard dig. Normally, one would welcome anything that would delay death, but these obstructions were annoying me. "Cockroach," Petie muttered under his breath, as I dug.

Sally Kisses shot me twice behind the ear with a twenty-two. . . .

I popped back onto the scene, the vertiginous room leveled back. I opened the door of the carpet store. My eyes felt black and red, like the covers of true-crime books. I pushed open the door a crack.

"Can I help you?" I asked. A man approximately my age with thinning blond hair stood before me.

He scanned the room and saw my merry band of killers at their respective stations. He swallowed hard as I locked the door behind him.

"I asked if I could help you," I repeated, confident in the human artillery backing me up. I was desperate to get back in their good graces just to survive this pitching session. Mistreating a third party was the only thing these guys respected.

"Yeah, I'm here to pick up my carpet," he said in a hick lilt.

I nodded with journalistic empathy. "What's your name?"

The man was still glancing around the room. The boys had stopped calling and inhaled the scene.

I stepped closer to him. "I asked you, What's your name?"

"Wayne Cubeck," he said.

"What kind of carpet did your order, Mr. Wayne Cubeck?"

"It was a blue rug, an outdoor rug, for my porch."

"I see. Mr. Wayne Cubeck, do you have a driver's license?"

"Why do you need it?"

Frankie Shrugs jumped in. "The man asked you for your fuckin' driver's license!"

"Hey, man, I don't want no trouble," Wayne Cubeck said, his Adam's apple quivering.

"Then give me your driver's license," I demanded.

I handed it to Frankie Shrugs, who wrote the information down at a little desk. "Now, Wayne Cubeck of Egg Harbor," I continued, "what did you like about the carpet you purchased?" The boys were getting into it, throwing approving glances my way.

Petrified, he gazed down toward my feet. "I dunno, I thought it would be good for my porch."

"The man thought it would be good for his porch," I repeated. "You wanted a nice ambiance for your porch, huh?"

"Hey pencil neck," Frankie Shrugs bellowed. "Why the fuck do you have an ambulance in your porch?"

"Ambulance?" Wayne Cubeck said, puzzled.

"No, ambiance," I corrected.

"Yeah, the ambiance," Shrugs repeated. *De ambyince.*

"I, I don't know what you mean." Wayne Cubeck was now visibly shaking.

"Well, is it a sunny porch or a shady porch?"

"Kind of shady."

"This man has a shady porch," Frankie Shrugs echoed.

The gang: "A shady porch. How about that?"

"Now, Wayne Cubeck, we can't seem to find your carpet. But why don't we take a look at what we have in stock, all right?" I said.

"Look, man, I don't want no trouble. I was just trying to pick up my carpet."

Sally Kisses brought over one carpet sample. "Hey, Wayne, here's one for you. Check out the ambulance on this one." He threw it down on a desk and grabbed Wayne Cubeck's hand to make him feel it. "You like this one?"

"It's fine. Look—"

"Do you like the texture?" Frankie Shrugs asked.

"It's okay. Man, I—"

"Damn it, Wayne, do you like the texture or the ambiance?"

"I dunno, both, I guess."

"Wayne, you can't have both," Frankie Shrugs said. "Do you like the texture or the ambiance?" He pulled out a pistol from his belt and cocked the trigger, pointing the barrel at Wayne Cubeck's head. "The texture or the ambiance?!" he said in a cold, psychotic rage.

Wayne Cubeck pissed himself and began to sob. Mickey's favorite proverb flew into my head: Entrances are wide, exits are narrow. This was enough for me. My little diversion had spun out of control, far beyond the mood-turning catalyst I was aiming for. It was clear, however, that the boys had just gotten going. I grabbed a weeping Wayne Cubeck's collar and brought him over to the door. The boys were so surprised at my aggression that they backed off.

"I am going over to that phone and making a call," I said. "I'm going to give a friend of mine your name and address. Then, I just might let you go. If one cop car, one busybody old lady, one militia group vigilante, one pain in the ass do-gooder comes by here . . . I'll be nonplussed and you'll get a visit from Louie Cuddles and Freddie Crushed Nuts. You understand me?"

Petie questioningly mouthed the word "nonplussed" at Sally Kisses.

Wayne Cubeck said nothing. The muscles in his face had frozen. I paced forward again to Wayne Cubeck, who was trembling from head to toe. "Wayne," I said, "I feel a lot of understanding between us." Unlocking the door, I pulled him out onto the sidewalk. His eyes were red, and he was wiping his cheeks.

"Wayne, the moral of this story is that you never know what's behind a door." I pounded Wayne Cubeck's sternum with my finger.

He nodded.

I flicked him on his cheek. "Understand!"

"Yeah, yeah, man, I understand."

I relieved myself in the marshes behind the shopping center and returned to the flack house.

Over the next two hours, we alerted every brand-name journalist in the Delaware Valley media about Vanni's virtual tour. I collected the media lists when we were finished. Petie had written the words "Under the weather" and "trifecta" on the back page of his, the degenerate. He disappeared into the storage room for a few minutes and returned with a raw, red nose and rapidly blinking eyelids.

"All right, guys," I said. "We have to shred all these papers."

There was a moment of silence that was broken several seconds later by howls of laughter. "Yeah, we'll shred things real good, Jones."

From the back of the shop, Sally Kisses emerged with two red canisters. He handed one to Petie. The two men began pouring liquid on opposite sides of the room, dousing the tents of carpet with pungent syrup. My jaw hung open like I was a catatonic freak. Frankie Shrugs took a step toward me, pinched my cheeks, and gave my face a light, affectionate smack.

"We're gonna kills two birds with one spoon," Petie shouted from the front of the store.

The other men just watched and nodded as my eyes darted between them.

"Does Mario know about this?" I asked. "I didn't know anything about this."

"No, pencil neck," Petie said. "We just do shit for fun and don't tell Mario. Why do you think Noel gave us this place?"

I took my hand to my chin and felt more stubble than should have been there at this time of day. It was as if my beard had grown suddenly, in the last thirty seconds. I couldn't think of anything to say or do other than to begin grabbing the shredders. As I pushed the largest one toward the back door, Sally Kisses put his foot against the machine. "Everything stays," he said.

"But I leased these."

"Don't worry about it," Sally Kisses said with a sneer. "You didn't think we'd just leave this place, did ya?"

"No, what could I have been thinking?" I said in a barely audible monotone.

Frankie Shrugs gave me a light push toward the back door with his left hand. The store began to stink like a chemical waste treatment plant. One by one, we filed out. I was second to last. Frankie Shrugs, the caboose, dropped a match onto the floor with his right hand in a professional-looking flick of his fingers. There was something grotesquely cool and commanding about the move, and I was terrified by my admiration.

The sound the match made when it hit the floor was a soft, thick puff. *PFOOM*. I felt the air scorch against my eyebrows. The flame obediently shot through the store as the door closed behind us. Then nothing. No explosion. No roof flying off. Ideal silence.

Frankie Shrugs hauled his hard potato sack of a body into the van. Petie shoved me into the back and sat down to my right. I felt my blood cells sprint toward my toes. Sally Kisses oozed in to my left. His mendacious eyes crinkled with delight at my pallor, as if my objection to arson had been the defining point scored in the Jonah's Less of a Man contest. My throat was tight. The men were silent. Sally Kisses smirked proudly at me and patted my knee as if he had just gotten me laid for the first time. Frankie Shrugs pulled out slowly, the interior of the car smelling like a blend of Armani cologne and sweat.

"You do this shit at the frat house in college? They call this shit what, grazing or something, Jones?" Sally Kisses asked.

"Yeah, we grazed a lot. . . . There were people shopping in the market next door. We have to warn them. Shit, guys, people saw us. That Wayne Cubeck saw all of us."

"You won't have no problems with Wayne Cubeck," Frankie Shrugs said.

Frankie Shrugs made a left onto Dorset, turning the wheel with one of his thick fingers. Again, I piped up about the shopping center. "Mario doesn't want people getting killed in that store. We have to warn them."

"How the fuck do you know what Mario wants?" Petie barked.

"Let me call from a pay phone and warn those people to get out."

Silence. Not "no." Not "not now" or "not yet." Nothing. Tombstone eyes. I couldn't get out to make the call. I couldn't grab my cell phone. My briefcase was on the floor in front of Sally Kisses. On my mind's screen, I saw Edie on a stretcher. Her teeth were black and she looked like a witch. She was not moving. I mouthed a prayer for candles.

Frankie Shrugs rolled into the driveway of the Golden Prospect, another stay of execution, at least for me. Strangely, I didn't care at that moment if they killed me. I deserved it, I reasoned. A black man should kill me—that would be absolute justice for Automatic Bart. I had been responsible for conceiving this baby, but how responsible was I for what it had grown into? I imagined that riots would be next.

I slid from the van, took the elevator to Mickey's floor, and bolted down the hallway to turn on the TV. The news was forty minutes away. Nothing yet. No special reports. I stretched out on the floor. I took note of the pillows on the sofa. The people who died in that fire would have their heads propped up on pillows like these in their caskets.

What do you do when you're waiting to find out how many people you killed?

Sit-ups. Charles Manson did drugs. Jeffrey Dahmer threw a head in the microwave. My signature would be washboard abs. I jammed my feet under the sofa where Mickey had died and cranked out ten minutes' worth of slow sit-ups, prepping for prison. I was just the kind of guy other hardened killers fear over in Graterford Prison: an Ivy League–educated Republican pollster.

Noel may have been setting me up for an arson rap. Maybe murder, too. There was no great strategic advantage to it, but Noel wasn't a strategist. He was a sadist and a murderer. I was at the scene of the crime. I was running it. How would that sound in court? "Yes, your honor, I was running this operation with a band of known killers, but in no way did I have an inkling that somebody would do something bad." In court, Petie would laugh at my use of the word "inkling." "Inkling" would be my prison nickname.

The news came on. *Eyewitness News.* Great omen. The anchor was Ann Malloy. I went to high school with her sister. They were all beauty queens. Top story: bank robbery in Camden. A chase down the Atlantic City Expressway . . .

The second story was a drug murder in the Atlantic City slums. A black woman was wailing "Cliff! Cliff!" at the ambulance. *Cleee-if. Cleee-if.*

So we had a robbery with no deaths and then a murder. What did this mean for my little genocide? Deaths usually go on earlier on the local news. They love fires.

"Now from Ventnor, we have this report on a shopping center fire. We've got Michele Argenti on the scene."

"Ann, a blazing fire broke out in a shopping center here in Ventnor Heights at about three o'clock this afternoon," Argenti began. The camera panned the shopping center. The structure remained standing, but the windows had been blown out and were emitting smoke. No injuries mentioned yet.

"The fire quickly ripped through the other stores, completely gutting the Shopping Bag and sending customers scurrying out of the store to move their cars to make way for the fire trucks. I have with me Maria Wendt, who was shopping at the time. Maria, describe for me what you experienced."

The camera zoomed in on Maria Wendt, who grabbed hold of Argenti's microphone. "All of a sudden, I hear this generator explode on the roof. I come running out, and this piece from the Shopping Bag sign, you know, goes flying across the parking lot and lands on this bike."

The camera took in a shot of a ten-speed bike and the sign fragment that had crushed it. No one had been hurt. We could have killed a kid. What did the law say here? Would I have been a murderer? Of course, I would. And Vanni hadn't done anything to shield me from this end of his business. He drew no line between my endeavors and his, and maintained no safeguards that divided sanctioned murders and collateral deaths. I shouldn't have been surprised, but I was. It was one thing to understand vice on an abstract level, provided that it was committed by others. Now I was a perp potentially involved with ancillary killings, which were worse than murder contracts on bad men who had provoked the rackets. I was no longer a mobster's grandson who had suffered an accident of birth, nor was I just a professional representing an undesirable in his crusade for vindication. I was repeatedly consorting with criminals and was at the scene of a mob-engineered arson.

I should have run. Right after the funeral, I should have run. I found Mickey's Bible and read Exodus.

Mr. Vanni's Elephant

"When a guy in Stone Harbor wears a wrinkled shirt, it's class. When I do, I'm a slob."

W E HAVE A WAY OF SHOWING UP AT SOUTH JERSEY'S SPECTA-cles, don't we, Jonah?" Cindi said as Mario's virtual tour of Lucy got under way. Our stunt would begin with Mario's tour and end with him chatting on-line with questioners who logged on to jerseydevil.org.

Cindi and I shared a fascination for ghoulish extravaganzas. We had sneaked onto the grounds of the Heritage Building on Kings Highway in Cherry Hill, where seven people had been murdered by a lunatic. It was the early seventies. Around the same time, we had tiptoed with flashlights onto the property of a black dandy named Major Coxson, who was killed along with his daughter in their home. Hanafi Muslim gangsters had done the Coxson job. By some macabre coincidence, I had returned to the United States just in time for a track meet where the Garden State Race Track burned to the ground. Cindi and I had watched the whole thing.

"We do," I responded. "But we didn't rig those."

"No, we didn't. How do you have this one figured?"

"It comes down to numbers, Cin. Vanni is dangerous. Let's give his danger a score of minus three. Vanni is familiar. People like that. Give his familiarity a plus five. Vanni nets out at plus two.

"Now take Automatic Bart. Bart is *really* dangerous. Or so everybody thinks, or will think. Give him a minus five for danger. And Automatic Bart is unknown. Give that factor a minus five because the unknown scares people. Automatic Bart nets out at minus ten."

"So," Cindi said, "Mario Vanni minus Automatic Bart equals give Mario whatever he wants."

"Right. If we build up Mario's positives, people feel safe."

"The devil we know."

"*Our* devil is always better than *their* devil."

Cindi and I stood outside in the shadow of Lucy's maternal belly early on the morning of Vanni's virtual tour. The tour would take about forty-five minutes, giving us plenty of time to edit it and feed it onto the Internet for the "live" on-line broadcast later today. Mario snickered behind one of Lucy's legs as Eddie and Diamonds got their film ready. Mario looked like a kid cutting school to smoke dope in the woods. As soon as I saw him, I dismissed Cindi because I did not want the two of them to meet. We spoke throughout the tour on cell phones.

As instructed, Vanni disappeared behind a fence, climbed into his Mercedes, and swung back gaudily around the block to a parking space beneath Lucy's belly. Vanni got out of the car, opening his eyes wide at the site of the cameras.

"Holy cow, what are all you doing here?" Vanni asked. *Holy cow.* "Welcome to Mr. Vanni's elephant." He gestured to Lucy's enormity as the cameras took it in.

Vanni then made his way to the door in Lucy's leg and went inside.

Cindi had been reminding me that one of our objectives was to make Al Just desperate for more information about Vanni. Given that everybody else in the world was getting this tour, Just had suddenly lost his advantage. Desperation meant careless reporting. Careless reporting was our friend. By inviting everyone inside, Just and KBRO would lose the edge and feel the other media snapping at their elusive Pulitzers, the way the *New York Times* did when Woodward and Bernstein at the *Post* kept finding skeletons during Watergate. Only the *New York Times* never got careless. These were different times.

"Sometimes I like to bring business associates here," Vanni said to the camera in Lucy's leg stairwell. "We listen to the music, Sinatra, usually." *Snotra uzhully.* "Have a drink and talk things over. We've got a little kitchen in the back. Sometimes we have a nice meal."

Vanni angled his head upward toward his office. The cameramen and I followed. A young actress, Cookies, whom we had hired from a Shore theater group, was dressed in quasi-impressive business attire. As she emerged from Vanni's office, she gave a surprised look to the cameras. "Oh, Mr. Vanni, what's going on?"

Vanni walked over to Cookies and put his arm around her. "I tell you, Cookies, I drive up and I got the whole world watching. I thought I'd show 'em where we work at Vanni Vending so they can see for themselves how I'm the Godfather and how we keep all these dead bodies all over the place."

"Oh, Mr. Vanni, that's awful. You shouldn't say things like that."

"I know, I know. Look, come back into my office, everybody," Vanni said.

Vanni led the way up Lucy's hollow leg into his office and hung his sport jacket on a rack, Mister Rogers–style. We jammed against a side wall in Vanni's office. A computer monitor had been placed on the corner of Vanni's desk. A TelePrompTer containing the boss's script sat across the room beside Eddie and Diamonds's camera.

"Okay, let me show you what we got here." Vanni made his way the three or four steps over to the chrome shelf with the family photos. "This is my wife, Rita. We've been married for almost thirty years. I met her in high school. When she married me, I didn't have a dime. I worked as a janitor at schools in Atlantic City for the first few years we were married." *Lannick City.* Nice touch. A janitor. He held Rita's photo for a few extra moments and smiled at it.

"This here is my son, Chris. He's a good kid. He's comin' up okay. He'll finish business courses at Rutgers next year."

Vanni moved to a large black-and-white photo that was ripped in a lower corner. "This here is my parents. My father was Mario, too. This is my mother, Igea." Vanni held his finger on his mother's image. "She died a couple years ago. She had cancer. Breast cancer. She was eighty years old. That's why I think my daughter, Angela, gets involved with these charities: because of the breast cancer in the family." He crossed himself and put the photo back on the shelf but was still looking at it.

"This one was taken in the 1940s when my parents came to Atlantic City from Camden. I wasn't born yet. Pop died when I was in my twenties. He was the hardest-working guy you ever met. Did everything. When he had to be a carpenter, he was a carpenter. When he had to cut the grass, he cut the grass. Most of the time he drove a truck for a vending company. No complaining, just did it. When I was a kid, I didn't understand why he had to work so hard and get paid dirt. Used to think he was a real square, me and some of my friends did. We wanted to make it easy and got in trouble. We did some stupid stuff. Hung out with tough people, broke into stores and stuff like that. We had an awful image and we deserved it. Not my dad. He always played it straight. That's why if you asked about Mario Vanni, you had to say it's the old man and people go, 'Oh, Old Mario, he's the salt a the earth.' You say 'Young Mario,' people go, 'Oh Jeez, what a bad kid he was. Beat me up once for lunch money.' You know what? I probably did it, too, and all that tough-guy stuff never left me. Follows me and my family around to this day." *Tuh diss day.*

"Now, Cookies, here's what I want you to do." Mario turned toward his assistant. "Sit down at this computer here and tell me what people are asking and we'll try to answer it." Vanni sat down behind his desk and Cookies sat in a smaller chair in front of the monitor. Cookies read off a list from which we had carefully rehearsed Vanni.

"Henry in Manahawkin asks," Cookies began, " 'are you telling us that you're not the boss of a crime family, that it's all one big misunderstanding?' "

Vanni breathed deeply and focused on the TelePrompTer. "Henry, I wish you'd show a little sensitivity. Did I just stand here and tell you I was some little spring flower in a garden spreading butter and roses throughout"—*tru-ut*—"the tristate area? Did I say that?

"I told you I was a real piece a work when I was young. I told you guys that I beat people up and that I broke into places. I told you that because it was true. I don't do that stuff anymore. I grew up. But I live in Jersey, I'm in tough businesses."

"Okay, Mr. Vanni," Cookies continued, "Mrs. L. in Merion asks, 'Do you believe that there's a conspiracy to make it seem like you run one of the biggest Mafia families in the United States?' "

"Mrs. L., maybe somebody will figure out that if this crime family is so big and bad, why can't anybody find it? Is it in this drawer here? Do I look like Goldfinger?

"I'll tell you what we got here with the government. We got a bunch of rich kids who went to Ivy League schools and now wanna play cops and robbers to take down the dago with the nice white Mercedes. Pale guys have been gunning for darker men in Philly for hundreds of years." Vanni's voice started to rise just enough to show emotion without coming off like a killer. Then he returned to calm.

"My daughter, Angela, went to Penn here in Philly. Undergrad. When she got in, some people in your crowd started with how her old man must have paid off the school. The kid cried for a week. What I think is that some people don't want dago broads in Ivy League schools because we bust up a nice club. That's what this Mafia business is all about—it's discrimination. Meantime, the real bad guys go free."

As Mario became more passionate, my E-mail sidearm buzzed. It was a message from Dorkus at Mount Misery: "We're on fire." This meant that the wires were burning across the region as jerseydevil.org was flooded with questions.

"Mr. Vanni," Cookies said, "an Al Just from KBRO-TV asks, 'Do you believe that everybody who asks you tough questions is a bigot?' "

"Mr. Just, sometimes I wonder what are you getting at. Look," Vanni shot back, still calm, still on-message, still reading, "you never know with people. Every time some guy grabs a hatchet and wipes out his whole family, you guys put the next-door neighbor on TV and he says, 'Gee, he was such a nice guy.' Well, the moral of the story is *no he wasn't.* The only people who can really say who the guy is are the ones who were on the wrong side of that hatchet. Nobody else can say a thing. All I know is that when a guy in Stone Harbor wears a wrinkled shirt, it's class. When I do, I'm a slob."

After several more questions, Cookies wound it down with an

emotional finale: "Mr. Vanni, Burt in Hammonton is asking, 'My brother overdosed on drugs that were sold to him by Automatic Bart's gang. Can you stop this insanity?'" The camera caught Cookies's face appearing concerned and then swung back to Vanni.

"Burt, I'm not a magician. I'm just one guy who believes what he believes. I don't have the power to stop all of this drug nonsense. I can only tell you to hang in there and make as much noise as you can so that the people who do have the power bring criminals, not stereotypes, to justice."

Mort Snores Like a Rhinoceros

"A dead guy is one less witness."

IRV THE CURVE BROKE A BAGEL CHIP IN TWO AND STIRRED HIS coffee with one of the pieces. Dollsy set my grapefruit juice down in front of me and pressed her glasses higher on her nose. The color of today's glasses was purple. All she needed was platform shoes, and she could have broken into *Pinball Wizard*.

"I understand there's a new bad guy in town, boychik," Irv said. "This Automatic fellow."

"You've been reading the papers, I take it."

"I always read the papers, not like everybody on these, uh, chat rooms I hear so much about." Irv winked at me. "Client seem happy?"

"To the extent that some clients can be happy. Mario is a man who expects to win. I get no points for helping him win. If he wins, it was him. If he loses, it was me."

"Were you the Francis Ford Coppola on that little videotape with the hippie selling drugs to those kids?"

"How'd you like it?"

"Quality acting, very artful. No Academy Award for lighting, though."

"Too much light on a swindle is not a good thing."

"Understood. How about that animal?"

"I had lunch with Noel a little while back. He asked me about the money and said he was just trying to help me learn the ropes. Oh, yeah, and he held a knife to my eye in the bathroom afterward. He said he'd kill me in a heartbeat."

"And you tell me this now?"

"What would you have done, Irv? I thought you were powerless. Besides, you don't like whiners."

"Still, you should have told me. Study this guy, Jonah. His habits."

"He lights up a cigarette when he starts something or stops something."

"Good. Keep studying. He's no better a fighter than you are."

"Are you serious? He's a much better fighter."

"No, see, wise guys aren't tougher than anybody else. That's not it. Do you know what gives them the edge?"

"The will," I said.

"The will to what?"

"The will to kill."

"Exactly," Irv said. "That he'll actually do it. Does Good Jonah have that will?"

I didn't know the answer but tensed up. I tried to read every twitch in Irv's face. Did he think I could kill? Big-time paranoia: If he thought I could kill, was I being too transparent? If I knew I could kill, did Noel? Did Vanni? What did it say about me that I was continuing to evaluate murder, as opposed to just passing it off as a stray thought, like shouting out loud in a synagogue? As I searched for reasonable words, all I could see was blood.

"You know," Irv said, "Mickey had a little heat in his place. Did you find it?"

"I've got it strapped on."

"Good. It's a clean piece. Stay in public. If something happens in private—you know—finish whoever it is. A dead guy is one less witness. Break up the gun into pieces, chuck it, and call me."

"Anyway," I said, trying to convince myself I hadn't heard this procedure, "the media side of the program is going well. The foundation has been built. Did you hear about Mario's tour?"

"Of Lucy? Yeah. I don't get it. They talk about it being on the computer and everybody talking about it in chat rooms . . ." Irv shook his head in confusion.

"What don't you get?"

"Where the hell are these rooms? I mean, where does everybody go to do these chats."

"They're at home or at work."

"The rooms are at home and work? Are these special rooms?"

"No, they're just on their computers watching the tape we made of Mario. We pipe it across phone lines."

"How the hell do you get a tape across phone lines?"

"It's just the technology."

"Oh, that's helpful—"

"Then the people talk about what they saw on-line in the chat rooms."

"Yeah, but where are the rooms?"

"In cyberspace."

"Where the fuck is cyberspace, Cape Kennedy or something?"

"No, it's not an actual place—"

"Look, just shut up with the chats and the cybers and the rooms. I don't get it. I'm glad it's working, but I don't get it and, if I can be frank, it doesn't sound like you get it either. Now ask me about something I can get through my head."

"I'm a little worried about your old buddy, Al Just. By the questions he's asking, he knows somebody's behind this."

I was not being entirely forthcoming with Irv. I was more than a *little* worried about Just; I wasn't sleeping and my stomach wasn't working right. Just wouldn't need much to make a link between Vanni and me—a few photos of me at the big elephant, vague connections between my electoral Poll Vaulter maneuvers and the stunts that were now benefiting Vanni. . . . The key was to keep the spectacles coming so that Just couldn't be diverted to a story about what was behind them.

"You think he's got something, Jonah?"

"Not yet, but this whole thing is just getting started. A lot will be going on during the next few weeks, so keep reading the papers."

"Care to give me a hint? I like to be in the swing." Irv's question mark ears were on full alert.

"Retaliation against Automatic Bart. Vanni's going to have a little run-in with the law."

Irv shook his head. "Charming. Does he know?"

"He knows everything."

"Good. See, this was a better choice than running."

"I'm not so sure. Anyhow, you'd send Red Tooth for me." Whenever I was bad as a kid, Mickey would threaten to send Red Tooth to "get" me.

"Wouldn't be Red Tooth." Irv studied a pumpernickel bagel chip as if it were an artifact.

"Why not?"

Irv drew his finger to his mouth as Dollsy approached with his toast. "Here you go, doll."

Irv continued when Dollsy left. "Red Tooth is gone. His son took over."

The revelation that Red Tooth was a reference to a real person chilled me. I felt a shiver behind my ears.

"You've only got a few weeks left in Mickey's place before Sidney Wagner tosses you out," Irv continued. "Do you know where you're going?"

"No clue. I've been distracted by saving my life."

"A good distraction."

I gripped my ankle and felt the heavy metal growth. "Do you have any ideas about where I can stay when my time is up at Mickey's place?"

"Carvin' Marvin and Mort the Snort have an extra room in Margate. I'd stay there, where you know the guys. You need a place that's hard to penetrate, where people will report strange things to Marv and Mort. Do you mind living with a couple of *alter kockers*?"

I scanned Irv's face for a hint of a setup. I had to trust him. I chose to see Irv and Blue's earlier harshness as the admonitions of uncles, not tracks of a plot. Go toward the wave, Jonah.

"Not at all. I'd like the company."

"Mort snores like a rhinoceros."

"I didn't know rhinos snore."

"Believe me, they snore. Do you snore?"

"I don't know."

"If you had a broad, she'd tell you, believe me."

"I think I may have a broad."

Irv executed a smooth backhanded shmeer of jam against his toast. His eyes lit up like a naughty seventh grader who had just seen a cheerleader's underwear.

"Jonah has a broad? When am I going to be a Grand Irv?"

"Not so fast. I have to survive the summer first."

"Who's the broad? The one from the cemetery?"

"That's the one."

"Out of death comes life. What's her name, that girl?"

"Edie Morris."

"Mickey loved that Edie Morris and her gypsy music."

"I can see why."

"Have you guys—?" Irv smiled and banged his bony fists together.

"What's this?" I mocked his hand-banging motion.

"This," Irv said, repeating the gesture, "means what it means."

Irv snickered, but his earlier words still echoed: *A dead guy is one less witness.*

I opened the door to Mickey's Buick and crawled onto the floor with a flashlight. I jammed a pencil into the grooves of the accelerator and wedged out dried berry bits. They were mixed in with silvery pine needles. Wherever Mickey had gone, he had driven himself. When Edie said that her family had picked berries in the pines, I had little doubt that Mickey's rant was more than hallucinatory nonsense.

I found a book on the natural resources of Southern New Jersey in the Ventnor Public Library. After talking my ear off about how smart people never came in, a tan, aging, and eminently crunchy librarian, who was a ringer for Janis Joplin, took me to the regional section and pointed right to the proper shelf. She recommended a book called *Fruit of the Valley*, which focused on South Jersey crops.

It took me twenty minutes to find the berries section in the book. The Pine Barrens had been so named because of their disastrous farming history. There were a few things that could be grown there, however, due to the nutrients provided by branches of local rivers. Those few things were berries. Blueberries and cranberries had been particularly lucrative for some. The book underscored the success of berry farming in a way that struck me as being defensive: "No matter what outsiders say about the Pinelands being barren, their gardens have long been quite fertile for some commodities, especially blueberries and cranberries." The subtext was, *What are we, a buncha retards here?*

I approached Janis Joplin with the book and pulled a dried berry from my pocket. I placed it on the photocopier. "Excuse me, what kind of berry would you say this was?"

"*Was?* You don't think it's still a berry?"

I nodded like a moron.

Janis Joplin plucked it gently from the copier and held it up. "Do you mind if I smush it?"

"Smush away."

She pressed the berry against the off-white plastic tray of the copier and it hemorrhaged out red. "Cranberry," she said, self-satisfied, like Miss Marple. "You can't tell what the dried ones are made of until you press them. I used to go picking them with my parents when I was little."

"Where did you go?"

"Some places in Burlington County," she answered. "Will you be checking this out?"

I checked the book out and walked up toward the ocean to flip through it on an old bench beneath the Boardwalk. It was shady, but there was enough light this time of day to see the pages clearly. Once I was confident that the tide wouldn't reach me, I began to skim through the section on berries. It said that the Lenape Indians believed that cranberries were a symbol of peace. They had believed this long before the arrival of the colonists. Cranberries were even passed back and forth to be eaten the way peace pipes were smoked in some other tribes. Cranberry growth was still strong in some places, but not like it was in the heydey of harvesting in piney towns like Hog Wallow, Double Trouble, Penny Pot, and Mount Misery. These towns sounded like names out of *Deliverance*, but they were short hops from Camden and Center City Philadelphia.

I remained on the secluded green bench for fifteen minutes, feeling very clever. Sherlock Eastman. Mickey had walked among the cranberries. Perhaps my grandfather the pirate had buried treasure in a piney grave somewhere in the depths of Burlington County. My self-congratulatory smirk shattered when I found a passage in the book estimating that two hundred thousand acres of the Burlington pines were used for cranberry farming. A lot of digging for one little *pisher.*

"What are you reading there?" Noel asked, dropping suddenly beside me on the bench. He had a canister of gasoline in his hand.

My heart jumped. "It's a book on nature."

"How sweet. You like nature, Jonah?" Noel's skin appeared oniony, as if no blood flowed beneath it, perhaps just a synthetic chemical. He grinned, twitching a little, obscuring then revealing his diamond tooth in rapid-fire motion. It gave me a philosophical thought: What if my mother had been wrong, and there *wasn't* good in everyone? Maybe some people really were vile to their core.

"Nature's fine."

"Care to read me a chapter?" Noel asked.

"Not really. Just killing time," I said, feigning indifference.

"On Mario's dollar."

"C'mon, Noel."

"Here kitty," Noel said to a group of stray cats that paced on the beach behind us. One of the cats, a striped gray one, approached Noel as he held out a cracker. "Trusting little fuckers, aren't they?"

I looked away. When I turned back, Noel had tied a makeshift leash around the cat's neck.

"What are you doing, Noel?"

"You never know who you can trust," Noel said, pouring the gasoline onto the cat.

"Jesus Christ!" I shouted, as Noel withdrew a match from his pocket and flicked it onto the cat, setting it instantly ablaze. Noel tossed the gasoline canister toward the tide. "I've got some extra at home. For you." He walked away to the north singing "What's New Pussycat?"

I grabbed a handful of sand and ran toward the cat. It was screeching madly, causing a middle-aged couple on the beach to stop and stare. This was my destiny. I would burn, which was worse than getting stabbed in the pupils. The cat's eyes popped way out, and its legs were cycling at unnatural speeds beneath the boards.

I threw my sand onto the cat, which doused some of the flames in a resonant *psschhht*. Noel returned, swiped my nature book, and strolled off again, this time to the south, a cigarette quivering from his lips. I thought about drawing my gun and shooting the cat as an act of mercy, but I couldn't risk letting Noel see that I was armed. I was jolted by my rationality: I was pulling onto the road to murder and was allowing my terror to convert to reason. Drunkish, the cat, with his eyes half closed, more in bewilderment now than in pain, fell into the dunes. "Who are you?" I whispered, disappointed in a ghoulish way that the blackened carcass didn't answer.

Meeting at the Crack a Dawn

"A grave injustice will be done against me."

FROM THE WOMAN WHO DOVE OFF A HIGH DIVE ON HORSE-back to boxing pygmies, the Jersey Shore has had a long-standing devotion to freak shows.

What I had in mind was a central rally in Philadelphia—and a satellite rally in Atlantic City—that would put the priorities of Mario Vanni and the Delaware Valley Anticrime Coalition at center stage. Doing this would require a concerned agitator with a resonant issue, an exiled hero who would redeem the region, an awful villain, and an apparatus to pull it off. In Rhoda McNee and DELVAC, I had my agitator and her resonant issue, crime. In Vanni, I had an unappreciated savior. The elusive Automatic Bart was my serendipitous devil. The challenge was manpower. I approached Vanni with the rally idea, and he recommended getting his "administration" together to plan it out. He asked me not to bring up the real endgame, the casino license, but rather to stress the widely accepted challenge of overcoming the diminished influence of the rackets.

I learned in political campaigns how hard it is to build a crowd. The key obstacle is giving people a reason to disrupt their cherished routines to attend something. Would they get to meet a star?

Would they be shown on camera? Would they get paid? Crowd building was the art of giving vast numbers of people a good reason to scream and yell enthusiastically about something or someone they did not understand. If Vanni's boys had any remaining power, it was the power to get people to understand.

I remember hearing Ronald Reagan tell one of his aides that every fight should be wrapped up in a principle. This exercise in gratuitous defiance would be wrapped up in the principle of political rebellion due to concern about crime.

The meeting of Vanni's administration occurred, at my suggestion, in a school classroom in Cherry Hill. It was held in an old elementary school on Church Road behind the Cherry Hill Mall.

We all knew that a top-level meeting like this could be a bugging bonanza for the government, especially if the boys stayed around and talked about real mob business. Trouble deserted his perch in Margate and swept the place. Vanni's boys were to file in on a late July Saturday morning at eleven o'clock, which Mario described as "the crack a dawn." He thought it would be good to get his guys up early to underscore the importance of the meeting.

An elderly black janitor named Thomas opened the red side doors to the building for me at eight o'clock. I couldn't look him in the eye. It was as if the old man knew what I had been doing, whipping up latent racial terror using Automatic Bart. Trouble's team set the classroom up with seats facing a chalkboard that I intended to use. The seats were those one-piece units with small, banged-up writing surfaces that swung over the seat from the right. A lot of these wise guys were pretty big, and I wondered if they all would fit in the seats.

The word "sucks" was the common scripture on the desk surfaces. One kid had written in pencil, "It's a town full of losers and I'm pulling out of here to win." *Thunder Road.* Nice.

Trouble began by closing the shades and sticking small black boxes against the windows. He then set up a device with a screen and began monitoring the noise level in the room. Trouble methodically removed all plants and flowers from the room, explaining that these were prime locations for listening devices.

Within a half hour, Trouble was pointing a remote-control device at the black boxes. He caught my quizzical look out of the corner of his eye and explained what he was doing without even looking at me. These devices would be set to various local radio channels so that if the government were trying to eavesdrop, all they would get was the Delaware Valley Top 40.

Throughout the classroom were posters about the Lenni-Lenape Indians. "The Lenni-Lenape once walked in snowshoes across the grounds of what is now one of the biggest commercial shopping areas in the country," one poster read. "The Lenni-Lenape were one part of a loosely knit band of Indians, known more broadly as the Delaware. They lived peacefully along the rivers and in the forests of Delaware, Pennsylvania, and New Jersey. A highly spiritual tribe, the Lenni-Lenape were known for exhaustive consensus-building before they committed their men to war."

At a few minutes before eleven, Trouble exited, and Vanni and Noel did their killer promenade into the classroom. They were dressed casually, Vanni looking like a banker on casual Friday in his pale green oxford cloth shirt and khakis. Noel had on his standard black pocket T-shirt and jeans. His diamond tooth held a lit cigarette steady. I got a minihug from Noel. I could feel the sinews of his back. I felt my spleen in my throat.

I was tempted to tell Mario about what Noel had been doing to me, but I held off. When I was a little kid, I was beaten up once in my neighborhood and had told Mickey and Blue about it. They told me that I had been stupid to ride my bike on a street where there were tougher kids. They also said that I had been weak to allow myself to have been beaten. They had no sympathy at all, a sentiment that likely transferred to Mario Vanni. On top of this scarring memory, my instincts told me that I had to make Noel feel totally confident in his persecution. How this would pay off, I did not know.

"Here's your book, Jonah," Noel said, handing over *Fruit of the Valley*. "Turns out, I like nature, too."

I took the book back, saying nothing.

The two men reviewed the Indian posters as I explained to them what I would be doing this morning. Noel briefed me on who all of our visitors would be.

The next to arrive was Froggie, the capo of Vanni's Delaware operations, so named, presumably, because of his hoarse voice. Noel immediately bummed a match from him and lit his cigarette. Then Vanni's underboss arrived with a bodyguard whom he asked to wait outside of the classroom, where I noticed Frankie Shrugs and Petie were standing guard. The underboss was Steverino, a gambling whiz who had operational jurisdiction over Atlantic City, according to the papers.

Bobby "the Toaster," the South Philly capo, arrived along with Phillip "Silly Philly," the Northeast Philly capo. The next migration included Vanni's pre-Noel *consigliere*, an elderly, skeletal, hawk-nosed man named Salvy Donuts. Donuts had been around forever, and I remembered reading about a jail sentence he was given for running a car theft ring some twenty years ago. Now Donuts was out of the operations end of the business and was just whispering in the ear of the capos, like a gangland Polonius.

Birdie, Vanni's central New Jersey capo, came next. A rotund, rosy-cheeked man who looked more like a deli owner than a loan shark, Birdie embraced everyone and pinched cheeks as he did it. He complimented Noel, fearfully, about his "guys doin' good." Then there was a guy called Face, a handsome man in his early forties who ran operations in the Pennsylvania suburbs immediately west of Philly; Boots, in charge of the airport and neighboring towns; Broadway of Center City; Switchie, so-named for his elaborate hijacking schemes that required repeated changes of trucks and getaway cars; the Baker of West Philly, who had sway in the city's unions; and No-No, who earned his nickname because of his justification of doing hits by saying, "The guy did a 'no-no.'"

Some of the men were central casting gangsters. The Baker was downright menacing. No-No looked clownish with his bright, un-matched clothing. As a group, they appeared to be bewildered extras from a Scorcese movie who had wandered onto the wrong sound stage. It was not lost on me that all of these men had murdered or else they wouldn't have been here, and I shivered when they squeezed into the semicircle of student seats. No-No looked curiously at the writing surface and pushed at it to make sure it wouldn't snap up at him.

Vanni began by thanking the men for attending and saying that their efforts would be fundamental to thwarting law enforcement's campaign to stop them. He further explained that I had been re-tained to help "deal with what the people think about Our Thing." He said that while I was not privy to any of their business infor-mation, he trusted me implicitly in terms of working on this "caper."

"Jonah here knows about the life and respects what we gotta do. We lost the mystique. Lost the mystique. Who thought it would come to this? Without the fear, the showbiz that we run everything, we can't get people to pay up or shut up anymore. If we're just a bunch of burned-out mopes, we've got nothing. Jonah's gonna help us a little with that. What we're gonna do is what Jonah here calls 'gratuitous rebellion.' " *Gruh-tootis.* "Is that good shit or what? Any-way, most of you guys knew his grandpop, Mickey Price. Jonah's smart like him. Just don't start with the cyber shit and nobody'll get hurt." Vanni's cadence audibly downgraded into the patter of the street when he was with his men. Then it hit me when No-No shifted in his seat and almost fell over like a circus reject: These guys were to Mario what BARRY SILVER. FURS was to me. They were what he was running from. It didn't make a difference whether it was the hotheaded Italian stereotype or the self-satisfied Jewish one, these guys were buoys that flashed us in Morse code: THIS IS WHAT YOU COULD LOOK LIKE.

"I appreciate your willingness to come here today," I began. "I won't talk any longer than I have to. We need to show a great deal of public support for your organization and Mr. Vanni as a positive symbol of it. We need to put together a crowd to protest and march on his behalf. Much of this is being done already through the Del-aware Valley Anticrime Coalition, or DELVAC.

"That's our gig?" the Baker said. *Dats r gig.*

Vanni's eyes twinkled.

"Mr. Vanni figures," I continued, picking up a piece of chalk and drawing a pyramid on the board, "that if you have an organi-zation with, say, ten divisions, and each of those ten divisions has twenty executives, and each executive has three or four associates, and each of these people is responsible for turning out fifty people to a rally, we could get almost fifty thousand people together in Atlantic City and Philadelphia."

I circled the number for effect and erased the rest of my diagram, which was, in essence, a hollow organizational chart for the Vanni Cosa Nostra family.

"Mr. Vanni also believes that if some of these people have special contacts within organizations that have many other members, such as labor unions, we may be able to send a message that the region's basic services—waste hauling, transportation, shipping—might be shut down if there is a failure to cooperate.

"We don't really want to shut anything down, but we will need to send a message that Mr. Vanni and all of you play an important role in the operations of this region, and that includes the labor unions, which, in Mr. Vanni's opinion, are the best way to get big numbers out."

"I'm kinda not sure if you wanna shut down shit or not. Which is it?" Switchie asked. *Chizzit.*

"We don't really want to shut the Delaware Valley down," I answered. "What we want is union participation in the rally and some sort of gesture of protest—something that may make it seem like the city's being shut down but really isn't. It may make people realize how valuable you all are."

"It could also piss off some pretty big fuckin' people in this area," Switchie said.

"You're right. But these big people are politicians. If the damage is minimal and it looks big on the news, these politicians will go with what they perceive to be public opinion. They won't support Mr. Vanni directly, but they might say that 'the people' have spoken and that 'protests are encouraged by the Constitution.' Stuff like that."

"We would be getting to some of them, through you fellas, before anything even happens," Vanni added.

"Hey, Mario, I'll do what you say," Switchie said, "but I'm worried about how this could come down on you. Ya know, we don't got the same profile. Is this worth the risk? I'm not so sure I see the points for the rest of us."

"Switch, wasn't it you who did a sit-down with me last month about people laughing at some of the young babies you got working for you who don't even scare the truck drivers anymore?"

Switchie nodded.

"And, Face, you got people in the neighborhoods—neighborhoods that were once ours, for Chrissakes—cooperating with the cops. Am I making this shit up?" Mario asked, a streak of anger in his voice, cleverly tossing the burden back on his capos. "Do we want to have more sit-downs? Do we want to go to more dinners and beef about what's befallen Our Thing like a bunch a school-girls? I'm trying to do something here!"

"We'll come out all right," Switchie assured. "But this is a big risk for you, know what I mean?"

"We're all right, Switch. We're all right. Just go with this, I think. What I need you guys to do is work through Jonah. He'll fill you in on the poop, how we get this thing going. The important thing is that you all here get the big picture, you know what I'm saying. This is the way I want to go."

"That's no problem, Mario," Switchie said. "You know, just be-tween us, we couldn't shut down a Dunkin' Donuts, let alone city services anymore."

"I know," Mario laughed. "But Jonah here says that we need to bring back the old romance of Our Thing."

"Un-fuckin'-believable," Switchie said.

"Any other ideas?" Vanni asked.

"Yeah, what's the hook for this? I mean, what are people rallying for?" Noel asked.

"Ah," Mario said professorially. "This'll be clear once we get closer. A grave injustice will be done against me. Don't worry, though, I'll be all right."

"If you say so, Mario."

"This'll work beautiful, I think," Donuts said, all hunched over as if he were about to take a peck at a zebra carcass. "I like what Jonah here's onto. The idea of making one thing look like a rev-olution without really rattling everything outta joint."

"Yeah, we can do this," No-No agreed. "Gettin' that many peo-ple, shit, we can do that. Nobody's gonna say no. Be easier to pull off on a weekend."

"You're probably right," I said, smooching a little No-No hiney. "But it'll be better to do it on a weekday. We want people to get off work and feel like they're giving a big screw to their bosses. Oh, and if anybody can provide beer, that would be great."

"People will come," Birdie agreed. "Even on a weekday, they'll come. I just gotta be clear about where to send folks, stuff like that. This'll be the balloons. This Jonah here's his grandfather's grandson. I always thought Mickey's kid went straight."

"I went into politics."

"You call that straight?" Birdie said, eliciting a laugh.

"I'm on board with getting the people," Face said. "I can help through the union. I just don't want to use all our chits. Remember, we got that thing coming up that could be tricky."

"Right. Right," Vanni said, knowing immediately what "that thing" was, which impressed me. "I'm with you guys a hundred percent. I'm not asking you to screw any deal."

"That's all. That's good," Face agreed. "And I'll talk to a guy about beer."

"Jonah, are you sure this beer business is a good idea?" Noel asked as if he were worried about me. "I don't want people all ripped."

"I'm not committed to it," I said. "I just—"

"Don't worry, Noel," Face said. "When they see who's running the kegs, everybody'll stay nice and sober. We got that effect on people."

"Then the beer stays but is controlled," Vanni concluded.

I suggested to Vanni that I could leave the room if he had other business to discuss. "Yeah, you mind?" he said. "Us guys don't get to talk a lot."

As I proceeded to the door, Vanni said in front of his men, "Hey, Jonah, you'll pull this off good. We'll bring the bodies. You put on the show. You'll pull this off good," Vanni said again. This was not a vote of confidence. It was a promise to his capos that my plan would work, and if it failed, Mario would do to me what needed to be done.

Noel, feigning support, nodded, too. "We'll bring the bodies," he echoed. I pictured him pushing a wheelbarrow filled with severed limbs. No one reacted as if this had been a strange remark. My elimination would be done the way a secretary orders new Post-it notes, as a perfunctory task on a checklist.

Shoebie Doobie Doo

"So sell dope in Philly only if you dare."

BY THE END OF JULY, THE SHORE SUMMER WAS IN ITS ADOLES-
cence. The toddling sense of experimentation, the impulse to
test whether it was really summer by wearing flip-flops, was over.
Anyone who was going to summer here was here. No new bathing
suits were being debuted. Shoebies, contemporarily updated to
carrying backpacks, were here in force by Friday night, sleeping in
cars, on porches, and on the floors of nonshoebie houses.

My shoebiehood was beginning. Sidney Blintzes had sent a
bunch of boxes up to Mickey's place for me to load up his belongings. Hint, hint. I supposed that was better than a gunshot behind
the ear. A move implied that I was going to be alive for a while. A
charity group was scheduled to come for Mickey's furniture that
weekend. Charity was my choice; I couldn't use this furniture with
its Munsters mien and whiff of petrified Bengay. Sidney said there
was no need for me to be there. All I had to do was pack up what
I wanted to keep, which consisted primarily of books and records.

Irv the Curve and I agreed that given what was happening with
Vanni and Noel, I was better off staying with friendly wise guys
than experimenting with neutral ground. We had ruled out Trouble's place to avoid someone stumbling on a connection between

the two of us. Single and approaching middle age, I was shleping my family's belongings "from Minsk to Pinsk," as Mickey might have said, to live in a condo with a couple of guys in their eighties with swollen prostates and a penchant for yelling at children they thought were running too fast by the pool. Carvin Marvin and Mort the Snort's admonitions always came with unscientific projections about what catastrophe would result from the running: You'll put somebody's eye out, you'll fall and break your neck, you're liable to kill somebody, you'll track sand all over the place. I had developed the theory that there was a Darwinian component to these preoccupations that had migrated from the years in Egyptian bondage. Pharaoh: "We better let these people go or they'll track sand all over the place!" "Moses: "Throw down your staff or you're liable to put somebody's eye out."

I propped a box beside me and turned on Mickey's stereo. A Philly station was rebroadcasting New York shock-jock Arnie Lutz's program from that morning. Lutz was berating a "vanilla lesbian," whatever that was. By the end of the abuse, all of the CDs were in the box. I left the klezmer music toward the top, speculating that maybe Edie and I would play them at her place. They wouldn't be hard to carry back to Washington. The books on a nearby shelf would be more difficult. I didn't want most of them. I had no intention of either reading Leon Uris or leading people to believe I read him by displaying QB VII on my bookshelf.

As I set up a new box, Lutz began joking about murdering drug dealers. I turned up the radio. Lutz was doing a "telethon" bit, trying to raise money to hire Mario Vanni to kill all of the drug dealers in New York, "the way he's doing in Philly and Jersey." I stood back up and glanced around the room with my mouth hanging open.

First, Lutz played the Jimmy Mack tape and offered his listeners a blow-by-blow account of what was happening to Dirty Zappa. When the wise guys delivered Dirty Zappa a particularly brutal blow, Lutz's in-studio aides shouted, "Oof!" The oofs were accompanied by canned audience laughter and applause.

Lutz then read from the New York papers the names of alleged drug dealers who had been arrested, and pleaded for Vanni to kill them. He asked his listeners to E-mail his Web site with the names of people they suspected to be dealing drugs. Lutz responded to the E-mails with polite form responses: "Thank you for suggesting that Mr. Vanni whack [name of drug dealer]. We take all of our listeners' suggestions very seriously. However, due to the number of requests Mr. Vanni receives, we cannot guarantee that he will whack [name of drug dealer]."

Callers phoned in and sang songs and offered up other random forms of entertainment to raise money for what Lutz said was a beautiful cause. He even mocked Jerry Lewis's tendency to cry after an especially moving performance. The telethon bit was clever, and I was gnawingly disappointed that I hadn't thought of it myself. Then I thought about some nut actually starting to kill people, and what the cold shock of handcuffs would feel like.

At the end of the radio telethon, Lutz graced the audience with his parody of Elton John's bicentennial hit, "Philadelphia Freedom," which he called "Philadelphia Bleed 'em." He sang the song himself with a fake British accent.

> *They used to get the kiddies stoned,*
> *Down by the old schoolhouse,*
> *They'd sell—*
> *To every Girl Scout who'd go by.*
> *They used to be junkies pushin' crack cocaine,*
> *But their crimes have changed,*
> *The mess they made!*
> *So high they will get hung.*
>
> Chorus:
> *If they're pushin' dope*
> *Then Philadelphia bleed 'em,*
> *Look, Mario, there's a pusher over there.*
> *Philadelphia bleed 'em and stuff 'em in a trunk,*
> *So sell dope in Philly only if you dare.*

Caught between feelings of pride and terror at my program's effectiveness, I took Mickey's books down from a shelf and indiscriminately slammed them into the moving box, including Leon Uris. My caper had made its way to Arnie Lutz, as big a pop-culture hit as one could hope for. A slim, flat children's book slipped behind the shelf. I edged it out with a pencil and saw one that Mickey and Deedee had read to me as a kid. I hadn't seen it in a lifetime. It was called *The People Papers* by Max Howard. It looked smaller than I had remembered. In my mind, it used to be a giant panorama, like a movie screen. I vaguely recalled the psychedelic pictures and the collection of stories. I fanned through the pages toward the end. One story was called "Ong's Hat." Sitting atop a giant black bowler was a man named Ong with a moon where his head should have been. A paralyzing chill gripped the back of my head, and the muscles in my neck tightened and spun as the words on the left side of the book spilled past my eyes:

> *From time to time, as I worry over this mystery of Ong's disappearance, I go into the pine woods and walk up and down, kicking over the sandy soil and calling out.*

The dizziness didn't overwhelm my Arnie Lutz victory until I got farther into the story. By the time I finished reading it, I was flat on my ass leaning against the bookshelf.

> *Alone, I think of Ong and of being invisible. I wonder if hanging his hat on a certain tree hadn't triggered some secret door in the middle of the air, that opened to another world.*

Another world. The man in the woods. The hat. The money?

My breathing became shallow and halting, and I felt a dozen pinpricks in my hands. My left hand was freezing, my right hand was sweating. I shuffled to the closet on my knees and pulled a blanket out, throwing it around me and falling back against the bookshelf. "Ong," I whispered like a mental patient. I wanted to adopt any couple staying at the Golden Prospect and climb in between them in bed until the nightmare went away. Two easy minutes ago, I was smirking over my Arnie Lutz coup and rehearsing an easy night with Edie. We had been spending more and more time together. Every encounter with her offered me a reason to believe that staying alive was something more than a biological drive. I had been doing my Vanni caper during the day and hurtling toward Edie at dusk. She appeared to be happy, too. We skipped tonight because I had to pack Mickey's things away and didn't want to depress her. What would she do if she saw me on the ground like this? "He seemed so nice," she would tell her family at the Cowtown Rodeo. "Men are all crazy," she would tell a friend, and I would be annexed into the realm of bad dating experiences.

Hell, wouldn't anybody be dizzy with Noel trying to kill him and a mystical affirmation that his dead grandfather was trying to tell him something?

I climbed into bed with the book about Ong, knowing the answer was in there somewhere. A snapshot of Mickey's funeral danced in my head somewhere south of my eyes. There had been the dark man with the hat on the Boardwalk. The man in black. He had removed his hat during kaddish. When I looked up again, he was gone. *Another world.* Red Tooth? I drifted in and out of sleep holding my pillow and hoping it would morph into Edie.

I had to call her. If she were horrified by my need for her now, she would be horrified by my need for her later.

"Hey, Ede."

"Hi there."

"I wanted to hear you say something."

"Okay."

"Tell me that we'll drift asleep many more times."

"We will."

"I finished *Happy All the Time.*"

"What did you think?"

"It's a lot like you. It makes me think of quilts and fireplaces, and I'm not somebody who thinks that way. What about *Good-bye, Columbus?*"

"Finished. I know why you picked it. Brenda's what you're running from."

"You're nothing like her."

"That's the point now, isn't it?"

book three
ong's hat

There's a man in the world who is never turned down,
wherever he chances to stray;
He gets the glad hand in the populous town,
or out where the farmers make hay;
He's greeted with pleasure on deserts of sand,
and deep in the aisles of the woods;
Wherever he goes there's a welcoming hand—
he's the man who delivers the goods.

—Camden resident Walt Whitman

Waterloo

"Moses Price. You are under arrest for running a criminal enterprise."

CARVIN' MARVIN AND MORT THE SNORT LIVED IN AN EX-hausted low-rise condo on Atlantic Avenue in Margate. The gray wooden structure ran parallel to the beach. A small community pool where children ran too much and tracked sand all over the place was wedged in between a series of decks and a concrete sea wall.

Like other souls who rose from modest means, Carvin' Marvin and Mort the Snort felt compelled to give their house a name. A foreign-sounding title was always preferable for such displays since Americans tended to equate hard-to-pronounce names with class. A small wooden plaque, therefore, was placed proudly above the worn front door.

"Welcome to Chez Guevara," Mort greeted me with a confident pump of his hand.

"I'm honored to call Chez Guevara my home."

"Listen to the political bullshit outta you. Marv said he heard the name somewhere from the Cuba days and says, 'Hey, don't "chez" mean house in Frenchy talk?' " ("Chez" was pronounced "shezz.") "I says, sure. So when we moved into this place, we wanted a classy name. So we got the chez, the Frenchy word, and we got Guevara, which is some hoity-toity Cuban thing. You smack 'em together and you get Chez Guevara."

"He was a famous man."

"Who?"

"Che Guevara."

"No. See, it's the name of the house is what I'm telling you."

"I understand."

"So the house is famous you're telling me?"

"No. Che Guevara was famous. But he spelled the name differently."

"What the hell are you talking about?"

"Che Guevara, the labor leader."

"Labor leader. Like the unions?"

"Right. Che Guevara was a labor leader."

"Get the hell outta here!"

"I'm serious, Mort." He shook his head in disbelief. Carvin' Marvin bounded down the stairs surprisingly swiftly for a man his age.

"Marv," Mort said, "Jones here says that Chez Guevara was a union boss."

"Met the guy in Cuba," Marv snapped. "Hey there, College. Shake the hand that shook the hand that wiped the ass of Abraham," he said, extending his palm.

"Why the hell did we name our house after half a commie?" Mort asked.

"He was a commie? You'd never know. Helluva card player."

"You didn't know he was a commie?"

"Morty, if a guy can play cards, who gives a shit what he's got in his closet? He was a famous guy."

"But he was famous for being a commie," Mort said, betrayed.

"Who gives a shit why he was famous. He was famous."

I chose to probe neither the name of my new residence nor Carvin' Marvin's relationship with Che Guevara. Mort shuffled off somewhere picking at some dry skin he found near his eye. Marv stood solidly in plush blue carpet and gestured for me to look around. I beheld the chrome furniture, the mirrored walls, and the puffy leather sofas. The adjective that came to mind was "mod." These guys were the Rat Pack on Mylanta.

The sound of squealing seagulls was interrupted by three loud raps against the door of Chez Guevara. Mort the Snort answered and took a few steps back. Noel? The door eased open and there, against the Atlantic Avenue traffic, stood a squat old woman with a face like a constipated schnauzer.

"Mrs. Pinsky," Mort said nervously.

Mrs. Pinsky clutched her straw handbag and pointed her doggy eyes at me. "Who's he?" she barked.

Mort the Snort had backed himself against a mirror. Carvin' Marvin stepped forward. "He's a friend's grandson, Mrs. Pinsky," Marv assured her.

"Whose grandson is he?"

"A friend of ours who just died. Tragic situation, I must say."

"You. What's your name?" Mrs. Pinsky asked me.

"Jonah."

"Like the Book of Jonah?"

"Yes, Mrs. Pinsky."

"You ever read the book of Jonah?"

"Yes."

"Are you a gangster, too?"

"No."

"All right then. No funny business. Understood?"

All three of us gangsters said: "Okay, Mrs. Pinsky."

She backed out the door, sniffing around. When it shut, I could hear the muffled sound of her bark yelling at someone, "No riding bikes up on the sidewalk. What is this, the Indian Apples Five hundred?"

"No, Mrs. Pinsky," an oppressed voice conceded.

"That," Marv said with a deep breath, as Mort began breathing into a paper bag, "was Mrs. Pinsky. She's the condo president."

"What's she so angry about?" I asked.

"She's not picky," Mort said sarcastically, talking into his paper bag.

My swinger roommates had three small bedrooms upstairs. Carvin' Marvin's overlooked the ocean. Mort the Snort's faced Atlantic Avenue. The one I would inhabit faced a side street and had a small window that ran high against the ceiling. There was a single bed and a night table, nothing more. This was where out-of-town killers probably crashed after a hit or a little *shtup* with a cocktail waitress.

And it was all mine.

"You sounded awful last night," Edie said, her hair pulled back in a ponytail. She had on khaki shorts and a polo shirt. The gradual curve of her face and the concern around her eyes made me stammer.

"I felt awful."

"What brought it on?"

I answered by kissing her for five minutes until she pushed me back.

"You're dodging my question."

"What was it again?"

"What brought on the way you felt?"

"Cleaning out Mickey's things, I found an old book he used to read me as a kid. Certain memories—bad ones—came flooding out." Edie faded into soft focus for a moment. Mentioning *The People Papers* caused Mr. Hicks, my high school English teacher, to pop into my head. I should call him. Mr. Hicks was an authority on folklore. We had stayed in touch on and off over the years. He might be able to shed some light on old Ong and what might have become of him.

"Was I the only one you called last night?"

Scary question. The answer would be an admission of her status. Contrary to what women on TV shows say, I have never seen evidence that women look favorably upon signals of commitment. My experience has been that modern women disrespect a man by precisely the amount he surrenders himself. Hell, I'd come clean.

"Yes. I called only you."

"Why me, Jonah?"

"You make me feel safe. Did anyone else ever make you feel safe?"

"My family."

"Do they know about me?"

Hesitation. "I told them a few days ago," Edie conceded.

"What did you say?"

Edie dodged the question by stealing my ploy of kissing the person she didn't want to answer.

"I told my parents I had a boyfriend."

"Did you give them any specifics?"

"I told them your name was Jonah. Don't worry, I didn't say anything about your being Mickey's grandson." This relieved and saddened me at the same time.

"If they're your parents and they make you feel safe, then I want to meet them."

The shape her eyes took was unmistakable: Edie was disarmed by my interest in her family. Here was a woman so antique, so out of touch with the modern equation of romance with desertion, that she actually wanted to draw me deeper into a narrative that could only be described as a future. There was something very wrong with this woman, and I wanted to marry her.

"So, Edie, what would you normally do on nights like this? Before me?"

"I'd make coffee, read the paper, and paint my toenails."

"Where's the toenail polish?"

"In my bedroom."

"Please get it."

Edie dragged out a skeptical "Oookay" and returned with the polish and cotton balls. She reclined noncommittally on the sofa. From the floor, I held the closest foot and began to paint her nails the fierce yellow-red color of sunrise. I glanced around to make sure that my college fraternity brothers weren't looking. She studied my strokes closely, more in wonder than critique. When I began Edie's second foot, I swallowed hard once, flummoxed over how I would explain this scene to Frankie Shrugs. On one hand, I had become obsessed with murder. On the other hand, I was painting nail polish onto a woman's toes and kind of liking it. Then Edie wiggled her bronze toes, and an invisible cartoon balloon drifted up against my ear and whispered in deflation, "You needn't explain this." The balloon withered into nothingness and I finished Edie's toes, then began thinking about where I put that diamond I had found after Mickey died.

"When you felt down last night, what memory was it that kept coming back?" she asked.

I couldn't tell her that it was no memory at all but the creepy reality that my dead grandfather was talking to me.

I withdrew into my reservoir of awful memories and popped up with a winner of a bad one to share with Edie: When Mickey, Deedee, and I returned to Philadelphia International Airport after our exile.

It had begun with the morning goose-stepping of the Parisian police who packed Mickey and Deedee off to the airport. They plucked me out of the schoolyard before I had a chance to hug a girl named Chantal. . . .

As our airplane descended into American airspace, I could see William Penn's hat atop Philadelphia City Hall through the scratched oval window. The monotony of a long, silent flight was shattered by the crackle of a flight attendant's knee as he knelt by Mickey.

The thin air was pregnant with bad news. "Mr. Price," he said, "I know you know this, but the captain has asked me to remind you that agents from the Federal Bureau of Investigation will be meeting you at the gate."

"I know, son," Mickey said.

Mickey requested a moist towel to wash his hands.

Flight 1229 from Paris landed at Philadelphia International Airport at quarter past seven in the morning. It was Valentine's Day, as evidenced by the useless purple heart candy the stewardess handed me. It was the kind with messages imprinted on the heart. Mine read HUGS.

I walked down the aisle in between Mickey and Deedee. We had been seated toward the front of the plane so it wasn't that far to walk. They both had their hands around the back of my neck. Their fingers painfully jammed the collar of my pale beige alligator shirt. I didn't say anything, though. They thought they were helping me, I'm sure. A woman in first class mimed to her husband the words "Mickey Price, the gangster."

The alligator shirts were big deals in those days. Mickey called it my country club shirt. He liked the way I looked in it, which was probably why I wore it. I tugged at the collar as a slight hint to get them off my neck.

"That's some country club shirt," Mickey said.

"It is, I know."

The heavy brown door swung open with a screech and a thunk. Everything looked brownish like a scorched forest. A huge, clownish-looking man in a synthetic beige suit stepped onto the ramp. "Mr. Price," he said, "I'm Special Agent Farrell of the FBI"

"I know you, Farrell," Mickey said. My grandfather's eyes were black and hard. Like Vanni's, actually, now that I think back on it. It was the first time in my life when I consciously recognized how rough a customer the old man really was.

"Yes, sir," Farrell said, seemingly afraid of Zeta Smurf.

Another agent stepped from behind the airport check-in counter and said, "Moses Price. You are under arrest for running a criminal enterprise that stole millions of dollars from the federal government by evading taxes that were to be paid by casino operations and gambling junkets where the government believes you have a controlling and illegal interest."

Mickey nodded rabbinically. The frigid snap of steel handcuffs around Mickey's wrists made me hurt somewhere down deep but unspecified.

We were shoved down a vomitous bright green corridor. A throng of reporters mobbed us when the door opened to the outside. A swinging camera hit my temple. My chin felt like it weighed ten tons. We were stuffed into the backseat of a boxy Ford LTD without whitewalls.

"What's it like to be the Godfather's grandson?" I heard somebody shout. Mickey glanced viciously in the direction of that somebody.

The car radio was on. The faint lilt of ABBA singing "Waterloo" flicked at my eardrums. I had heard ABBA in Paris but never this song. Was this a new song or an old one? I didn't know. I would have to call someone to find out. "Wo wo wo wo, Waterloo, finally facing my Waterloo . . ."

The case against Mickey had been thrown out shortly after the main witness against him, Droopy Moran, was crushed by a falling I-beam on a Philly construction site. "Better safeguards for workers are needed," Mickey had said solemnly on the courthouse steps after the judge's dismissal.

Edie's eyes were wide open as if they had been pinned that way.

Her face was like the posters you see for horror films where the scared baby-sitter finds a clue suggesting that she's not in the house alone.

"You'll be hearing more stories like this," I warned her. "For some reason, you are able to draw these things out of me."

"I don't mind."

"You may someday."

She denied this.

"I would listen to your stories, you know, Edie."

"Yours are better."

Edie's kisses led to a horizontal collapse across her sofa. Her pity quickly transformed our clothes into an urgent heap of khaki and pastels. "Being here like this with nothing on, this is what normal people must do," was my first thought. My second thought was that I should run. One way or another, I would only end up hurting Edie. The sanctuary of the moment made me remember another time I was with a woman in this way. It was incomprehensibly long ago—not long after Mickey, Deedee, and I returned to America, and an inevitable series of demolitions forever altered the silhouette of Atlantic City.

The Sanhedrin of Ozzie's

"I can only tell you what our laws say about taking a life."

Y OU CAN TALK ABOUT THE TALMUD ANYWHERE IF YOU DON'T
know much about it. I called Rabbi Wald from my digital
phone and asked if he could meet me for lunch. He agreed to meet
me at Ozzie's in Longport, the gateway to the cash flow temples.

The rabbi walked in right on time and offered the folks who
recognized him a macho "Howyadoin'." He was wearing a pocket
T-shirt, khakis, and Western boots. When he shook my hand, a
crew of cash flow temple congregants (obscured by a mountain of
French fries) nodded as if I must be somebody pretty big to be
acknowledged by South Jersey's outlaw rabbi. An old woman sitting
alone stared at the rabbi's boots, then at mine.

"They got me my usual spot in the back," the rabbi said.

"You have a usual spot?"

"Sure. A guy's got to have a steady place to hear confession."

"Confused about our affiliation, are we?"

"No. You?"

"A little. Confessions are supposed to be anonymous."

"Not Jewish confessions. We want everybody to know." The
rabbi smirked and waved me on.

A waitress who looked a lot like a younger version of Dollsy handed us menus as Rabbi Wald took a seat with his back against the wall. We both ordered borscht.

Rabbi Wald leaned back with a Brando-esque look of self-satisfaction. He knew I had come to seek his counsel and was doing his Don Corleone method act. I swear, all of these people around here lived in the movies. I waited for the rabbi to flick his nose the way Brando did when all of the supplicants came for favors at his daughter's wedding.

I decided to play along.

"You are vexed, Jonah. Why else would you see a rabbi?" Don Corleone momentarily faded.

"There are other reasons to see a rabbi."

"Not for American boys like you. You come when you are vexed."

"I'll concede the point if you can help me."

"Talk to me."

"Over the years, you've known some very tough men, men like my grandfather. Men who killed. A man in your line of work must have a reason for spending time with such men. Other rabbis would find associations like that repugnant."

"Even gangsters have spirits."

"Yes, but law-abiding people have spirits, too. You could be-friend them."

"I have befriended law-abiding people."

"But you"—I smiled accusingly—"you like the *shtarkers*, the wise guys. Will you grant me that?"

Wald's face tightened and turned a flushed pink. It must have been the way I had spoken to him. He knew I had keyed in his Brando tics and he felt like a putz. Good. I had been watching people impersonate Don Corleone for a quarter cen-tury and had tired of it by the time Carter was elected. My im-patience was fueled by a deeply ingrained knowledge that Rabbi Wald was meeting me in part because it made him feel like he was the *consigliere* to the Don's college-educated scion. Michael Corleone had the Irish Tom Hagen who wanted to be a wartime *consigliere;* I had the Jewish Rabbi Wald who wanted to be an Italian racketeer. Edie was the only person I knew who wanted to be who she was.

"I will."

"Then how does a smart man like you reconcile what these men have done with your friendship with them? Were you afraid you would be harmed?"

"Never."

"But you knew that Mickey and his friends murdered?"

"I never saw anyone murdered."

"*Saw?* Rabbi, you're talking like Bill Clinton. You don't have to see a murder to know that one took place. It's not like they were going to call you up and ask you to drive out to the Pine Barrens with them to watch Louie Snake Eyes get clipped."

"Louie Snake Eyes got clipped?"

"I don't know. I didn't know there was a Louie Snake Eyes."

"Oh."

"So you must have believed that the crimes—Mickey's crimes— were somehow justified."

The rabbi wrung his fingers and waived Dollsy Jr. over for some more water. I wanted to drive her down to Murray's so she could look at herself in thirty-five years. This is *it*, sweetheart. . . .

"At some level, I suppose you're right."

"At what level?"

"Your grandfather and his friends came from a different time. They would have either trampled the competition or been trampled. I'm a lot younger than those guys. And I come from a different place. Camden in the fifties was not the same place as it was during Prohibition. Who knows what I would have become under different circumstances."

"A killer? Could you have become a killer?"

"Maybe. Jonah, God knows what makes people kill. Circumstances mean a great deal. Moses killed. Moses killed the Egyptian. You knew that. You know the Bible stories."

"But God didn't punish Moses for killing."

"How the hell do you know? His life wasn't a day at the racetrack. Maybe that trip through the desert was punishment, listening to his tribe squabble like a prehistoric condo association."

I could feel my brain working. I could *hear* it working as I loaded up my next question. It was a slow-moving, grinding noise. I heard blood splashing through my heart.

"How, to the best of your training, did God view Moses' murder of the Egyptian?" I asked.

"I can only tell you what our laws say about taking a life. It basically comes down to this: The Sanhedrin tell us that if someone comes to kill you, be first and kill him. Self-defense."

I reached down under the table and nervously felt around for nothing in particular. My fingers ran atop a series of gummy bumps.

"Who were the Sanhedrin?"

"They were the big guns. Moses appointed them to serve as a court of sorts. They stuck around until the Temple was torched in the year seventy."

"You say that like it was torched for the insurance money."

"You never know."

"Did these guys judge Moses for killing the Egyptian?"

"Dunno. But in cases of self-defense, you do what you have to do."

"So in cases of self-defense, it's okay?"

"I didn't say it was okay in the sense that God would be happy about it. I'm saying that in certain cases someone's gotta do what he's gotta do. You want this to be tied up all neat. It's not. . . . Jonah"—Rabbi Wald placed his palms atop the back of my hands— "are you worried about the fate of Mickey's soul?"

I crossed my fingers the way my mother did when she taught me that kiddie hand maneuver: *Here is the church, here is the steeple. Open the door and see all the people.* What did the Sanhedrin say about lying?

"No, Rabbi, I am worried about my own soul." This being the truth.

"Have you done something?"

My eyes bore in on his. "No. I have this compulsion to do something."

"Is it out of hate, or are you trying to rub out your own Jersey devils?"

"That's very deep, Rabbi, but no, I hate a man who wants to kill me."

"I see. But, Jonah, *will* he kill you?"

Usually tears come with a warning—a lump in the throat, a deep suck of wind. Not this time. A fugitive drip of salt water escaped from my eyes.

"He will certainly kill me. I don't doubt this at all. Don't you see what's tearing me up, Rabbi? It's not only that I am obsessed with killing this man. It's that I *want* to. Every time I see him, he says something or does something that makes his goal very clear. This isn't paranoia—the guy got where he did because he kills people. Look, Rabbi, I'm a mind reader. It's my job, my little talent. This man is going to kill me. Don't ask me how I know. I know."

"So you never factored killing into your calculations."

"Of course not."

"It's dealing with the variables that makes a man great."

"Or sends him to hell."

"That, too. Can Mickey's friends help you?" The rabbi's pupils bugged out in a scary way. "Or *is* it Mickey's friends?" he asked softly.

"I don't know. I don't think so. But they don't have the power you think they do."

Rabbi Wald smiled in a striking way. He appeared kingly as he reached forward and grabbed my face and whispered, "No man has the power we think he does. Only God has that power."

"Mickey worked his whole life to keep me away from his life. His professional life."

"In this he failed, Jonah. Circumstances can always be debated. Everything can be debated. These things are wrestled with, not swatted away. The wise are the wrestlers. At the end of the day, it's between you and God."

"Can you wrestle God and win?"

"No, but you can get wiser and stronger."

Borscht arrived. Rabbi Wald picked up a napkin with one hand and chopped at the sour cream with the other. He began eating, and a drop of beet juice fell from his lower lip onto a napkin hanging on the edge of the table. The red liquid bled through the paper the way firecrackers spread against the night sky. Was a murder in self-defense truly acceptable? Or did Mickey and the boys find the one rabbi who would be likely to give the interpretation they had sought? I picked up my spoon and pushed down at the borscht, watching it swirl into the bent silver.

Ground Zero

"Homework is not our friend, love."

THANK GOD FOR THE STOLEN CELL PHONES. MARIO HAD SWIT-
chie rip them off from a truck that had come in from Moto-
rola's Schaumberg, Illinois, headquarters. I hadn't actually specified
that the phones had to be stolen; I had just asked that they be
untraceable, but these guys stick with what they know. They were
the kind that you could use as walkie-talkies—you could just press
a button and get the guy you needed once you had programmed
his number.

I was walking down the shadier streets in Center City, Philadelphia, wearing a logoless baseball cap, sunglasses, a ratty Eagles
T-shirt, khaki shorts, and almost a week of beard stubble. While I
wasn't a big enough name to be recognized by most folks, it was
always possible that one of the reporters had seen me doing my
pundit gigs over the years, and, if there was anyplace I could get
nailed for my Vanni program, it would be here, now.

My first illegal call was to Cindi. It was around noon.

"Hey, it's me," I said.

"How are you holding up?"

"I don't know. Tell Dorkus to pull the trigger."

"This soon?"

"Yeah. I'd feel better if it got out there."

"Done."

Next I phoned Frankie Shrugs, who was somewhere in South Philly.

"Yo," he answered.

"You ready to make that call?" I asked.

"Yeah, now?"

"Now. Do you know the message?"

"Yeah, I got the message. That guy we got's gonna rat out the boss at City Hall."

"That's the one. Do you have the patsy?"

"Yeah, we got him. We just took him to lunch. He thinks he's Pacino."

"Good. That's what we want."

In the next few hours, I confirmed that DELVAC had a protest permit, that Cindi had alerted the media, that Dorkus had begun firing our message onto the Internet, and that Mario was in the hands of his handlers. I was reluctant to call the capos. As critical as they were to this, I didn't want to appear to be checking over their shoulders. We had spoken a few times via stolen phone, but it was all in the planning stages. I never had to supervise them in the execution.

I paced from Independence Hall to City Hall and back. Screw it, Jonah, call them. Mario will blame you if this caper goes south. Besides, he told them I was responsible. I'd be negligent *not* to call.

At about seven in the evening, I leaned against a tree near the Liberty Bell and started calling the boys. The Baker was in an abandoned field out at King of Prussia with buses filled with union guys.

"King of Prussia, you read me?" I said.

"Yeah, I can fuckin' read," the Baker replied.

"Are the buses ready?"

"Yeah, about a hundred."

"Do they have the message?"

"Yeah, free him. Free him now."

"Right."

"Look, they wanna know if they can cheer the union guy that's speaking."

"Yes, King of Prussia, they can. Remember, though, this is about helping our man. The unions are there just to provide bodies."

"Don't worry, for every guy here, a whole bunch more are coming by subway, by car, and on foot."

"Thanks, King of Prussia. See you there."

"No you fuckin' won't neither, understood?"

"Understood."

Next I phoned Boots, who was operating out of an old warehouse near the river.

"Riverfront, over."

Nothing.

"Riverfront, over?" I asked again urgently.

"Keep your pants on, Princeton," a gruff voice responded.

"Princeton?"

"Or wherever the hell you did college," Boots said. I decided against a correction over the cell phone.

"Okay, the barges ready?"

"It looks like Ellis fuckin' Island out here. Five barges. Must be three thousand people. We shoulda done this in the park near the zoo. Swear ta God you better have food."

I had purposely avoided having the rally at the park near the zoo because it was too big. Independence Hall was closed in by office buildings, which would make even a crowd of ten thousand appear to be ten times as big.

"They're getting the food ready," I said. "How long will it take to get here?"

"About a half hour, forty-five minutes."

"Go."

In the next ten minutes, I made about six calls on the stolen cell phones to make sure we met our minimum numbers. So far, so good.

"Food unit, over," I said, praying No-No wouldn't answer. He scared the hell out of me. Without food, though, we were all screwed.

"Yeah, food," a garbled voice responded.

"Just checking in," I said. "The guy at the airport and the other guys want to make sure we're square for food. A lot of people coming in." I felt better pawning my demands off on other wise guys.

"I'm here on Sansom. We got pretzels. We got hot dogs and hamburgers. You should see some of them where you are."

I glanced around. I saw a few of the usual places, but nothing as extensive as what I had expected.

"I don't see much," I said.

"Much? What the hell's much?"

"There are a couple of stands."

"A couple. You see a truck that says 'Northeast Beer'?"

I craned my neck in every direction. "No, Sansom, I don't."

I could hear No-No reaming a guy standing next to him. I couldn't hear his statement clearly, but the words "knife" and "balls" were in there.

"Check with me in five." No-No clicked out.

I was sweating like a pig. Not only was it terribly hot, but I envisioned thousands of people getting here and having nothing to eat or drink. If No-No didn't come through, it would be over the Ben Franklin Bridge for me by nightfall. I wondered how high it actually was. Was there a way to fall that would lessen the impact and allow me to survive a trip like that? I thought about the Olympic divers. Year after year they jumped from high places and survived. What did they know? What was the trick? I began breathing heavily but calmed down once I made my decision: I wouldn't even try to survive the fall. Let gravity win. The sooner poor Edie could get on with her life, the better. What did I think I was going to do, swim to Cape May and become a carpenter?

I proceeded toward the sound stage in the park and saw the men testing the speakers. I buzzed Cindi.

"Hey, it's me. The speakers sound all right?"

"They're fine. Calm down. The satellite truck is here."

"Where?"

I heard Cindi yelling at someone to hit the lights. An enormous flash blinked against a glass tower. It was bright in the dwindling daylight.

"Good," I said. "Do you know anything about media?"

"I didn't want to drop the bomb about the big guy yet."

"But when?"

"About a half hour."

"I don't know. Isn't that too late?"

"We want to give them enough time to get here but not enough time to do their homework," Cindi said. "Homework is not our friend, love. Speaking of homework, did you train the big kahuna for this?"

"Yeah. The first time on camera, I beat the crap out of him. He was trying too hard to be smart. It's weird, but when he says what's on his mind, even if it's a lie, he's pretty good. Other times he really means what he says."

"Are you sure he's not going for a major political party nomination?"

"Hey, that hurts, babe," I said, imitating one of Bill Murray's insincere expressions.

"Right. You've got that one reporter covered, don't you? The asshole? Indiana Jones?"

"Yeah, my guy called him earlier."

"It'll be fine, then. Calm down," Cindi assured me.

I clicked her off and phoned No-No again. I still didn't see the additional concessions.

"Sorry to bother you again," I said.

"You see the stuff?" No-No asked.

I looked around. "I definitely see more people but not more food stands."

"Hold on."

I held for two minutes. I watched my watch the whole time. I felt myself age.

"How about now?" No-No asked.

"No."

"Motherf—"

Another two minutes.

Suddenly I saw it. There were three flatbed trucks. Two were loaded with little puffy silver concession stands filled with soft pretzels, hot dogs, hamburgers, soft drinks, and, Praised Be He, beer. The third carried marching signs and dozens of boxes marked simply Candles—Special Order.

Vigil

"Lieutenant, we have a situation."

DURING THE SUMMERTIME, THE SKIES ABOVE PHILADEL-phia are white, grasping for blue. A camp counselor in the Pine Barrens named Kenny once insisted that it was the humidity that painted the sky this way, not the heat. I suppose that this attribution was supposed to make the weather less hot, somehow. "When I sweat," I told Kenny, "I say I'm *hot*, not humid." No sale. This was an important distinction to Kenny.

During the early evening hours, a celestial blue begins to push out the white. This movement gives hope to those who simmer beneath William Penn's iron hat that crowns City Hall. It's a brand of hope that suggests nighttime will deliver more relief than day-time had. When I was little, I thought that "evening" meant to *even* things out, to make those things fair at night that had been unfair during the day.

At eight o'clock on this August Thursday night, it was still light, and a cumulus cloud sat comically on William Penn's head making him look like a colonial baker. A sea of locals had begun to gather at City Hall after the news about Vanni had begun to break.

We started it on the Internet with a viral E-mail from Dorkus, who claimed to work for the police department. He "leaked" that

Vanni would be arrested for the murder of several drug dealers. The dialogue quickly migrated to KBRO's newscast, which led with Al Just's story about Vanni's probable arrest.

"The source that has been supplying me with stunningly accurate information," Just said with a drum roll in his voice and a bulge in his pants, "appears—and I must stress, *appears*—to have turned himself into the police. He is allegedly a solider in Vanni's mob family who has been flipped or turned on his boss."

As Philadelphians gathered outside of City Hall, amplifiers on a flatbed truck were blasting Elton John's "Philadelphia Freedom." Beefy organizers wearing DELVAC T-shirts made certain there was sufficient room for people to maneuver on the street. A few kids pumped their fists in the air and formed the "number one" sign with their fingers the way people do when the camera hits them at ball games. It was impossible to determine just what they were number one at, but they strutted their victory nonetheless. Foreseeing this, Cindi had made the number one sign DELVAC's logo. The media had begun to report a backup along I-95.

By nine o'clock, the sky fell into a deep and romantic navy hue, the color of the sky on the original jacket of *The Great Gatsby*, with its vague, exploding scenery and the twisted golden idols in Daisy's eyes. Union men and women with the machinists, jobbers, energy workers, truckers, and construction trades had begun to arrive by the busload. Some employers had wisely granted permission for "liberal leave" for the following morning so that union members wouldn't worry about staying out late. I overheard a mounted patrolman on a walkie-talkie contact his boss as he beheld the bloating crowd: "Lieutenant, we have a situation," he swallowed painfully. Throughout the region, the Philly police were being paged to come down to City Hall. A permit had been granted, but we had never specified the size of the expected crowd. People were free to walk in the park, were they not? The authorities were scrambling for crowd control support, although the rallyers were perfectly, eerily, docile.

Camera crews and satellite trucks had begun to set up. Some people began standing on cars and buses. Silhouettes began forming in the yellow windows of nearby towers. A sweet scent began to season the humid air as a beige Ford split the crowd, the only car that had been able to penetrate the throngs. The hum of Hollywood-style expectation pulsed through the clutter of humanity in waves.

"Is it—"

"Do you think—"

"It looks like—"

A flutter of children rushed the car and knocked on the windows.

"I'm pretty sure—"

"Oh, my God, you don't think—"

"He's better looking in per—"

The Ford stopped at the base of City Hall's steps. A squadron of policemen surrounded the car, their beefy arms crossed and their faces growling like hungry bulldogs. The passenger side of the car opened, and a mammoth, uniformed bohunk stepped out with a walkie-talkie and put his hand on the rear door. Wearing Ray Bans despite the creeping darkness, he reminded me of Jethro Clampett, only with thinner lips. A fat, black Sig Sauer semiautomatic sidearm was strapped to his hip. Seconds after Jethro pulled at the metallic car door handle, a tasseled cordovan loafer slipped to the sidewalk followed by a stiletto-sharp khaki pant cuff. When the figure of Mario Vanni emerged complete from the sedan, his name could be heard like a congregational chant:

"Vanni."

"It's Vanni."

"Look, Vanni."

"They've got Vanni."

The cameras swung before Vanni and Jethro, who had hooked Vanni's arm as if to promenade him to a gangland hoedown. Vanni's hands began to sparkle as the camera's lights fell upon them. He was handcuffed. Jethro's near-twin brother then slid from the backseat and took Vanni's other arm. The cameras homed in on the handcuffs. Despite his constraints, there was something freestyle and electric in the movement of his limbs in their sockets.

Al Just stepped forward, having been bumped up to regional royalty status through his Vanni coverage. "What's going on, Mario?"

Vanni, looking like a suburban executive wrongly collared at his flagstone barbecue, stepped toward the mike, which his captors allowed.

"How ya doin', Al?" Vanni said. "All I know is if they can do this to me, they can do it to you. But don't worry about me, I'll be out by the eleven o'clock news."

I smiled like a James Bond villain at Vanni's mastery of my coaching.

"Clever shindig you're putting on for a bunch of Philly wise guys, Don Vanni," Just shouted as the giant Clampett brothers guided a vulnerable, Muppet-like Vanni away from the cameras and into City Hall. Vanni smirked, and for the first time in the evening, I cursed myself for feeling so cocky. Stop the self-analysis, Jonah, and just make sure this works. *Entrances are wide, exits are narrow, boychik.*

I crept to the top of the steps of City Hall. When I turned around, I beheld waves of handheld white candles dotting the landscape of downtown Philadelphia like tiny ghosts as the identity of the Mafia turncoat was whispered about. The candles emitted fragrance, a subtle reformulation of Skin Bracer. Once I told Vanni what I wanted, he had a contact of his in North Jersey obtain—I didn't ask how—some of the raw materials that went into making the aftershave. Evelyn Woulders had not been the only focus group target to associate Skin Bracer with simpler times; about 40 percent of those surveyed made the link, too, which was a high enough figure for me.

"I hate that scent, Jonah," Cindi said into my telephone earpiece from her invisible perch in the crowd.

"You're not the demographic," I reminded her.

In a breaking news report, Just announced the name of Vanni's betrayer.

"The focus," Just stated, his eyebrow knowingly cocked, "is a man named Remo Stacciatore. Sources close to the investigation say that Stacciatore is a contract killer for Vanni who allegedly carried out the hits on drug dealers. He had reportedly admitted this in exchange for immunity from prosecution. I must underscore that, as of now, these are only rumors."

• • •

Philadelphia, New Jersey, and the whole Delaware Valley region have a history rich in pop music. With stars hailing from or living in the region including Frank Sinatra, Bruce Springsteen, Jon Bon Jovi, Frankie Avalon, Al Martino, Lola Falana, and Patti LaBelle, the Delaware Valley prides itself as being a breeding ground for musical talent. Dick Clark's *American Bandstand* had originally been broadcast from Philly. A promoter once unbelievably claimed that the powers that be chose Atlantic City for casino gambling due to the region's "greatest natural resource": music. From the heyday of Cherry Hill's Latin Casino in the sixties to the rise of regional rock talent like South Jersey poet Patti Smith, the Deuvilles, Hall & Oates, Todd Rundgren, the Hooters, Steely Dan's Donald Fagen of North Jersey, The Feelies, Southside Johnny and the Asbury Jukes, and Delaware's George Thorogood and the Destroyers, we blasted this music from speakers on flatbed trucks while the throngs waited for word on Vanni. Nor did we forget lesser-known but beloved local bands such as John Eddie and the Front Street Runners, the Yow Kings, Martin's Dam, and Fascist Julio and the Stranded Jellyfish.

On a giant screen in nearby Independence Hall, we played a short film that was essentially a montage of footage of famous Philadelphians, or famous people *in* Philly, near area landmarks. The local music accompanied the visuals.

The footage also showed local politicians ranging from William Penn to a string of Philly mayors like Frank Rizzo and Ed Rendell, and cinema stars of Philly-focused movies like Sylvester Stallone (*Rocky*), Katharine Hepburn (*The Philadelphia Story*), and Tom Hanks (*Philadelphia*). We spliced in the pope from his 1980 visit, trips to the city by Presidents Kennedy, Reagan, and Clinton, and soft-focus footage of Mario Vanni grilling hamburgers for hungry neighbors beneath the steel tusks of Lucy the Elephant. We ended with footage from the funeral of Philadelphia's Grace Kelly, the only one of us actually to achieve the royalty that the Shore's cash flow temples could only pose for.

Through a series of fronts, I recruited Reverend Clifford Harvey—Jesse Jackson printed on the fifth carbon—who claimed to have worked for Martin Luther King, Jr. Trouble checked this out and determined that he had been an eleven-year-old leafleter for a 1967 Philadelphia march. Good enough, the Internet didn't care, and we cobbled together a Web site collage mixing Reverend Harvey in with the civil rights heavies—King, Abernathy, Malcolm X. All I wanted was to hedge against any potential sentiment that Automatic Bart was being deliberately set up as a strategic foil for Mario Vanni.

When Reverend Harvey arrived outside of nearby Independence Hall, he climbed atop a raised prefab stage and solemnly acknowledged his parishioners with a popelike backhanded wave.

"America is not the land of opportunity," Harvey began.

"America is the land of paupertunity," he continued to cheers.

Overjoyed by the roar, Harvey said, "Justice may be blind but she ain't deaf and we want her to hear the cries of her people." *Criiiiiiieees of her peeeeeee-ple.*

"You know why we can't let Justice be deaf?"

"Yeah!" a random man boomed in a baritone. I couldn't see him but I pictured Barry White.

"Because we have a government that has framed an entire generation of black men." BIGOT COPS and FRAME-UP were among the more succinct messages plastered on signs.

"That's right!" the baritone man shouted again.

"And it's not just people of color who suffer. The government isn't always too particular about its targets of discrimination. We can't let Miss Justice send up an Italian man whose clothes are too nice for the government."

"Damned right!" Barry White boomed.

"And the thing is that Miss Justice does not want to discriminate. She wants us to be free. Justice is not the enemy. It is the men that have taken the cloth that blinds her and bound her hands with it so she can no longer hold the scales that would keep us free."

"Listen to the man, now!" Barry White concluded.

Next it was Ike Shackley's turn to address the rally. Shackley was head of the Philadelphia chapter of the Brotherhood of Shipping Workers, an enormously powerful union both nationwide and in the region.

"The persecution of the working people of this city is unprecedented," Shackley began. "Now I'm not one of these guys who see a conspiracy every time they turn around, but I'm starting to think that way." By the end of his speech, Shackley had linked the increase in local crime to an impossible amalgam of the city's business elite and Automatic Bart.

In press interviews away from the vigil's epicenter, DELVAC's Rhoda McNee invoked the memory of Bobby Kennedy and called for restrained, thoughtful attacks on crime. "Rushes to judgment punish everyone but the guilty. We must be ambiguous in our campaign to punish the real criminals. We must not just blame escaped goats," she wandered from the text. Not perfect, but it would do. Beneath Rhoda's name on the KBRO-TV screen was her psychic bribe from Cindi: "Kennedy family friend."

A local psychologist named Alonzo Mendez, whom Cindi dragged out from a community college, spoke on the air about the "healing power" of the "vigil."

At a booth near the Liberty Bell, children did finger paintings depicting freedom.

Boos echoed against the concrete when Sergeant Mike Pariso of the Philadelphia Police Department slipped down the steps of City Hall to speak to the cameras.

"I am here to clarify a few important misunderstandings," Pariso began. From the center of the rally, I watched Pariso on my handheld TV. Cindi high-fived me: Whenever a spokesman steps forward to clarify misunderstandings, it means that he has already lost the podium; the other side has seized the agenda.

"Number one," Pariso continued, his forefinger pointing, "Mario Vanni has not been arrested." He might as well have rammed that finger straight up his nose and downloaded a real goober.

"Number two, the police have no credible informants linking Mr. Vanni to the murder of these drug dealers. We will be dismissing an individual shortly whom we have not found to be credible.

"Number three, we urge the public not to believe everything they hear. There is a lot of misinformation floating around out there."

I smirked upon hearing the word "misinformation." My expression was accompanied by groaning in the audience that burped out along with Pariso's final sentence: "We will keep you posted as to any authentic developments in this case."

In the Information Age there is no such thing as misinformation. If it's out there, it's information. Even if it's wrong, it's information that is being processed, digested. Christ, if somebody eats spoiled cottage cheese, it's still food that has to go through the body. *Misinformation!* Just because the cottage cheese is bad doesn't make it misfood.

Al Just and the other evanjournalists began firing questions at Pariso as he climbed the steps of City Hall. He ignored the inquiries and the howls of betrayal that followed him like a wet terrier, the kind everyone has secretly kicked at least once in his life.

The oak doors at the top of the stairs opened, emitting a thin amber beam of light. The expectant multitudes roared their approval when Mario Vanni himself appeared and descended. One of his wingmen was "Quick Pat" Conti, his lawyer from Cherry Hill, so-named because his clients were often sprung from jail as fast as they had been hauled in. Conti had become notorious after he defended a mobster who was caught with cash and drugs in his pockets by successfully arguing that, "They were not my client's pants." The other guy standing there was a South Philly–type in a bad suit that he probably thought looked great because it glowed.

Vanni laughed like Kris Kringle and stepped up to the cameras. The professorial Conti stood beside him like a human exclamation point. Vanni waited until the cameramen got comfortable with the massive units on their shoulders.

"Look," he began, "I don't have a whole big speech." He sucked in his breath the way people do when they must stall their pulmonary systems so they don't cry.

"You've seen with your own eyes what the government can do to a man if they don't like him. They drag this poor Remo guy in and try to make him say stuff that he doesn't believe. Now I'm going home to my family and that's that!"

A Puerto Rican child popped onto the scene and whispered something in Vanni's ear. Whatever it was, Vanni acted happy to hear it, throwing his head back open-mouthed and staging a howl. Cindi and I could see his gold fillings sparkle on camera. This was vintage Reagan: find a kid, engage the kid, and no matter what happens, demonstrate that the kid has reached you. Vanni pinched the kid on the chin and slipped into the rear of his Mercedes, which had oozed before the curb outside City Hall.

Conti said a few words about witch-hunts and climbed into the passenger seat of the Mercedes. The monster car sped away, and I felt the tailwind rustle my hair in an imposing shiver of autumn. The red and yellow taillights winked against the smirking chrome bumper, vanishing in the direction of the Ben Franklin Bridge over to Jersey.

A hard-looking woman in an orange halter top shouted, "Any other dagos you wanna bust, Pariso? Uncle Fuckin' Tom!" Those surrounding her applauded with congratulatory whoop whoops.

The South Philly guy who had been standing behind Vanni stepped into the lights, blinking. "Hey, hey," he began. "All I'm gonna say is that my name is Remo Stacciatore. These cops, all they want is for me to say that Mario Vanni had me kill those drug guys. They wanted me to level all of these charges and alligators. I says to them, 'Look, I got mad cow disease. I don't remember killin' nobody, and I don't remember because I didn't do it. Mario Vanni didn't kill nobody and either did I.'"

The reporters inched closer toward Stacciatore. I could tell by the way his eyebrows arched at the laughter of the crowd that he was inclined to step into the cameras, the opposite direction from where I wanted him. His time on stage was over. I reluctantly sneaked in behind Al Just and stared Remo down, borrowing one of Vanni's video snarls. I drew my index finger across my throat in a slitting motion. Remo nodded, hurt by my short circuit, then he vanished into the diminishing returns of patsydom.

While my finger was still on my throat, Al Just turned around and saw me. He tilted his head in a curious way and his eyes flashed in a digital readout: "If my father hadn't been Mouse Yutzel, I could have . . ." I felt my lower back tighten in terror and pretended, lamely, that I had just been scratching my neck. I did not run; I just kept scratching my neck. Just—I could feel his eyes still on me—backed away slowly and began darting his eyes between Remo Stacciatore and me, lost in the aroma of cheap, but familiar, aftershave.

I escaped between a series of metal tables that Cindi and DELVAC had set aside for press. I didn't recognize any of the reporters, except for Al Just, who was melting down in a polyethylene cup of beer. He had been scooped and scammed—Frankie Shrugs had his finale by validating the Internet "leaks" about Vanni's arrest—something that reporters never report. Most of the ones at the table were with the print media. One woman said disapprovingly to a scruffy-looking man with a camera, "Some show." Scruffy responded, "Yeah, but we came."

I felt safe inside a metallic silver, bullet-shaped truck parked before the Rohm & Haas building on Independence Mall. From a little round window, I could see Al Just glancing around angrily. I stepped away into a darker part of the truck. A nerdy slacker named Justin typed a handful of coordinates into a computer keyboard. A sneeringly pretty young woman sat beside him paging through *Cosmopolitan*. I thought about how right Irv the Curve had been about smorgasbroads. I could tell by the way she moved her lips when she read that she believed that the magazine contained real life—the pillow fights with tan, whippet men with hairless bodies and the cavalcade of advice columns that began and ended with the words, "You deserve . . ." From their appearance, I didn't have confidence that these kids could do anything right, which made me momentarily angry with Cindi for hiring them. My life was in their fingertips. A hungry satellite that hovered, batlike, above the Gulf of Mexico registered Justin's efforts by spitting out a long list numbers in a digital spray of goo.

My old video buddy Diamonds emerged from a neighboring editing room with a parrot on his shoulder and handed Cindi a videotape. Cindi accepted the beta-size videotape of a swaggering, loved—and free—Mario Vanni.

The *Cosmo* girl put down her magazine and typed something else into the computer, which triggered a hydraulic humming sound on the roof of the mobile studio. She nodded to Cindi, who held the tape against a heavy white machine that sucked it into its gut. The computer screen in front of Justin registered the insertion with the blue and pregnant word "Receiving." I reached over Justin's shoulder and pressed the lethal Send button, spraying billions of giga-Vannis across the galaxy.

In news stations across the country, assistant producers reviewed a real-time posting of news footage that was available on the satellite. Our offering had been included. With a few points and clicks, local news shows could download our videotape.

We stayed inside the truck and tuned into the four local TV stations that featured extensive coverage of the vigil. All of them had pulled Diamonds's edited montage down from the satellite. Cindi was sure that many other stations across the region would use the footage, too. The montage featured rally shots combined with short bursts of prerecorded wisdom from Mario Vanni, who turned his beaming face mimicking the moon slipping into darkness. I had stolen this slo-mo, soft-focus look from my favorite old advertisement for Shasta, the one they would run when my mother and I watched Wimbledon so long ago. Dorkus E-mailed digital versions to his network of Vanniphiles around the country.

Many outlets picked up Vanni's Almighty Message: "I guess what these people are trying to say is they want to feel safe. I understand that. I'm one of 'em." "Look, I tell everyone that I know to stay away from drugs. Drugs scare me, and I'm not a timid guy. I'm an old-fashioned guy." "I turn on *Action News* and turn it right off. You didn't have this crazy stuff going on when I was a kid. I wish I could turn back the clock, don't know what else I can do. . . ."

I crept out of the truck and looked both ways for reporters. I didn't see anyone problematic, so I maneuvered between thirsty protestors toward the bowels of the city. Hiding among the departing throngs on the platform of the High Speed Line, the local transit system over to Jersey, I wiped my brow with a red bandana. Come on, damn train. My nerves were on edge despite the success of the vigil. I began to stuff my stolen cell phone into my backpack when a muscular hand fell upon my shoulder. I swung around, slapping it away.

Al Just.

I jerked my neck in the opposite direction, pretending that someone else in the crowd had reached out for me.

"You, with the phone," Just said.

"Me?"

"Yeah, I know you."

The lights of the oncoming train reflected against the metal rails. Come on! People began to take note of Just. As the train rolled closer, I reached into my pocket and pulled out a wad of cash with my right hand. With my left, I pushed Just backward. He fell on his ass, his feeble ponytail grazing the pavement. I threw my cash at him and shouted, "Take it! Police!" Just's jaw fell open, bewildered by my diversion, as I backed onto the train. My ground began moving; the former Alvin Yutzel stood still. But I saw the bastard's mouth move as my train rumbled into Philadelphia's ribcage. As if he were a saved soul, he shouted, "He took de money and run Venezuela!"

"*Kinahora*, Jonah," Irv the Curve said as we walked barefoot along the surf on the morning after the rally. He kept holding up the front page of the Philly tabloid, the *Daily News*. There were two photos. The one on the left was of Sergeant Pariso pursing his lips like a Holy Roller. The other was of Vanni's car pulling away from City Hall. The massive headline read, "OOPS!"

"Looks like the cops fucked up good," Irv added. If Irv's ears had had tongues, they would have been panting.

"They didn't fuck up at all. We fucked them up. That cheap move with the Italian police sergeant didn't help them any."

We trudged a few feet toward England to stand shin-deep in the ocean. I kept it simple, noncyber. "We planted information in the press linking Vanni with the hits," I added. "We got a good buzz going. Vanni didn't kill any of these guys. We just loudly denied responsibility within the news cycle for things that had already happened. I have a friend who's good with police scanners.

"Every time I got word on a killing, we called Al Just to claim that Vanni ordered the murders. Meanwhile, publicly, we expressed outrage. Al Just needed a story. He thought his source was solid because every one of these guys really turned up dead. We paid some locals to say they wrote Vanni letters asking for his help. We've got more envelopes moving around this city than the post office. No law against that."

"Yeah, but Jonah, a guy like Just is no idiot."

"But he's desperate. He wants to be a star again. The mob and this racial shit are his franchises, and he'll report what he needs to report to keep them profitable. We timed it so that most of these calls—and the other chat—came close enough to his broadcast so he wouldn't have time to really check. *If* he wanted his story."

"You weasel!"

Irv was so proud I couldn't spring Just's pursuit of me yet. I needed this adulation, however fleeting.

"Once the press ran with the 'playground pusher' stories, Vanni's denials were seen as admissions. Vanni's capos found a wise guy wanna-be, this Remo Stacciatore. They had Remo go to the cops and say he'd consider admitting that he did the hits for Vanni in exchange for immunity from prosecution. We got word to Just, not to mention half the world, that a top Vanni button man had been flipped by the authorities. Just figures it's his source. The police wouldn't comment, which was interpreted as an admission."

"You hire a couple of ballagoolahs that look like marshals to escort Vanni, 'perp walk' style, into City Hall, handcuffed," Irv reasoned. "Everybody thinks their savior has been arrested."

"Right. We shipped the protestors in using Vanni's capos."

"What the hell was Vanni doing in there all that time? In City Hall?"

"He was reading over this book I gave him that he liked."

"Brass balls."

"Anyway, Remo, right on schedule, came down with mad cow disease. Vanni was released—walked out, really. The police then denied what the public had already seen with their own eyes. The more the cops denied that an arrest had taken place, the more the whole thing looked like a cover-up, which I knew from my polls would be the reaction."

"And everybody thinks that Vanni's God," Irv laughed. "God who can take care of the devil, because he says up front that he'll be out by eleven—and he is! Nice touch!"

"That was all Vanni's idea," I said. "The guy's incredibly smart. He's caught on to my racket well."

"Mickey always said Vanni was smart. That's why he wants to

go straight. Straight is smart, Jonah." A grandfatherly expression of concern grew around Irv's eyes. "What's wrong?"

"Just is coming for me," I said, feeling like a jumpy Nixon aide.

"There's nobody more dangerous than a guy who's been knocked on his ass," Irv said. The cool sea-foam suddenly stung. Could Irv have known about what happened on the subway platform? He had eyes everywhere, I swear.

"What do you see, Irv?"

"I see a boy who was always chased become a man who is always chased. I see the stakes rising."

She Had Strong
Opinions the Way
Sad People Do

"We don't tell people something else in my family."

CARVIN' MARVIN AND MORT THE SNORT WERE OUT DOING whatever old gangsters do before sunset. Mrs. Pinsky was back by the pool sniffing a railing. Edie would swing by in an hour and we'd have dinner at Ventura's in Margate and go for a walk in Ocean City where we didn't know anybody. I had always wanted to see what the cash flow temples looked like from over there.

I headed up the stairs and slid open the door of my little closet. I had stored Mickey's klezmer CDs here. They didn't have professional covers, only Mickey's writing. I thought maybe Edie would want to listen to them in the car. There were no song names written, only the word "Concert" and a list of dates, presumably when the concerts had been recorded. Oddly, one of the dates listed was my birthday, last year. The date didn't make sense: Mickey could not have been at a concert. He had been with me the whole day.

I took the CDs downstairs and opened a cabinet where Carvin' Marvin kept his collection of Mathis and Sinatra albums. I carefully opened the player and inserted one disk into the machine. At first, I thought that I had accidentally turned on the radio as opposed to the CD player, but the register showed that the CD player was on.

I heard gruff voices, not the tones of klezmorim getting ready to do a number.

My heart began to race and, one by one, I slapped each CD onto the player. There wasn't a note of music on them. That vertiginous feeling, my lifelong companion, consumed me as I lay flat. As soon as my head touched the carpet, a knock fell against the door of Chez Guevara. I instinctively reached down and felt my ankle. My gun slipped out easily from the strap. I stuffed the CDs under a corner table and pressed a sweating eye against the peephole. Reality had canceled out my vertigo.

It was Edie, her eyes small and red. Her lips were purple like a cold child's. I returned the gun to my ankle strap and opened the door. Edie's right hand was in her leather purse.

"What's wrong?"

She just seethed, perfectly silent, witchy.

I drew my hand to brush aside a stray, sun-bleached strand of hair, but she swatted me away. I backed up, more terrified now than I had been when I was told that my mother was sick, that my father had died, that I needed to pack my suitcase because we were leaving the country, that Mickey would be arrested when our airplane landed in Philadelphia, and that "Mario Vanni wants to talk to you." Long before Edie was dropped into my life by a God who had decided to even things out for me, the *prospect* of Edie was what fueled me. Edie meant hope. I was not romantically deformed; it was possible to be one of the young couples that ran along the beach, with their babies in those jogging contraptions. Edie's existence was God's way of asserting that there was, in fact, time. Until I saw her red eyes.

I backed onto one of the groovy couches.

Me again: "What's wrong?"

Edie still didn't answer, but she did sit down. Her eyes bore into me. Drill bit eyes. Tears streamed down her cheeks. I reached forward to hug her, but she shifted back, her hand still obscured in her purse. She exhaled, her eyes growing even smaller, giving her a two-dimensional appearance. I was terrified.

I don't know how long she silently huffed at me, but I felt myself age. My chest was tight, my head spun like a gyroscope. I was losing her. I heard Noel's laughter in the canyons of my skull.

Edie drew in one deep, long, horrible breath. "The father of one of my new students took me aside. Just now. He sent the little girl to the car. He said to me, 'Ms. Morris, your new boyfriend is a mobster. He works for Mario Vanni. If you hang out with him, you're likely to die. Just thought you should know. Thanks for the lesson.' Before he left"—Edie huffed—"he took out a skinny knife and sliced my shirt. Right down my chest."

"God, Edie, are you okay?"

It was all coming true. I had brought her into this, and now I was going to get her killed.

"I'm okay, in a homicidal way."

"I'm so sorry."

"Before you're sorry, what about denying you're a mobster first."

"I'm not a mobster."

"How reassuring." She pulled her hand from her purse and showed me a pistol. "I've been carrying this since my last music lesson."

"You own a gun?"

"I have for years. My dad taught me to shoot. I never used it for protection until now."

I described Noel to her. It was he who had visited her with a rent-a-kid and his eye-piercing stiletto. I thought about Moses in the desert killing the Egyptian. If I was ever to get a divine signal to smite Noel, this was it. I thought I might be losing my conscience, but looking at Edie's wet, puffy face, it dawned on me that perhaps I had found it. There was a moral center to my universe, and she was sitting beside me.

"He works for Mario Vanni. He's been on my case since Mickey's funeral. You will never see the child or him again."

"Why not?"

"Because she's not his daughter and he accomplished his mission. Scaring you away from me."

Edie slapped the gun back into her purse. "I know how to shoot," she said matter-of-factly.

"Do you want to shoot me?"

"Why is this Noel after you?"

"He thinks I have Mickey's money. Or that I'm too close to

Vanni. Or that I'm a pawn in his plan to become the boss. Or something."

"Do you have Mickey's money?"

"No."

"Do you work for Vanni?"

"Yes. I'm doing some polling for him. I had no choice."

"When did you plan on telling me this?"

"I didn't want to tell you at all. I wanted to resolve it."

"In the meantime, this murderer comes to see me."

"I'm sorry."

"I'm not from that world, Jonah. My family's not from that world. We don't understand it. I don't understand it. You may be sorry, but I don't know if I can take this." The mild veins beneath her eyes were growing blue.

"My mother couldn't take it either," I said. "It's what got her. I know it. She knew about Mickey's world."

Edie leaned down on a pillow and closed her eyes. She seemed to have truly fallen asleep. As she rested, I became momentarily at peace with murder as I saw Noel's knife slicing across Edie's chest. There is no grief deeper than that linked to a future lost. This is why people mourn the deaths of children more than they do the deaths of the elderly. It is because of a future robbed. A future canceled is a multiple homicide. This had swiftly become the underpinning of the murderous jihad I wanted to launch against Noel. The Sanhedrin could kiss my ass.

When Edie woke up ten minutes later, her eyes were puffy from crying. She was no longer the serene blue-blooded Methodist I had met on the Boardwalk. Bluebloods aren't warlike; they already have everything. When angry, she took on the quality of a street urchin. This woman was trained to "go heavy," as Mickey would have said, not a sign of contentment.

I was afraid to touch Edie, seeing how she swatted me away before. I could see she wasn't happy with her appearance by the way she tilted her head away from the light. I knelt by the sofa. She held out her arms and I climbed within her reach.

"What's with you, anyway?" Edie returns from the pines.

"What do you mean?"

"Why aren't you married? Is it these secrets that you keep?"

"People leave me. Like I think you're doing now."

"How do you know I'm leaving you?"

"Christ, Edie, you came with a gun."

"Maybe I came with a gun to stay with you. From what I can tell, I may need a weapon to stay and fight."

I exhaled and my head fell into my hands. "What do you mean, stay and fight?"

"I mean, I want to know you, right now. Tell me about your parents. What happened to them? What about other women?"

"What does that have to do with staying and fighting?"

"Tell me, goddamnit! You were raised by gangsters. I can only imagine what you were taught. Tell me now."

"My dad died first."

"How old was he?"

"About the age I am now."

"I see."

"It was an embolism or aneurysm. Something like that."

"Who told you that?"

"My mother did."

"You don't believe it, do you?"

"I have no evidence either way."

"That's the official spin?"

"I don't know. I didn't ask for an autopsy report."

"Do you suspect that your grandfather had something to do with it?"

"Suspect? I suspect everything and everyone. Don't look at me like it's a disease. It's a rational response to my world."

"I don't think you're diseased, Jonah."

I shrugged, but Edie persisted. "What did your father do? What was his job?"

"He did something with sports. Boxing, mostly. I don't know exactly what he did. I read something once after I grew up about some fight in Bayonne that was supposed to be fixed, but the guy didn't go down like he was supposed to. I know that some of Mickey's friends were in boxing, too. I wonder about it sometimes, but what good does it do? Everybody's dead."

"What about your mother? What happened to her?"

"Some infection grew inside. That's all they told me. It was not long after my dad died. She was crying all the time, screaming at my grandparents. Then she got sick and quieted down."

"You don't suspect that she died because of something in Mickey's world?"

"Sure I do. Maybe that's what she was screaming about. She was like me. She knew what went on, but she deserted me so that I'd have to live inside it. She just couldn't act on what she knew the way I can."

"How do you act on what you know?"

"I do it in my job. Let somebody else get the infection. I don't care."

"Bullshit! I don't think you're that tough."

"You give me too much credit. All right, sometimes I care about the fallout of what I do. Sometimes."

"What about other times?"

"Other times I figure, fuck 'em."

"I see."

"You wanted the truth. You wanted to know me. Is this over, Edie?"

"No. Tell me about your women."

"I have my good friend Cindi, you know that."

"Do you sleep with her?"

"No."

"Did you ever?"

"No."

"Who was your first girlfriend? I'm talking sex here. That will tell me something. And don't hit me with another question to my question."

"It's not something I've ever even been open with my friends about."

"I'm not one of your friends. I was planning to be something more. I won't spend my life with a phantom."

I began to break away, searching for a convenient place in the room to hide my eyes. I couldn't look straight at her so I found a random dot on the wall to stare at. She permitted this avoidance.

"I met her on the Boardwalk one weekend when Mickey and Deedee went out of town. I was sixteen. She was older, I guess twenty-five. It was when they blew up the old Lenape Hotel to make way for the Golden Prospect. Mickey left town so it wouldn't look like he had anything to do with the Lenape coming down. The papers were making a whole thing out of organized crime controlling casinos, so Mickey wanted to lay low.

"This girl—woman—started talking to me during the countdown. She was pretty forward. I could have never initiated anything like that. I took her to dinner at Carmine's. I spent the money that Mickey had left for me.

"She was so beautiful, but in a flashy way, and I felt like a complete freak out in public with her. The hostess was obnoxious. There was a little sign with movable letters that read PLEASE LET OUR HOSTESS SEAT YOU. When the lady turned her back, I rearranged the letters to read PLEASE LET SOUR HOSTESS EAT YOU. She thought that was brilliant."

"What do you remember about her?"

"I remember that she had strong opinions the way sad people do. Mostly about men. Her name was Margeaux with an *x*. I figured out later that she was a pro."

"A pro?"

"A whore. Mickey and the guys sent her. Mickey had been worried about my not being social. I didn't even touch her until the next morning. We fell asleep on the living room sofas. She woke up crying."

"Why didn't you touch her?"

"Because I thought it was wrong. She looked like . . . like me, a little kid without her makeup. She told me later that her real name was Debbie Miller. She was from Tuckerton. Anyway, the more shit I figured out Mickey was into, the straighter I got. Did Mickey think I couldn't read the papers? Did he think I couldn't go to the library and read about those men who were buried in the Pine Barrens? I figured that women either leave or turn out to be whores or something."

Edie said nothing, perhaps because I was a man working for the rackets. A man with a bull's-eye on his head. A man "knocking on forty."

"Tell me your middle name," I said.

I saw the subtle dimple in her cheek for the first time this evening. She was not leaving.

"Seven Angels," she said, averting her gaze toward a photo of
Dean Martin.

"Edie Seven Angels?"

"Yes."

"You're serious?"

"Yes."

"What's the significance of Seven Angels?"

"That's for another time. I came here carrying a gun because I
want to stay, not leave. I know it will be a fight, which is why I
came armed, but I can't fight unless I know what I'm up against."

I covered my mouth and closed my eyes. The redness in Edie's
face had gone down, and she had stopped crying. I could not tell
if fear, anger, or empathy dominated her mood.

"Do you want protection from Noel? I can arrange it," I said.

"I'm a very good shot. No, I don't want protection. I can handle
the frontier. What about you? You are in danger from these men."

"I am carrying a gun. I have shot guns all my life, but I never
had to carry one until now."

Edie turned her head and sighed.

"Do you want me to drive you to your parents?"

"And tell them what? That the mob paid me a visit?"

"No. You can tell them something else."

"No, Jonah, we don't tell people something else in my family.
We don't do something else."

"Yet you know how to use a gun. Talk to me, cowgirl."

"I can't let everything loose on command. All I know is that I
want to have you and not these other people. These Noels."

"It will take a little more time. Edie, you are all that I have. I
know it's awful. Everybody thinks somebody like me would feel
safe having had a grandfather like Mickey, but no one could feel
less safe. I don't expect you to understand this."

"Why would I understand this?"

"You knew Mickey. You said he seemed like a nice old man."

"But I didn't have to deal with what was behind that."

"No, but I did. It's a part of me, and no one is sorrier than I am."

"You still need a road map out, Jonah."

"I have one, Edie. You just got pulled into it before it was re- solved. Not all unresolved crises are due to bad planning. Knowing what you now know, what would you do?"

"I don't know the how, only the why."

"What is the why?"

"It's better to be a living hunter than a dead bear. There is nobody more hateful than a willing victim."

"But how do you live with the sin?"

"Of all people to ask such a question . . . You've been living with sin your whole life. You grapple with it."

I packed away Mickey's klezmer CDs and threw a blanket over them. Edie began driving to Batsto. I followed her in my Cherokee and held my breath the whole time. While Edie Seven Angels slept back at her apartment, I studied her silhouette against the pine moonlight. I had the impulse to bay at the giant white sphere. She awoke briefly and whispered, "Of all the people you've lost, whom do you miss the most?"

"Deedee and my mom," I answered automatically.

"Why them?"

"They knew I wasn't tough. From the first day, they knew."

"I know, too."

"I know you do, Ede."

As she returned to slumber, my mind drifted to the CDs, to Ong, to cranberries, to Noel, Just, Vanni, and to the funereal soul on the Boardwalk. And the haunting name Seven Angels? Either all this added up, or I was a Shore breeze away from being committed to Ancora Mental Hospital. The only variable I understood was the plague that Mickey had left me: the CDs. I knew that they had been made to protect me.

Dead Men Are the
Loudest Talkers

"I'm goin' in fuckin' reverse here!"

MARIO VANNI STOOD BENEATH LUCY THE ELEPHANT'S OPEN, tusked mouth like a man resigned to being swallowed whole. His eyes were as black as wet slate, which would have made him appear to be furious had it not been for the loosened muscles around his neck.

He knew about Just, I thought. No, that wasn't it. Not yet.

Hollywood never reflects that the rackets are a perversion of Italian life, not a model for it. Honesty, however, has no sex appeal, so the lenses focus on the glamorous malignancies. A man named Michael DiRenzo decided he wasn't having any of Mario Vanni's vigil bullshit and decided to make *his* Italians the story.

DiRenzo was head of the Italian Anti-Bigotry Coalition. Up until recently, the IABC had consisted of a group of Italian professionals and intellectuals who got together a few times a year to host festivals and speakers about Italian history. A mole within the IABC got word back to Vanni that DiRenzo was planning a news conference at an unspecified time and place where he would announce that Vanni did not represent all Italian Americans.

Vanni had called me down to the elephant via pager. I left my gunslinging girlfriend and launched my Cherokee as fast as I could.

Things were still raw with Edie, but the threat at the other end of that pager was mortal.

"Look, Jonah," Vanni began, "you got me to go with you on this idea of yours, and I thought it was going pretty well. Now, all of a sudden, I got my own people about to protest against me. See what you got me into?"

"I understand," I said, embracing my shit-eating role here.

"I don't want to hear you understand." *Unnerstann.* "I want to hear that this conference isn't gonna happen and my own people won't turn against me."

"The IABC has never actually been *for* you."

"But *against? Against?* This isn't the face time you sold me on. I'm goin' in fuckin' reverse here!"

Petie walked by, clearly enjoying seeing me roasting on Vanni's spit.

"Hey, Mario, I don't want to be outta line, but I could just clip this DiRenzo guy," Petie offered.

I instinctively slapped my forehead.

Vanni held out his hand in a "calm down" gesture.

"Petie, I love ya, but you've got to be the biggest babbo this side of Palermo. You hit a guy like that, it's all over. We get nothing."

"Yeah, but he can't talk too loud when he's dead."

"Read a fuckin' history book, Petie. Read a book, would you." *Wudja.* "Dead men are the loudest talkers. They get to be heroes. Martin Luther King. Malcolm X. The Kennedys. Geronimo. Jesus!"

Petie walked away dejected, blaming me for his humiliation.

"Mario, I'm not happy about DiRenzo, either," I said, "but it's collateral damage. All generals take side damage—"

"Don't start with any Holy Roman Empire bullshit on me now. I don't want any collateral damage, you understand?"

"I do—"

Vanni stepped toward me and reached out as if he were going to grab my collar. He stopped short. His eyes dissolved into tiny black pinholes, the same look that I had seen that day in media training. At the time, I found it to be an interesting feature, clinically. Now that his black eyes and twitching veins bore in on me, I felt as if Vanni himself, not Noel, would kill me. I despised Vanni at this moment and wanted to join up with DiRenzo and publicly chastise every movie director who ever glamorized these bastards.

I felt a momentary loss of bladder control but then gained it back. It's one thing to disappoint a boss. It's another to piss on him.

I called Mario aside.

"What is it?" he barked.

"How attached are you to that Mercedes?"

I got in touch with Vanni's mole in DiRenzo's organization. He wouldn't talk to me. I spoke with Noel, who told me with his earnest eyes that he would do everything he could. He put his hand over his heart when he said it. A half hour later he called me at Chez Guevara and said that the mole had "clammed up." Not even he, Noel, could get him to cooperate.

Cindi determined through her media contacts that the news conference was to be held at a little American Legion outpost behind a high school on the west side of Cherry Hill. We drove out to Mount Misery to talk over the crisis with Dorkus. His real name was Bruce. His appearance was precisely what I thought it would be: He was tall, skinny, and pimply with mousy brown hair. Dorkus-Bruce also had a head that was way to big for his body. It was a peculiar shape, too, with a disproportionate amount of skull jutting out in back.

Cindi and I were nervous wrecks, but Dorkus-Bruce was perfectly calm as he processed the challenge at hand. He got on-line and began browsing through different sites, seemingly uninterested in what we were telling him.

He located the IABC's Web site and coldly clicked around the screen. He then zoomed in his chair clear across the room to a window. "Hey!" he yelled outside. A profoundly unattractive—and even geekier—boy of about fourteen emerged. This one had kinky black hair that grew out of his head in waves. He looked like a Chia Pet. While I had not been a stud at that age, I was thinking that these two yahoos would never—and I truly meant never—get laid for as long as they lived. Cindi must have been thinking the same thing as the two geeks spoke, because she whispered something to me about never wanting to shake hands with them.

Dorkus-Bruce showed the other kid something on the IABC Web site, and the two of them began laughing like hyenas.

I could see by the self-congratulatory look on DiRenzo's face that he was pleased by the turnout. A well-built guy who looked like a phys ed teacher, DiRenzo patted a heavy-set woman, whom I took to be his flack, on the shoulder. I lingered in the back of the stuffy room with a fake press pass hanging over my belt and a slender notepad sticking up from my back pocket.

Three local camera crews came, filling the room with all kinds of silver stands, boxes, and wires. A half dozen print reporters showed. DiRenzo opened with a statement about how he deplored violence. He praised DELVAC for its vigilance in fighting crime but characterized many of its efforts as being "misguided," a word that really means you've got shit for brains.

"My greatest concern is that the popular culture's indifference to Mario Vanni's alleged role in stopping crime is, in effect, an endorsement of the man and his way of life. Furthermore, implicit in both the lighthearted support of Mr. Vanni and the deeply felt belief among some that he is fighting crime is the assumption that his values are Italian values. They most certainly are not.

"Mr. Vanni and his Cosa Nostra are hideous mutations. In his world, you're not allowed to acknowledge the existence of the Mafia, or even to use the word. Today, I'll use the word: Mafia. There is a Mafia. The government says that Mario Vanni runs it, and I believe them.

"Every community has people who shame them. However, Italian Americans have been particularly harmed by how the news and entertainment media willfully interpret the remarks of Italian criminals to be sagacious, their violence to be justified, and their way of life honorable. This is a perversion that I, on behalf of Italian Americans, deplore.

"Mario Vanni is a criminal and a disgrace. No one of any ethnicity should support him or believe for a moment any of his propaganda. His is one story that doesn't have two sides. It has one side—a bad side. I call on everyone in the Delaware Valley, especially the fine people of DELVAC, to repudiate all implications that Mario Vanni is anything but a common criminal."

DiRenzo, wiping his brow, bit his upper lip and opened the floor to questions. Virtually all of them were sympathetic. One was disturbing and brought a tear to the eye of a pretty but nervous-looking woman I pegged as DiRenzo's wife.

"Sir, do you believe you are in any personal danger from Mr. Vanni?" a young woman in the second row asked.

"Yes, but if I am hurt—or worse—it won't be a very hard crime to solve. Everyone will know who did it: the Mafia."

I restrained my compulsion to tell DiRenzo that his fellow Italian had spared his life.

I met Cindi in her office after the news conference. She contacted the old photographer Lloyd Hernsen and asked him to release to the press the photo he had taken earlier in the summer of Vanni with little Carmela Diaz. I had been holding it for a snag like this. Within eighteen hours, thirty million people in the Delaware Valley and beyond gathered round to view this tender moment between the Don and a little girl he had never met. From the right.

One hour and a half before DiRenzo's news conference began, Mario Vanni's white Mercedes was blown to metal morsels on the Dorset Avenue Bridge at the Jersey Shore. Traffic was snarled for hours, complicated by the D-Day-style invasion of police and news helicopters and media vans from inland. These were media that would have otherwise flocked to Di Renzo's anti-Vanni soiree in Cherry Hill.

The authorities were attempting to determine if there had been anyone inside the car. Al Just had speculated that someone must have been in the car because the bridge was too narrow to accommodate parking. "But it remains to been seen if there's something else to this," he sneered. At me.

A witness claimed on TV to have seen a black man flee from the scene of the explosion. A police officer said something on camera about Vanni's car being the only one on the bridge. This was odd, he explained, because the Dorset Avenue Bridge was heavily trafficked. "It's a miracle that there were no other cars on the bridge," he said.

An hour after the explosion, a quarter mile from the bridge, Mario Vanni climbed from the waterway onto a Boston Whaler belonging to a few Villanova kids. They had delivered a soaking Vanni to the authorities amid an applauding crowd. He had shared a simple alibi. Sparks flew from the car's vents. He rolled from the car, jumped into the water (the Dorset Avenue Bridge was low), and hid near the shore until it was safe to surface.

What Mario didn't share, of course, was that he himself had detonated his beloved Mercedes by remote control after abandoning it on the bridge. Trouble had rigged the explosive, and a few of Vanni's boys had stopped the cars that approached the bridge.

That evening, I approached Vanni as he was cooking hamburgers on a grill beneath Lucy's mouth. From my angle, Lucy appeared to be a mutant house pet waiting to be fed.

"Top of the evening to you," I greeted Vanni, self-satisfied.

"What am I, a fuckin' leprechaun?" *Lepper-conn.* Vanni's eyes remained trained on the grill.

Noel appeared from behind Lucy's leg. He grabbed a handful of potato chips and made them vanish like liquid. Frankie Shrugs, Petie, and Noel were holding paper plates up to Vanni, who dished them each a hamburger. I know he saw me out of the corner of his eye, but he didn't acknowledge me right away. I kept walking closer.

"I'm told that DiRenzo still had his news conference," Vanni said without looking up.

"Yes, he did."

Vanni gave his men a snarl, to which they snarled sympathetically back. Everybody loves it when College fucks up. Murderers or not, all clients are the same: A consultant is only as good as his last miracle. When you fail, your failure is the essence of who you are and have always been.

"He get cameras?" Vanni asked.

"Yes, sir."

Another exchange of happy snarls masked as disgust.

"You made me blow up my fuckin' car and he still gets cameras. I turned on *Action News* but didn't see anything. How come?"

"The conference didn't go quite as Mr. DiRenzo expected."

Mario and his boys all turned toward me.

"Yeah, how's that? DiRenzo get stage fright?"

"No, he did pretty well, actually."

"Then why are you so cool about the whole thing?"

"DiRenzo was talking to our cameras. They were camera crews, but they weren't real news people. They belonged to us. I had to give him cameras."

I shot Noel grade school eyes. *Nanny nanny foo foo.* Screw him, he already wanted to kill me.

"Where were the real reporters?" Mario asked.

What Dorkus had found on-line as Cindi and I sweated bullets was DiRenzo's media advisory. He hacked onto the site and changed the time and location of the news conference. He found IABC's computerized media list by rooting around for a while and then sent out the bogus media advisory. Dorkus then, along with his mutant little friend, launched a massive denial-of-service attack on the IABC's Web site. This type of attack was done by causing computers throughout the Delaware Valley simultaneously to dial into IABC's home page so there could be no real access to the site. At the same time, Cindi's crew repeatedly called to RSVP in the affirmative to DiRenzo's news conference so he'd think that every-thing was humming along smoothly and, accordingly, not bother to monitor the IABC's home page. She sent a handful of friends to the news conference along with some of Eddie and Diamonds's video goofballs.

"Mother-a-God," Vanni said. I thought about adding that the whole thing had been rigged by a couple of horny freaks at summer camp in the Pine Barrens, but I decided to keep my mouth shut. I wanted Vanni and his gang to envision me inside of a CIA-sponsored submarine orchestrating my digital scam.

"By the way, Noel, your mole clammed up on us. Wouldn't tell us a thing, useless bastard." I kept my eyes on Noel when I said this. I wanted Vanni to see my anger and associate it with Noel.

"Fuckin' Jones." Vanni shook his head and smirked. Noel gave me a hollow thumbs-up.

Vanni called me aside. "I don't like the look in your eye."

"We've still got a problem, Mario."

"You're the fuckin' Grim Reaper, I swear. What's the problem?"

"Al Just. He has a good sense that you have outside help."

"He said as much a few weeks ago," Mario said with a counterfeit laugh.

"But now he knows it's me."

"Well, son, he better unknow it pretty fuckin' quick."

I stayed and had a hamburger just so Vanni could see me chewing slowly, suffering. Midmeal, a kid I didn't recognize delivered a special edition of the *Atlantic City Packet*. A huge photograph of Mario's disintegrated Mercedes appeared on the front page. The headline read "Miracle Mario." The photo of Vanni with little Carmela Diaz and Mario's predestruction Mercedes appeared on page two.

When I was finished with dinner, I flipped over my paper plate and began taking notes on the Vanni program's coup de grâce— God willing, a diversion that would get Mario his license and me my freedom from South Jersey.

Life Cheats

"It's an old Pine Barrens tale."

S ACAJAWEA!"
     This is what Joey D. would say to people before Mr. Hicks's
English class began. Joey D. would walk right up to someone—
usually a good-looking (or timid) girl—grab his crotch, and utter,
"Sacajawea," the name of the famous Indian heroine. This battle
cry occasionally crossed the line and became, "Suck my jawea,"
which, of course, had been the implication all along. When Mr.
Hicks heard it, I was sure he would kill Joey D. on the spot. Instead, Mr. Hicks shook his head at the warped brilliance of Joey
D.'s ability to link anything to a dick joke.

     Mr. Hicks was deeply proud of my success in politics, although
I think he had really hoped I'd become a writer. I sent him a few
speeches I had written over the years, which I think dampened his
vicarious ambitions.

     Mr. Hicks was eager to meet me for lunch. I didn't tell him that
the subject was a man who had lost his hat in the woods. We met
at a place on Ventnor Avenue called Lou's, an old diner-style operation where Mickey and the boys took me when they were tired
of Murray's.

My teacher was ageless. Mr. Hicks looked exactly the same as when I had graduated from high school. He had a full head of light brown hair flecked with gray. From some angles, he appeared to be blond. His bone structure was acute, which gave him a disapproving look even when he was feeling nothing of the kind. He had small scars around his eyes from his days as an amateur boxer. Mr. Hicks said that it was great to see a student who didn't seem surprised that he was still teaching at Ventnor High.

"Some of these people come back and ask, 'You're still here?' as if this were a failing of some kind," Mr. Hicks said. "I like teaching. This is my job."

"It wouldn't make sense to me if you were anywhere else."

A waitress came by to take our orders, Reubens, which arrived swiftly. Mr. Hicks looked at his Reuben sandwich. The chef hadn't cut the toast all the way through. Mr. Hicks seemed annoyed, and I held my breath, wondering if he was going to send the chef into the hallway to "think about it."

"Do you ever go back and read any of the books from high school?" he asked, satisfied with his slicing.

I thought for a moment. "Just *Gatsby*. It was very different."

"How so?"

"When I reread it a few years ago, I was Gatsby's age, as opposed to sixteen or seventeen. It wasn't a book about . . . what did we call it? Oh, the American dream, which seemed corny, really, the second time around. It wasn't a book about America anymore, it was about an obsessive hustler approaching middle age."

"So what did a real obsessive hustler nearing middle age learn from a fictional one?" Mr. Hicks asked.

"You think I'm nearing middle age, do you? Where does that put you?"

"When you were eighteen, I was thirty-eight. You were a kid; I was nearing middle age. Now we're both middle aged."

"You cheat," I said.

"Life cheats, Jonah. So what's *Gatsby's* lesson?"

This was an easy one for me. "That we're always chasing what was rooked from us when we were young."

"But for you, whatever you were . . . rooked . . . is dead."

I knew he wasn't referring to my parents, but I thought about them anyway.

"I know that."

"Maybe." Mr. Hicks said this pointing at me the way he had when I was in high school. "So you said you wanted to ask me about something."

"Folklore."

"My hobby."

"My grandfather used to read me a story when I was a kid. I found the book on his shelves. It's called *The People Papers*, a bunch of kids' stories."

"Never heard of it."

"There was a story in the book about a man named Ong."

Mr. Hicks smiled.

I continued. "Ong—I guess he was Chinese with a name like that—went into the pine woods. He threw his hat up into the air. It got caught on a tree, and he fell into another dimension."

"Ong's hat," Mr. Hicks said flatly.

"Right, Ong's hat went into a tree."

"It's an old Pine Barrens tale. It's one of those stories that counselors tell kids at camp. They have for years. Why are you so interested in the story?"

"In the weeks before he died, Mickey talked a lot about the stories he read to me. This one stuck with me for some reason. I'm a little sentimental these days."

"I'm sure you are. You've been through a lot."

"So the guy just went into the woods and threw his hat into a tree and disappeared."

"So says the legend. They even named a town after it. And he wasn't Chinese. He was a piney named Jacob Ong. He disappeared into another dimension. People don't talk there, they whisper. That way, other people don't know what anybody's saying, just what they think is being said. It's mind control. The legend says that sometime around the millennium, Ong's Hat will surface and merge with our world. So much for that theory."

I felt my throat tighten up.

"It's an actual town?"

"Sure. An old piney town called Ong's Hat. It's not far from Fort Dix. There's not much there. Years ago it was a regular piney town. During Prohibition, some of the guys—guys your grandfather probably knew—had liquor stills there. I don't think there's much in Ong's Hat now, except for maybe blueberry and cranberry farms, but it's there."

Does He Eat Peas?

"The devil they know versus the devil they don't."

THE BRICK HOUSE BEHIND THE AZALEAS IN THE COUNTRY-
side of western New Jersey was as tidy a place as I had ever
seen. The Morrises' devotion to the preservation of their colonial
must have been all-consuming. I could smell the fresh paint on the
blue shutters as Edie and I stepped up the front walk. Smooth
lines from the wheels of a lawn mower were visible on the grass.
A hyperactive blue jay poked its beak beneath its wing on a birdhouse off to one side of the property, as one of its feathers wafted
slowly earthward. A white swing bench drifted gently to and fro on
the front porch, which felt ten degrees cooler than the August heat
beyond the Morrises' property.

This was where Edie grew up. She had never lived in another
house, with the exception of her current place in Batsto. The house
was somewhat more regal than I had expected, not in its extrava-
gance but in what had been left out. There were no cheap allusions
to upward striving: no monogrammed stained-glass windows, no
street names with hints of Britain, no gratuitous uses of Tudor, no
gasping reaches for celebrity via displays of the family name on
doors or mailboxes (as if anybody gave a rat's ass that *The Johnsons*
lived there), and no pillared entryways evoking Tara. The cars

were three-year-old Buicks. You couldn't even see the Morrises' house from the road. The bricks were sealed with extra cement that overflowed, embracing each one.

Edie took a deep breath before she opened the door. Her anxiety made me feel cruelly significant: She was worried about me, she was worried about my introduction.

On the other hand, I found it strange that she could just open this rich oak door and walk right in. I had never known that comfort, the sheer buoyancy of being able just to walk into the home where you grew up and know that your parents wanted to see you and that somebody with a name like the Blade, the Shark, or the Weasel wouldn't come swinging out of a closet and throw a garrote around your neck.

The rich smell of the evening's feast lingered as Edie opened the unlocked door. An antique table stood sturdily on the foyer's hardwood floor. There was a photo of Edie as a teenager on the table. She wore a Western hat and an unequivocal smile. She looked gorgeous. I wanted to steal the photo, show it to Trouble, and quietly return it.

A surge of doubt drifted through my bones. Why did this creature in the Western hat, who grew up in this house, with its birdhouse and heavy cinder-block foundation, want to be with a glib drifter who came from a world of urgent relocation and scary nicknames? Strangely, evidence of a woman's perfection was her implicit rejection of you. I escaped from my thoughts when the baronial figure of Mr. Morris ducked his head under a hanging light fixture and let out a warm, "Hey there, Jonah."

"I'm Jonah Eastman," I said, obviously.

"I'm Bob Morris."

"You are indeed," I said, displaying my genius.

Bob Morris was a ringer for Charles Lindbergh, only with a darker complexion. He was tall and trim with thinning silver hair, a *de minimus* Nordic nose like Edie's, and a prominent cleft in his chin. Edie had her mother's coloring, though. I kept focused on his face, and he on mine.

"Edie looks just like you," I said. "She doesn't have the dimple in the chin," I added, pointing to my chin as if Bob Morris didn't know what a chin was. Edie's arm was around my waist, *the way it had been when we were in her shower last night.*

"She's prettier."

"She's more my type, anyway."

"That's a good thing. You look like an actor."

Edie killed her dad's observation. She swung around and studied my face.

"He does, sort of," she said and leaned across to kiss her father who said, "Jonah's a mite taller than I thought he'd be."

That did it. The height reference. *You don't look anything like your grandfather, the killer troll.*

I was rescued from having to make an inane response by the soft patter of footsteps across a tile floor, footsteps that belonged to a slender, fine-featured woman of about sixty with silver hair swept back under a disciplinary white headband. She extended her hand.

"I'm Elaine Morris."

"Jonah Eastman."

"I hear a lot about you."

"Respectable things, I hope."

"But of course."

I handed Mrs. Morris the bottle of merlot I had brought.

We sat in a living room with old, fine furniture. Mrs. Morris offered us something to drink. The three Morrises had red wine, the merlot. I had club soda with lime, a more graceful choice than Manischewitz. I sensed that this style of decor must have had a formal name, but I didn't know what it was. Provincial. Victorian. Elizabethan. Carotid. Trapezoidian. I didn't know and felt self-conscious about not knowing.

Bob Morris set down his glass of wine on a butler's table. "Tell me about your work. Edie says you're a poll taker." Elaine Morris sat beside him.

"I am. I do a lot of political strategy, too."

"Are you doing any political work now?" Mrs. Morris asked.

"I'm in between big projects. I'm just doing some consulting." This was true.

"What kind of consulting?"

"When I'm not getting my grandfather's affairs squared away"—a gulp from Elaine Morris—"I have a few business clients, big companies, that are concerned about public opinion. If they sense that public opinion is turning against them, they have to modify their behavior accordingly."

"Can you share an example?"

"I have a client with a successful business. A lot of people like this company a whole lot more than they like its competitor, an upstart. So one thing I'm doing is helping them communicate points that differentiate my client from its competitor."

"The devil they know versus the devil they don't," Mrs. Morris said astutely. Edie squirmed.

"You might say that. I am also suggesting to my client that they do things to remind people about the services they provide to the community. If you don't remind people, they don't know. So that's what I'm working on."

"Do you plan to stay in Jersey long?"

When will you be leaving?

Dinner began with a garden salad. Everything had been grown in the Morrises' own garden. There was iced tea, a drink I never liked but tolerated in this case. The main course was roast beef, which I loved, and roasted potatoes, which I really loved. The greens were garden-grown peas.

As we passed around the plates of food, Mrs. Morris set her cool gray eyes on Edie and asked, "Does he eat peas?"

Dead silence. Edie squinted at her mother. I pressed my tongue to the back of my teeth in surprise.

"Who, mother?"

"Why, Jonah."

Bob Morris curled his lip and barked, "What kind of question is that? 'Does he eat peas?' " This was the first hint of aggression I had seen from him. He was a retired lawyer. Not a Philly-style litigator, but a South Jersey land-use lawyer who could afford to be a bit gentler than his rabid counterparts across the river.

"He eats peas," I volunteered, defusing the tension. "Tell me about your daughter?" I asked, dishing myself some peas, which I would be certain to eat. Mrs. Morris appeared confused. Bob Morris grinned playfully. "Whattaya want to know?"

"Has she ever been convicted of anything, you know... *major?*" I winked at Bob, who laughed conspiratorially.

"We'll talk privately," he said.

"Well, Bob, I find this to be very insightful."

"Good, son, there are some things in life you have to know." Bob Morris nodded at me. The guy liked me. He had a streak of irreverence, and I sensed he was carrying on in order to tweak his imperious wife, who appeared to disapprove of her husband as much as she did of me.

"I hope you didn't mind me quizzing you about her, it's just that I love her."

Bob brought his napkin to his mouth. Mrs. Morris, who had started to rise, fell back into her seat. Bob's eyes sparkled like constellations as if he had just flown around his property. *The Spirit of South Jersey.*

Elaine Morris, losing control of the conversational cockpit, broke the warm moment. "Edie tells me you've had a tough time of it with your family."

"I have. Nobody's left. My father died when I was ten and my mother died a few years later. My grandfather, who really raised me, died a few months ago."

What will come out eventually must come out immediately. This was Henry Kissinger's quotation about what he learned during Watergate. Out with it. I sensed that Elaine Morris liked me better when I was down, so I brought it all out into the open.

"My grandfather was a bit of a character, a gunslinger of sorts," I acknowledged. "He tried to be a solid citizen, but he couldn't bring it off. He blew it for himself. I think he may have blown it with some things he involved my dad in. And then there's me— the hope."

"Lots of us have had characters in our families, Jonah," Bob said dismissively.

"Any of them try to kill Castro?"

Even Elaine laughed. I pictured her handing Castro a cigar, Castro smoking it, and it blowing his head off.

Bob Morris tapped my hand lightly. "Well, son, you've had your share."

"He really has, Dad," Edie agreed.

With that, Elaine and Edie began clearing the table. I pushed back to help.

"Stay down, Jonah," Bob ordered. Stay down. I loved that. He had felt the artillery from his wife.

When the women moved into the kitchen to paddle conspiracies back and forth, Bob and I spoke about Edie's shyness as a child and her fascination with music. Then he took me through their garden and asked me more about Mickey. And, in my desperation for a parent, I unloaded on him about when Mickey bought his Dartmouth sweatshirt.

It was May, nineteen years ago. It was a seminal spring that had brought death to the Chicken Man and sent Mickey to college.

Phil "Chicken Man" Testa, the Philly rackets boss, was blown to morsels when an ambitious punk named Rocco Marinucci detonated a nail bomb beneath his front porch early one morning. Mickey and his boys were scared because none of them had sanctioned the hit, and other mob functionaries had been disappearing. My uncle Blue didn't know, either. They had been afraid that the New York bosses, having had had enough of Mickey's influence on the Italians, had decided to make a move on Atlantic City.

As it turned out, Marinucci, the Chicken Man's killer, had been working for a random faction within the Philly outfit, but no one knew this until Marinucci was found dead in the trunk of his car with the remnants of detonated firecrackers in his mouth. A coroner's report indicated that the small explosives had been set off in Marinucci's mouth while he was still alive, probably one at a time in case he had had any doubt that he was being tortured. Police speculated on the record that the Marinucci hit had been the work of the "old, blue-chip Philly Cosa Nostra" that didn't like upstarts. That meant my uncle Blue Cocco.

Before the Chicken Man puzzle was solved, even Mickey and Blue were nervous. Blue fled to his retreat in the Poconos and Mickey came up to see me at Dartmouth in New Hampshire. It was the only time I remember him having bodyguards. He rented a suite at the Hanover Inn for his crew and kept tabs on matters back home in a safe house in nearby Canaan. He gave me no notice of his arrival.

I had been about to go for a nap in the sun, when three dull thumps landed on the door of my dorm room. I turned down my stereo, which was playing "Who Can It Be Now?" by Men at Work. A falsetto voice on the other side of the door identified itself as belonging to "Little Red Riding Hood." I thought it was one of my fellow fraternity pledges, so I opened the door.

Before me stood little Mickey backed by a chorus of ballagoolahs in T-shirts that read A Voice Cries Out in the Wilderness. This was Dartmouth's motto. Mickey had brought along (minus Uncle Blue) a group that he had dubbed "the Scholarship Committee," because they had scoped out colleges for me years prior. The Scholarship Committee consisted of Irv the Curve; Fuzzy Marino; a cop named Stuart, who wore a graying buzz haircut; and a young enforcer on steroids named Rocco Gibraltar. Mickey had approved of Dartmouth when he read in the brochure that it had been founded by colonists to educate the Indians.

They were all wearing windbreakers or sport jackets over their T-shirts, except for Mickey. This was to conceal their guns.

I fell back against my beanbag chair, which I had dragged up here from home. The guys laughed their asses off. A fragile Asian girl named Heather from my dormitory tiptoed by and craned her neck at the spectacle. I would have to explain this later.

"Jonah, did you think you could run from us forever?" Fuzzy asked me with a bear hug.

"How's it going, boychik?" Irv the Curve asked.

I pretended I was glad to see them and invited them in. Fuzzy acknowledged *"tsuris,"* heartache, back in Philly. I took him into my small bedroom while I changed. He told me about the Chicken Man but played it down. Fuzzy made it seem like Mickey was just depressed about the death of an old friend, Art Levy, who did vague jobs for Mickey out west. When I tied my sneakers, I could see that Fuzzy had a small Beretta strapped to his ankle.

We went for an early dinner at a grill in town. My mortification at walking across campus with these men postponed my concern about what the Chicken Man's detonation might have meant for Mickey.

A few kids I knew said hello as we walked on the sidewalk near the central quadrangle, called the Green. I greeted them back and smiled urgently. Mickey wanted to stop and talk to every kid who greeted me as if they had all been close friends. He was understandably relieved that I had found a place for myself at Dartmouth. I discouraged Mickey's gabbing by pointing out buildings that lay ahead so he and his Merry Men would keep moving forward. A flotilla of gorilla biceps and loafers parting a sea of slim wrists and sandals.

Mickey eyed the Dartmouth sweatshirt in the window of the Co-op. We went in together and he bought it, hungrily slipping it over his Voice T-shirt. When we got to the grill, Mickey could see that I was uncomfortable. That's how I knew he was upset about the Chicken Man. He normally was very conscious of not injecting his world into mine, but the pressures shoved decorum down his priority list and he turned snappish. It was a confusing subject for both of us. On one level, Mickey knew that it was he who had erected a wall in between our worlds. He liked it when Irv the Curve called me *shaygets* or Mr. Brooks Brothers. On another level, Mickey punished me for assimilating. He did it with cold glances.

"Don't get hoity-toity now," he said when we sat down at a table in the back. The word "hoity-toity" ripped into me. I despised Mickey throughout dinner and couldn't look at him. Hoity-toity. Fucking murderer. When he crossed his legs, I could see that he, too, had a gun strapped to his ankle. I hoped that New York's five families were waiting in the kitchen to spray us all with gunfire. Let them have Atlantic City. I wouldn't care if they got me, too. Maybe Mickey would live and watch my hoity-toity classmates carry my bullet-riddled corpse across the Green to the Hitchcock Medical Center where a hoity-toity doctor would say, "I'm sorry, Mr. Price. There was nothing we could do."

After studying alone, I walked over to the hotel and knocked on the door to Mickey's suite. It was about ten in the evening. He went to bed early when he was at home but tended to stay up later when traveling. His crew did what he did.

No answer. I banged again. Fuzzy answered wearing his Dartmouth T-shirt and boxers emblazoned with Italy's flag.

"You miss us?"

"Deeply. Is Mickey here?"

"He signed off a while ago."

I pushed open the door to Mickey's room and whispered his name. I gently felt around the bed and it was entirely flat. "He's not here, Fuzzy," I said.

"What the hell are you talking about?" He flicked on the light. *"Jesus Christ!"*

Empty.

Fuzzy rounded up the rest of the guys. We were all frightened, but of different nightmares. The Scholarship Committee was worried that they had botched their assignment to protect Mickey and would be killed. While the big guys like the Chicken Man were usually killed outright, a few other serious characters had simply vanished, never to return. The uncertainty surrounding their disappearances was making normally cool men jumpy in the unfamiliar terrain of the White Mountains. I wasn't worried about violence happening on campus; I was afraid of getting exposed for being related to thugs. To my knowledge, no one at Dartmouth knew who my grandfather was, and that was fine with me.

The Scholarship Committee grabbed its sidearms, and together we began searching the campus. It was cold for a spring night. A pack of students from my dorm greeted me as I passed them on a narrow street. I said nothing back and marched like Frankenstein toward Frat Row. "What's with him?" a voice asked. They soon saw.

Behind me shlumped Irv the Curve, Fuzzy, Stuart, and the chiseled Rocco Gibraltar. You don't see many gangland figures at colleges that were listed "most competitive" in the Barron's book. My friends fell silent. I wondered if they had heard the stories after all. People always found out. When they did, they usually thought the whole mob thing was cool. It wasn't quite as cool when they saw their collegiate friend being followed by murderers.

The looks on their faces broke whatever bubble of denial I had been floating in. Suddenly, I was so frightened that Mickey had been killed that I did not care what my peers thought of me.

Beyond the narrow road that led from the library down to the business school and the river below lay a peculiar strip of property in our nation's cultural underbelly, known as Frat Row. The row was percolating with degenerate life. These degenerates, however, were quite different from the ones heading toward them: They did not derive their income from their degeneracy.

Mickey had always been fascinated by the fraternities. He couldn't understand why I didn't spend more time at the frat houses and, as worldly as he was about some things, he was oblivious of what really went on at college. No matter how many times I told him, he genuinely failed to understand the huge role that drinking played in fraternity life. I think he envisioned future world leaders talking about important subjects, planning to run for office or take over banks. I had a gut feeling I'd be able to find Mickey on the row.

We searched the fraternities in order of their closeness to us until we came to mine, which was at the end of the row. In the basement of the house there was a card room, where the boys and, occasionally, the braver girls would play poker or gin. The basement was a veritable sensory assault. It always smelled of stale beer, or "mung" as it was called. Loud music always blasted. On this occasion the song was "Bye-Bye Love" by The Cars.

There was a sign with push-in plastic letters at the entrance of the basement that read NO DRINKING FOR FRESHMEN, which made Irv the Curve and me smirk wickedly at each other. Beneath the NO DRINKING sign was a list of fraternity officers.

The voices coming from the card room did not exclusively belong to Dartmouth students. I pushed open the paneled door of the card room and, to my relief (horror?) found my grandfather in his new Dartmouth sweatshirt—one collar tucked in, one sticking out—presiding over what appeared to be a blackjack lesson. There was an exquisite young woman standing next to him, someone whom I had recognized from around campus but had never spoken to. She was one of those face book goddesses, who instilled such pathological longing in men like me that she might as well have been attending college in Ecuador.

Mickey was dealing.

"Hey, Jonah," he said, looking up at me.

"Hey, Jonah," a number of others said, including those who did not know me.

"I'm showing Lynn here how to count cards. She's really a math whiz." Lynn.

Fuzzy let out a deep breath. He looked as if he were about to drop dead of a heart attack. Irv the Curve just laughed. The other tough guys, even Rocco Gibraltar, sighed audibly. Losing Mickey could have cost them their lives.

Lynn the goddess began flirting with Rocco Gibraltar. I could tell that Lynn liked his name. Mickey excused himself and asked one of my fraternity brothers where the rest room was. He volunteered that he needed to wash his hands. Before departing, Irv the Curve stood guard while I rearranged the letters on the No Drinking for Freshmen sign, borrowing some from the roster of names. The sign now read FORNICATING SHMENDRICKS and listed fraternity officers with vaguely pornographic names like Bink Domee and Dirk Thickbone.

When we left the house that night with Mickey, I heard two guys talking on the porch. One said to the other, "Do you know who that old guy is?" The other voice said no. "That's Bugsy Siegel, the head of all the gangsters. His grandson goes here."

For days afterward, my fraternity brothers were talking like Rocco and Fuzzy. Amazing. Mickey shoots his way out of Prohibition to get me to the Ivy League, and a bunch of preppies from Scarsdale only want to act like hoods. . . .

I found out a few weeks later that Rocco Gibraltar had sneaked out of the Hanover Inn the night of the frat house card game and had himself quite the *shtup* with Lynn the goddess at her dorm.

I did not share this part with Bob Morris, who had devoured my every word.

"Some of us have really had a time of it, son," Bob said.

"She hates me," I told Edie, squeezing the thick golden sponge beneath her collarbone. She was covered entirely in suds from the neck down. I could see only the tips of her knees above the waterline. For the bath, Edie had pulled her hair up and clipped it on top of her head. She had a great back, with a spine that made me think of a long sliding board.

I sat behind her in the tub and ran the sponge under the water and along her belly.

"Who?" she said in a loaded voice.

"Your mother."

Edie denied this. "She's just not effusive" was her explanation.

"Your dad's great. He's very tan. Is he that dark all year-round?"

"He's tanner in the summer, but he got his dark complexion from his mother. She was Delaware."

"What do you mean, she was Delaware?"

"Delaware Indian."

"You have Indian blood?"

"A lot of people do. Sometimes the Delaware were called Lenni-Lenape. That's where I got my middle name. My grandmother's name in Lenape meant Seven Angels, so my dad decided to use the name in English. My mother didn't like it much, but he felt strongly about it."

My eyes stretched out into a panorama of tepees. My mind bounced between visions of the dark man on the Boardwalk and hatless moon-headed Ong. The man on the Boardwalk looked like an Indian. Was Ong an Indian? Now my girlfriend casually drops that she's part Indian. Mickey had met Edie. He had liked her. I had thought their bond had been klezmer music, but maybe I was wrong. Besides his identification with the Indians' struggle, what the hell was up with Mickey and Indians?

"Your heart is racing," Edie said. "I feel it on my back."

"There was an Indian at my grandfather's funeral."

"Oh?" she responded. The muscles in her back tightened. She turned around and faced me, urgently.

"One minute he was there, then he was gone. I had never seen him before."

"Why do you find that so strange?"

"It was spooky."

"Indians are spooky?"

"No, the way he was standing, it was like he knew Mickey but couldn't come right over."

"Everything with your grandfather was a big secret. That was bad for you." Gradually, Edie's slow and soapy descent before me took precedence over the secondary issues of gangsters, Indians, and disapproving mothers.

"Here's something that's not a secret, a gray hair," she hummed, splashing water lightly on my chest. I strained downward but couldn't see the exhibit. I shrugged in defeat. "Did you know it was here?"

"I don't see all of myself."

"I'm beginning to."

"And you're not running?"

"If I am, I'm not too fast, am I?"

Fun

"It was the best of my bad options."

I MET TROUBLE FOR DINNER OUTSIDE OF STEWART'S, THE HOT dog stand on Ventor Avenue. Despite the descent of evening, it was hot as hell outside so we ate in Trouble's car. It was that challenging inland South Jersey heat, the kind that jabbed a finger in your chest and asked with a gritty smirk, "Had enough?"

Trouble's face showed an unfamiliar gravity. I was reluctant to comment on his tension because I knew how much I loathed people analyzing my stresses and sadnesses. *"Are you okay?" "What are you worried about?" "You need to relax, have more fun."* Why the hell did everything have to be fun, anyway?

"Out with it," I ordered.

"Out with what?" Trouble said, unfunly.

"The look on your face. Cut to it."

Trouble reached inside the crack between the two front seats. It was an article about Automatic Bart. The headline read: "The Hunt Continues."

"The hunt continues, Jonah?"

"I suppose it does."

"And that's okay with you?"

"What, that people are looking for somebody who doesn't exist? Yeah, it's okay with me, given my options."

"I'm just not too keen on a hunt for a black man."

"A black man who doesn't exist, Trouble."

"Even so, Jonah. Even so. You knew it would come to this." His eyes were bloodshot.

I began rubbing my temples with my thumbs. The line at Stewart's was growing, teenagers mostly. The boys were rail thin, with long bathing suits hanging down past their hips. The girls were whippet-sleek in two-piece numbers. A lot of them had tattoos, mostly the girls. A boy whipped one of the girls with a moist beach blanket. She feigned discomfort. "Owwww, Jordan," she said. But she was grinning. This was a ritual of some sort.

"We'll be out of the wilderness soon."

"Maybe." Trouble sniffed the word.

"What do you mean, maybe?"

"You can be stone-cold, I swear."

"What can I tell you? That I had no idea it would come to this? I can't tell you that. This is part of what I do."

"There's a price, though. Somebody gets hurt. Another white cop has an excuse to beat up a black kid. Another black kid figures he'll only be seen as a monster so why not act like one? You can't see the price right away, but there is one. It's not all about Clever Jonah. It's not a game."

"I know it's not."

"You half know it's not. You don't totally know it's not."

"I didn't make Automatic Bart black. Everybody else did."

"But you knew they would, man. You knew they would. You can't tell me that one of your polls didn't show something down deep on race."

I bit down hard on the inside of my cheek.

"Yes, Trouble, I knew. I knew, okay. Do you think *I* like it? I'm trying to save my life here. If this doesn't work, I'm dead."

"Clever Jonah. Yeah, we've both got our excuses. Everybody's always got a good reason to do the wrong thing. I watched Lee Atwater set Willie Horton into motion and then go out and play in a blues band to show it was nothing personal. It *is* personal. You don't know . . . Hey, what did you call that Willie Horton thing, when a spin campaign comes to life and everybody believes it's true?"

"A Flackenstein."

"Flackenstein," Trouble repeated, half chuckling, half in disgust.

"Then you're off the case, Trouble. I've got to handle it now, anyway. I'm due to get a grocery sack of cash from Mario pretty soon. I'll drop it off to you."

"Just like that, I'm off the case?"

"You did great. Better than great. Now I've got to take care of things as much as I can. I'm sorry that the whole Bart thing turned out how it did, but the people invented him, I just didn't stand up and shout, 'You're wrong, everybody! Bart's white! Bart's white!' I did what a guy does with a gun to his head. It was the best of my bad options."

"I can't kill anybody," Trouble said automatically. The statement left me winded. I don't know where it came from.

"You don't have to."

Trouble gazed out the window at the teenagers loitering on the sidewalk. "Look at them. Snapping towels and shit. They're worried about how their hair looks and who they're going to meet on the beach."

"I hate those kids, too."

"I didn't say I hated them."

"You didn't have to. They're not carrying around what we are, killers and spins and sick daughters. All they're carrying is a little sunscreen, if that."

"We weren't ever that light. Ever, Jonah."

"Let's not screw around. We hate those kids."

"We sure as hell do, don't we?" Trouble collapsed into a madman's laugh. I joined him. It was one of those visceral laughs that are really cries. We couldn't cry, though. You needed answers to cry to a resolution, and we didn't have any.

"I pictured things would be different," Trouble said between gasps for air. "For me. I didn't imagine I'd be sitting in some Shore place, miles away from my wife and my sick baby, screwing around with some racketeer. I didn't picture digging around in people's trash for the mayor. I thought when I got out of Camden, I got out."

"I thought when I left South Jersey, I left it, too. My friend Cindi says Jersey is shaped like a boomerang. It always comes back."

"Hah! I like that."

"Hey, Trouble, just one more question that I always wondered about."

"What's that?"

"Did anybody at the White House know who my grandfather was? I was always holding my breath, thinking that one day I would get tapped on the shoulder and thrown out. I know you never actually met Mickey, but I always wondered."

"I knew."

"When did you know?"

"Somebody said something at a track meet once."

"Did anyone at the White House know?"

Trouble bit his upper lip. "One day when Mickey came to Washington, I saw him hand his hotel room key to you through the iron bars at the White House gate. One of the uniformed guards said, 'Shit, that's Mickey Price.' He said something about Mickey being an undesirable because he had been questioned in the Kennedy assassination. I said I'd handle it."

"Did you handle it?"

"Didn't do a fuckin' thing. I knew you weren't in that life. You were a guy like me, just running."

"It's good to know. Thank you."

That evening, I dropped off one hundred thousand dollars in cash to Trouble's place in Margate in a paper shopping bag. Later, I drove him to the station and watched the red taillights of his train vanish westward out of Atlantic City toward the Delaware River.

The Plantation

"Welcome to my racket."

GOOD COVERAGE BEGETS GOOD COVERAGE," CINDI REMINDED me biblically over lunch at Ponzio's a few days after the Vanni vigil. "Until it doesn't."

"*Begets?* What is this, Leviticus?" I asked. Cindi threw a Sweet'n Low at me.

She was right, though. Quirky cultural obsessions like this one with Vanni didn't last very long and said more about the nation's need for amusing diversions than for heartfelt beliefs. I feared that Vannimania could die with the first nip of autumn air. To make matters worse, Al Just had taken to injecting critical remarks about Vanni's "spin campaign" into every news story that he could. When Vanni came ashore after his car blew up, that had sealed it for Just. He hadn't found me yet, but I knew he was looking.

"If we get this Vanni story out of the news cycle—end it—Just won't have time to find out what's behind it," Cindi said.

"But what's behind it is pretty interesting, Cin."

"The answer lies in doing something big, and doing it fast. Not just a diversion, but a diversion that makes everything that follows an anticlimax."

Like all chief executives, Vanni wanted the bad press simply to vanish. This was impossible to achieve, and even Vanni understood that any attempt to silence a reporter could result in disaster. In a series of tusk-side meetings during the past week, I had opposed any effort to quash Just using violence. Noel and Frankie Shrugs had called me a "faggot" for this view, but Vanni reluctantly agreed with my counsel to spare Just's life.

"You're turning me into a friggin' fairy," he said, attempting to save face with his boys. Cindi and I agreed that we needed to accelerate our coup de grâce.

With all of the talk about crime, breast-beating about "the cities" had become chic, and Vanni was a big city guy. His turf, after all, included Philadelphia, Wilmington, Camden, and Atlantic City. Some even said Trenton, but I didn't know. I set up some surveys to test possible reactions to a Washington "state visit" by Vanni. Specifically, there were congressional hearings at the end of September where big-city players would offer their insights to members of the Senate. I proposed the idea to Cindi during our lunch at Ponzio's.

"But, Jonah," she said, "we can't risk him looking like a smart ass before Congress."

Cindi was right, so I did a quickie poll among people in the Delaware Valley, our primary target audience. The survey hinted that Vanni being scolded by a member of Congress might actually give him some of that fuck-you cachet folks around here seemed to like. And if they didn't scold him, his very appearance would be good enough.

On the Friday before Labor Day weekend, Cindi and I drove to Great Falls, Virginia, just outside of Washington, to meet with a Southern lobbyist friend of mine, DeWalt Nash. We were unusually silent, except for a brief follow-up to a discussion we once had twenty-five years ago.

"Do you remember how you insisted that Elton John and Olivia Newton John were married?" Cindi asked me.

"Yes, I remember. And now we know that Elton's gay and Olivia's fighting breast cancer."

"Oh, that's cheerful," she said, as we emerged from the Baltimore Harbor Tunnel, the air becoming visibly thicker as we traveled south. I opened my window. It was like God had turned on a blow-dryer and aimed it straight at my Cherokee.

If anyone could help us arrange a Vanni state visit, it was DeWalt. The way I saw the caper, DeWalt could go to a senator involved in the cities hearings and let the idea of Vanni testimony roll off his tongue like it was some sort of joke. We couldn't jeopardize DeWalt's standing in the community by making people think he had an actual link to the mob. If the senator thought the idea could boost television ratings—and that's all these guys cared about in an election year—he might go for it. I had spoken to DeWalt about this on the telephone without mentioning Vanni's name. I followed it up with a fax of an article about Vanni so he would put things together.

In the late 1980s, DeWalt was on the verge of losing his biggest client, a farm coalition. He had pitched their business with an objective of winning subsidies for farmers. There were ten members of Congress blocking the legislation. I issued a carefully worded poll indicating that these congressmen—dubbed the "Toasty Ten"—would face the scorched electoral wrath of a broad coalition of farmers, textile industry workers, and food-processing employees if they turned their backs on the farmers. Specifically, I calculated that if all of the workers under the umbrella of this coalition voted in the next election for the Toasty Ten's opponents, the political muscle gained by the spectacle would outweigh the actual risks on other legislation. In the end, the Toasty Ten buckled, DeWalt Nash got his way, the farmers got their subsidies, and I won a lifelong friend.

DeWalt Nash stood about six-four and had probably been described as "gangly" in his youth. Nevertheless, adulthood had been kind to him; he was one of those men whose courtly charisma made them strangely handsome in late middle age. He spoke slowly, like a pensive Baptist preacher, and, indeed, his speech was peppered with Scripture and familial sayings. His enunciation was exquisite: When he pronounced the word "wheat," for example, he actually aspirated—"wwwhhheat" as opposed to "weet." The content of his speech gave away little of his personal politics. If he harbored any old-style racial or religious prejudices, which he probably did, I never saw any evidence of them. He now bided his time in semiretirement in a magnificent redbrick plantation overlooking the Potomac River.

We pulled into the narrow road that led to DeWalt's house. The grounds were beautifully kept, and I could see a team of hands working beneath the white sky on shrubs up near the main house. Horses, mostly warm bloods, grazed in a nearby valley.

"My God," Cindi said when she saw the place, "I didn't think people lived like this anymore."

"People who live like this don't want you to know that there are people who live like this anymore."

We walked up several steps onto a columned porch and tapped on the front door. A plump, middle-aged black woman in a uniform answered the door and escorted us to a rear porch where DeWalt was going over some papers on a wicker couch. The house was large in the sense that it had huge rooms with high ceilings, but there weren't actually too many rooms.

"Well, greetings, Jonah." DeWalt rose. His voice prompted Cindi to take a step back, as if he had just mandated a plague. She had a stricken, let-my-people-go expression of awe on her face.

I answered with a question: "How are you surviving the heat?"

"Of what heat do you speak?" DeWalt said, grinning at me.

"This isn't hot to you?"

"I find it to be gentle and sultry," DeWalt said. Extending his hand toward Cindi, he said, "I'm DeWalt Nash."

"Cindi Handler."

"Enchanted, Cindi. Enraptured and charmed as well."

Cindi blushed.

"As I mentioned on the phone, DeWalt, Cindi handles PR and media relations."

DeWalt nodded. "Ah, yes. Moses was a lobbyist such as myself, but he needed a PR man to speak clearly to the people, which is why he had Aaron."

I asked DeWalt if he had ever given the plantation a name.

"Did you have a name in mind, son?"

"No, just curious."

"Son, city boys who wake up one morning and suddenly find

themselves with a pile of money like to come out this way, purchase a little history, and give it a fancy name that they post out on an electric gate. As for Loretta and myself, we just call it a house."

I nodded humbly. DeWalt gestured toward seats at a round iron table where the maid had placed glasses of freshly squeezed lemonade. We sat.

DeWalt brought his hands together prayerfully and acknowledged Cindi and me with solemn resolve. "I had occasion to haul these old bones in to sit down with the esteemed Senator Lindbaugh on a matter of the utmost urgency. When we completed our business together, I raised the subject of how things were progressing on his urban projects. He observed that things were stagnating, and I jokingly suggested that he should take up the matter of a Philadelphia-area businessman, a Damon Runyon sort, who seemed to be drawing some serendipitous attention to himself. When he asked what I meant, I said, with droll demeanor, of course, that Mr. Mario"—*Mur-yo*—"Vanni represents an interesting phenomenon and could be a good centerpiece to new hearings on the cities. Remember, the senator is up for re-election, and a little face time with your friends in the field of journalism would not be deleterious."

"Did he buy?" I asked gently.

"Jonah," DeWalt continued, putting his hands down on the table, "the senator kept me for another forty-five minutes. I professed surprise that he took my jocular idea seriously, and he asked if I had any way of facilitating such a contingency. He was particularly interested in Mr. Vanni's recent high-profile escape from peril on that little seaside bridge. By having Mr. Vanni testify, which is not without precedent I might remind you, it would not mean that the U.S. government endorsed his bid for a casino license in any way."

DeWalt winked again. I had told him nothing about the casino license.

"I see that you understand the endgame," I said respectfully. Very respectfully. Cindi's jaw dropped. She hadn't been given the big picture until now.

"Well, Jonah, guys like me do things slowly. We walk slow, we talk slow, and we think slow, but every now and then, I reckon we make a good guess. Anyway, I told the senator that I'd have to noodle on it and get back to him. Now, having heard my news, what do you propose that I tell my good friend from Missouri?"

"Given that it has to look like his idea, you could suggest that his staff contact Vanni's attorney. You can call Lindbaugh's assistant this afternoon and tell him. There's nothing funny about suggesting someone call an attorney. After all, Kefauver and McClellan did it when they were arranging testimony years ago. The lawyer is a man named Pat Conti. I can contact Conti and instruct him to say he has to think it over. One thing we'll have to negotiate is whether the senator will want to scold Vanni. I think that may be good."

"I didn't sense that the senator wanted to reprimand Mr. Vanni. I do, however, believe he can appear to be judgmental. The victory lies in the senator's ability to look like a player on the tube. What happens in that session is of little consequence. You enlightened me, Jonah, years ago, that television is a visually stimulating medium, and I'm certain that the senator understands the value of being visually stimulating."

Cindi widened her eyes at me in a request for permission to speak. It was cute, I thought. I nodded.

"I think we're fine, DeWalt," she said. "We certainly don't want Vanni being embarrassed, but we'd like there to be a little wise guy tension. For the cameras. We'd like to surprise the audience with Vanni's respectful demeanor, which is how Jonah is counseling him."

"Yes, I agree," DeWalt said. "I was going to bring that up. Manners and decorum are very important in these situations, and it was my assumption that these nuances will be conveyed to our friend in Philadelphia or Atlantic City or wherever he might be."

I assured DeWalt that this had been conveyed.

"Then it looks like everyone will potentially be quite pleased, and we'll have achieved our objectives," DeWalt concluded.

"Sounds like it."

Cindi asked DeWalt how media coverage of such an event was orchestrated.

"My feeling, Cindi, is that when the senator fully understands the media opportunity that lies at his sore feet, his office will handle much of the national media. What you do to convey things up north to your targets is up to you."

The discussion was over. There was no mention of money, because to a man like DeWalt, a discussion of fees would have been crass. It was understood that Vanni would pay, and pay a lot. The going rate for a man like DeWalt making a call like this was about fifty thousand dollars.

In four hours, I was back inside the elephant briefing a visibly excited Mario Vanni about his upcoming star turn.

"Fifty grand for a call?" Vanni asked me, incredulous.

"Welcome to my racket," I replied.

"Mother-a-God, all this money," Vanni snarled, his enthusiasm evaporating. "You know, some of the guys think you're taking me. They've never seen money like this. I don't know, Jonah," Vanni threatened.

My exhaustion over the whole affair having gotten the better of me, I said, "Then don't pay, Mario."

Vanni's eyebrows furrowed into his puzzled-hurt expression. "Not pay you?"

"If it's too much, then don't pay."

"I'm not saying I won't pay."

"*I* am, Mario. Don't pay for the lobbyist. And don't pay me anymore."

"It's just the amount," he said.

What made this discussion even more unnerving was that when it came to paying for my services, Mario Vanni was no different from my erstwhile legitimate clients. Because I performed an intangible service—as opposed to that of a plumber, who either unclogged the sink or he didn't—nobody ever wanted to pay. There was always this dance going on. The client was always hinting that there would be some unspecified pot of gold at the end of the rainbow awaiting me if only I would waive my fees. The fertile future was forever being dangled in lieu of payment today. That was the problem with being in business today, something that Evelyn Woulders might have understood if I had chosen to rest my head on her shoulder after the Basic Beliefs interview: Nobody *made* anything anymore. No wonder nobody wanted to pay. All they ever got for their money was ether. Where had all the plumbers gone? But I couldn't do what I did for free, so after a few years of experimenting with alternative methods of begging, I stumbled upon the only approach that appeared to work: the wild-eyed threat of abandonment. This was not cunning on my part. I'd rather get whacked or fired than spend all of my time managing lack of payment. Mobster or senator, I had grown to despise this discussion, having to plead with a client to pay photocopying charges as if I had just cleaned out his home safe and shot his poodle. An insane part of me wanted a bloodbath. Fuck 'em all.

"Don't pay me. Not a dime. I'd be offended if you paid me and you didn't feel right about it," I persisted. "This is how I make my living, counseling senators on how to get what they want. If they ever beefed about money, I'd tell them not to pay, too."

Vanni's eyes went dead, this time not with malice, but worry. I had stabbed his rawest nerve, the crooked one. If he'd stiff the only legitimate guy he ever did business with, then *he* wasn't legitimate.

"These fuckin' senators, do they pay when you bill 'em for polls?" Vanni smirked.

"No."

We both laughed.

"But," I added, "they don't have to. They've got their dream."

book four
nothing
spontaneous

Don't take a moment's rest. Run!

> —Irving Berlin, who
> frequented Atlantic
> City, on making it in
> America

Mario Hits the Hill

"Everything's a big fuckin' con, you know that?"

IN CONTEMPORARY AMERICA, THERE IS NO SUCH THING AS OVER-
kill. Overkill is what it's all about now, and it can be exploited
provided that you have a feel for the economics of it. The key is
to overexpose the icon but not the person. As soon as the icon
becomes a person, people start pissing all over him. The public
hadn't interacted with Mario Vanni the man at all. His legend had
been accomplished through third-party chats, edited video, satellite
feeds, and, therefore, an implied grass roots. And one more strafe
would be all the people would get.

In the days before Vanni's visit to Washington, Cindi and I made
sure that the American public couldn't get enough of the icon
Vanni. Once Senator Lindbaugh's office announced his testimony,
television stations across the country clamored for our old satellite
feed of Mario driving home from work, playing with his dog, and
audaciously confronting "reporters." People could download these
bites, too, from jerseydevil.org.

In one prefab report, a voice asked Vanni, "Are you angry at the
government for setting you up?"

"You can only be angry when you're surprised. I'm used to this.
I'll tell you who should be angry—you!"

Not only was the footage getting great pickup, but commentators were lining up to offer wisdom about what the coverage of Vanni said about the country's "state of affairs." This was just another chin-scratching device to shoehorn in tabloid talk about the gangster's "historic" visit, an adjective I added to a news release Cindi penned for DELVAC.

There was very little that was historic about a gangster coming to Washington. It had been done several times before. There were the Kefauver hearings in 1952, the McClellan hearings later in that decade, the 1964 sessions where Joe Valachi revealed the existence of Cosa Nostra, and other occasions in subsequent years that dealt with subjects ranging from the CIA's attempt to kill Castro to conspiracies about the Kennedy assassination. Nevertheless, in a culture that couldn't remember that we had ever had issues with Russia, the "historic" shtick really took off.

The challenge was that very few wise guys are good on their feet answering questions. All the repetition about being "unable to answer the questions on the grounds that it may tend to incriminate" them came off as a smarmy dodge. In fact, one New York boss, Tony Ducks, got his nickname for his prowess in ducking testimony. In the case of Frank Costello in '52, the camera kept showing him pulling at his fingers while barking out clipped answers to congressional questions. Not good. Through DeWalt and Conti, the lawyer, we had negotiated ground rules with the Senate Subcommittee on Urban Affairs whereby Vanni could offer testimony and then defer tougher questions to Conti.

I made a reservation for Mario at the Hay-Adams Hotel across the street from the White House. I had requested that Vanni bring none of his goons. I wanted no visuals that would validate the subtext of Vanni's being a gangster. Today, Mario Vanni was just another traveling businessman with a garment bag slung over his shoulder. Conti would arrive at Capitol Hill tomorrow.

I anticipated that the choice of hotels could become a press angle in and of itself. We leaked where Vanni was staying to the D.C. media. "Vanni Eyes the White House" became a local tabloid's headline.

I had Mario take the train down from Philly. Union Station was right next to Capitol Hill, which was one of the worst neighborhoods in Washington. That meant some of the local toughs would come by to greet their hero. I was dumbfounded by Vanni's strong appeal among blacks, but, poll after poll, they loved him.

Vanni's train arrived in D.C. at seven o'clock in the evening. People noticed him immediately and smiled like mannequins. He was sparkling, his tan summer face still in full glow.

The crowd gave Vanni a wide berth, all the while grinning, grinning. I was off to his right, just out of camera range. A few black kids moved alongside Vanni, one offering to carry his garment bag and the '76ers tote bag he held in his left hand. "Nah, that's okay, kiddo," Vanni told him.

The kids then formed foothills of protective shoulders and adopted that churlish expression that you see with gangsters and their aides. "We're parta this," their faces seemed to say.

As the automatic doors opened, Mario strode through the outside portico. There were six camera crews near the taxicab stands, along with a number of primarily black well-wishers and Capitol Hill yuppies.

A woman from WJLA shouted, "Hey Mario, what are you going to do tonight?"

"I'm gonna check into my hotel and have a nice, quiet dinner. Then tomorrow, I'm going to Capitol Hill and try and pass a few bills." The growing crowd laughed at Vanni's breathtaking wit, along with a few D.C. cops who were now beginning to emerge onto the scene.

One young black man asked Vanni if he was a Democrat or a Republican. Pulling a Nancy Reagan, I mouthed to him, "You're an Independent."

"Me, I'm Independent, I guess. I'm a shake-things-up kinda guy like that Ross the Boss guy with the big ears." That was beautiful— and all his own. I had a pang of jealousy hoping that Vanni wasn't getting more coaching on the side. The spotlight brought out his best attributes. *Self-improvement. Zats-uh-key.*

"Is this your first time to Washington?" a well-coifed newscaster from WRC asked.

"Yeah. I passed by it once when we drove the kids to Florida but I've never been to the city. Seems like you got great people here. Too bad the bums over there don't appreciate their neighbors like I do," Vanni said, pointing toward the Capitol. I had counseled Vanni that when in doubt, he should bash Congress.

"Gotta go," Mario told the crowd, feigning disappointment. Vanni climbed into the back of a cab and I took the one behind him. A cop car tailed us with blinking lights, adding to the gestalt of motorcade chic.

Vanni paid for his room at the Hay-Adams in cash, which appeared to give the delicate blonde woman behind the counter an embolism. Vanni watched everyone in the smallish lobby watch him. He loved it.

Vanni eyed his suite approvingly. "Fancy place, Jones," he said, proceeding toward the window. This was the most docile he had been with me in a while, I suppose because he needed me now. His mouth fell open when the White House, bathed in blazing light against the navy sky, filled the window.

"Holy shit," Vanni said. "There it is, I guess." He stared toward the left, toward the East Room. "You worked in there, huh?"

"I did."

"Show me where stuff is there."

"Sure," I said. There I was huddled in the center window of a Hay-Adams suite giving a multiple killer a civics lesson. I couldn't help but think it would have made a warped T-shirt: The Don Went to Washington and All I Got Was This T-Shirt and a Fuckin' Dead Pollster. I gave Vanni a pointing tour from the East Wing to the cramped little offices of the West Wing, where the executive offices were.

"You mean he doesn't actually work in the White House, just that little thing over there?" Vanni asked.

"That's right."

"Everything's a big fuckin' con, you know that?"

I was hoping that our dinner downstairs wouldn't last too long, because I wanted to go to my apartment—for the first time since Mickey died—and get some rest. I had left my Cherokee with the doorman for just this purpose.

From his walk-in closet, Vanni spoke. "Hey Jonah, I gotta blanket here and a pillow for you on the couch." Shit.

"Excuse me?" I asked. Vanni emerged. "Here, I got this for you.

You can stay right there." He pointed toward the sofa that was no more than ten feet from the foot of his bed.

"You want me to stay *here?*" I asked, trying not to look too horrified.

"Yeah, sure," Vanni said, as if I'd be honored.

"I live near here. I can give you some privacy if you want."

Vanni said, still missing my point, "Nah, no bother."

I took the pillow and blankets and put them on the edge of the chintz sofa. Bugsy Siegel had died on a sofa like this. He sat down to read the L.A. Times and—*bada-bing!*—his eye was rolling across the carpet. Frankie Carbo had placed a carbine outside on the lattice.

On the elevator ride down, I anticipated the facial expressions of the Washington power elite when Vanni walked into their hallowed dining grounds. Their brittle wrists would probably snap and crumble into their salads. To my surprise, no one recognized him, and dinner was uneventful with the exception of a man at the next table asking the waiter, "What the hell is *crudd*-ite?" Crudité.

The waited corrected him and, to Vanni's and my delight, snobbishly uttered "crood-ih-*tay*."

Back in the room, I had Vanni go over his speech once. I made check marks next to the sections where I wanted him to look up at the senators. I peppered him with questions beginning, "Do you expect me to believe . . . ," and Vanni handled them calmly. In order to help him maintain his sense of humor in front of the senators, I gave him a mantra to repeat to himself, which I had plagiarized from the dolt, Rhymin' Hyman: "They put their legs on one at a time." Vanni loved it.

After the rehearsal, I covered myself with a blanket that sickeningly reminded me of the one they placed on Mickey in the helicopter when he died, as if a dead man needed to keep warm. Then I got to thinking something even more sickening: My relationship with Vanni had progressed to the point that I had stopped worrying about getting whacked and was more put out by the inconvenience of sleeping on a sofa bed.

Two o'clock in the morning and I was wide awake, obsessing about having to use the bathroom. I didn't actually have to use it but was thinking about whether Vanni would be awakened if and when I turned on the bathroom light. I tried to stop worrying about my bladder but then began obsessing about Vanni's testimony. I could have sworn I saw a shadow on the other side of the sofa and became convinced that it was holding an ax. "You did a no-no, college boy. . . ."

I held my breath for a few minutes and then was shocked into reality by Vanni's voice. For a moment, I thought I was dreaming. "Jonah," Vanni said unmistakably, "you awake?"

"Yes," I responded, my heart pounding. "Are you all right?"

"Yeah." Vanni turned on the small lamp next to his bed. I sat up and turned around. There was the boss in his Eagles T-shirt. *De Iggles.*

"Can't fuckin' sleep," a subdued Vanni said. "I'm thinking about the casino application. We sent it in yesterday. I put it in my kids' names."

"Oh, good. That's good. Can I get you anything?" I asked, thinking this might be my big chance to use the rest room and get the whole thing over with.

"Anything new with Just?" he asked. Shit. "I've got *agita* with all this."

"No, nothing new. He's still fishing. He's not connected enough in Washington to blow tomorrow. If we do well on the Hill, that'll close out the news cycle. It'll be hard for him to get interest in a big new story if we—you—disappear after tomorrow."

"Right, right," Mario said anxiously. "Hey, do you think you could take me over to see that monument?"

"Which monument?"

"The Abe Lincoln one. I wanna see it. You mind goin' over there?"

"No, I mean, I could take you in the morning. I just don't want to do anything to put you in danger."

"Nah, we're awake. Let's do it." Vanni's eyes made it clear he was not putting the matter up for a vote.

I rarely stayed up past nine and now, in the nervous hours of the morning, I was putting on my khaki pants and oxford shirt to take the boss of the Philly Cosa Nostra to see Abraham Lincoln.

Vanni emerged from his walk-in closet with his uniform blue button-down shirt, khaki pants, and loafers.

We left the hotel, and within five minutes, Vanni was gazing up at the memorial. He stepped purposefully up the steps toward the heavens. He nodded humbly to the Park Service cop who didn't recognize him. We walked through the massive marble pillars up to the base of Abe Lincoln's feet. There were a few other people there, mostly young kids, probably drinking and screwing on the outskirts of the memorial.

Vanni stopped at Lincoln's huge marble feet. "Serious shit," he said, amused. "Honest Friggin' Abe. The man on the penny. Guess you gotta get whacked to get one of these graves?" Vanni observed.

"Lincoln's not actually buried here," I explained. "He's buried in Illinois where he was born. Let me show you something else." Vanni followed me through the colonnade and out to the southwest side of the memorial. I pointed across the river toward Arlington. In the distance, occasional whips of light shot through the G.W. Parkway. In the heavens, there were the blinking lights of aircraft probably on their way to Dulles Airport from Europe. Reagan National was closed this time of the morning. Then there was the ghostly glow of the Custis-Lee Mansion at Arlington Cemetery, beneath which a small fire burned.

"Do you see that flame?" I asked Vanni.

"Yeah. What's that?"

"That's President Kennedy's grave. They call it the Eternal Flame. His wife lit it after he was killed. Now she's buried there, too. The mansion was Robert E. Lee's house during the Civil War."

"You could run for president or something like that," Vanni said. "You've got the personality, the education, the look."

I gave Vanni a look as if he had just picked my nose. "Are you serious?"

"Sure," Vanni said. The shadows of his face made by the lights of the memorial conveyed a two-dimensional expression—annoyed on one hand, affectionate on the other.

"Believe it or not, that's why I came down here in the first place. I thought about running for office someday."

"Why not run for somethin'?"

"I realized the reason why I wanted to run for office was for the applause. I mean, the first time I saw Reagan walk out to the trumpets and get into his helicopter, I had tears in my eyes. All these people applauding. The never-ending bar mitzvah reception. Then I started realizing the price you pay for all that applause. People digging into your past, harassing your family, making things up. I got to thinking, Why do I need applause in the first place?"

"Everybody needs applause," Vanni said. "My mom, she always told me I would grow up to be king. My wife, she just says, 'Hey, King, take the trash out.' Some king. You're so smart you could probably figure a way to make people vote for you by screwing around with their computers."

"I really don't know much about computers, if you want the truth."

"Are you shittin' me?"

"I don't understand computers. I understand people. I find people who understand computers. Anyhow, if I ran for office, I'd have to open up the paper every day and read that I am the heir to the man that some asshole thinks killed Kennedy to get his casinos back."

Vanni was staring straight ahead at the Eternal Flame when I saw the hot yellow lights of the memorial flash against his teeth. He smiled. "That's what it's all about with you, isn't it?"

"What?"

"You're afraid that they're gonna give you shit about your grandfather. You ashamed of him?"

"No."

"Yeah, but you think there's a way to run away from who he was. There's no way to play it down, play him down. I'll tell you somethin', pal, he was a hell of a man. He did what he had to do in a miserable fuckin' world."

"I never denied who he was and who I am. I just didn't want to spend my life answering for things that happened a half century before I was born."

"I have news for you," Vanni said. "Nobody walks away standin' up. You don't even walk away when you're dead. Your kids don't even walk away when you're dead. Know what I think? I think you deal with it straight up. That's your fuckin' spin, as you guys call it. Your spin is; This Is Who I Am. You can't spin your way outta who you are."

"Who I am is not a guy running casinos in Cuba. That wasn't me."

Vanni put his left hand behind my neck. With his right he held my face. "But he was parta you," his voice echoed through the marble. "Mickey Price is parta you like my kids are parta me, legit casino or not. And don't kid yourself. You may not be a killer, but you're a wise guy all right. It's how you're built. You're not a wise guy like me, but you're a wise guy like he was," Vanni said, pointing toward the Eternal Flame dancing wildly above Kennedy's bones. "You're an Ivy League wise guy. You go freestyle."

We stood silently for a few moments studying Arlington. "Ah, it's better that way," Vanni said. "You either live on your terms or it's like you're dead. You're either a wise guy or you're an old lady."

Letting Vanni Be Vanni

"It's not like guys like me get up in the morning when we're sixteen and ask, 'Hey, am I gonna be a senator today or am I gonna hit some loan shark with a pipe?' "

SYNDICATE CHIEF VANNI TO TESTIFY TODAY—THAT WAS THE front-page headline in the *Washington Herald*. I had trained Vanni as well as I could to handle his testimony. He had demonstrated that he could handle tough questions without lashing out—provided that he was scripted and not left on stage for too long. I reminded him to take a Xanax for the tics. I felt a novel sense of relief that whatever happened now was in God's hands.

Vanni's core mission was to validate the Almighty Message that we had been building all summer: that the status quo was fucked up. That good was bad and bad was good. That he should be given his casino license quickly, before things got "outta hand."

I briefed Vanni on the correct way to address members of the committee and worked with him so that he knew how to look up from his text during his statement. I reminded him that his testimony would be broadcast nationwide and that we had arranged through his union boys to have employers tune their sets into the proceedings at workplaces from central New Jersey to Delaware and west toward Harrisburg. Cindi leased giant screens and had them placed in key locations throughout the Philadelphia and

Atlantic City areas, including Independence Hall and City Halls. The broadcast would also be carried on jerseydevil.org for those who didn't want to leave their desks.

Vanni appeared at the foot of the Capitol steps, alone, in a taxi. I had arrived a few minutes before, after washing up at my apartment, and stood atop the steps talking to Cindi by cell phone. Vanni took a deep breath as he beheld the Capitol, alone. A handful of reporters trained their cameras and microphones on Vanni as he climbed the steps. I could see from above that they were looking for his goons. There were none. His statements were short and humble. He came off as being shy: "I'm gonna do my best. This is some place. I'll tell 'em what I know. I'm not much of a talker."

Inside the Capitol, I pointed Vanni in the right direction with my chin, still on the phone with Cindi. He kept rubbing at his breast pocket nervously to make sure his speech was still there.

"You'll be great," I mouthed as he proceeded down the hallway.

"Some adventure," Vanni said back. Young aides and a few tourists snapped photos of him and drew their shoulders toward their necks the way schoolgirls do when the quarterback passes their locker. Vanni was stepping with a determined rhythm that I thought warranted a musical score. Jefferson Airplane's "White Rabbit" came to mind. I crept ahead of Vanni and into the room before him.

The massive oak doors at the rear of the room creaked open, the way those in a haunted house would. A young woman, presumably a Hill intern, shuffled sideways into the room. A firing squad of cameras that had been pointing toward the front of the room swung around furiously toward the doors. The conservative faces in the audience broke into anticipatory beams. The electric muttering of the audience grew, and necks craned and pecked around. They looked like ostriches or prehistoric birds. The effect was comical.

A guard near the door stepped aside and held his stomach in. And, coffee-colored laser eyes beaming straight ahead, Mario Vanni briskly entered the room in a blue double-breasted suit, crisp white shirt, and floral tie, walking drill-sergeant-straight down the center aisle toward his seat. The audience offered sighs of recognition and made the obligatory comments associated with celebrities: "He's shorter that I thought." "He's handsome." "He's taller than I thought." "He's so handsome."

In his right hand, Vanni now held his roll of paper, and his arms pumped with sufficient aggression that he gave the impression of a sprinter about to hand off a baton to another eager runner. A mass of muscle shifted beneath his shoulder. Vanni's hair was immaculately coifed and shone against the media's lights, which also gave his movements a strobelike syncopation. He looked like tinsel, emitting sparkling heat.

There was no baton handoff. Vanni held on tight to his papers, his face serious and respectful. The crowd ogled his entrance and some people even took another glimpse at the door where he entered as if a whole chorus line of Vannis might come kicking their way in. I took a seat in the back.

Most people crinkled their eyes approvingly. The cameramen also revealed their teeth as they knelt at the table where Vanni would soon seat himself. Vanni stroked the table's wood with subtle awe. I understood this gesture, which was truly spontaneous. I once had touched the door to the Oval Office for the sole purpose of gaining tactile confirmation that I, Jonah of South Jersey, had, in fact, made it here. This journey for Vanni had been significantly longer than the one-hundred-and-forty-mile train ride from 30th Street Station. Circus or not, Vanni's fingertips were made of genuine flesh, and the hearing table was cut from real American oak.

As the Don turned to wait for his lawyer, "Quick Pat" Conti, who had been seated in the back, he pulled his suit jacket downward decisively, militarily, to make certain it was straight. A pale Conti come down the aisle, leaving his ego in his briefcase and giving Vanni his entrance. The Don nodded politely to Conti as he set his briefcase beside the table. Respectfully, Vanni tilted his slick head toward a man in the front of the room who gestured for him to be seated. Vanni and Conti sat. The gangster flattened down his speech on the table. He then withdrew shining gold-rimmed reading glasses from his breast pocket in a czarlike way, setting them on his papers.

The senators entered, eyeing Vanni with reserved disapproval and, I sensed, fascination. A star's a star. I could see Senator Lindbaugh ceremoniously fiddle with papers he had probably not read and then lean toward his microphone.

"The committee now calls its next witness, Mario Vanni of Philadelphia, who, I believe, is seated before us. Sir, would you please identify yourself for the committee?" he asked.

"Yes, Mr. Chair, my name is Mario Vanni." Close enough. There was something kind of cute—Sesame Streetish—about Vanni's calling Lindbaugh "Mr. Chair" rather than the correct "Mr. Chairman."

"Would you please identify the man sitting to your left?" Lindbaugh asked.

"Yes. He is Pasquale Conti. He is my attorney."

"Mr. Vanni, do you know why you have been asked here?"

"I believe so, sir, yes, sir," Vanni said. Some in the crowd chuckled as if this were funny. Vanni turned around, a little startled. "You are holding a hearing about the cities and thought I could talk about that."

"That's correct," Senator Lindbaugh said. "Without meaning any disrespect, you are an unusual speaker for us."

Vanni nodded.

"We trust you are doing well after your harrowing ordeal in Ventnor."

"Yes, sir, thank you for asking."

"While this is not a court of law, it must be noted that you have been at different times in your career under investigation under the nation's Racketeering and Corrupt Organizations, or RICO, Law. The federal government alleges that you are one of the most powerful leaders of the Cosa Nostra, or the Mafia, in the nation. Whatever people may feel about you, it must be noted that you are not on trial today, but rather you have been invited because we believe that you are, for better or for worse, a representative of the complexities of city life and would provide us with some insights that we would not have without you. That being said, sir, have you prepared a statement?"

"Yes, Mr. Chair, I did do that, yes," Vanni said humbly, his Philly–South Jersey accent resonating in a reliable bass.

"You may begin."

Vanni picked up his golden reading glasses and eased them onto the bridge of his nose. He raised his papers and found a suitable reading distance. The photographers moved in more closely, which startled Vanni momentarily. He returned to his position and began.

"Mr. Chair . . . Chair-*man*, distinguished"—*dustinngished*—"members of the committee, members of the press and the public, I am grateful for the chance to speak to you today.

"Because so many of you have already heard things about me, let me tell you who I think I am."

The audience laughed politely. Vanni hadn't cracked a joke, and I had not written the remark to be funny; he was simply acknowledging something that was undeniably true—that his reputation preceded him.

"My name is Mario Peter Vanni." He stopped for a moment and nodded at several of the senators, as if to say, "You got that?"

"I was born in Camden, New Jersey, and grew up in an area of Atlantic City called Ducktown. It was a small Italian community. As I got older, I spent a lot of time in South Philadelphia, where my father made deliveries for a vending company he worked for. He was a good man, an honest man, and I loved him. He died when I was nineteen. He wanted the best for me and my brothers and my sisters even if he couldn't provide it.

"My childhood is filled with the smell of peanuts and saltwater taffy from the Atlantic City Boardwalk. It is filled with the smell of cheese steaks and pretzels from the street corners in Philadelphia. If you ever get to Philly, and you want a cheese steak, I recommend Pat's at Ninth and Passyunk. And no, I don't have a financial interest in the place."

Even the senators cracked a smile.

"My memories are also of sea air that I could smell year-round near my home 'down the Shore,' as we say in the Philly area. I remember drive-in movies, too. The very first drive-in theater in America was right in Camden. They put her up in nineteen thirty-three before I was born. I just think of the place and I can smell the popcorn.

"But there are other things I remember, Senator. Other smells. When I was sixteen, there was a man in South Philly they called Dan the Man. This guy was a loan shark. He had other hobbies. He would go up to people that owned shops or worked in the area, and he would ask them for money. Only it wasn't really asking. If they didn't give them money, he would beat them up or wreck their stores. I heard of Dan the Man. We all did. We just avoided him, which is the best thing to do. I wish more kids would understand that—that it's smarter to walk away from guys like that. That wasn't something I understood when I was young, and I regret not understanding that.

"One day I was on a delivery with my father when Dan the Man opened the door on his side of the truck. He asked my father for money, and my father told him to get lost. He dragged my father out of the truck and slammed his head into the door of the truck. My father was bleeding and part of his head was flipped open. The skull, it was. I smelled a smell I had never sensed before. It was the smell of fresh blood. I could see under his skull, and his eyes were staring straight up. I screamed and my father didn't say anything. Dan the Man was just walking down the street like nothing happened. People were gathering around my father.

"I told one guy to call an ambulance, and I ran down the street after Dan the Man. There was a hardware store on the street. I picked up a lead pipe and threw it like an Indian, and it hit Dan the Man in his shoulder. A crowd started to follow me. When I got up to him, I kicked the pipe away so Dan the Man couldn't grab it. He turned around and looked at me with his cigarette hanging out of his mouth, shocked at what was happening. He was wearing cheap aftershave, and I'll never forget the raw way it smelled. It was awful. I never hated someone so much in my whole life. Still don't."

Vanni took a deep breath and bore in on Senator Lindbaugh for an eternal five seconds. "I fought Dan the Man right there," Vanni said with an oddly appropriate snarl.

"He didn't even get a shot in. He fell back against a car and hit his head on a door handle. He was unconscious and went into a coma, and died a few days later. While all this was happening, in the background I heard people tending to my father and I heard a siren.

"An ambulance was taking my father off to the hospital. My dad did better that day than I did. He recovered real good. Well. He was a real tough guy. A *real* tough guy. Not like me. I was taken to jail and was convicted of manslaughter and did four years' time.

"Now I don't think I should have done time for what I did, if you want to know the truth. But I did the time and didn't beef about it. That's the way things were. In the city, that's called being a stand-up guy. When I got out, I had a reputation, as you can imagine. People saw me and didn't tangle with me. That reputation stays with me until this day. It's why whenever somebody in Philly or Jersey gets shot, they say, 'Vanni.' Whenever something comes up that nobody can explain, they say, 'Vanni.' Truth is that a hundred Mario Vannis couldn't have done half the things people say I've done. But when there's a big problem, it's easy to throw out a simple solution, especially if it can be summed up in one word, especially one with a vowel at the end. A word like 'Vanni.'

"Why am I telling you all this?" Vanni's voice had downshifted back into full Philly street cadence. This part had not been planned, but adrenaline served Vanni well. The downshift was working.

"I'm tellin' you because I may not be your kinda guy, but the story I'm tellin' you is a true story that tells you the kinda guy I am. I'm the kinda guy who when he sees somebody killin' his old man, I pick up a pipe and settle things in the street, right there in front of everybody. No sneaky business. I admit that there aren't many guys like me around anymore. My breed's extinct—just not in the movies.

"The men you saw on that videotape kicking that drug dealer off the streets—I know these men. I didn't direct them to do what they did because I didn't have to. In the city, we know what the problems are, and if the government won't handle them. . . . well, the people will.

"I'm not gonna tell you I'm a real sweetheart because that would insult your intelligence and make you angry at me. I don't wanna show disrespect. But if you wanna learn about the cities you gotta learn what makes people do what they do. It's not like guys like me get up in the morning when we're sixteen and ask, 'Hey, am I gonna be a senator today or am I gonna hit some loan shark with a pipe?'

"I didn't have a great big choice and I regret not having a choice.

But I don't regret being Mario Vanni because I did the best with what I had, which wasn't much.

"I've got a wife, Rita, that I've been married to for twenty-eight years. I've got a daughter, Angela, who went to the University of Pennsylvania and just graduated from Villanova Law School. I've got a son, Chris, who will finish up at Rutgers next year. They are good, honest people who are making a positive contribution to this society—more than I ever did or will. But I'm trying here. I'm trying. I am close to all of them and am very proud of Rita, Angela, and Chris and want the best for them even if I went the wrong way a lot of the time.

"As this"—*aziss*—"committee goes forward and studies the cities, I hope that you all will understand that we're Americans, too, and not everybody who grows up in those cities had the luxuries many of you did. I know that don't—doesn't, I mean—excuse everything. Believe it or not, I'm a law-and-order guy who believes in personal responsibility. But I have to tell you that if I grew up different, in a different place, I might never have been in that Philly neighborhood with Dan the Man trying to kill my father. So I did what I had to do and I don't regret it. I just regret that I had to do it, and I think there's a difference.

"I just want all of you to know that I love my country and do what I can in my own small way to make things better. I'm not a saint. But I'm not a devil like some we've got coming up. I hope that all of you, and everybody at home watching, can tell the difference between a kid and a crime, a city and a sin."

When Vanni was done, he took off his reading glasses, folded them, and placed them smoothly in his breast pocket. For fifteen seconds, there was silence in the hearing room. The only sounds were the creaking of old wooden chairs. The senators slowly turned their eyes toward one another, wondering who would speak first. Senator Lindbaugh didn't want to. The others didn't want to bail him out. DeWalt Nash was miles away on his plantation watching TV and was in no position to whisper into anyone's ear.

Congress had been expecting a wise guy. What they got was an aging ruffian who stopped a brass knuckle short of coming clean. Vanni's voice had cracked when he mentioned his father lying on the ground. When he spoke about his wife and his children, he didn't look at his notes. His eyes twinkled. He struggled with good English, sometimes getting it right, sometimes not. People liked seeing that struggle.

After the pause, the audience members captured each other's expressions. Many of them held their breath. It was the breathlessness of just having seen something unbelievable, like flies that had lined up one by one and volunteered to be squashed by the finger of a man whom they should have seen coming. The silence was an inverted form of applause. Anti-applause.

Vanni humbly nodded his thanks. Conti shook his client's hand and jotted something down on his yellow pad.

Finally, looking like a central casting shmo, Lindbaugh finally said, "Thank you, Mr. Vanni, for your statement."

Vanni remained seated, waiting for the follow-up questions I had prompted him for. The senators were darting their eyes back and forth at each other. A fawning aide with a self-important look on his face whispered something to Lindbaugh. They weren't going to question Vanni. They didn't want to. They couldn't.

"Mr. Vanni, we would like to thank you again for your testimony," Lindbaugh repeated. "One of my colleagues has informed me that we have a bit of a scheduling problem and will need to speed up these hearings. I hope you won't mind."

"I understand. You guys got stuff to do," Vanni said. The tension in the room was shattered by laughter as if Vanni's response had been a real zinger. Vanni rose like a tsunami. He looked like a giant despite the fact that he was a medium-sized man. Everyone else remained silent. Vanni strode out of the hearing room without making eye contact with anyone, as I had advised him. Conti crept out, mouselike, behind him.

On the way down the steps of the Capitol, Vanni was mobbed by cameras. I had counseled him to get into the taxi we had waiting as quickly as possible and get to the train station. After a boffo performance, ad-libbing with the press could only mean trouble. Don't get piggy. Stuff him in the car, waving, smiling, teasing the public with what might have been, what could be. . . .

"If I have to smile one more second, my face is gonna crack," Vanni told me, climbing in. "Pseudo-events." He laughed.

I saluted him good-bye. The rear door closed and the car slid away.

I took a seat on a low marble pedestal and phoned Cindi back in South Jersey.

"How'd we do?" I asked.

"You can't believe it," she whispered.

All three network affiliates in the Delaware Valley had covered Vanni's testimony. Along the Boardwalk in Atlantic City, people were lined up at store windows and in public areas to see him testify. I was back in Margate at Chez Guevara in time to get the evening papers.

" 'We're Americans Too,' Vanni Tells Urban Affairs," shouted the banner headline in the *Philadelphia Bulletin*. The *Bulletin* and *Daily News* articles were accompanied by a series of photos: Vanni arriving at the train station. Vanni climbing the Capitol steps. Vanni entering the hearing room. Vanni making a point before the senators. Vanni sipping water. In most of the photos, we had attempted to situate Vanni so that cameras could get him from the right. In most of them he was smiling.

The articles included excerpts of Vanni's speech, which had been provided on-line. The take-away of the articles was that Vanni had told off Congress, which he really hadn't. He was more humble, if not awestruck, than I had ever seen him before. But they always need a fuck-you to make it a hot story. KBRO's Al Just was off-center, referring bitterly to Vanni's presentation as a "dog and pony show," as if Mario's Capitol party had been thrown against him. The *Bulletin*'s photo editors were still reliably dispatching photographers to staged Vanni events and running Vanni photos. My surveys were consistently showing that while only 25 percent of the people in the Delaware Valley read the articles, more than 80 percent caught visual images of the boss on newspapers, on TV, or in E-mail attachments of the Vanni-isms that had been flying around the Internet all summer.

DELVAC's Rhoda McNee released a Cindified statement that evening underscoring that while DELVAC did not condone Vanni's performance, "We cannot ignore what it says about crime and the cities."

"With guys like Automatic Bart out there, people feel safer with

Vanni whether you like it or not," a Pleasantville man was quoted as saying in the *Atlantic City Packet*.

Dorkus had fanned a rumor in Vanni chat rooms indicating that the New Jersey Casino Control Commission had decided to award Vanni his casino license. This was untrue, but it set expectations where we wanted them. Now the commission would have to deny it, and we knew what that meant.

A Left Turn in the
Pine Barrens

"There was an old tale about a piney fiddler named Sammy Buck who bested Satan in a fiddling contest."

E ASTMAN," THE COCKY VOICE SAID AS I REACHED FOR THE handle of my Cherokee outside of Chez Guevara. I let go of the handle and turned around. It was Just. He was alone.

Just's pursuit had become a distant second on my list of worries for the next few days. I was ready.

"Yes," I said cautiously.

"That was a nice stunt you pulled after the vigil," Just snarled.

"You scared the hell out of me."

"Yeah, but it wasn't because you were scared of getting mugged, was it? I know you, Eastman."

"I know you, Yutzel."

He winced. His given name caught him off guard.

"What a stunt," he continued. "Automatic Bart. Jerseydevil.org. The pusher murders. The vigil. Washington. Jesus, Eastman."

"It's *Jonah* Eastman."

"Cute. It was you all along with Vanni. It should have hit me sooner. Mickey Price is still with us. You start it on-line and watch it bounce up to the rest of the press. Everybody assumes. You did all of it, didn't you?"

Now I winced. I covered my throat and faked a scratch so Just wouldn't see me swallowing. I was more bothered than I had thought I'd be. It was his words: You did *all* of it, didn't you? Even guilty men are outraged when they get caught. "You were all over the Delaware Valley."

"I'm *from* here, Al. Is there a crime in being a local boy?"

"I know you're Price's grandson."

"Another crime?"

"Maybe not, but it sexes up the true story, doesn't it, Eastman?"

"The truth is incidental," I said politely. Mickey had always been polite to his pursuers.

"Incidental to what?"

"Incidental to running the story. So where does this leave us?"

"It leaves me to kick over the log and watch the maggots run out."

"So, one South Jersey son of the rackets annihilates another. I made it a little too far from South Jersey for your liking, huh, Yutzel?

"We are nothing alike," Just said angrily.

"Do you plan to air it, Al?"

"Once I have it all together, you bet. Care to cooperate?"

"No, I want to get on with my life."

Just laughed. "How sensitive of you. You know, Jonah, you can get into the back of the cop car sitting up or lying down, but you're getting in. You're lunch meat with those Turks, you know. Word's out. I'm giving you a choice to cooperate with the story or deal with the consequences of noncooperation."

The rage of thirty-eight years of interrogation boiled in my throat. It wasn't a wild rage, though. It felt pointed, sharp—organized even. Just was all swagger. The bastard was envisioning who would play him in the movie; I saw the reel whizzing past his eyes.

"Do you want to nail gangsters or make sure that Mickey Price's grandson doesn't get the American dream?" I said. "I have a story, too, Al. But it's not a story I want to tell. I'll tell it only if you make me."

"What's your story about?" Just asked, a tad deflated.

I spoke slowly and quietly. I heard a trace of a South Jersey accent in my voice, but I was neither startled nor shamed by it.

"It's about a bunch of wise guys from Jersey and Philly who fed a hard-up reporter a prefab story. It's about a reporter who didn't check his facts because he was thinking more about moving up to the networks than getting at the truth. It's about a reporter whom the rackets targeted specifically because they knew he had a block-buster jones—so bad that he'd swallow anything that was shoved at him without checking. A reporter who may have even been in cahoots with the *amici* to this end. Had connections, family and all, that go way back.

"This is the story I'll tell. Me and my *goombas*. I'll write a book like Sammy the Bull. I've got great contacts in publishing and in the media. I'll go on the circuit with Remo Stacciatore, who has fantasies about Robert De Niro playing him in the movie—I'll write. We'll call De Niro 'Bobby' when we're on Larry King. He likes that. The movie—I'm thinking Scorcese, David Mamet, you know—will be about a shmucko reporter who went for the whole enchilada that Mario Vanni and I served him, an enchilada that resurrected his dead career. That's the story I'll tell."

I bore in on Just's eyes, from which his self-satisfaction had slowly drained. "*If* you make me tell it. If you don't make me, well, this'll just be another weird summer down the Shore. A personal memory."

Just feigned calm, but I knew by the shifting sinews of his jaw that he hadn't thought the whole thing through. It wasn't that he was dumb; it was that his delusions had polluted him. "Vanni would never let you talk," he said desperately.

"If you embarrass him, Al, Vanni will order me to talk. It'll be scorched earth. Everybody'll go down—you and your dividends you call news. The proof you give in your stories is the lack of evidence. You can't find anything, which proves your point that your targets are terribly clever. I have proof, Yutzel. I'll tell my story equipped with the recordings we made when we fed you the information, even the locations of the phone booths we called you from. And Vanni and his boys will embellish. You know how these guys are. God knows what they'll come up with. Payoffs to sources that you never verified, that kind of thing. Jeez, come to think of it, maybe that Jimmy Mack tape that made you a star again was a fraud. Then it's over to the Faces and Places beat for you. It's up to you, Al. If you don't do a story, we don't do a story, and everything's cool."

I opened the door to my Cherokee. Before I shut it behind me, I barked, "I saved your life, too, you son of a bitch. *Dayenu*." Enough. I sped off toward Ventnor where the answers to Mickey's riddle awaited me. Just and his network dreams shriveled in the rearview mirror, as the carcass of a freshly charred kitten came into view, its ashen paw jammed in the passenger window. I released the window and let the dead feline drop onto Atlantic Avenue.

Janis Joplin stood behind the counter of the Ventnor Public Library waiting to exercise a brain that had been lodged in neutral for some time. When I approached, she greeted me warmly.

"I'm looking for some maps of South Jersey." My chest was still tight from Noel's second cat homicide.

She swiftly found two oversized beige maps of Southern New Jersey encased in plastic.

I asked her if she would mind if I looked over them privately. "It's a sentimental thing," I told her. I muttered something about "closure," which appealed to her touchy-feely sense of righteousness, and she guided me back to a lunchroom the librarians used. It was a depressing, windowless, puke-green room with folding tables and learn-to-read posters taped to the walls.

My heart rate accelerated as I unfolded the first map. As dusty as it looked on the outside, that's how clean and crisp it was on the inside. It didn't look like anyone had ever opened it before. In the lower center of the map, at the corner of a green demarcation of the Lebanon State Forest, sat the word "Ong," like a medallion. Ong was in Pemberton County at the corner of Buddtown and Turkey Buzzard roads, a few miles from places with surrealistic names like Comical Corners and Hanover Furnace.

I hurriedly opened the second map on another lunch table. It was a broader, less detailed map of South Jersey. There, about thirty miles due east of Cherry Hill, just southwest of Fort Dix and Maguire Air Force Base, was Ong's Hat.

I shut my eyes and slowly sucked in as much air as I could. I gradually let it out and, like Moses, watched the dust on the map part like the Red Sea.

I made it to the Pemberton County Courthouse in about forty-five minutes. A weasel of a man in the Department of Records stood behind a Formica counter. He resembled that telephone operator character Lily Tomlin used to play on *Laugh-In*, Ernestine. The name pinned to his chest was L. Putz. I got out one sharp laugh before I brought it under control by converting it into a cough. My fortune was in the hands of Putz.

"I'm looking for the land records for Ong's Hat."

"Ong's Hat," he grinned. "Are you completely serious?" He was a smug little nelly. They must have beaten the shit out of him in grade school.

"Yes, sir. Why does that seem strange?"

"Ong's Hat is kind of a joke around here. There's nothing really there anymore. Just a couple of old houses. It's just a left turn in the Pine Barrens. America just left it . . . sitting there."

"I see. But it is on the map."

"No, really?"

I showed him the photocopy of the map section I made back in Ventnor.

"I'll be a monkey's uncle," he said, tapping his sunken chest.

"Would you mind helping me out? I'm working on a history of unknown towns for a Discovery Channel documentary. Would you be willing to be interviewed? I may be bringing a camera crew out in the next few weeks. Can I get your name?" I pulled out a little notepad from my rear pocket. Putzo grew about six inches on the spot. He had himself as a guest on Letterman nestled like a diamond in between the prongs of Cindy Crawford and Al Pacino.

"Lawrence Putz. I'm the director of geographical records, Pemberton County Courthouse."

"Putz? What kind of name is that? Is it German?"

"I think it's Dutch, actually," he said, fingering the name tag. "I think my grandfather altered it, shortened it somehow back in the forties." Probably from Putzenheimer, Putzendorfer, or Putz-enschnitzel. "He was an agronomist. He wanted me to go into agronomy, but I wanted to be a lawyer, run for president or something." Putzie giggled. "Anyway, I turned out to be more of a homebody like my father is. My parents still live around here, and I just bought a condo a few blocks away from them in Mount Holly. Ever heard of Mount Holly?"

"Sure. Horse country. Would you have to get some kind of permission to go on camera, that is, if we go that way?" I sensed he went that way.

"I'd probably have to get it signed off by Mrs. Carper. She's the head of staff around here."

"Of course. Mrs. Carper. And you could talk about the region, the records and all?"

"I know a lot about it, sure."

"That's good. Well, I'm just trying to build a story. I'll get back to you, if you wouldn't mind giving me your number." Putz reached into a drawer and handed me his card. "There you go. And your name is?"

"Keith Partridge."

"Like the Partridge Family?"

"Exactly."

Putz took me to a brown corner of the records department and rummaged through a handful of drawers before he got to a small section called "Ong."

"I'll be darned," Putz said. "There are a few plats here. Looks like most of the area is owned by the state, part of the Pinelands Preservation Act."

There were four plats. There was a small pig farm owned by a family called Clement. Two houses were owned by people named Tuck and Buck. I had heard the name Buck before. There was an old tale about a piney fiddler named Sammy Buck who bested Satan in a fiddling contest. Then there was a plat for the Mother Leeds Historical Society that was "dedicated to the preservation of the great legends of the Pine Barrens." Leeds was a big name in South Jersey and had been for hundreds of years. Mother Leeds was the name of the old woman that was said to have given birth to a mutant thirteenth child, who became the Jersey devil.

According to the records, the Mother Leeds Historical Society had been built in 1933. This particular section of land, about twenty acres, was not owned by the state.

"The Mother Leeds Historical Society," I read aloud. "Have you ever been there, Mr. Putz?"

"Hmm, I don't think so. Let me look at the file."

Putz scanned the page and cackled.

"What's so funny?" I asked.

"Do you see this notation here?" He pointed to the initials "N.J.S.P."

"Yes."

"That's for New Jersey State Police."

"So."

"Well, nineteen thirty-three was the year Prohibition was repealed. Looks like the authorities wanted to check the place out, make sure it was kosher. I'm pretty sure somebody told me that there were liquor stills there. Anyway, it says here that they paved the roads in nineteen thirty-four."

"Does it say why?"

Putzy rifled through some more papers. "I can't say for sure. Hmm, that's interesting. It looks like there was a manufacturing plant there for a few years after Prohibition."

"Does it say what the plant made?"

Putz paged slowly through the files and shook his head in the negative.

"What are you looking for?" an old woman with silver cat glasses asked as she glided through the library. Putz jumped to attention.

"Oh, Mrs. Carper, I was just looking up something. This man is working on a documentary on the region. Say, you might know: There was a factory of some kind in Ong's Hat in the middle nineteen thirties. Do you know what they made there?"

Mrs. Carper's eyes broadened into pale blue screens. In them, I could see a skinny preteen girl, riding her bike all wobbly legged on the dirt roads of South Jersey many decades ago.

"Molasses."

Freebird

"The foundation's mission is to get the good word out about the Indians so nobody fucks with us."

I KNEW THAT MICKEY'S RIDDLE WOULD BE SOLVED IN ONG'S Hat, and I wanted to have Edie with me. I knew that rough stuff would happen soon, things that that could not involve her, but I couldn't inject subterfuge into this chapter. She wanted to know me—this was it.

Edie and I reached Ong's Hat at ten in the morning. A dirt driveway lay beyond a mailbox and ivy-covered trellises. I pulled my Cherokee into the driveway and saw the two-story house with its wraparound porch. A small carved wooden sign swinging above three immaculate brick steps denoted the Mother Leeds Historical Society. Beneath the sign was the painted image of an old woman staring into a forest, her arms raised, presumably grief stricken at the birth of her thirteenth child, the Jersey devil. I could make out what appeared to be a tail sticking out from the trees.

A dark-skinned man stood at the side of the house. He wore overalls and a straw hat. He was raking cranberries from a sandy marsh onto a giant burlap sheet. Long black hair fell beneath the rim of his hat onto his shoulders. He made me think of a dancing skeleton. He glanced fearlessly at us over his shoulder, as if Edie and I were delivery people he had been expecting. He was an Indian.

He rested his palm on the top of the rake the entire time and waited for me to approach. I stopped about ten feet away from him, believing it was the respectful thing to do. Edie hooked her arm in mine as I greeted him with a Lenape gesture of peace that Mickey had shown me long ago. It was a horizontal slice across the air at chest level, a Frisbee-throwing motion.

"Sir," I began, "my name is Jonah Eastman. I came here because I was told there was some history with my family here." The man responded with a pregnant pause, obliging me to speak further. "I just wanted to see the place."

The Indian nodded. "So now you see it. Now what?"

"Now . . . now I don't know," I laughed.

"You got a plan?" he asked metallically, as if he hadn't spoken in centuries.

"A plan? Sort of."

"Don't be a *shmendrick*. Always have a plan." He turned and raked a few more cranberries.

"Sir, can I ask you how long you've lived here?"

"Forever. Been around forever."

"You were at a funeral a few months ago, weren't you? Down the Shore. I saw you."

His eyes crinkled, and for the first time he appeared kind. "And I saw you, Jonah. Saw you when you were a little *pisher*." He stopped raking. Oxygen entered my lungs via shallow puffs.

"You stood back on the Boardwalk and took your hat off."

"Said *kaddish*, too. *Yisgadal v'yiskddash sh'me rabbah . . .*" The prayer for the dead. He removed his hat and wiped his brow.

"May I ask your name?"

"Freebird. Like the song from the seventies. Those days are past. Do you know that?"

"I know."

"Mickey wasn't sure you did," Freebird said.

I held my breath. Seeing my reluctance, Edie asked, "What do you do, Freebird?"

"I sell cranberries."

"That's not all you do, is it?" I asked.

"No, it's not, Kylotaylo."

"What was that you said?" Edie followed up.

"I called your boyfriend Kylotaylo. It means Holds the Sky, Seven Angels."

Edie drew her hand toward her mouth and fell one step back.

"Let's sit down at the picnic table," Freebird suggested.

As we walked the fifteen paces into the shade, an intangible crinkle around his eyes made me think that I had known Freebird through the ages. I ran through every old memory I could conjure up, wanting to remember him. He knew my history. He knew Edie's Indian name. He knew everything. Had he been stalking us, or did his insight go farther back? I wanted to ask him about what Mickey had said about me. Did Mickey say he was proud of me, or had be been more resentful of my legitimate success? What about my parents—did Freebird know them, did he have any insight into their deaths? Where did I begin? My mind was mush.

"They say the Jersey devil lives out here, Freebird," I said.

"What, I'm not as good as the Jersey devil?"

"I sense you're plenty good."

"Freebird, how did you know my name was Seven Angels?" Edie asked.

"What a beautiful baby you were. Your father, what a good man. He inherited that land up near Cowtown from his mother. A Lenape."

"Yes, I know," Edie said.

"The government comes in and says all of a sudden that it's their land," Freebird began. "Bob—your father—knew about Mickey and the Indians. He came to Mickey. Your mother was none too happy about it, but he didn't want to lose his land. Mickey lent him the money and pulled some strings to make sure he kept it. That was long ago. During Vietnam. Mickey sent over your first guitar teacher."

"Mrs. Stern?"

"She taught you klezmer, no?"

"Yes, she did."

"It is *bashert* that we all meet like this," Freebird said.

"*Bashert?*" Edie asked.

"It means your destiny," I explained. "Freebird, do you have a last name?"

"Levy."

"*Freebird Levy?*"

"Yes."

"Next thing you're going to tell me is that Geronimo's last name was Cohen."

"Pincus."

"*What?*"

"Just kidding, Jonah. Your grandfather had a helper years ago who managed his gambling investments on the reservations. A man from Camden, Arthur Levy."

"I remember him. Mickey was all broken up when he died. I was in college."

"He was my father," Freebird said. "When he died, I took over as Mickey's link to the tribes. When he moved out west, Mickey started calling him Red Tooth."

"I always thought Mickey made Red Tooth up."

"He did. My father was Levy. My mother was the Indian. Like all converts, Mickey was more Indian than the rest of us. Everything had to be Indian, so he started calling my father Red Tooth. They both got a kick out of it."

"If you don't mind me asking, what tribe are you?" Edie asked.

"Last of the Absegami. Lenni-Lenape to most people. They named the Shore island Absecon, after us. My mother was Absegami from Ohio. The Lenape were all dispersed. It's hard to tell who's what anymore."

"Why did Mickey care so much about the Indians?" I asked.

"*Why* is not my question to answer. Maybe it was business. Maybe because the Lenape Indians, like all tribes, are sovereign nations that couldn't be taxed and bothered by the government. Mickey was watched every day of his life. He needed to expand his business somewhere where he wouldn't be bothered. He needed to mix with vulnerable people like Indians, people who would scream bloody murder if they were harassed. Mickey put the tribes back on their feet. He took a healthy consulting fee and got plenty of the skim, too. Who knows, maybe he liked the Indians because he related to all of the chasing and wandering. Look, I just know that he did care. He cared long before Wounded Knee. You know about that place?"

"The Indians were massacred by the Cavalry. It was around the turn of the century."

"No, later. In seventy-three."

"There was that protest," Edie said.

"There was an armed siege," Freebird corrected. "An armed siege. Radical Indians took control of Wounded Knee. The purpose was to force the government to make good on about three hundred treaties they *shtupped* us on. Conditions on the reservation were awful. We had the lowest life expectancy and income in America. Two of ours were killed by the government. Frank Clearwater and Buddy Lamont. More than a thousand of us were arrested. I was one of them. There were demonstrations all over the world. There was an airlift about fifty days into the siege. Planes dropped food and arms. It was like God himself had come out to the Plains. It was raining food and guns. A miracle."

Freebird's eyes were affixed to a fast-moving cloud.

"I think I remember this from the news," I said. "What's the tie to Mickey?"

Freebird tapped on my—Mickey's—turquoise ring. "Jonah, it was Mickey who funded Wounded Knee. Mickey got us the weapons for the siege. Mickey did the airlift."

I felt a tinge of vertigo, but it passed through me quickly.

"But what came of it?" I said.

"We won and we lost. But we needed a visible loss to get at an invisible win. After Wounded Knee, the Feds saw we were serious. Sure, they busted us in the short term, but after that we started getting more leverage in Congress, in state governments. Mickey financed the lobbyists. They liberalized the laws, and we started getting the casinos about the time you went to college. 'Make 'em happy,' the stuffed shirts figured. Mickey directed it. He went with states that had loose bingo laws and then said, 'Hey, if we have bingo, why can't we have a card game. We have a card game, why can't we have baccarat?'

"In one of the hearings, this state senator raised holy hell about gambling being un-American. Well, Mickey knew history. He sat in the back of the room with a disguise, an Indian getup. He had on a khaki outfit, Western boots, a headdress, face paint. He didn't shave for a few weeks before the hearing. He scribbled on a piece of paper that the Revolutionary War was financed by lotteries, that Harvard and Princeton—those big-shot schools—were financed by lotteries, too, and that Indian gaming was in this country before the white man ever settled here. So our chief gets up and shoves it up the senator's ass. The jackass tried to explain why this was different, but everybody laughed at him. Mickey had the whole argument calculated.

"Before Wounded Knee, Mickey said we needed to agitate to get what we really wanted. Who cares if we were arrested in the siege? It gave the illusion that the Indians had been shut down. But we hadn't been. Mickey started funneling more money and consultants onto the reservations. Everybody's been looking for Mickey's money in a vault, in Swiss banks." Freebird laughed. "He'd been putting it into Indian country for years. Decades. He started with small businesses, illegal crap games, moved up to bingo, lotteries, then land with oil, then casinos. We were fronts, but we didn't give a shit. We knew it would revert to us someday. Mickey and his *alter kockers* couldn't keep it. We knew the old rackets were falling apart. Mickey invested in our casinos, we gave him income, everybody was happy. The Feds never looked for Mickey's money on the reservation."

"I knew a little about this obsession with the Indians, but—no offense—I thought it was, uh, I don't know—"

"*Mishegoss?*" Freebird suggested.

"Yeah, I thought Mickey was a little nuts."

"Well, it was heartache for him, too. The government found out about Mickey supplying guns and started dogging him. We thought we were smoked for a while, that they'd find out about his investments, but they didn't. Every time they got close, we screamed 'Wounded Knee!' and they backed off. They thought he had gotten into arms smuggling. You guys left the country after Mickey had enough of being chased around. We offered to do rallies and protests for him, but he said no. It would have brought more grief to the tribes and his campaign to bring gambling to Atlantic City. Anyhow, after my father died, I became the liaison between Mickey and the tribes. We always met here, walking in the pines."

Freebird had a family that lived in Medford. The Mother Leeds Historical Society was just his office. His wife was Sandy, and he called his son Louis Born to Run, and his daughter Mary Queen of Arkansas. He had a nephew called Freddy on Fire. "The Lenape love Springsteen," Freebird explained.

"All told, everything is worth billions now," Freebird said.

"Does every tribe share in that?" I asked.

"Just a few. Mickey wouldn't deal with the Chicaloopas."

"Why not?"

"Gonifs," Freebird concluded. "Thieves to the core. Anyway, if the government tries to take legal Indian property this time, there won't need to be an armed siege."

"The media—" I said.

"Right. The media would side with us in a heartbeat. You'd see to that, wouldn't you, Jonah? There's a foundation. Mickey set it up to go into effect upon his death. He called it Absegami. The foundation's mission is to get the good word out about the Indians so nobody fucks with us."

Freebird squished my face again with his hands. "You're the head of the Absegami Foundation. You get a salary for managing media affairs, but no assets. Except one little thing that we'll talk about in private later, if you don't mind, Seven Angels."

Edie nodded, a bit dazed.

"Mickey had a Lenape name, too. He was known as Tentala-moshee. It means Fox in Great Wave. I named him that myself. My father brought me to the Shore when I was ten years old. I had never seen the ocean and was standing on the Boardwalk. Mickey was in the ocean and looked so small against the waves. I started crying and said to my father, 'Your friend will drown.' My father smiled and told me that Mickey was the smartest man he ever met and that he knew what he was doing. A huge wave came and Mickey disappeared. I held my breath, terrified. But my father still smiled. 'Look,' he said. Sure enough, Mickey rose up. So I called him Fox in Great Wave."

"He always said you should go toward the big waves, not away," I said.

Freebird nodded. "Your name comes from the ocean, too."

"Right. The book of Jonah from the Bible."

"Oh, yes, that, too. I meant your Indian name, Kylotaylo. Mickey named you Kylotaylo when you were three years old. Your mother was holding you in the ocean. She held you in the waves and then threw you into the air. I was standing back with Mickey, my father, and Irv. You were laughing so hard we thought you would choke on the salt water. You were holding your hands up above your head like a champion fighter. The rest of us began laughing, too. 'I hold the sky,' you shouted. Mickey asked how you said 'hold the sky' in Lenape. And so, Kylotaylo."

Freebird disappeared into the Mother Leeds Historical Society and brought out a large carafe of cranberry juice mixed with seltzer. He poured a glass for each of us and held his up in toast. "Just understand, Jonah, that your grandfather never wrote anything down. He always wanted deniability. But he dictated something to me years ago that you will get soon enough . . . from heaven. You'll just have to trust that it is from Mickey."

Gypsy Music

"Mickey had been in on everything."

WHAT'IL IT BE, HON?" DOLLSY ASKED ME. I SAT IN THE REAR booth of Murray's with my back against the wall. The boys never used this booth because it was so close to the bathrooms. The authorities, therefore, were not likely to have bugged it.

"I'm waiting for Blue and Irv. I'm okay for now."

I placed a portable CD player on the seat beside me and attached two headsets. I had additional CDs in the gym bag beside me.

When the heads in the restaurant began twisting backward, I knew that Blue and Irv had arrived. They entered Murray's like two downgraded hurricanes and limped back to the booth.

"We gonna listen to some music?" Irv asked, pointing to the CD player.

"Nah, we'll just talk," I said.

Dollsy stopped against the table. "What'll you boys be having?"

I ordered my usual spinach omelet and grapefruit juice and then fiddled with my bag. Blue and Irv ordered nothing.

"What's on your mind, Jonah?" Blue asked.

"I need to ask for your help with a problem."

"Whose problem?" Blue asked.

"Mine. Ours."

Both men appeared to be awfully old all of a sudden. I felt like a bully.

"I want my life and I don't want Noel—or anybody—dogging me forever. I want him gone."

"Jonah," Blue said, leaning forward, "that ain't how it works. You should know that by now. We can't just clip the guy. There's a guy in this mix named Vanni, you remember him?"

"I do. You never tolerated men who said things couldn't be done," I explained. "You never tolerated men who whined and said they didn't have the power to affect events. And here you are telling me that you can't do this."

"Look," Irv said, holding up his palms in a simmer-down motion. "Noel's a made guy. You don't clip a made guy without the boss's permission. There are rules."

"That son of a bitch has been torturing me for three months now. Even Al Just knows I'm cooked. The only thing Noel hasn't done yet is take out an ad on one of those airplanes that fly over the beach. I can do it if I have to, but it can't look that way. I'm the one playing by the rules here."

Now both men were holding their palms out toward me.

Irv spoke. "There's no nice way to say it, Jonah. What's to stop Vanni and the Turks from killing you anyway?"

"I've got a hedge. My hedge could make life very hard for Vanni now that things are looking up for him. Whatever future plans you have could be affected, too. I don't want to do it that way. Please, do this for me because I asked."

"What future plans?" Blue asked.

"I don't know. All I know is that you're retired like I'm retired."

Irv sighed. "Jonah, Jonah. We can't do this. I'm sorry. I could have been wiped out when they got the Dutchman in Newark. Blue could have gotten hit any number of times along the way. We're old men because we made the right choices. Getting rid of that animal would not be a wise choice."

"I understand. Then it has to be this way. Please remember that I asked for your help first." I placed the CD player on the table and pushed the two headsets toward Blue and Irv. I took a deep breath and stretched my neck around, setting off a few crunches in my spine. "Please listen."

Irv was fiddling with the headset I had placed before him. "What's going on here? What is this?"

"Collateral."

The two men did not look at each other. At the same time they said, "Collateral on what?"

"On my life."

Blue and Irv's jaws were frozen. I pushed the Play button.

"Mickey's gypsy music?" Blue asked, squinting.

The color suddenly fell from Irv's face. "No," he whispered, patting Blue's hand. "No."

"Keep listening," I said.

Within seconds, they both understood. Irv gazed heavenward and flicked his upper teeth with his tongue, smiling in a tragic, deathly way. Blue rubbed the knuckle of his thumb on his sternum and appeared as if a force below him were pulling his face downward. His skin went gray and his hands went lifeless.

"I'm sorry," I mouthed, "but I had no choice."

Blue and Irv listened for a few more seconds. They were completely shriveled.

"Noel is now *your* problem," I said.

"Listen now and don't ask questions, understood?" Irv said to me while nodding toward Blue.

"Yes," I said, startled by Irv's sudden assertiveness.

"You drive Carvin' Marvin's car from now on. Don't ask, you just do it," he ordered.

"And bring us that old rifle Mickey used to keep," Blue added. "Don't think, just listen. Time to step into the clouds and have faith, Jonah," Blue concluded.

"Listen to every fuckin' thing we tell you. This"—Irv made a gun out of his hand—"is not what you do. But keep that little gun just in case."

Irv reminded me of a corpse with a face that had been stretched with pins and chemicals into an empty grin. Dead men grin, but why? Where the hell is a dead man going that he's happy about?

• • •

Mickey's electronics whiz had been doing a lot more than sweeping for bugs over the years; he had also been planting them. The guy was either long dead or in Tahiti. According to the dates neatly printed on Mickey's CDs, he began secretly recording his meetings with his cronies when I was in college. When the tapes had gotten too voluminous to keep in cassette form, he had them transferred onto the compact disks I had found. Mickey had kept them alongside his old klezmer albums. "Who the hell would ever look there?" I could hear him saying. Blue, Irv, Vanni, and Mickey himself were all over the tapes. So were details of the arrangements with the Indians. So were bosses from New York, Chicago, Florida, Kansas City, and New Orleans.

I played many of them. They contained a virtual history of the mob in the Delaware Valley, not to mention some jolting goings-on in other parts of the country. I heard who killed whom and why; how and where their bodies had been disposed; what judges, politicians, and cops were owned; what casino officials had been bought; even who had been framed.

I envisioned all of these crimes as I listened to the CDs. Imagine what the FBI, the media—not to mention Hollywood—could do with what I had: interactive CD-ROMs where you could click on a location in the Pine Barrens and find out who had been buried there, how they were killed, and who had done the jobs, all with cross-tabulated hotlinks to other murders. . . .

Mickey had been in on everything. He had been no more above murder than I was above exploiting bigotry in politics. The last recording had been made about a few months before Mickey died.

"Freebird, I have an odd mission for you," Mickey began. "I need you to visit my grandson's place in Washington and remove something. He has this horrible old beanbag chair. Take it and throw it away somewhere in the woods."

There was a minute of silence on the tape. A speedboat skipped across the inlet and a young man hooted in an ostentatious celebration of the new spring.

"Freebird, do you want to know why I am doing this?"

No answer was audible, but I suspect that Freebird had shaken his head.

"I could always see around corners. My little gift, no? I look around the corner and see he's coming for me. You know what I'm talking about. I'm ninety-five, I shouldn't be so greedy, even with life. I've been having these nurses and medical men all over my apartment lately. I tell them I'm fading. They deny it. You know what that means.

"Every time Jonah looks at that damned chair, he feels robbed. You know something? He was. Most sharp people were robbed. But he has to go forward. I want him thinking about it—thinking, thinking, thinking."

I had a lawyer friend who was affiliated with DeWalt Nash in Washington make up my will. It was a living will. In it, the contents of the CDs would be placed in the immediate custody of the director of the Federal Bureau of Investigation upon my death or incapacity. The tapes were in a vault under the control of the lawyer. I had hidden a set of duplicates.

I did not explain all of the details to Blue and Irv. All I said was that the only thing that would endanger them more grievously than my death would be my precarious life. If I were threatened, or if my friends and family were harmed, I had it within my power to release the tapes or any portion of them to authorities. Or, if my life were ebbing away somewhere in a nursing home, after being beaten like a piñata, my living will would release the tapes like gangland pestilence. There was profound incentive to keep the Jones happy and healthy, and do with Noel what needed to be done.

Men like Blue and Irv the Curve did not need to be tweaked with the details of my living will. They were the consummate big-picture men. If everyone was calm enough and wise enough to see the view, we would all grow old and stay free.

Jersey Girl

"The hit on Hitler never came off."

THAT EVENING, BEFORE SUNSET, EDIE PULLED HER OLD
Chevy Malibu into the parking lot of Birdwood Park in Had-
donfield as I had invited her to. Two ancient draft horses with
Western saddles were roped to a fence at a corner of the park.
Edie smiled crookedly when she saw the beasts. The slackening
of her face, eerily, made me think of Blue. When she kissed me,
Blue went away.

"I'm here for my treasure hunt," Edie said.

"I'm here to supervise."

"You look sad."

"No, not really," I lied. Down deep, I saw this as a good-bye,
and I wanted her to remember me in precisely the way I had plot-
ted the evening. At the very least, it would be a story she could
tell a daughter someday.

Edie was wearing jeans, a lightweight cotton shirt, and paddock
boots. Without a splash of makeup—a little blush, maybe—she had
a country-and-western sex appeal that was refreshingly out of place.

We mounted the rickety horses from the lowest beam of the
fence, and I offered Edie simple instructions: "Follow the irises."

I had bought hundreds of irises the night before and scattered them strategically throughout the park early this morning.

"What do you know about this park?" I asked.

"I know it's where they found the first dinosaur."

"The first *complete* dinosaur."

"What does that have to do with us?"

"I'm a dinosaur. We're dinosaurs."

"I see." I could tell that she detected my sense of abandonment but didn't want to ask about it again.

Edie rolled her eyes and followed the irises up a hill with browning grass to a birdhouse. An envelope was tacked to the pole. Edie dismounted at the birdhouse and opened the envelope, sliding out the left half of an Atlantic City postcard. She spread apart the folds of the card and held it out for me. Her eyes surveyed mine for hints.

The card said, in my writing, simply, "Jersey girl,"

"It says just 'Jersey girl.'"

"There's a comma after the 'Jersey girl.'"

"So there's more?"

"Mount up again and follow the irises."

Edie held the card in her teeth and mounted.

September weather in South Jersey is a politician, hinting at both summer and winter at the same time. The sky was wintry, clear blue, without the white dome of humidity that makes it hard to breathe. The temperature, however, was decisively summer. Low eighties, I'd say. It was back-to-school weather that gave me a quiver in my throat. I was frozen in adolescence. Frozen not in terms of my actual behavior, but in my immovable psychic perception that I should be heading to study hall, and that adulthood was a factual error. Almost two decades since that chapter in my life was ripped away, and I was still thinking about it. Commit to nothing, Jonah—those years are still out there like wild horses that need to be broken and ridden. . . .

As the draft horses followed the irises down a ravine, Edie reached out and grabbed my hand, kissing it quickly and letting it go.

"Why do you think you're a dinosaur?" she asked.

"I'm not a fan of this century. I've never felt I belonged in it."

"Where do you belong?"

I stopped my horse and pointed ahead. Past a rock at the base of a soft iris-covered hill flowed a stream. The water was still and quiet. Another envelope sat on the rock. It took Edie a few seconds to spot it because it was partly obscured by irises. She dismounted and stepped toward it.

Inside the envelope was the right half of the Atlantic City postcard. Two words were written on it: "let's go!"

Edie held the postcard halves together and read aloud: "Jersey girl, let's go!"

"Well?" I asked.

Her cheeks were turning pink and her features froze in a quizzical expression. "What are you saying, Jonah?" she drawled.

I pointed across the stream.

Edie stuffed the envelope in her jeans and mounted the horse again. She immediately noticed a string of irises scattered on the other side of the stream. We proceeded across, the horses stopping to marinate their noses in the cool water.

The irises led to a cluster of trees up on a rise. Edie galloped toward it. I was never much for speed, so I trotted at a moderate pace behind her. Wedged beneath a plaque on a huge rock was a third and final envelope. Edie dismounted. It was the exact spot where the hadrosaurus had been discovered. She tore open the envelope, which contained the little pouch Mickey had carried around for so many years. The pouch contained a round three-carat stone set in platinum with two baguettes tapering down on either side. Edie shook it out into her palm and gasped. I dismounted.

"So, Jersey girl, let's go!"

"I will," she said, studying the ring as if it were an artifact that had nothing to do with her.

"If it's not you, it's nobody."

"You're that desperate, Jonah?"

"No, you're that much of a prize. The prize of a hundred lifetimes. Put the ring on, you don't have to say anything."

She put it on.

"It's stunning. When—can you afford this?"

"No, but I paid the price for it. The diamond has quite a history."

Edie hugged me. The woman just fit. My depression lifted. Maybe this would not be a good-bye. I had just grown accustomed to seeing everything as a final exit.

"Tell me the history," she said.

"In the nineteen forties, Mickey had a friend named Benny Siegel."

"*Bugsy* Siegel?"

"Yes. Benny had an affair with an Italian noblewoman named Countess Dorothy Di Frasso. Di Frasso's husband was very close to Mussolini. He justified his visits to Italy, not to mention Di Frasso's trips to Hollywood, by explaining that his real goal was to get next to Hitler and kill him. Benny was completely insane.

"While Mickey hated Hitler and had funded anti-Nazi efforts, the idea of Benny Siegel whacking out the führer in Berlin was hard to imagine. Mickey said he couldn't support the effort, but if Benny wanted to keep banging the countess, then he should keep banging the countess."

Edie laughed.

"When Benny told the countess of his interest in killing Hitler, Di Frasso applauded the idea. She rewarded Benny for his romantic audacity with a small velvet sack containing diamonds, which he brought back to America with him.

"The hit on Hitler never came off. The countess was bored one day and bragged about the scheme to one of her servants, who promptly informed her husband, the Count Di Frasso. The count forbade his wife ever to see Benny again and surrounded her with fascist muscle to prevent the two from ever having contact."

Benny, who was not one of the great strategic thinkers of his crowd, wasn't that disappointed when the countess ended their affair. He had moved on to a new vision: building Las Vegas. He was explaining his plans to Mickey at his apartment in Atlantic City when the countess called. Even from listening to one side of the conversation, it wasn't hard for Mickey to understand what had taken place.

"Sorry about the broad, Benny," Mickey said.

"Hell, it's okay, Mick. I got some good stones out of the deal."

Benny reached into his suit pocket and gently shook out several diamonds from the velvet case.

"Take one," Benny said.

"No, they're probably the only thing you ever got that you didn't steal."

Benny smiled and claimed to be hurt. "Here, take this one. I don't want to have to hurt you." Benny handed him a three-carat brilliant-cut diamond and Mickey slipped it into a pouch that he'd carried around for fifty years.

"I think we should celebrate," I told Edie.

"How?"

"There's dessert over the hill. I need to talk to you about some things."

We mounted the horses, Edie holding her hand awkwardly so as not to damage the ring, and trotted up a nearby hill. A gazebo rested on an open green with a view of Birdwood Manor. Two very neat-looking men in white with closely cropped hair stood in waiting in the gazebo. As we approached, an elderly violinist, also in white, appeared from behind a tree and began playing a tune I didn't recognize.

Edie grabbed me urgently. "I never imagined . . ."

"What did you imagine?"

"Never to be treated this way. I thought men like you died off hundreds of years ago—to your dinosaur point."

"We did, but I believe in what happened here today. I would either find you or I would find no one."

"You're insane but I love you.

"I love you. I know you know that."

"I know that."

We had ice cream and cake as the sun set. It occurred to me as we ate that I was just half a person. You're not supposed to think or talk that way these days, but I was really just half a person. Edie rounded me into a full moon.

My generation and its adventures made no sense to me. It wasn't superiority on my part; it was a lack of connection, a sense that my time of birth had been a cosmic screwup. The women were Lady Brett Ashleys, confused drama queens looking for the ultimate prom date all the while preaching about quests for commitment; the men were latter-day Robert Cohns, awaiting the quintessential microbrew in which to drown their agony.

My exile had played a big part in this abandoned way of think-ing. By the time I'd returned to America, the show had rolled on. For the first time in twenty-five years, it occurred to me that maybe I hadn't missed as much as I thought I had.

I took Edie's hand and studied the subtle veins beneath her eyes. It seemed to me evidence that we were both still very much alive. If I could survive the next forty-eight hours, I would serve middle and old age nobly.

"Pack your bags, Edie, we're going on a little vacation. Bring your rough-riding gear. You'll need to go on up ahead of me, though."

"Where are we going?"

"America."

Sometimes Life Throws
You a Curve

"Look beyond Lucy."

WHAT HAS A MAN BECOME WHEN THE ONLY THINGS THAT stop him from killing are logistics?

On the evening that I proposed to Edie, I called Noel using the number assigned to a cell phone Vanni kept inside Lucy the Elephant.

"It's me, Jonah."

"*Meow*. Got anything for me?" Noel sniggered.

"In fact, I do."

"Is it more brilliant polling information, let's say, like the public doesn't like taxes or some shit like that?"

"No, it's what you're looking for. I want to meet you at the place where it is."

"Jonah, you want me to just meet you someplace, huh? Am I a fuckin' idiot or something? No, pal, you come here to me and then we'll talk about who's going where."

"Fine. I'm near Philly. I'll drive down the Shore now."

"You'll drive down the Shore when I tell you. I've got shit to do. Get here before sunrise and we'll talk."

Noel hung up. I knew he wouldn't agree to my first plan. He

liked to be in control. He liked to inconvenience people. This would give Blue and Irv time to work whatever they had planned.

Abandoning Chez Guevara at 4:58 A.M., I drove Carvin' Marvin's Cadillac Deville, fueled by premium unleaded gasoline and faith, south on Atlantic Avenue. The royal howdah atop Lucy's back came into view two minutes later. There were no rajahs riding the Shore beast on this September morning.

A groggy Petie admitted me to Lucy. Noel dismissed him and waited for me alone at the top of the steps. I climbed the narrow steps to greet him. Morning did not become Noel; he appeared cadaverous and puffy, the price of the gangster life that they don't show you in the movies. A cigarette dangled from his brown lips.

"What do you got, Jonah?" he asked, once Petie left.

"Money."

Noel smirked. He wasn't buying. "Yeah, how much?"

"I don't know. A lot."

"A hundred bucks. A million?" he said, disbelieving.

"Hundreds of thousands, I think."

"Golly, wow," he droned. "All for me?" He drew back on his cigarette and blew smoke in my face. I coughed. Noel blew another puff of smoke at me. He took a few steps back and leaned against an archway. For the next few minutes, he stood smoking, studying my face. Occasionally, he would snicker at me.

"Are you going to stare at me all night long?"

"I dunno. I'm just trying to think about what I'll do with all that money you've set aside for me so generously. Such a good, good Ivy League boy, thinking of shit-for-brains Noel."

"I want you out of my life, Noel. This is the only way I know to do it."

"What's to say I don't take the money and keep after you for the rest that you hid? What's to say I don't take the money and kill you? What's to say you don't have somebody waiting to clip me? You're awfully trusting."

"Are you scared of me, Noel?"

"Don't fuck with me, Jonah!" he snapped. The cigarette fell from his mouth. He picked it up and put it back between his lips.

"How can I answer any of those questions? You won. I found some money and I'm telling you. What would you prefer, that I found it and didn't tell you? You've got to make a choice here. You wanted money. I found money. If you want to take all of your friends to protect you, be my guest."

Noel had waved Petie away when I came in. He was a lone operator. His loyalties began and ended in the mirror. There was no way Noel would take anyone else because he'd have to split the money with him.

"Let's get out of here," Noel said with a shove. "I'll follow you."

I stumbled out of the elephant, I knew, for the last time. Petie had crawled back to sleep. Noel made a gesture to his jacket, implying there was a gun in there. He need not imply. I knew. He frisked me from head to toe. I was unarmed.

I climbed into the driver's seat and Noel slid into the passenger seat. He threw out a lit cigarette, pulled his gun, a semiautomatic Beretta, and pointed it at my side. I shivered, visibly, I'm sure. Noel smirked at his achievement. I pictured the bullet hammering into my side, an angle I hadn't ever considered. One good shot could pierce everything—lungs, heart. I thought back to those gross body diagrams they used to have in school, attempting to recall which body parts were where.

Atlantic City melted in my rearview mirror as I paid the toll in Pleasantville. The smell of sea air dissipated with every dark, anxious mile along the expressway. Noel was perfectly silent. My laptop and transmitting gizmos were in a backpack under the passenger seat.

I cracked my window an inch or two. I really needed the air. "Hey, hey, pal!" Noel yelled, jabbing the gun in my side.

"I just need air."

"I bet you do, pencil neck. Close the window. I'm not going out like Bruno." Back in '80, the Philly boss, Angelo Bruno, was killed when his driver cracked Bruno's window so that a shotgun could slide into the car behind his ear. Bruno had been a good friend of Mickey's. Bruno would have frozen in disbelief at the very concept of Noel.

"Bruno's driver opened the passenger window, you asshole," I said. "How the hell do you think somebody's going to shoot you with an inch opening from over here." I closed the window.

Noel recoiled at my treatment of him, but Blue and Irv had

commanded me to talk to him this way, and I had promised to leave this night in their hands.

"Did I hear you straight?" Noel asked.

"You heard straight."

"Are you fuckin' blind, or is it me that has the gun here?"

"You've got the gun, Noel, but it's all you've got. You sit around like a babbo misusing the word 'respect.' Nobody respects you. They don't even fear you. They fear your gun. Mario said the Turks were all faggots."

"Zat right?"

"What, did I hit a little close to home?"

"Fuck you," Noel said with a counterfeit laugh. The gun was pressed against my temple. Strangely, I wasn't dizzy. Everything else makes me dizzy—women, restaurants even. Here I am, a second from death, and I feel alive and lucid.

"Do you want the money, or aren't you smart enough to wait a few minutes until we get to the place? See, if I'm dead, you don't get the money. Shit, Blue was right."

"What the hell does that mean?"

"Blue said you were so kill-happy you didn't understand that the Life was about money, not killing. He said you wouldn't see forty."

Noel belted out another artificial laugh, the one that said, "This'll make me look secure, like it's not getting to me."

"Yeah, well, Blue and his fossils will be in for a fuckin' surprise."

"Don't think so, Noel. You can do a lot to those fossils, but you can't surprise them."

Noel's eyes bugged out. "How do you know that?"

"I'm going to be dead inside a half hour, aren't I? C'mon, you can confess it to me."

As I saw hints of sunrise, it occurred to me that the old gang legends were younger than I was when they met their ends. Capone was jailed at thirty-two. You couldn't tell that from the pictures; he appeared to be a middle-aged, balding thug, but he was a kid. Dutch Schultz died at thirty-three. Legs Diamond was killed at thirty-four. Little Augie Orgen, thirty-three. Dion O'Banion, murdered in his Chicago flower shop at thirty-three. Abe "Kid

Twist" Reles flew headfirst from the window of the Half Moon Hotel in Coney Island—he was thirty-four.

At about quarter to five, I pulled into the field near Maguire Air Force Base, not far from Ong's Hat.

"Time's almost up, asshole," Noel said, singsong.

"You tell time?"

He jammed the barrel of his gun hard into my head. I saw a few stars crash onto the dashboard. Noel's foot was bouncing outrageously against the floor mat. He withdrew a cigarette from inside his jacket and flipped it into his mouth. I followed his skeletal left hand from his chest to the dashboard lighter, a digital journey that dragged like a marathon. With his right hand, he pressed the muzzle of the gun even harder against my temple and cocked the trigger. With the yellow nail of his left index finger, he pressed the cigarette lighter.

The scent of rotten-egg gunpowder blew through the car. I didn't even hear the shot. Noel angled his chin downward to take in the mammoth crimson hole in his chest. His head shifted upward to leer at the splattered and cracked windshield. His Beretta fell to the floor. A geyser of blood poured from his mouth. It had not occurred to me that Noel would have blood. Noel's eyes followed the blood on the windshield, which served as a mirror allowing him to witness how he looked spiraling down toward death. He gagged, making me think of what Mickey had told me about bullies when I was in grade school: Nothing frightens a man more than the unexpected sight of his own blood.

I had no sense of where the shot—or bomb—came from as Noel's blood soaked into the fibers in my shirt. I stumbled out of the car and grabbed my revolver from a compartment in the side of the seat that Carvin' Marvin had cut for me. From the unbloody part of the front windshield, I could see Noel's eyes become momentarily alert.

Noel lurched toward the floor of the car. His movement was deliberate. He was going for his gun. I took heavy leaps around the engine toward the passenger door where the window was fully open. I cocked the hammer of my revolver, pointing it to where Noel's head would be when he rose, if he rose. As soon as I saw

Noel's brow, I fired. The pop from my gun was joined by an echo that came from beside me. Noel's head shuddered in a way that struck me as comical. I instinctively fell to my knees, blocking my head from whatever had exploded beside me. I rose with the revolver still pointing toward Noel, again cocking the hammer.

Rising from the mist beside me was Fuzzy. Irv the Curve and Blue stood behind him like *alter kocker* Earps at the O.K. Corral. Fuzzy's pistol still smoked. Noel was dead. When I moved closer to Noel, I could see that the light in the car caught his diamond tooth. His mouth was a lake of blood. So much blood.

"A shame, isn't it, Jonah?" Irv said, as Blue and Fuzzy vanished into thin darkness.

I could not speak.

"Waste of a good car," Irv added. "Although they screwed up the bodywork after ninety-six or so on the Deville. Marv's lease was up anyhow."

Irv patted me on the back of my neck. "Rifle was in the trunk," he said. "Rigged up to the lighter. Noel wasn't used to insults. Couldn't think straight with you talking that way to him."

Irv grabbed Noel's hair and looked him over. "One slug in the head, one in the seat that missed. Which one from Jonah, which one from Fuzzy?" Irv asked nursery rhyme–style. "Plus the one from the rifle."

A truck pulled off of the main road into the clearing where we stood. I jumped back as soon as I saw the headlights.

"Calm down, Jonah."

The truck backed up to the car where Noel sat, dead. Blood was still dripping from the car door. Carvin' Marvin jumped out of the truck and opened the rear door.

"Look what you did to my fuckin' car!" Marv said. Then he laughed. A hydraulic whir began and a ramp slid out from the back of the truck. After I retrieved my backpack, Marv started his slaughtered car and drove it up the ramp into the truck. The sight of Noel's head sliding against the dashboard made me gag.

The moon rested on its celestial shelf in the Pine Barrens, a slice of light catching Irv on his question mark ears. The moonlight made Irv the Curve appear positively exquisite—handsome as

Bugsy Siegel and as wise as Solomon. This man had survived everything God had thrown at him and could still crinkle his eyes together like a kid who had just set fire to a bag of dog shit on somebody's front step. Past gang wars, FBI raids, bypass surgery, marriages, Irv the Curve kept moving and, as a ghost of a cloud floated beneath the moon, for the first time I understood why: He loved the education. He hated the pain but he loved trading in knowledge. He fired wisdom out like bullets—as if he was angry (and maybe he was)—but he loved to learn. That was Mickey's attraction to him, and his to Mickey. What these guys accumulated was a vault full of angles, markers, scams, and experiences.

The clouds were swiftly swept aside as if the sky were being tidied up for a big event—the arrival of South Jersey's Messiah, Ong; the last Cowtown Rodeo; or the resurrection of young Springsteen, the concert I missed when we fled America, the concert that I once thought had been rightfully mine.

How do you thank a man for existing and for being wise? You don't, because he knows you appreciate him. If he didn't, he wouldn't waste time on you, let alone work to save your life.

"Irv?"

"Yeah, Jonah?"

"If the money just wanders, what the hell good is it?"

"The money's beside the point. Guys like us, we were running governments that nobody would elect us to. The same big shots that wouldn't invite us to parties had to deal with us. Of course we couldn't spend the money, it was all hot. But we could move it around and make our little world sing our tune."

"But Mickey spent so much of his life worried and exhausted."

"Jonah, he had the attacks just like you. He was worried and exhausted from being himself, not from his work. Your generation was taught the wrong—what do you call it—benchmark. Being carefree just isn't in the cards for people like you, me, and Mickey. So we wrestle. The wrestling is what makes us alive and defines us.

"Mickey left you as prepared as he could. Yeah, when Vanni came to him, it cut Mickey to his core. I couldn't get a straight answer out of Mickey. He didn't know whom to trust or what the hell was going on. Vanni would have never come to Mickey in the old days when Mickey was at the top of his game. No matter what the papers said, in the end he was just another old man. We're all old men."

"I figured it was something like that."

Irv swatted me with the *Racing Form*, his ritual good-bye, and walked off, instructing the boys to be on their way.

"I'll be with you in a minute, Blue," Irv said, turning back toward me.

Irv bit his upper lip and scratched his ears, slowly winding toward something that made my bones sweat. "Sometimes, life throws you a curve."

"I understand."

"Vanni gets his casino."

"I know."

"Inside of two weeks, he'll own the Golden Prospect straight out."

"The Golden Prospect?"

"That's right."

"Just like that?"

"Not quite, kid."

"And this is all right with you?"

Irv cupped my face in his hands. "The government's all over the casinos now. No matter what people say, they're not mobbed up anymore. Mickey was the last of our boys to hold points. That's illegal ownership, Jonah. *Illegal.* The only way to own 'em now is to own 'em straight. With Mickey gone, we didn't stand a chance to hold on against these big companies and their friends in the government with their computers counting everything."

"Just like that, you let Vanni have it?"

"We don't care about the Golden Prospect. Let it be Vanni's headache. We want to focus on our Indian business. The past is the future. We've got other plans for the Jersey Shore. We'd been planning it with Mickey for a while. You did good."

Irv scratched his head. "These days, it all wanders. Money, people, the gossip that sneaks around on those chat rooms—I still don't know where the fuck those rooms are," Irv laughed. "Everything's a fugitive. Now go. Somebody'll deliver the Jeep in time."

I could not tell Irv why I had suspected he would come through for me, Mickey's tapes or no tapes: How do you tell one of Dutch Shultz's killers that you polled his demographic? My interviews with men like David Fine had suggested a latent preoccupation with redemption.

"Look beyond Lucy," Irv shouted. *"Go!"*

A Monster Who
Doesn't Exist

"Without warning, the Boardwalk ended—just ended—in
Ventnor."

LIKE LAPOWINSA, THE PHANTOM ONG, AND THE JERSEY DEVIL
before him, I turned around once more and watched Irv the
Curve disappear into the pine woods. I looked up into the night
sky, which was dominated by Orion the Hunter. *Orion?* He became
visible only in the fall. Was it fall? It was.

I ran a few hundred yards into the woods and stopped at Ran-
cocas Creek. I stripped down to my underwear and stepped into
the water after stuffing my bloody clothes into a plastic bag. The
water was frigid, but I didn't care because I could see the cells of
Noel's blood swimming away from me and dissolving downstream.
I returned, soaking, to the muddy shore and began running in my
diaperish underwear toward the sunrise.

An orange strip lit the lowest fragment of the sky as if God
himself had highlighted it with a fluorescent marker. I proceeded
through a thicket, turning around once or twice to see Irv shrinking
in the gummy darkness.

The lights on the rise were sudden and blinding, accentuating
the yellow paint of the Golden Prospect helicopter, *Goldie,* and the
blackness of her steel rotors—a ruthless ebony that these woods
hadn't seen since the Batsto furnaces shut down after the Revo-

lution. *Goldie*'s giant blades hissed, causing thousands of fey lighting bugs to flee like campfire cinders.

The door slid open with smooth precision, and the leathery hand of Sidney Blintzes extended itself down into the pines and pulled me aboard.

"I'll never know physics," I said, glancing around the cabin. This thing was like a flying condominium, not unlike the Sikorsky the marines used to shuttle the president from the White House to Camp David.

"Physics? Him I don't know," Sidney said, winking, unsmiling. He handed me my duffel bag, which contained a change of clothes.

I slipped my laptop out of my backpack and turned it on. "Look at that gadget," Sidney said as I typed a short E-mail to Cindi and Trouble. The note read, "Money wanders." It was my signal to them that I was safe but, again, running.

"Remember what Capone said: 'On the lake it's bootlegging, on Michigan Avenue it's hospitality,' " Sidney said. "Well, the geniuses call these computers 'the future'; I call it a buncha yentas talking and teenagers pulling their *petzels* to girlie pictures. We put a computer in your grandfather's little room at the casino that added up the take on the little tube. Mickey told them to get rid of it. 'I can smell the take within a grand!' " he said. Sidney then nodded sorrowfully.

"What's the matter, Sidney?"

He leered out the window. "They just got Vanni this morning. Outside Olga's Diner. He's gone."

I felt as if Lucy the Elephant had just collapsed and died on my chest.

I knew Olga's. It was at the circle on Routes 70 and 73 in Marlton. Cindi and I had gone there plenty of times after failed dances.

"Who's *they?* Those Turks?" I asked accusingly, as if Sidney himself had committed the act.

Sidney continued speaking as I touched my wet legs to make sure that I was really here. "He was going for a cup of coffee on his way to the Shore. Colored guy did it. Shouted, 'Africa shall rise,' something like that. He was holding some damned book. Vanni didn't have guards since your Washington affair. Came on TV before I left. Al Just at KBRO."

Just finally lands his hemorrhaging scoop. So ends the news cycle.

"Did they get the guy?"

"Yeah, wait 'til you hear this. The shooter grabbed what was left of Vanni's coffee, sat down in his new Range Rover, and waited for the cops. Drank the cup down. Had a big afro like they used to wear. How do you like that?"

I pictured Vanni's blood mixing in with the spilled coffee, swirling around the traffic circle and trickling eastward to the Shore.

"A nut, Sidney, a nut," I declared, while my old phrase for spin run amok kicked around my skull.

"We don't know yet."

"Maybe he was trying to impress Bart."

"Jonah, this guy thinks he *is* Bart."

"A monster who doesn't exist."

The helicopter sucked skyward and I thought, This is how it ends: roughneck old nomads in the Pine Barrens cleaning up and running off to manage nobody's billions that had been scattered across the reservations in a financial diaspora. Vanni eliminated by a Black Panther wanna-be. And me in wet underwear in a casino helicopter.

As we fled, I tilted my head against the window and faced Orion. Wisps of starlight around his head made it appear as if he were wearing a headdress. Half asleep, I pictured the great hunter floating in the future. He was holding something other than his flaccid bow and arrow, which had been reshaped across the ages by the shifting heavens. Orion now held a laptop computer, and it was logged on to a new Web site hawking gambling junkets for the Pleiades. Orion's puzzled face came into view as a light cloud drifted away.

The two faceless pilots flicked at the sparkling controls, which prompted a hydraulic whistle that could have only been man-made. I gripped Sidney nervously as the helicopter swung toward the sun that rose, reluctant, above the Atlantic breakers.

I thought I had seen the Shore from every angle, but not this one. Once out over the ocean, the pilots banked westward, triggering a rush of dizziness. The Golden Prospect, which I always envisioned towering over the coast like a concrete Godzilla, was actually one of the smaller casinos. I'll be damned. From this altitude, the Boardwalk sat like a discarded Popsicle stick with microscopic ants riding bicycles. Without warning, the Boardwalk ended—just ended—in Ventnor. I had always known this factually, but seeing it from up here made it seem absurd and cruel. There was no sign explaining why it ended there, no natural formation like a stone jetty to make it logical, just an honest South Jersey, *Hey, dat's it, Jones.*

Beyond the Island House, Lucy the Elephant emerged forlorn and misty, surveying the sea. A few lone beachcombers stooped to absorb her oddness as they had for more than a century. Lucy's eyes were plastered in a fixed, banal gaze from this vantage point, as opposed to the expressive surprise she wore when viewed from up close. There was no other activity around her, summerers and shoebies having vanished after Labor Day, just a small American flag that I had never noticed before crackling defiantly in the wind.

Just over Lucy's shoulder, I spied my final message from Irv the Curve. It must have been—may have been—what he meant by "Look beyond Lucy." You never knew with Irv. The letters on our favorite furrier's billboard had been rearranged. The sign now read: R U BARFY SLIVERS? The extra *R* had been broken apart and used as a question mark. I'd laugh later.

I waved bye-bye to Lucy, the way I had all those years ago when my dad pointed out Mr. Berlin on his rolling chair. As much as I hated being airborne, I preferred gliding within God's breath to drowning in the juices of Lucy's intestines. Within seconds, *Goldie* leveled off and the slate seawall that kept the cash flow temples of Longport from spilling off of the Monopoly board passed beneath us as we edged west into the heartland, toward my inheritance.

epilogue

C'mon Get Happy
Harpers Ferry, West
Virginia

"As you see, even in this promised land
of ours, there's always somebody out
there making it hard to settle."

MY FOOTSTEPS ALONG THE RIBBONOFF HIGHWAY LEAVE ME
on a rocky cliff. My perch overlooks the violent blue union
of the Potomac and Susquehanna rivers in Harpers Ferry. This is
where *Goldie* touched down a little more than a year ago. Edie had
been waiting for me, leaning against her old Chevy Malibu with
its horse trailer.

The roads leading here really did look like ribbons of highway
from the air. Eerily, a few weeks after we moved in, I found a book
on Woody Guthrie in a little store in Shepherdstown which contained the lyrics to "This Land Is Your Land." It turns out that he
wasn't singing "ribbon of highway." It was just "ribbon highway."
My camp counselor had either sung it wrong, or I had misheard it.

It's Halloween Night and the heavens are flirting with winter,
much like the New Hampshire skies always were when I was in
college. Our stone house sits at the top of twenty acres, a short hop
from where John Brown captured the U.S. Arsenal in 1859. Edie
and I can see the arsenal from a window in my lookout study, which
was the only room that had been fully furnished when we got here.
When I climbed to the study for the first time, I found hundreds
of books and magazines about the Indians weighing the shelves

down into a sag. On the corner of the desk sat a black-and-white photograph of Mickey and me at a diner near Canaan, New Hampshire, that had been taken in the spring of 1981. It was the debut of his Dartmouth sweatshirt.

This property was my inheritance from Mickey. Freebird had handed over the deed to me that day in Ong's Hat. The house rests beyond a red-clapboard-covered bridge. It runs above a creek that pops with autumn life. Edie loves the bridge and planted flowers around it last spring. I mentioned putting a beanbag chair in the study, but Edie gave me a dirty look. Despite the fragility of my life, nothing frightens me as much as a disapproving look from Edie. She did, however, locate an old Partridge Family poster. Edie's been very emotional lately, and I have a weird feeling she may be pregnant, especially since she stopped riding Squaw a few weeks ago. I bought a quarter horse, the true American breed, for myself. I call him Lapowinsa.

As tacky as I knew it was to name a property the way Carvin' Marvin, Mort the Snort, and Rhoda McNee had, I nevertheless christened the place "Thousand Kim," after Dutch Schultz's surreal deathbed invocation, "A boy has never wept nor dashed a thousand kim." I have never known what this meant, which was the attraction. Maybe the Dutchman didn't know what it meant either. To me, it was a poetic geyser that came from the dying mouth of another New Jersey killer who missed his mother and whatever nosegay of promises she had made to young Arthur Flegenheimer—promises made long before he snapped down the brim of his fedora and began calling himself Dutch Schultz. I can see now how these things happen.

Mickey and I had first seen this farm years ago. We had driven to Harpers Ferry one autumn weekend when I had my White House job. I remember the prism of leaves against the backdrop of Mickey hiking up a rusty boulder in his loafers, studying the property. He had called it "an honest place."

Word is out among the locals that a young Indian family has moved onto the property. A few weeks ago, one of the dentally impaired workmen admired our house and asked me what tribe we were from. I told him that Edie was Absegami and I was Ashkenazi. "Oh sure," he nodded respectfully, as if these had been the tribes that had defeated Custer. He also asked me what I did for a living. I told him that I used to work for the mob. He slapped his knee and returned to fixing the flagstone on our covered bridge. Up here, I always tell people the truth because nobody believes me.

Despite having gained Edie and Thousand Kim, I've been hollowed out about Vanni. Or maybe I've been down about Mickey, having combined much of my grief into one big balloon payment. The newspaper photo of Vanni's death scene showed my copy of *The Image* lying on the bloody sidewalk.

There were public vigils for Vanni at the time of his murder. I had commenced my campaign with an on-line ruse to create the illusion of grassroots support for Vanni when, in fact, this grass roots had consisted of four or five people. As Prohibition was a swindle anchored in the promise that the lumpen had been tranquilized, the Internet, with its informational whiff, distracted from the reality that it, too, was just another downmarket riot. The word "processing" that is so married to our age implies reason and careful analysis. There couldn't be a smellier red herring: Anybody with a motive, a modem, and the Almighty Message can become an electric sniper and fire into the culture.

Despite this, the outpouring of grief after Vanni's murder had truly been spontaneous. Rita Vanni had called for privacy and calm, a request that had been honored across the region. I glanced away from the TV screen when Rita started speaking, her face a testament to the exhaustion of every Italian who had been forced to answer for the actions of the handful of mutants that all cultures share. The only garish exception to her request was a quickie special on KBRO-TV called "What Might Have Been." It had featured the Jimmy Mack videotape, which was routinely being used by media across the country as filler for generic crime stories, and some of our b-roll footage of Vanni walking along the Margate surf, his ungelled hair (my suggestion) blowing wildly in the sea breeze. A sober Al Just narrated one segment that chronicled the culture of organized crime in Philly from Prohibition to the millennium. In it, he acknowledged his father, Morris "Mouse" Yutzel. He referred to him as a "sweet old Camden gambler." This had been his only foray back onto the mob beat.

Edie gently tolerated my distance, but it wasn't something we could easily talk about. She empathized with my state but not its cause. I couldn't blame her, I guess. A man can excuse his outrages, self-inflicted or not, only so many times before the people around him implode or flee.

When I got here after last summer's showdown with Noel, I went out and smashed my revolver and my laptop against the cliffs and scattered the pieces in the rivers. As I did this, I felt the eyes of the Sanhedrin upon me. How had they come down on what I had done? Was I as justified as Moses, or just a wily pollster grasping for biblical links to justify my instincts, which had been from the beginning to kill. I found no resolution and just treaded in the moral muck between flack and murderer.

Shortly after we moved in, I got a call from the New Jersey governor's campaign manager. "Are you the Poll Vaulter?" he asked.

"I am."

"Heard good things about you from some guys down the Shore," he said. No specifics were needed: The Casino Commission had granted Angela and Christopher Vanni their casino license only days after their father was killed. Smart people started asking other smart people questions about how Vanni had pulled it off. The answers had led back to me.

The governor, a Republican woman, is thinking about the White House and needs some help overcoming her odds. After all, a female, pro-choice northeasterner would be hard to elect. But not impossible. Anyhow, between the Absegami Foundation and the governor, I've got plenty of work.

In the pioneer spirit, Edie and I held our wedding ceremony at Thousand Kim last Labor Day weekend. We settled on a small affair. Rabbi Wald came up on his Harley to do the service. I suggested that he form a gang and call it Hell's Rabbis. He nodded his head in genuine consideration.

Edie's immediate family and a few of her friends, including her former klezmer partners, were there. Edie sang one song, *"Schnerele Perele."* Mrs. Morris, whom I now called Elaine, seemed vaguely surprised that those who represented me did not appear to have decomposing bodies in the trunks of their cars. From my side, there was Cindi Handler and a man called Will she had begun seeing.

Will was a reporter for the *Camden Courier* whom she had met during the course of our caper. Mr. and Mrs. Hicks came; Freebird Levy, his wife, Sandy, and their son, Louis Born to Run; and Trouble, Jessica, and their daughter, Dawn, who was feeling well. Trouble and Jessica regarded each other with fragile but anchored affection, the way couples who have finally hit upon the essence of marriage do. In this spirit, Rabbi Wald's wedding sermon concluded with him pointing toward the horizon and saying two lines that I recall verbatim: "The cause of modern marital strife is the belief that things are supposed to be different. When you discover that marriage is hard, just know that it's supposed to be, and that the perfect life isn't just over the ridge."

The only one from Mickey's gang to attend was Irv the Curve. His gift was a fireplace kit—stokers, brushes, and little shovels— that he had stolen from a Prohibition-era swindler named Fuller who was thought to be the man that F. Scott Fitzgerald had based Jay Gatsby on. He had ripped them off when he was a kid working for the Dutchman.

Edie's bridal appearance made me dizzy. Good dizzy. I always thought she was exquisite, but I nearly passed out when she rose with her father at the end of the white linen aisle scattered with irises. She had an endangered brand of beauty, the kind that tapped you on the shoulder rather than slammed you over the head. I preferred that.

After Rabbi Wald said we were married, the ground rolled the way it did when Blue and Irv the Curve told me the facts of life that night in Carmine's. But when Bob Morris winked at me like Lindbergh landing at Le Bourget, the vertigo stopped.

Endings, at least in my life, have never been neatly sewn up, with one act definitively ending and another one beginning. I always seem to track sand. After the wedding, when I walked Rabbi Wald to his motorcycle, I saw that he had brought for me Shore newspapers that were stuffed into a little compartment behind the seat. They included a huge series of articles about the events at the Jersey Shore during the past year. The lead feature was on Angela and Chris Vanni's success with the Golden Prospect. There was a photo and everything—these two all-star kids grinning like Kennedys from the Boardwalk. Whatever spears of guilt I felt about the methods I used to get them their casino were offset by knowing how proud Mario would have been of how his kids had "spun out."

Irv informed me that Vanni's killer, one Lucius Turner, wasn't the lone nut everybody thought he was. He had been put up to the job by Noel. The idea had been to get rid of Vanni but avoid an all-out war by having the ostensibly angry Turks then demonstrate their commitment to the old guard by killing Turner. It turns out that Noel didn't even have the Turks on his side. Petie and the others had led Noel to believe they were behind him, but they hadn't lifted a trigger finger to help him. At some level, Noel had known that his faction hadn't been strong enough to take Vanni's men down and needed a ruse to prevent a bloodbath. In the end, Noel had gotten too tangled up in his own Machiavellian underwear to spot the old-fashioned hit that had been rigged for him. Lucius remains isolated in a special wing of Ancora Mental Hospital in South Jersey, where a handful of syndromologists are studying "Media-inspired reflexive violence," or MIRV.

Yet another article announced that the Lenape Nation had come forward to claim the land adjacent to the Wildwood beaches as their own. Their leader, Robert Between Mountains, said that Wildwood had been stolen from them in 1820. He wanted to put up a casino, and his neo-Lenape stood to make billions. When the mayor of Wildwood scoffed, Robert Between Mountains produced a series of deeds showing that his syndicate, called LenCorp, had purchased hundreds of acres of beachfront property through legal fronts during the past three decades. Due to the accretion of soil deposits, their holdings now accounted for more land than Mickey and his boys had actually paid for. How great is that? From his grave, Mickey gives the white man one last *shtup* while Blue and Irv quietly expand their empire.

The recordings Mickey made to save my life have been encased in a slim shoe box that once housed a pair of his Bally loafers. I won't say where I hid the box. Mickey had bought the shoes in Havana before Castro kicked him out.

I'll do my own pioneering here at Thousand Kim, where I have a strange notion that I have finally found a home. I feel only the impulse to build here. I'll never return down the Shore, the Ribbonoff Highway being a one-way street. I don't want to go to any beach, really. Other people's beaches seem, well, wrong. Factually incorrect, a geographical snafu not to be taken seriously.

Only my Shore makes sense, but I think of it—her?—in daydreams as a banshee. She walks along the foam in bell-bottom jeans, focused seaward. Her midriff is bare and soft the way Margeaux-with-an-*x*'s was before women trained in gyms like prizefighters. I suspect she sees me but acts distracted by opaque spirits leaning against the horizon like Andy Gibb or another pretty, long-dead icon from the seventies.

The advantage of having zipped past my youth like a comet is that I am accustomed to hurtling forward. Men with happy memories are the ones who get greedy and botch the present.

When I turned on my computer for the first time in my study at Thousand Kim, my E-mail light was flashing green. The return address read "Tentalamoshee"—Mickey, the Native American agitator. For all of his Luddite rants and feigned senility, he had known about E-mail all along.

To My Jonah from Your Pop Pop Mickey,

When you see this note I will be gone, maybe up in heaven or someplace else God has in store. Who am I, the big genius with it all added up?

You did it, big shot. How the details happened, I don't know. You were chased I am sure. The man who thinks he can't be caught is the man who will be caught. I knew they would come for you—the price you pay for talent.

When you run casinos you learn quick that not all the players get dealt the same hand. The House always wins like God always wins. God dealt you a mixed hand. The trick is that you have to push up against God. The push defines you. The House always wins, so you might as well get in close and find out what you have. This is what I tried to show my Indian friends. To BE the House.

A man can only fight with the weapons he has got. In this life we do the best that is doable, not the best that can be imagined. Don't believe this you-can-do-anything nonsense they teach young people nowadays, because fantasies screw you. It is why men like your Uncle Blue and Irv and me needed each other. We knew what we did not have. Blue was the fighter. Irv was the talker. I saw the chances and played them. Like you, we were forced by conditions to find what we were.

I know you have hiked to that nice place up there. As you see, even in this Promised Land of ours, there's always somebody out there making it hard to settle. No matter what our weapons or our battles, Jonah, in the end we're all shoebies, aren't we?

acknowledgments

M Y WIFE, DONNA, AND MY CHILDREN, STUART AND ELIZA, UN-derstood that I never found time to write. Time found me. I am grateful for their patience.

My old friend Ed "Tombstone Eyes" Becker recounted for me what it was like to be a young aide to Benjamin "Bugsy" Siegel at the creation of Las Vegas in the 1940s, a time I could not have imagined on my own.

Against great odds my agent, Kris Dahl at ICM, and my editor, Sean Desmond, at St. Martin's, championed *Money Wanders* from the beginning and made it a better book. I am always aware of how lucky I am to have found them. My literary *consigliere*, Bob Stein, played a pivotal role in bringing this book to life, and I am grateful for his Dutch uncle guidance.

I am indebted to novelists Barbara Esstman, Bob Cullen, and Dan Stashower for their vigorous editorial guidance. Matthew Klam was also a stalwart friend throughout the writing process.

My friends Ann Matchinsky, Bill Boswinkle, and Maya Shackley provided critical input and support. My partners, Nick Nichols and John Weber, put up with a dose of yammering. I also appreciate the indulgence of my friends in law enforcement and politics, especially Gary Klein, Unit Chief, La Cosa Nostra Unit of the Federal Bureau of Investigation; Paul Rakowski (ret.) of the U.S. Secret Service; Sean McWeeney (ret.) of the Federal Bureau of Investigation's Organized Crime Strike Force; and Alan Hart of Burlington County College.

Mr. and Mrs. Joseph Truitt, my high school English teachers at Cherry Hill West, were critical touchstones—I wasn't their best student, but perhaps I was one of their most inspired. Jim McCarthy enlightened me about American Indians. Jim's father, *Washington Post* columnist Colman McCarthy, prodded me to write when others didn't.

Marc Wassermann, with whom I shared a crib in Pennsauken, New Jersey, reminded me of Pine Barrens tales we were told in summer camp.

My mother, the late Sondra Byer Dezenhall, once suggested on the Atlantic City Boardwalk, "You know, you should write." My sister, Susan, echoed, "Yeah, you should." My father, Jay, said, "Write? Write *what?*"

Finally, many thanks to my old gang in South Jersey and Philly for its sense of humor and support. My memories of summers "down the Shore"—especially a peculiar few months in a basement apartment on Baton Rouge Avenue—inspired this book.

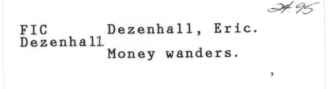

$4.95

FIC   Dezenhall, Eric.
Dezenhall
             Money wanders.

DATE